Praise f

'The year's most chilling crime novel
. . . gripping and original'
Sunday Express

'Move over Thomas Harris, there's a new kid on the block. Chelsea Cain has brought a brilliantly disturbing twist to the whole serial killer genre, as well as penning a thoroughly gripping and convincing thriller . . . This is, of course, classic stuff in the Hannibal Lecter mould, but Chelsea Cain has a compelling prose style and makes her characters highly believable and very sexy'
Daily Mirror

'Dark, distressing and disturbing, *Heartsick* is also a triumph of the human heart. Just pray you never meet Gretchen'
Val McDermid

'With Gretchen Lowell, Chelsea Cain gives us the most compelling, most original serial killer since Hannibal Lecter'
Chuck Palahniuk

'What may be the creepiest serial killer ever created. This is an addictive read!'
TESS GERRITSEN

'A real barnstormer of a thriller, Chelsea Cain's chilling debut novel . . . is not for the squeamish . . . Inspired by a real-life case, Cain explores the strange bonds that spring up between criminal and victim – to terrifying effect'
Red

'Creepily addictive'
Belfast Telegraph

'There are blood and guts aplenty in Chelsea Cain's debut psychological thriller . . . Disturbingly good'
Marie Claire

HEARTSICK

Chelsea Cain lives in Portland, Oregon, with her husband and young daughter. She used to be a creative director at Lane PR in Portland, but left the job when she had two books due to be published: *The Hippie Handbook* and *Confessions of a Teen Sleuth.*

She currently writes a regular column called 'Calendar Girl' for the *Oregonian* arts supplement. She gets a fair amount of fan mail from prisoners.

Also by Chelsea Cain

Gretchen Lowell series

Sweetheart

Evil at Heart

The Night Season

Confessions of a Teen Sleuth:
A Parody

The Hippie Handbook:
How to Tie-Dye a T-shirt, Flash a Peace Sign, and Other Essential Skills for the Carefree Life

Dharma Girl:
A Road Trip Across the American Generations

Edited by Chelsea Cain

Wild Child:
Girlhoods in the Counterculture

CHELSEA CAIN

HEARTSICK

PAN BOOKS

First published 2007 by Macmillan

First published in paperback 2008 by Pan Books
an imprint of Pan Macmillan, a division of Macmillan Publishers Limited
Pan Macmillan, 20 New Wharf Road, London N1 9RR
Basingstoke and Oxford
Associated companies throughout the world
www.panmacmillan.com

ISBN 978-0-330-51654-9

3 5 7 9 8 6 4 2

A CIP catalogue record for this book is available from
the British Library.

Typeset by SetSystems Ltd, Saffron Walden, Essex

Printed and bound by
CPI Group (UK) Ltd, Croydon, CR0 4YY

For Marc Mohan,

who loved me even after he read this book

Acknowledgements

Thanks to my writing group: Chuck, Suzy, Mary, Diana and Barbara. I know I keep saying it, but your input made all the difference. Thanks also to my agent Joy Harris and everyone at the Joy Harris Agency (hi, Adam!) as well as my editor Kelley Ragland, George Witte, Andy Martin and everyone at St Martin's. Maria Rejt, Katie James and everyone at Pan Macmillan, you are all twisted and fantastic. I am lucky to know such excellent people in publishing. Dr Patricia Cain and Dr Frank McCullar provided medical consults, and Mike Keefe and the dogs walked with me along the Willamette while I picked out places for corpses to wash up. Thanks to my mom, always, my dad and Susan, and my large and fantastic family (especially my aunts, the Cain Millers and my graceful and strong grandmothers). Roddy McDonnell, thanks for making me such an awesome parallel parker – it is still my proudest talent. Laura Ohm and Fred Lifton, thanks for the food and company; and to my friends at the *Oregonian*, thanks for letting me write for you and hang out with you. Maryann Kelley, I've been thinking about you a lot lately. Thank you Wendy Lane, of Lane PR, the only person I ever write for who responds with two words: 'It's perfect.' Special thanks to my husband Marc Mohan for his editing prowess and for his tolerance of my love of televised surgery, and thanks to our daughter Eliza for taking all those extra long naps. Eliza, you can't read this book until you're twenty-one. I mean it.

1

Archie doesn't know for sure that it's her until that moment. There is a dull bloom of warmth in his spine, his vision blurs, and then he knows that Gretchen Lowell is the killer. He realizes that he has been drugged, but it is too late. He fumbles for his gun, but he is ham-fisted and can only lift it awkwardly from his belt clip and hold it out as if it were a gift to her. She takes it and smiles, kissing him gently on the forehead. Then she reaches into his coat and takes the cell phone, turning it off and slipping it into her purse. He is almost paralysed now, slumped in the leather chair in her home office. But his mind is a prison of clarity. She kneels down next to him, the way one might with a child, and puts her lips so close to his that they are almost kissing. His pulse throbs in his throat. He can't swallow. She smells like lilacs.

'It's time to go, darling,' she whispers. She stands then, and he is lifted from behind, elbows under his armpits. A man in front of him, red-faced and heavy, takes his legs, and he is carried into the garage and laid in the back of the green Voyager – the vehicle Archie and his task force have spent months looking for – and she crawls in on top of him. He realizes then that there is someone else in the van, that she wasn't the one behind him, but he doesn't have time to process this because she is straddling his torso, a knee pressing on either side of his waist. He cannot move his eyes any more, so she narrates for his benefit.

'I'm rolling up your right sleeve. I'm tying off a vein.' Then she holds up a hypodermic in his sight line. *Medical training*, he thinks. Eighteen per cent of female serial killers are nurses. He is staring at the ceiling of the van. Grey metal. *Stay awake*, he thinks. Remember everything, every detail, it will be important. He thinks: *if I live.*

'I'm going to let you rest for a little while.' She smiles and puts her flat, pretty face in front of his so he can see her, and her blond hair brushing his cheek, though he cannot feel it. 'We'll have plenty of time for fun later.'

He cannot respond, cannot even blink now. His breath comes in long, shallow rasps. He cannot see her push the needle in his arm, but he assumes she has, because then there is only darkness.

He wakes up on his back. He is still groggy and it takes him a moment to realize that the red-faced man is standing over him. In this moment, the very first moment of Archie's awareness, the man's head explodes. Archie jerks as the man's blood and brain matter blow forward, splattering Archie's face and chest, a vomit of warm, clotted fluid. He tries to move, but his hands and feet are bound to a table. He feels a piece of something hot slide down his face and slop on to the floor, and he pulls hard against the bindings until his skin breaks, but he cannot budge them. He gags, but his mouth is taped shut, forcing the bile back into his throat, making him gag again. His eyes burn. Then he sees her, standing behind where the man's body has fallen, holding the gun she has just used to execute him.

'I wanted you to understand right away how committed I am to you,' she says. 'That you are the only one.' And then she turns and walks away.

He is left there then to contemplate what has just happened. He swallows hard, willing himself to remain calm, to look around. He is alone. The man is dead on the floor. Gretchen is gone. The driver of the van is gone. Archie's blood is pulsing so violently that it is the only sensation. Time passes. At first, he thinks he is in an operating room. It is a large space, walled with white ceramic subway tiles and well lit by fluorescent lights. He turns his head from side to side and sees several trays of instruments, medical-looking machinery, a drain in the cement floor. He strains again at his bindings and realizes that he is strapped to a gurney. Tubes are coming in and out of him: a catheter, an IV. There are no windows in the room and a faint earthy smell skirts the edge of his consciousness. Mildew. A basement.

He starts to think like a cop now. The others had been tortured for a couple of days before she dumped the bodies. That means that he has time. Two days. Maybe three. They could find him still in that amount of time. He had told Henry where he was going, that he had a psych consult about the newest body. He had wanted to see her, to get her advice. He was not prepared for this. But they would connect it. Henry would connect it. It would be the last place to which he could be traced. He had made a call to his wife on the way. That would be the last point of contact. How much time had passed since he had been taken?

She is there again. On the other side of the table from where the body still lies, thick, dark blood seeping on to the grey floor. He remembers when she had first introduced herself – the psychiatrist who had given up her practice to write a book. She had read about the task force and had called him to see if she could help. It had been hell on all of them. She offered to come in. Not counselling, she had said. Just talk. They had been working on the case for almost ten years. Twenty-three bodies in three states. It had taken a toll. She invited those who were interested to come to a group session. Just talk. He had been surprised at how many of the detectives had shown up. It might have had something to do with the fact that she was beautiful.

The funny thing was, it had helped. She was very good.

She pulls the white sheet covering him down so that his chest is exposed, and he realizes that he's naked. She places a hand flat on his breastbone. He knows what this means. He has memorized the crime photos, the abrasions and burns on the torsos. It is part of the profile, one of her signatures.

'Do you know what comes next?' she asks, knowing that he does.

He needs to talk to her. To stall. He makes a garbled noise through the duct tape and motions with his head for her to take it off. She touches her finger to his lips and shakes her head. 'Not just yet,' she says softly.

She asks it again, a little more harshly. 'Do you know what comes next?'

He nods.

She smiles, satisfied. 'That's why I prepared something special for you, darling.' She has an instrument tray beside her and she turns and withdraws something from it. A hammer and nail. Interesting, he thinks, amazed at his ability to detach from himself, to remain clinical. So far the victims have been seemingly random – male, female, young, old – but the torso damage, though it has evolved, has been notably consistent. She has never used nails before.

She seems pleased. 'I thought you'd appreciate some

variety.' She lets her fingertips dance up his ribcage until she finds the rib she is looking for and then she places the point of the nail against his skin and comes down hard with the hammer. He feels the explosion of his rib breaking and gags again. His chest burns with pain. He fights to breathe. His eyes water. She wipes a tear from his flushed cheek and caresses his hair, and then she finds another rib and repeats the process. And another. When she is done, she has broken six of his ribs. The nail is wet with blood. She lets it drop back on the instrument tray with an innocuous clink. He can't shift his body even a millimetre without a searing pain, like none he has ever felt. His nasal passages have clogged with mucus, he can't breathe through his mouth, he has to brace himself for agony with every lung expansion, and still he can't make himself breathe shallowly, can't slow the panicked, heavy pants that sound like sobs. *Maybe two days was optimistic*, he thinks. Maybe he would just die now.

2

The scar on his chest was pale and raised, the fibrous tissue no wider than a piece of yarn. It began a few inches below his left nipple, carved a naked path through his dark chest hair, arced, and then arced again back down to its original point. It was shaped like a heart.

Archie was always aware of it, the raised skin against the cloth of his shirt. He had a lot of scars, but this was the only one that still seemed to hurt. A phantom pain, Archie knew. A broken rib that had never quite healed right, aching underneath. A scar wouldn't hurt. Not after all this time.

The phone rang. Archie turned slowly to look at it, knowing what it meant: another victim.

He only got calls from two people: his ex-wife and his ex-partner. He'd already talked to Debbie that day, so that left Henry. He glanced at the caller ID on his cell phone and confirmed his suspicions.

He picked up the phone. 'Yeah,' he said. He was sitting in his apartment living room in the dark. He hadn't planned it that way. He had just sat down a few hours before and the sun had set and he hadn't bothered to turn on the light. Plus, the dingy apartment, with its sparse furnishings and stained carpet, looked slightly less sad cloaked in blackness.

Henry's gruff voice filled the phone line. 'He took another girl,' he said. And there you had it.

The digital clock that sat on the empty bookcase blinked insistently in the dim room. It was an hour and thirty-five minutes off, but Archie had never bothered to reset it, he just did the maths to calculate the time. 'So they want to reconvene the task force,' Archie said. He had already told Henry that he would go back if they agreed to his terms. He touched the files that Henry had given him weeks before. They were on his lap, the crime-scene photographs of the dead girls tucked neatly inside.

'It's been two years. I told them you had recovered. That you were ready to come back to work full-time.'

Archie smiled in the dark. 'So you lied.'

'Power of positive thinking. You caught Gretchen Lowell, and she scared the crap out of everybody. This new guy? He's killed three girls already. And he's taken another one.'

'Gretchen caught *me*.' A rectangular brass pillbox sat on the coffee table next to a glass of water. Archie didn't bother with coasters. The scratched-up oak coffee table had come with the apartment. Everything in Archie's apartment was scarred.

'And you survived.' There was a pause. 'Remember?'

With a delicate flick of his thumb, Archie opened the pillbox and took out three white oval pills and tucked them in his mouth.

'My old job?' He took a drink of water, relaxing as he felt the pills travel down his throat. Even the glass had been there when he moved in.

'Task-force supervisor.'

There was one more requirement. The most important one. 'And the reporter?'

'I don't like this,' Henry said.

Archie waited. There was too much in motion. Henry wouldn't back down now. Besides, Archie knew that Henry would do almost anything for him.

'She's perfect,' Henry said, relenting. 'I saw her picture. You'll like her. She's got pink hair.'

Archie looked down at the files on his lap. He could do this. All he had to do was keep it together long enough for his plan to work. He opened the top file. His eyes had adjusted to the dark and he could make out the vague image of a ghostly body in the mud. The killer's first victim. Archie's mind filled in the colour: the strawberry ligature marks on her neck, the blushed, blistered skin. 'How old is the girl?'

'Fifteen. Disappeared on her way home from school. Along with her bike.' Henry paused. Archie could hear his frustration in his silence. 'We've got nothing.'

'Amber alert?' Archie asked.

'Issued a half-hour ago,' Henry said.

'Canvass the neighbourhood. Dogs, everything.

Send uniforms door to door. See if anyone saw anything along the route she would have taken.'

'Technically, you're not on the job until morning.'

'Do it anyway,' Archie said.

Henry hesitated. 'You're up for this, right?'

'How long has she been missing?' Archie asked.

'Since six-fifteen.'

She's dead, Archie thought. 'Pick me up in a half-hour,' he said.

'An hour,' Henry said after a pause. 'Drink some coffee. I'll send a car.'

Archie sat there in the dark for a few minutes after he'd hung up. It was quiet. No TV blaring from the upstairs apartment; no footsteps overhead; just the pulse of traffic going by in the rain, a steady blast of forced air and the rattled hum of the dying refrigerator motor. He looked at the clock and did the maths. It was just after nine p.m. The girl had been gone for almost three hours. He was warm and woozy from the pills. *You could do a lot of damage to someone in three hours.* He reached up, slowly undid the top few buttons of his shirt and inserted his right hand under the fabric, placing it over his ribs, running his fingers over the thick scars that webbed his skin, until he found the heart that Gretchen Lowell had carved on him.

He had spent ten years working on the Beauty Killer Task Force, tracking the north-west's most prolific serial killer. A quarter of his life spent standing over corpses at crime scenes, paging through autopsy reports, sifting through clues; all that work, and Gretchen had tricked him into walking right into a trap. Now Gretchen was in prison, and Archie was free.

Funny. Sometimes it still felt like the other way around.

3

Susan didn't want to be there. Her childhood home was cluttered, and its tiny Victorian rooms reeked of cigarettes and sandalwood. She sat on the gold thrift-store couch in the parlour, occasionally looking at her watch, crossing and uncrossing her legs, twisting her hair around her fingers.

'Are you done yet?' she finally asked her mother.

Susan's mother, Bliss, looked up from the project she had spread out on the large wooden wire-spool that served as a coffee table. 'Soon,' she said.

On the same night every year, Bliss burned a likeness of Susan's father in effigy. Susan knew it was crazy, but with Bliss it was easier to just go along. Bliss made the foot-tall father figure out of bundled straw, wound round with brown packing string. It had been an evolving process. The first year, she had used dead bear grass from the yard, and it had been too wet and hadn't burned. Kerosene had been required to get the thing ablaze and sparks had set the compost pile on fire. The neighbours had called 911. Now Bliss bought straw ready-packaged at a pet-supply store. It came in a plastic bag with a picture of a rabbit on it.

Susan had said she wouldn't come this year, but there she sat, watching her mother wrap the packing string tighter and tighter around the little straw man's femurs.

Bliss cut the string, tied it in a knot around the straw man's ankle and took a drag off her cigarette. That was Bliss for you: she drank green algae and smoked menthols. She embraced contradictions. She wore no make-up except for blood-red lipstick, which she wore every day without fail. She refused to wear fur except for her vintage leopardskin coat. She was a vegan, but she ate milk chocolate. She had always made Susan feel, in comparison, less beautiful, less glamorous, less crazy.

Susan would admit that she and Bliss did have two things in common: a shared belief in the artistic potential of hair, and poor taste in men. Bliss cut hair for a living and wore her bleached hippie dreads down to her waist. Susan coloured her own hair, dyeing her chin-length bob colours like Green Envy or Ultra Violet or, most recently, Cotton Candy Pink.

Bliss appraised her handiwork with a satisfied nod. 'There,' she said. She got up from her cross-legged position on the floor and bounced into the kitchen, her dreadlocks flapping behind her. She reappeared a moment later with a photograph.

'I thought you might want to have this,' she said.

Susan took the colour snapshot. It was a photograph of her as a toddler, standing in the yard with her father. He still had his heavy beard and was bending down so he could hold her hand; she was looking up at him and beaming, all plump cheeks and tiny teeth. Her brown hair was tied up in messy pigtails, and her red dress was dirty; he was wearing a T-shirt and holey jeans. They were both sunburned and barefoot, and they appeared completely happy. Susan had never seen the photograph before.

She felt a wave of sorrow wash over her. 'Where did you find this?' she asked.

'It was in a box of his old papers.'

Susan's father had died when she was fourteen. Now when Susan thought of him, he was always kind and wise, a picture of paternal perfection. She knew it wasn't that simple. But after he was gone, both she and Bliss had fallen apart, so he must have had some levelling influence.

'He loved you so much,' Bliss said quietly.

Susan wanted a cigarette, but, after spending her childhood lecturing Bliss about lung cancer, she didn't like to smoke around her. It seemed an admission of defeat.

Bliss looked like she wanted to say something motherly. She reached up and smoothed a piece of Susan's pink hair. 'The colour's faded. Come into the salon and I'll touch it up. The pink is flattering on you. You're so pretty.'

'I'm not pretty,' Susan said, turning away. 'I'm striking. There's a difference.'

Bliss withdrew her hand.

It was dark and wet in the back yard. The back porch light illuminated a half-circle of muddy grass and dead sedum planted too close to the house. The straw man was in the copper fire bowl. Bliss leaned over and set the straw on fire with a white plastic lighter and then stood back. The straw crackled and burned and then the flames crept up the little straw man's torso until they engulfed him fully. His little arms were splayed wide, as if in panic. Then all human shape was lost to the orange blaze. Susan and Bliss burned Susan's father every year so that they could let him go, start afresh. At least that was the idea. Maybe they would stop if it ever worked.

Susan's eyes filled with tears and she turned away. That was the thing. You thought you were emotionally steady, and then your dead father went and had a birthday and your crazy mother went and set a straw doll on fire in his memory.

'I've got to go,' Susan said. 'There's someone I need to meet.'

4

The club was choked with cigarette smoke. Susan's eyes stung from it. She pulled another cigarette out of a pack on the bar, lit it and took a drag. The music pounded through the floor. It snaked along the walls and up the stools and tunnelled its way through Susan's legs and vibrated the copper surface of the bar. Susan watched the yellow pack of cigarettes jump. It was dark. It was always dark in that club. She liked the way that you could be there and hide in plain sight from the person right next to you. She was good at drinking, but she'd had one drink too many. She considered this. It had probably been the blackberry martini. Or possibly the Pabst. Her mind blurred from the booze and she placed a hand flat on the bar until the sensation passed.

'I'm going outside for some air,' she said to the man next to her. She yelled it to be heard over the music, but the club's throbbing baseline sucked the life out of all other sound.

The front door was on the other side of the dance floor, and as she made her way through the Monday-night crowd, she compensated for the drinking with a too-careful stride, head held high and level, arms extended a few inches from her sides, eyes straight ahead, cigarette burning. No one danced at that club. They just stood around, shoulder to shoulder, nodding their heads to the beat. Susan had to touch people to get them to part for her, a shoulder, an upper arm, and they would melt a few inches back so she could pass. She could feel their eyes follow her. Susan knew she attracted attention. It wasn't that she was pretty exactly. Her look belonged in the 1920s: a wide face with a large forehead that tapered to a small chin, skinny limbs, a rosebud mouth and a flat chest. Her chin-length hair and very short bangs made her look even more like a deranged flapper. 'Striking' was definitely the word for it. Without the pink hair, she might even have been beautiful, but it distracted from the sweetness of her features, making her look harder. Which was sort of the point.

She got to the door, squeezed past the bouncer and felt the crisp fresh air wash over her. The club was in Old Town, which up until recently had been called 'Skid Row'. Back when people still called Portland 'Stumptown', there had been a thriving shanghai business in that part of town, and thousands of loggers and sailors had gone into a bar or brothel only to wake up in the hold of a boat. These days, Portland's biggest industries were tourism and high-tech; many of Old Town's weathered turn-of-the-century brick buildings were being redeveloped as lofts, and you could tour the shanghai tunnels for twelve dollars.

Everything changed eventually.

Susan dropped what was left of the cigarette on the wet cement, ground it under the heel of her boot, leaned up against the brick wall of the club and closed her eyes.

'Do you want to smoke a joint?'

She opened her eyes. 'Fuck, Ethan,' she said. 'You scared the shit out of me. I didn't think you heard me in there.'

Ethan grinned. 'I was right behind you.'

'I was listening to the rain,' Susan said, lifting her chin at the glistening black street. She smiled slowly at Ethan. She had only known him about two hours, and she was beginning to suspect that he was smitten. He was not her usual type. He was in his late twenties, in that particular punk-rock way. He probably wore cords and a hooded sweatshirt every day. He lived with five other guys in a crappy house in a cheap part of town. He'd worked in a record store for eight years, played in three bands, listened to Iggy Pop, the Velvet Underground. He smoked pot and drank beer, but not the cheap stuff. 'Do you have a one-hitter?'

He nodded happily.

'Let's walk around the block,' she said, taking his hand, arm swinging, leading him out into the steady spit of Portland rain.

He loaded the one-hitter as they walked and passed

it to her for the virgin drag. She took a hit, feeling the satisfying burn in her lungs before she exhaled. She placed the one-hitter in his mouth and guided him around the corner of the building they were passing. There wasn't much traffic in that part of town at night. She put her face right in front of his. He was taller, so she was looking up.

'Do you want a blow job?' she asked gravely.

He smiled that sort of dumb smile that guys get when they cannot believe their good luck. 'Uh, sure.'

Susan smiled back. She had given her first blow job at fourteen. She'd had a good teacher. 'Really?' She tilted her head in an exaggerated expression of surprise. 'That's funny. Since you haven't been taking my calls.'

'What?'

Their noses were almost touching. 'I've left you eleven messages, Ethan. About Molly Palmer.'

His smile vanished and a coin-slot-shaped furrow appeared between his eyebrows. 'Excuse me?'

'She was your college girlfriend, right? Did she ever tell you about her relationship with the senator?'

Ethan tried to back up, realized he was against a wall, and instead shifted awkwardly before settling on crossing his arms. 'Who exactly are you?'

'There've been rumours for years that the senator fucked his kids' teenage babysitter,' Susan said. She stayed in front of him, not giving up ground; she was so close that she could see the saliva pooling in his slightly open mouth. 'Is that true, Ethan? She ever mention anything?'

'I swear to God,' Ethan said, stressing every syllable, looking everywhere but at Susan, 'I don't know anything about it.'

The phone rang. Susan didn't move. 'Is that you or me?' she asked.

'I don't have a cell phone,' Ethan stammered.

She arched an eyebrow. 'Must be me,' she said, shrugging. She reached into her purse, pulled out her cell phone and answered it.

'Hello?'

'I've got a job for you.'

She turned away from Ethan. Took a couple of steps. 'Ian? Is that you? It's after midnight.'

'It's important.' There was a pause. 'You know those missing girls?'

'Yeah?'

'There's another one. The mayor had an emergency meeting tonight. They're reconvening the Beauty Killer Task Force. Clay and I are down here now. I think this is big, Susan. We want you to write it.'

Susan glanced over at Ethan. He was staring at the one-hitter in his hand, looking sort of dazed.

'Cops and serial killers?' she said.

'The mayor is going to let us have a press person on the ground in the task force. They don't want another repeat of the Beauty Killer thing. Can you come down early tomorrow – say, six – just to talk about it?'

Susan checked her watch. 'Six in the morning?'

'Yep.'

She looked over at Ethan again. 'I'm kind of working on something else,' she whispered to Ian.

'Whatever it is, this is more important. We'll talk about it in the morning.'

Her head was foggy from the liquor. 'OK,' she agreed. She snapped the phone shut and bit her lip. Then she turned back to Ethan. It had taken her months to track him down. She didn't even know if he still kept in touch with Molly. But it was all she had. 'Here's the thing,' she said to him. 'The media's ignored the rumours long enough. And now I'm going to find out what happened. And I'm going to write about it.' She made eye contact with him and held it, wanting him to see her face, to see past the pink hair, to see how serious she was. 'Tell Molly that. Tell her that I'll keep her safe. And that I'm interested in the truth. Tell her that when she's ready to talk about what happened, I'll listen.' The rain had progressed from a spit to a half-hearted drizzle. She pressed a business card into his hand. 'My name is Susan Ward. I'm with the *Herald*.'

5

The lobby of the *Oregon Herald* didn't open until seven-thirty a.m., so Susan had to use the loading-dock entrance at the south side of the building. She was running on four hours' sleep. She'd spent an hour online that morning, trying to get up to speed on the latest missing girl, forsaking a shower, so her hair still smelled vaguely of cigarettes and beer. She'd tied it back and dressed simply in black pants and a black long-sleeved shirt. Then thrown on some canary-yellow sneakers. No point being completely boring.

She flashed her press pass at the night security guard, a plump African-American kid who had finally made it through *The Two Towers* and had just started reading *The Return of the King*. 'How's the book?' she asked.

He shrugged and buzzed her into the basement with barely a glance. There were three elevators in the *Herald* building. Only one of them ever worked at one time. She took it to the fifth floor.

The *Herald* was located in downtown Portland. It was a beautiful downtown, full of grand buildings that dated back to when Portland was the largest shipping port in the north-west. The streets were tree-lined and bicycle-friendly, there were plenty of parks, and public art on every block. Office workers on break lounged next to homeless people playing chess in Pioneer Square, street musicians serenaded shoppers and, Portland being Portland, there was almost always somebody protesting against something. In the midst of all this elegance and bustle was the *Herald* building, an eight-storey brick-and-sandstone behemoth that the good citizenry of Portland thought was unsightly back when it was built in 1920 and had thought was unsightly ever since. Any interior charm had been gutted during an ill-conceived renovation in the 1970s, which must have been the worst decade in which to renovate anything. Grey industrial carpeting, white walls, low panelled ceilings, fluorescent lights. Except for the framed stories that lined the halls and the unusually cluttered desks of the employees, it could have been an insurance agency. When she had imagined working in a newspaper office, she had imagined bustling chaos and colour and fast-talking colleagues. The *Herald* was soundless and formal. If you sneezed, everybody turned to look.

The paper was independent, meaning that it was one of the few major dailies in the country that wasn't part of a corporate chain. A family of timber barons had owned it since the 1960s, having purchased it from another family of timber barons. The new barons had brought in a new publisher, a former public-relations executive from New York named Howard Jenkins, to run the place a few years before, and since then the paper had won three Pulitzers. It was a good thing, Susan figured, because, newsprint aside, there wasn't a lot of money in being a timber baron any more.

The fifth floor was so quiet that Susan could hear the watercooler buzzing. She scanned the main room, where rows of low-walled pens housed the *Herald*'s news and features staff. A few of the copy editors sat hunched over their desks, blinking sadly at computer screens. Susan spotted Nedda Carson, the assistant news editor, walking down the hallway with her usual large travel mug of *chai* in hand.

'They're in there,' Nedda said, jerking her head towards one of the small meeting rooms.

'Thanks,' Susan said. She could see Ian Harper through the glass panel next to the door. He had been one of Jenkins's first hires, stolen from the *New York Times*, and he was one of the paper's star editors. She walked over and knocked once on the glass. He looked up and waved her in. The room was small and painted white, with a conference table, four chairs and a poster encouraging *Herald* employees to recycle. Ian was perched on the back of one of the chairs. He always perched like that. Susan thought it was because the elevation made him feel powerful, but maybe it was just more comfortable. News editor Clay Lo sat across the table from Ian, his doughy head in one hand, glasses askew. For a minute, Susan thought he was asleep.

'Jesus,' Susan said. 'Tell me you haven't been here all night.'

'We had an editorial meeting at five,' Ian said. He flung his hand at a chair. 'Have a seat.' Ian was wearing black jeans, black Converse sneakers, and a black blazer over a faded T-shirt with a picture of John Lennon in front of the Statue of Liberty on it. Most of Ian's T-shirts were intended to communicate that he was from New York.

Clay looked up and nodded at her, eyes bleary. A cup of coffee from the commissary downstairs was on the table in front of him. It was the last dregs from the air pot. Susan could see the grounds around the lip of the Styrofoam cup.

She sat down, pulled her reporter's notebook and a pen out of her purse, set them on the table and said, 'What's up?'

Ian sighed and touched the sides of his head. It was a gesture intended to indicate thoughtfulness, but Susan knew he did it to check that his hair was still tucked back into his neat, short ponytail. 'Kristy Mathers,' Ian said, smoothing his temples with his hands. 'Fifteen. Lives with her dad. He's a cab driver. Didn't know she was missing until he got home last night. She was last seen heading home from school.'

Susan knew all this from the morning news. 'Jefferson High,' she said.

'Yeah,' Ian said. He picked up a *Herald* mug that sat in front of him, held it for a minute, and then set it back on the table without taking a sip. 'Three girls. Three high schools. They're adding a police detail at each school for security.'

'Are they sure she didn't just go to meet a boyfriend or head to a sale at Hot Topic or something?' Susan asked.

Ian shook his head. 'She was supposed to babysit for a neighbour. Never showed. Didn't call. They're taking it pretty seriously. What do you know about the Beauty Killer Task Force?'

Susan felt goose bumps rise on her arms at the very mention of the infamous serial killer. She looked from Ian to Clay and back to Ian. 'What does the Beauty Killer have to do with this?' she asked.

'What do you know about the task force?' Ian asked again.

'Gretchen Lowell killed a whole bunch of people,' Susan said. 'The Beauty Killer Task Force spent ten years trying to catch her. Then she kidnapped the lead detective on the task force. That was over two years ago. Everyone thought he was dead. I was home for Thanksgiving from grad school when it happened. She turned herself in. Just like that. He almost died. She went to jail. I went back to grad school.' She turned to Clay. 'They keep attaching murders to her, though, right? I think they got her to give up something like twenty more victims in the first year after she was arrested. Every month or two, she cops to a new one. She was one of our great psychopaths.' She chuckled nervously. '"Great", as in scary, brutal and cunning, not super-duper.'

Clay folded his hands on the table and looked at Susan meaningfully. 'We gave the cops a bit of a hard time.'

Susan nodded. 'I remember. They got loads of negative press. There was a lot of frustration and fear. Some very catty op-eds. But in the end, they were heroes. There was that book, right? And, like, a thousand human-interest stories about Archie Sheridan, hero cop.'

'He's back,' Ian said.

Susan leaned forward. 'Shut up. I thought he was on medical leave.'

'He was. They talked him into coming back to lead the new task force. The mayor thinks he can catch this guy.'

'Like he caught Gretchen Lowell?'

'Without the "almost dying" part, yeah.'

'Or the op-eds?' Susan asked.

'That's where you come in,' Ian said. 'There was no access last time around. They think that if they let us in on the process, we'll be less inclined to point and snicker. So they're letting us profile Sheridan.'

'Why me?' she asked sceptically.

Ian shrugged. 'They asked for you specifically. You weren't here the last time around. And you're a writer.

The MFA makes them less anxious than a J-school degree.' He touched the sides of his head again, this time finding a tiny stray hair and gliding it back into place. 'They don't want a reporter. They don't want digging. They want human interest. Also, you went to Cleveland High.'

'Ten years ago,' Susan pointed out.

'It's where the first girl disappeared,' Ian said. 'It's colour. Plus, you're a terrific feature writer. You do great at the series stuff. You've got a knack for it. Jenkins is convinced this is our ticket to another Pulitzer.'

'I write quirky essays about burn victims and rescued pets.'

'You've been wanting to do something serious,' Ian said.

Should she tell them? Susan tapped her pen against the notebook for a minute and then laid the pen carefully down on the table. 'I've sort of been looking into the whole Senator Castle thing.'

It was like she had started masturbating right there on the table. There was a moment of complete stillness. Then Clay slowly sat up. He glanced at Ian, who sat on the back of his chair, hands on his knees, back straight. 'Those are rumours,' Ian said. 'That's all. Molly Palmer had a lot of psychological problems. There's nothing there. It's a smear campaign. Trust me. It's not worth your time. And it's not your beat.'

'She was fourteen,' Susan said.

Ian picked up his mug but again didn't take a sip. 'Have you talked to her?'

Susan sank an inch in her chair. 'I can't find her.'

Ian gave a vindicated little snort and put the mug back on the table. 'And that's because she doesn't want to be found. She was in and out of juvie. In and out of rehab. You think I didn't look into this the moment I got to town? She's disturbed. She was in high school and she lied to a few friends and the lie snowballed. Period.' He frowned. 'So do you want the serial-killer task-force dream story, or should I give it to Derek?'

Susan winced. She and Derek Rogers had been hired at the same time, and had been competitive from the start. She crossed her arms and considered the rather appealing possibility of not having to write another story about a police dog. But she had hesitations. This was important. It was life-and-death. And while she would never admit it to anyone in that room, she took that very seriously. She wanted the story. She just didn't want to be the one to fuck it up.

'We're thinking four parts,' Ian continued. 'We'll jump each story from A-one. You follow Archie Sheridan. You write about what you see. It's your only beat. If you want it.'

The front page. 'It's because I'm a girl, isn't it?'

'A delicate flower,' Ian said.

Ian had won a Pulitzer back when he worked for the *Times*. He'd let Susan hold the medallion once. Sitting there now, she could almost feel the weight of it in her hand. 'Yeah,' she said, her pulse quickening. 'I want it.'

Ian smiled. He was handsome when he smiled, and he knew it. 'Good.'

'So?' Susan said, snapping her notebook shut in preparation to stand up. 'Where am I supposed to find him?'

'I'll take you over there at three,' Ian said. 'There's a press conference.'

Susan froze. Now that she had committed, she was dying to get started. 'But I need to see him working.'

'He wants some time to get organized.' Ian's expression didn't leave much room for discussion.

Half a day. It was a lifetime in a missing-persons case. 'What am I supposed to do until then?' Susan asked.

'Finish up all your other work,' Ian said. 'And learn everything you can.' He picked up the newsprint-stained tan telephone that sat on the table and punched some buttons. 'Derek?' he said. 'Can you come in here?'

It took about a nanosecond for Derek Rogers to appear at the conference-room door. Derek was Susan's age, which she, in her more contemplative moments, admitted brought out her competitive instincts. He had gone to college in South Dakota on a football scholarship and settled for sports journalism after an injury forced him off the team. Now he split his time between the crime and city desks at the *Herald*. He still looked like a jock, square-jawed and clean-cut, with that way of walking a little bow-legged, like a cowboy. Susan suspected that he blow-dried his hair. But he wasn't wearing his suit jacket today, and his eyes looked bleary. Susan considered that perhaps he led a more interesting life than she gave him credit for. He smiled at her, trying to catch her eye. He was always doing that. Susan remained evasive.

Derek was carrying a projector, a laptop and a box of doughnuts. He slid the doughnuts on to the table and opened the box. A sickly-sweet aroma filled the room. 'They're Krispy Kreme,' he said. 'I drove all the way to Beaverton.'

A girl was missing and Derek was buying doughnuts. Nice. Susan glanced at Clay. But he didn't launch into a lecture about the grave nature of the situation. He took two doughnuts. 'They're better when they're fresh,' he announced.

Ian took an apple fritter. 'You don't want one?' he asked Susan.

Susan did. But she didn't want to make Derek look good. 'I'm fine,' she said.

Derek fiddled with the equipment. 'I'll just get set up.' He opened the laptop and turned on the projector, and a square of colour appeared on the white wall. Susan watched as the blur focused into a PowerPoint title page. On a blood-red background, a Halloween font read THE SCHOOLGIRL KILLER.

'The Schoolgirl Killer?' Clay asked sceptically. White clumps of doughnut glaze clung to the corners of his mouth. His voice was fat with sugar.

Derek glanced down shyly. 'I've been working on a name.'

'Too literal,' Clay said. 'We need something snappy.'

'How about the Willamette Strangler?' Derek said.

Ian shrugged. 'It's a little derivative.'

'It's too bad he doesn't eat them,' Clay said drily. 'Then we could come up with something really clever.'

'So the third girl's been missing how long?' asked Susan.

Derek cleared his throat. 'Right. Sorry.' He faced the group authoritatively, his fists on the table. 'Let's start with Lee Robinson, Cleveland High. She disappeared in October. She had jazz-choir practice after school. When it was over, she left the gym, where practice was held, and told some friends that she was walking home. She lived ten blocks away.'

Susan flipped open her notebook. 'Was it dark?' she asked.

'No,' Derek said, 'but close. Lee never arrived home. When she was about an hour late for dinner, her mother started calling her friends. And then, at nine-thirty, she called the police. They're not thinking the worst yet.'

Derek hit a button on the laptop and the title page dissolved into the image of a scanned *Herald* news story. 'This is the first story we ran, on the front page of Metro, October twenty-ninth, forty-eight hours after Lee's disappearance.' Susan felt a jolt of sadness at the sight of the girl's school picture: flat brown hair, braces, jazz-choir sweatshirt, pimples, blue eyeshadow, lip gloss. Derek continued: 'The cops asked anyone with information to call a hotline. They got over a thousand calls. Nothing panned out.'

'You're sure you don't want an apple fritter?' Ian asked Susan.

'Yes,' Susan said.

Derek hit a key again. The story dissolved into another slide, an image of the front page. 'The November first story was front-page news. "Girl Missing".' The school picture was there again, along with a picture of Lee's mother, father and brother at a neighbourhood vigil.

'There were two more stories after that, with very little new info,' Derek said. Another slide. This one was dated 7 November, another front-page headline: MISSING GIRL FOUND DEAD. 'A search-and-rescue volunteer found her in mud on the banks of Ross Island. She'd been raped and strangled to death. The ME estimated that she had been in the mud for a week.'

There was a story every day for the next week: rumours, leads, neighbours remembering how lovely Lee was, classmate vigils, church services, a growing reward fund for information leading to the killer.

'On February second, Dana Stamp finished up a Lincoln High dance-team practice,' Derek said. 'She showered, said goodbye to friends and headed to her car, which was parked in the student parking lot. She never made it home. Her mother, a real-estate agent, was showing a house on the east side and didn't get home until nine p.m. She called the police just before midnight.' Slide. ANOTHER GIRL MISSING screamed the front page of the 3 February issue of the *Herald*.

Another school photograph. Susan sat forward a little and examined the girl on the wall. The similarities were striking. Dana didn't have the braces or the acne, so at first glance she seemed prettier than Lee, but once you looked more closely, they could have been related. Dana was the girl Lee was going to be, once the braces came off and the pimples cleared up. They had the same oval face, wide-set eyes, small, unremarkable nose and brown hair. Both were skinny, with the awkward beginning of breasts. Dana smiled in her picture; Lee didn't.

Susan had followed the story. You couldn't live in Portland and avoid it. As the days slipped by without any clues as to Dana's whereabouts, they blended into one girl: DanaandLee. A grave mantra repeated again and again by local newscasters, the lead story, regardless of what was happening nationally or internationally. The police would say publicly only that they were considering the possibility that the two cases might be related, but in everyone's minds, there was no doubt. Their school pictures always appeared side by side. They were referred to as 'the girls'.

Derek looked dramatically from person to person. 'A kayaker found the body partially obscured by brush on the bank of the Esplanade on February fourteenth. Nice, huh? She had been raped and strangled to death.'

The slide dissolved to that day's paper, 8 March. THIRD GIRL VANISHES: CITY RECONVENES BEAUTY KILLER TASK FORCE. Derek summarized: 'Kristy Mathers left school yesterday at six-fifteen after a play rehearsal. She was supposed to ride right home on her bike. Her father's a cabbie. Works late. He stopped by the house around seven p.m., after he wasn't able to reach her by phone. He called the police at seven-thirty. She's still missing.'

Susan gazed at the girl's photograph. She was chubbier than Dana and Lee, but she had the same brown hair and wide-set eyes. Susan glanced up at the round white clock that hummed on the far wall above the door. The black minute-hand jumped forward. It was almost six-thirty. Kristy Mathers had been missing for over twelve hours. A cold chill folded down Susan's spine as she realized that there probably wasn't going to be any happy reunion at the end of this story.

Ian turned to Susan. 'Your subject's Archie Sheridan. Not the girls. The girls are – ' he ran his hand over his hair back to his ponytail – 'background. You write this right, it'll make your career.'

Derek looked confused. 'What do you mean? You

said that this was my story. I was up half the night working on this presentation.'

'Change of plans,' Ian said. He shot Derek one of his handsome smiles. 'Nice PowerPoint, though.'

Derek's entire forehead constricted.

'Relax,' Ian said with a sigh. 'You can update the website. We're setting up a blog.'

Two perfect red spots appeared on Derek's cheeks and Susan could see his jaw tighten. He looked from Ian to Clay. Clay busied himself with another doughnut. Derek looked balefully at Susan. She shrugged and gave him a half-smile. She could afford it.

'OK,' Derek said with a resigned little nod. He snapped his laptop shut and began to coil its cord around his hand. Then he paused, the cord a strangled knot around his fist. 'The After School Strangler,' he said. They all looked at him. He grinned, pleased with himself. 'For the name. I just thought of it.'

Ian looked at Clay, head cocked questioningly.

No, Susan thought. Don't let this bozo name him. Not Derek the Square.

Clay nodded a few times. 'The After School Strangler.' He chuckled mirthlessly. 'It's corny. But I like it.' His laughter faded and he sat perfectly still for a moment. Then he cleared his throat. 'Someone should write an obituary for the girl,' he said softly. 'Just in case.'

6

Archie counted out the Vicodin. Thirteen. He placed two of the white oval pills on the back of the toilet and nestled the other eleven in the brass pillbox, padding them carefully in cotton so they wouldn't rattle. Then he put the pillbox in the pocket of his blazer. Thirteen extra-strength Vicodin. It should be enough. He sighed and pulled the pillbox out of his pocket, counted out another five pills from the large amber plastic prescription bottle, added these to the pillbox and dropped it back in his pocket. Eighteen Vicodin. Ten milligrams of codeine and 750 milligrams of acetaminophen in every dose. The maximum acetaminophen dosage human kidneys could handle was four thousand milligrams in twenty-four hours. He'd done the maths. That was 5.33 pills per day. Not nearly enough. So he played at controlling his habit. He would allow himself one more every few days, up to twenty-five, then he would wean himself, break pills in half, get back down to the recommended four or five a day. Then work his way up again. It was a game. King of the Hill. Everyone took turns. Vicodin for the pain. Xanax for the panic attacks. Zantac for his stomach. Ambien to sleep. They all went into the pillbox.

He traced his fingers along his jawline. He had never been good at shaving, but lately he had become almost dangerous. He pulled at a small piece of toilet paper that was stuck to a razor nick. It came off, but the wound immediately started bleeding again. He splashed some cold water on his face, tore another square of toilet paper off the roll, held it to his chin and looked in the mirror. Archie had never had the ability to appraise his own appearance. His gifts were appraising other people's appearances, empathy, recall and an obsessive, dogged determination that required him to pursue every possible outcome until, like a peeled scab, the truth was exposed. It had rarely occurred to him, during his strange career as a homicide detective, to pay attention to how he might appear to others. Now he turned his eye for detail to his own image. He had sad, dark eyes. He'd had sad eyes long before he'd heard of Gretchen Lowell, long before he'd become a cop. His grandfather, a defrocked priest, had fled Northern Ireland, and they were his eyes: homesick, no matter how many people were around him. Archie had always had sad eyes, but it was as if in the last few years his other features had withdrawn, so now the eyes stood out more. He had the strong chin from his mother's side and a nose that had been broken in a car accident, and cheeks that dimpled when he permitted a lopsided smile. He wasn't pretty. But he wasn't unhandsome, if you liked sort of average-looking, depressed people. He smiled at his image and immediately cringed at the result. Who was he kidding? But he tried to make an effort. He tried to flatten the cowlick at the front of his thick head of curly brown hair and smooth his eyebrows. He wore a ridiculously professorial tan corduroy blazer, and a brown-and-silver silk tie purchased by his ex-wife, who he knew had good taste only because he had heard people comment on it. The blazer, which had once fitted perfectly, now hung too loose in the shoulders. But his socks were clean. He appeared, to himself at least, to look almost normal. He hadn't felt rested in two years. He was forty, but looked at least five years older. He was fighting a losing battle with pills. He could not bear to touch his children. And he looked almost normal. Yes. He could carry it off. He was a cop, he reminded himself. *I can bullshit beautifully*. He pulled the toilet paper off his face and tossed it in the wastebasket under the sink. Then he gripped each side of the basin and examined his reflection. The nick was barely noticeable, really. He smiled. Lifted his full eyebrows. *Hello! Good to see you again! Yep! Feeling fine! All better!* He sighed and let his face fall back into its natural slack expression, and then absent-mindedly picked up the two pills off the toilet and swallowed them without water. It was six-thirty a.m. More than twelve hours had passed since the last time anyone had seen Kristy Mathers.

The new task force offices turned out to be in a former bank, which the city had leased months before for overflow office space. The cement-block building was a one-storey rectangle with few windows, surrounded on all sides by parking lot. Its drive-through ATM was still in operation.

Archie glanced at his watch: almost seven o'clock.

The night-time house-to-house had turned up nothing but tired, scared neighbours. Henry had dropped Archie home at three a.m. with the address of the new task force offices. 'Get a good night's sleep,' Henry had said. And they had both laughed.

Now Archie stood across the street, hands deep in his pockets, surveying the spectacle. A cab had dropped him off – his compromise to the pills. He was an addict, but he was a responsible one. A smile passed his lips. A. Fucking. Bank. There were already three local news vans parked in the lot around the bank building. ALL THE NEWS WORTH KNOWING read a slogan on one of the vans. No national news yet, he noticed. But if he was right, it would only be a matter of time. He watched the reporters, clad in absurdly warm and waterproof coats, confer with their bearded cameramen. They lurched forward expectantly every time a car pulled up, then settled back to cigarettes and thermoses of coffee when the occupant became clear. They were waiting for him, he realized. Not the girls. Not the task force. Not, to be fucking sure, a story. They wanted him: the Beauty Killer's last victim. The bones in his fingers went cold. He ran a hand through his hair and noticed it was wet. He had been standing in the slow rain for ten minutes. *You'll catch your death*, he thought to himself. The words were not in his voice, but hers. Lilting. Teasing. *You'll catch your death, darling.* He took a deep breath, pushed her, for a moment, from his mind, and started towards his new office.

The mob of reporters swarmed around him as soon as his shoes hit the wet concrete of the parking lot. He ignored the questions and the cameras, walking as fast as he could through the gauntlet, shoulders hunched against the rain. 'How does it feel to be back?' 'How's your health?' 'Have you been in contact with Gretchen Lowell?' Don't get distracted, he told himself. He fingered the pillbox in his pocket, gaining solace from its presence. Just keep moving.

He showed his badge to the uniformed officer at the door, and slid in past the reporters kept firmly outside. The bank was full of people – cleaning, tearing down the old transaction counter, moving furniture. The air was dense with the dust of smashed drywall and the hum of power tools. Archie's eyes burned from the particulate matter as he scanned the room. Henry was standing just inside the door, waiting for him. He had shown Archie the ropes when Archie made detective and he had been looking out for him ever since. A large man with a gleaming shaved head and a thick salt-and-pepper moustache, Henry could cut an imposing figure when he chose. But his crinkled grin and kind blue eyes betrayed his warmer nature. Henry knew both facades, and he used them to his advantage. Today he was dressed in a black turtleneck, black leather jacket and black jeans. He wore a hand-tooled black leather belt with a silver and turquoise buckle. It was an ensemble Henry revisited with little variation.

He was attentively brushing white dust off his black pants when he saw Archie. 'Make it past the local newsies?' he asked with amusement.

Archie had been the object of much more voracious press attention, and Henry knew it. 'That's nothing.'

'You would know,' agreed Henry. 'You ready for this?'

'As I'll ever be.' Archie looked around. 'This is a bank.'

'I hope you're not sensitive to asbestos.'

'Does this seem odd to you?' Archie asked.

'I've always liked banks,' Henry said. 'They remind me of money.'

'They all here?'

'They're huddled together, waiting for you in the vault.'

'The vault?'

'Kidding,' Henry said. 'There's a break room. With a microwave. And a mini-fridge.'

'Sure. It being a bank. How's the mood?'

'Like they're about to see a ghost,' Henry said.

A sink, fridge and countertop with cabinets dominated one wall of the break room. Several small square tables had been assembled to form an *ad hoc* conference table. The seven detectives were sitting or standing around it, many with travel mugs of coffee. Conversation stopped dead when Archie entered.

'Good morning,' Archie said. He looked around at the group. Six of them he'd worked with on the Beauty Killer Task Force, two were new. 'I'm Archie Sheridan,' he said in a strong voice. They all knew who he was, even the two he hadn't met. But it gave Archie something to start out with.

The new additions were Mike Flannigan and Jeff Heil, both of medium height and build, one dark-haired, the other light-haired. Archie immediately mentally dubbed them 'the Hardy Boys'. The other five were Claire Masland, Martin Ngyun, Greg Fremont, Anne Boyd and Josh Levy. He had worked with some of these detectives for years, night and day, and, with the exception of Henry, he had not seen any of them since being released from the hospital. He had not wanted to see any of them. They looked at him now with a mixture of affection and anxiety. Archie felt bad for them. He always felt bad for people who knew what he had been through. It made them feel awkward. He knew it was up to him to make them comfortable, so they could work effectively for him, no distractions, no pity. The best tactic, he knew, was to act as if nothing had happened, no time had passed at all. Back to work, just like that. No emotional speeches. Show them that he was up to speed, in control.

'Claire,' he said, spinning around to face the petite detective, 'what's the security situation at the other schools?'

The rest of the team had been brought in that morning. But Claire and Henry had worked the case from the beginning.

Claire sat up a little bit, surprised, but pleased to be put on the spot, as he knew she would be. 'After-school activities have been cancelled until further notice. We've got four uniforms stationed at each school, and six units patrolling around each between five and seven, when he seems to take them. They're hosting safety assemblies today. Sending letters home to the parents suggesting they don't let their girls walk or bike to or from school.'

'Good,' he said. 'Search and rescue?'

Martin Ngyun leaned forward. He wore a Portland Trail Blazers baseball cap. Archie wasn't sure he'd ever seen him without it. 'Just got an update on that. Nothing turned up last night. We've got almost fifty people and ten dogs doing a daylight block-by-block in a square-mile radius around her house. Another hundred volunteers. Nothing yet.'

'I want a roadblock near Jefferson today between five and seven. Stop everyone who drives by. Ask if they've seen anything. If they're driving by there today, there's a chance they drove that route yesterday. Lee Robinson had a cell phone, right? I want to see her phone records and all the girls' e-mail records on my desk.'

He turned to Anne Boyd. She had been the third profiler that the FBI had sent to work on the Beauty Killer case, and the only one who was not an insufferable prick. He had always liked her, but he had not responded to her occasional letters over the last two years. 'When do we get a profile?'

Anne finished off a can of Diet Coke and set it on the table with a tinny clatter. She'd had an Afro the last time Archie had seen her; now her black hair was woven into a thousand tiny braids. They swung as she tilted her head. 'Twenty-four hours. At the most.'

'A sketch?'

'Male, thirty to fifty. And then there's the obvious.'

'Yeah?'

'He makes an effort to return the victims.' She shrugged her plump shoulders. 'He feels bad.'

'So we're looking for a male between the ages of thirty and fifty who feels bad,' Archie summarized. *Sound familiar?* 'If he feels bad,' he theorized aloud to Anne, 'he's vulnerable, right?'

'He knows what he did is wrong. You might be able to intimidate him, yeah.'

Archie bent forward over the table, leaning on his arms, and faced the group. They looked at him expectantly. He could tell that many of them had been up all night, working the case. Every minute that ticked by would eat away at their morale. They would sleep less, eat less and worry more. His team. His responsibility. Archie was not a good manager. He knew this. He put the people who worked for him above the people he worked for. This made him a good leader. As long as he got results, the higher-ups were willing to overlook the manager bit. He had worked on the Beauty Killer Task Force for ten years, led it for four, before they'd caught Gretchen Lowell. He had felt the edge of the brass's axe on his neck during his entire tenure. He had proved himself and almost been killed in the process. And because of it, he had the tenuous trust of the people in that room. This made him loathe all the more the announcement he had to make. 'Before we continue, I should let you know that a writer from the *Herald*, Susan Ward, is going to be following me around.'

Body language stiffened.

'I know,' Archie said, with a sigh. 'It's irregular. But I have to do it and you'll just have to believe me when I tell you that I have a good reason. You are all welcome to co-operate to your level of comfort.' Looking around the room, he wondered what they were thinking. Celebrity whore? Promotion hound? An exclusive exchanged for the burial of some damaging information? *Not even close*, thought Archie. 'Any questions, concerns?' he asked.

Six hands went up.

7

'Tell me about Archie Sheridan,' Susan said. It was mid-afternoon and she had made her way through the folder of research material that Derek had pulled from the *Herald* database and handed over with an apple fritter wrapped in aluminium foil. Was he trying to be funny? Now she sat perched on the edge of Quentin Parker's desk, a notebook in her hand.

Parker was the city crime-beat reporter. He was balding and fat and thought little of journalism degrees, much less MFAs. He was old-school. He was belligerent. He was condescending. He was probably an alcoholic. But he was smart and Susan liked him.

Parker leaned back in his task chair, gripping the arms with his beefy hands. He grinned. 'What took you so long?'

'They tell you about my Pulitzer Prize-winning series?'

He snorted. 'Did they tell you that your vagina got you the story?'

She smiled sweetly. 'My vagina is my most tireless advocate.'

Parker guffawed and appraised her fondly. 'You sure you're not my kid?'

'Would your kid have pink hair?'

He shook his head, causing his jowls to sway. 'Over my dead fucking body.' He looked around the newsroom at the rows of people staring at computer screens or talking on telephones. 'Look at this place,' he said, scowling sadly at the hushed, serious environment, all carpeting and cubicles. 'It's like working in a fucking office.

'Come on,' he said, pushing himself upright and out of his seat. 'I'll buy you a crappy sandwich in the cafeteria and we can play reporter.'

The cafeteria was in the basement of the building. The food was standard institutional fare: slop under heat lamps, iceberg-lettuce salads, shrivelled baked potatoes. A wall of steel-and-glass vending machines that had probably been in the building for thirty years hosted tangerine-sized red apples, triangular sandwiches, slices of pie and slightly bruised bananas. Parker bought two ham-and-cheese sandwiches out of a machine and handed one to Susan.

Because the food was lousy, few of the paper's employees actually used the cafeteria, much less sat down to enjoy the ambience, so Parker and Susan easily found a vacant beige Formica table.

The stench of stale cigarettes clung to Parker like an aura. He always smelled like he had just come from a smoke break, though Susan had never seen him leave his desk. He took a large bite of sandwich and wiped some mayonnaise off his chin with the back of his hand.

'So, go ahead,' he said.

Susan opened her notebook and smiled dazzlingly. 'Susan Ward,' she purred. '*Oregon Herald*. Do you mind if I ask you a couple of questions, sir?'

'Not at all. Fine paper, fine paper.'

'Detective Archie Sheridan. He was on the Beauty Killer Task Force from the beginning, right? He and his partner investigated the first body?'

Parker nodded, his chin multiplying as he did. 'Yeah. He'd been a homicide cop for a couple of weeks. Partner was Henry Sobol. It was Sheridan's first case. Can you fucking imagine that? First case and he draws a serial killer? Lucky fuck. Of course, they didn't know that then. It was just a dead hooker. Jogger found her in Forest Park. Naked. Tortured. It was some twisted shit. Tame compared to what would come later, but twisted enough that it caught a little attention. For a hooker case. That was back in 1994. May.'

Susan checked her notes. 'Then they found the other bodies over that summer, right? In Idaho and Washington?'

'Right. There was that kid in Boise. Ten-year-old boy. Went missing; then they found him dead in a ditch. An old man in Olympia was found murdered in his back yard. Then there was some waitress in Salem. Someone tossed her body out of a moving car on the freeway. Caused a four-car pile-up that delayed traffic for hours. The citizens were pissed.'

'And Sheridan caught the signature, right? Marks on the torso?'

'Yeah. That's what we called them in the paper. "Marks on the torso".' He leaned forward, his expansive girth bulging against the table. 'You know what an X-Acto knife is? Like a pen with a razorblade at the end?'

Susan nodded.

'They all had been cut up with one of those. Every single one of them. Very specific injuries, inflicted while the victims were still alive.'

'Specific how?'

'She signed her work. Carved a heart on every one of them. There was a lot of other torso damage, so the hearts were sort of hard to spot, the forest for the trees sort of thing. Someone would have seen it eventually. But Sheridan caught it earlier than most. It was his first case, you know, his dead hooker. Not a big priority for the squad, let me assure you. I mean, they couldn't even find any family to claim the body. She was a runaway from foster care. But he wasn't going to let it go. And when the brass realized they had a serial killer on their hands who was torturing and murdering taxpayers at random, they formed that task force quicker than you can say "evening news".' He took another bite of sandwich, chewed twice and started talking again. 'You have to understand that she confounded the hell out of the investigators. There are things we understand about serial killers. Gretchen Lowell did not conform. Her vic profile was all over the place. She was consistent with the torso damage: she cut them, stabbed them, carved them, burned them sometimes. But there was a Chinese menu of other psycho shit. Sometimes she made them drink drain cleaner. Sometimes she dissected the bodies. Removed their spleens. Took out their appendixes. Tongues. A few were basically filleted. Plus, she had accomplices. And she was a woman.' He swallowed his mouthful of food and set the sandwich on the table. 'You're not eating,' he said.

Susan stopped writing and glanced sceptically at her Saran-wrapped sandwich. She was feeling a little queasy and it lay there like something that had been dead for a while. She looked at Parker, who raised his eyebrows expectantly. She unwrapped the sandwich and took a tiny bite off one corner. It was ham, but it tasted like fish. He seemed satisfied. She put the sandwich down and went on with her questions. 'So tell me about the accomplices. They were all men, right?'

'Poor fucks. They think she found them mostly through newspaper personal ads or, later, on Internet dating sites. She'd use false information to register on the sites and then trawl, looking for her targets. Apparently she had a knack for picking out men she could manipulate. She'd isolate them from their friends. Find their weaknesses. And push them until they cracked.' He smiled wryly and a small glob of mayonnaise squirted out of the corner of his mouth. 'She has a lot in common with my wife, actually.'

'I had this boyfriend once who met his ex-wife through a personal ad. She emptied out their bank account and moved to Canada one day while he was at work.'

'Yeah,' Parker said, smiling and dabbing at his mouth with a paper napkin. 'Doesn't often work out, does it?'

'What did you think of the task force? Of how it was run? You wrote a lot of those stories.'

Parker waved his hand dismissively. 'There was a lot of political crap. A lot of pressure from the families and the media and politicians. I haven't seen that much back-stabbing since my daughters were teenagers. The FBI sent three different profilers. And they went through three task force leaders before they finally gave it to Sheridan. Detectives would burn out on it after a few years. I mean, they were tracking down leads all day, every day, and coming up with *nada*. They had a database with something like ten thousand individual tips. The profile the FBI gave them was all wrong. One year there'd be forty-eight cops working the case, and then a year would pass between bodies and the public would get all pissy about how they weren't coming up with anything and how tax dollars were being wasted, and the next year the task force would be down to three guys. Another body would turn up, and it would bloom again. Sheridan was the only cop who was on the task force for all ten years. He was the only one who never asked to be transferred.'

She had stopped writing in the notebook. 'You know him?'

'Sure.'

'In a "Let me ask you a few questions as you run away from me in the hallway" kind of way, or in the "Let's talk about this over a few drinks" kind of way?'

'The former. He had a wife and two babies. Totally smitten with them. The wife was his college sweetheart. I met her once. Nice lady. As far as I ever knew, he had the Beauty Killer and he had his family, and not a lot in between.'

'What did you think of him?' Susan asked.

'Good cop. Smart guy. He could have taken a lot of shit for that. He's got a master's degree in criminology or some such crap. Total college boy. But his colleagues liked him. Fair. Driven. And,' Parker added, wiggling his hand in the air, 'he was a little bit off.'

'Off how?' asked Susan. Her pen now lay next to her sandwich.

He shrugged. 'Let's just say he was very focused. But then he worked one case for ten years.'

'Where's he been the past two years, do you know?'

'Here, as far as I know,' Parker said. 'On Disability. She did a number on him. He was in the hospital for a month. Rehab after that. But I heard he worked with the prosecution on the deal they cut her, so he didn't exactly fall off the face of the earth.'

'She pleaded guilty to the five murders in Oregon and six in Washington and Idaho, and kidnapping and attempted murder, and coughed up twenty more bodies, right?'

'In exchange for life, yeah. Lot of people thought she should have gotten the needle.'

'What do you think?' Susan asked.

'I wish there'd been a trial. I love a good emotional courtroom drama, and I would have paid top dollar to see Archie Sheridan testify.'

Susan bit her lip. 'Why did she go after him? It doesn't make sense.'

'He was leading the task force. His picture was in the paper all the time in those days. She felt the need to present herself to him. She walked right into his office, offered her supposed psychiatric expertise. Maybe it presented itself as a challenge. And then there's the fact that she's cuckoo.' He popped the last bite of his sandwich into his mouth as an exclamation mark.

'Why did they call her "the Beauty Killer"?' Susan asked.

'That was mine,' he said proudly. 'I asked the ME who examined Sheridan's dead hooker to characterize the condition of the corpse. She'd been cut up pretty bad. He whistled and said, "It's a beauty." Most interesting autopsy he'd done all year. His last job had been in Newport, all drownings and suicides. He was positively tickled. Just a coincidence that Gretchen Lowell turned out to be a looker.'

It still didn't click for Susan. This was a woman who had a strong survival instinct. She'd been on a ten-year killing spree. At least. Kidnapping the cop who was chasing her was not in her best interests. 'What do you think of the theories that she wanted to be stopped? To be caught? Suicide by cop?'

'It's bullshit,' Parker said. 'Gretchen Lowell is a psychopath. She's not like us. She doesn't do things for reasons. She liked killing people. She's said as much in prison. She kidnapped Archie Sheridan, drugged him, tortured him for ten days, and would have murdered him if he hadn't talked her out of it.'

'Talked her out of it. Just like that.'

'She was the one who called nine-one-one. If she hadn't had medical training, he'd be dead. One of the EMTs told me that she'd kept him alive for almost thirty minutes, doing CPR, before they got there.'

'She saved his life.'

'Uh huh.'

'Christ, that's got to be a mind-fuck.'

Parker's lips were shiny with grease. 'I'd expect so.'

8

Mayor Bob 'Buddy' Anderson was announcing the new task force at an afternoon press conference at the new offices. This was where Susan was finally supposed to meet her subject.

Susan loathed press conferences. They were artificial and on-message and almost never revealed anything that was true in the way that made for good writing. The information relayed was accurate, yes; but never true.

Ian insisted on driving, which was fine with Susan, as her battered Saab was always loaded with the accoutrements of her life: magazines, empty water bottles, discarded jackets, notebooks and pens – dozens of pens. She found that passengers sometimes failed to understand her complete lack of interest in picking up old French fries off the floor, much less dusting the dashboard. Parker, who was actually covering the press conference, and who did not like Ian (based entirely on the fact that Ian had graduated from journalism school in 1986), took a separate vehicle.

It was still raining. The sky was entirely white and the foothills that surrounded the city looked like jagged, milky shadows. As they made their way over the bridge, Susan placed her hand flat on the passenger side window, watching the rivulets of water carve their jagged paths down the glass. So many people moved to Portland for the quality of life and the progressive politics. They bought bicycles and big old wooden houses and espresso makers, and then, after the first dreary winter, they moved back to LA. But Susan liked the slick of rain, the way it distorted the view out of every windshield, every window. The way light blurred around brake lights and glowed on the pavement. The scrape of the wipers.

She had to ask it. 'This assignment,' she said, still looking out of her window, drumming her fingers on the cold, hard glass. 'It has nothing to do with your cock, right, Ian?'

Ian looked honestly startled. 'Jesus! No. No, Susan. Howard asked for you. I just agreed. I would never . . .' He let that trail off.

'Good,' Susan said. 'Because if I ever thought that it was interfering in our professional relationship, the fucking would stop.' She turned and looked at him with her hard green eyes. 'You understand that, right?'

He cleared his throat, and his face and neck reddened. 'Yes.'

She let her gaze drift back out over the Willamette. 'Don't you love the rain?'

*

Anne Boyd and Claire Masland sat across from one another in the rectangular break room of the former bank. Claire was the tiniest white woman Anne had ever met. It wasn't so much that she was short; she was probably five three. It was just that Claire was so slight and angular that she seemed smaller than she was. But Anne liked Claire. She looked like an adolescent boy, but she was one of the most tenacious cops Anne had ever worked with. Like one of those cute lapdogs that sinks its teeth into someone's forearm, locks its jaw, and can't be prised off without tranquillizers. They'd become friends during the Beauty Killer case. The other cops thought it was because they were women. And it was, in a way. They knew something about each other. Despite the black–white thing, the thin–heavy thing, despite it all they recognized the thing that, as women, made them different enough to lead them into a violent world still dominated by men. They understood what it was to be attracted, in some way, to death.

'You want to go over it again?' Claire asked.

Claire had recounted her particular knowledge of the case to Anne twice already and now sat fidgeting, her gaze resting on the microwave where her lunch was currently heating. She had been at Jefferson, interviewing kids who knew Kristy, and Anne knew that she wanted to get back to the field. Missing-persons cases were hard enough. Missing kids made everyone work twice as hard and feel twice as guilty.

'I think I've got everything I need from you for now,' Anne said. She stacked the copies of the notes that Claire had brought her next to the ones from Henry and Martin. The notes that cops took at a crime scene were often more copious than the version that made it into their reports, and Anne had learned long ago that the smallest detail could mean the difference between a solid profile and a half-assed guess. 'How do you think Archie looked this morning?' Anne asked, keeping her voice casual.

Claire shrugged, her eyes still on the microwave timer. Thin people, Anne noticed, never seemed to stop eating. 'Fine,' Claire said. She lifted a hand to her mouth and tore at a bloody cuticle.

'Fine?'

Claire's grey eyes steeled and her hand fluttered to her lap. 'Yes, Anne. Fine. They ask you to keep an eye on him?'

'I'm just concerned about a friend,' Anne said. She examined Claire, the dark circles under her eyes, the bitten cuticles. The stress was already taking its toll.

'Work's the best thing for him,' Claire said. The microwave dinged and Claire hurried to push her chair back and stand up. 'Besides, Henry says he's OK.'

'Henry loves Archie,' Anne said.

'Exactly. So he'd protect him, right? Besides, they wouldn't ask him back if he weren't OK.'

'You know that's not true.'

'You come in on the red-eye?' Claire asked.

Anne leaned forward. 'How does he seem to you?'

Claire thought for a moment, wrinkling her smooth forehead. 'His voice sounds different.'

'It's from the drain cleaner she made him drink. It must have damaged his vocal cords.'

Claire closed her eyes and turned her head. 'Jesus Christ.'

Anne hesitated. But she felt that she had to say it. 'This new killer. It's going to get worse, Claire. He's accelerating. You don't have a lot of time.'

Claire turned and moved to the microwave. 'I spent last night with Kristy's family,' she said. 'Her father. Her grandmother. Her aunts.' She opened the microwave and extracted a withered burrito on a paper plate. 'And the whole time, I wasn't thinking about her. I was focused on the next girl. The girl safe in her bed, who is going to disappear. Who is going to be raped. Who is going to be murdered.' She poked at her burrito sadly with a white plastic fork. A plastic tine snapped off and stuck in the tortilla skin. Claire shook her head, disgusted. 'The microwave in here is a piece of shit,' she said.

It was drizzling, so they had set up the podium and bouquet of microphones under the ATM portico. By the time Susan and Ian arrived, the press were already in position, perched politely on grey-steel folding chairs. Press in Portland, Oregon, meant the *Herald*, three weeklies, a half-dozen neighbourhood papers, an NPR affiliate, a community radio station, four commercial radio stations, the Associated Press stringer and four local TV news teams. Because of the scope and theatre of the case, several additional TV and print reporters had come down from Seattle. Their news vans were just a little slicker than the Portland crews'.

The mayor, looking grim and presidential, was vociferously pledging a quick resolution to the case, employing a rotation of repetitive hand gestures to reinforce his earnestness. 'We are committed to putting every available resource into the apprehension of the monster who has been preying on young girls in our city. I urge the citizens to take precautions but not to panic. In reconvening the Beauty Killer Task Force, I have great faith that we will have a resolution to this madness.'

Susan opened her notebook and wrote one word: *campaigning*. She closed the notebook and looked up – and that's when she saw Archie Sheridan. He was standing behind the mayor, leaning against the cement-block wall of the bank, his hands in his jacket pockets. He was not watching the mayor. He was watching them – the press. Looking from one person to the next, appraising each of them. No expression. Just watching. He looked thinner than in the photographs, she noted. And his dark hair was longer. But he did not look damaged or crazy or deranged. He just looked like someone waiting for something to happen. A passenger on a subway platform, looking for the tell-tale light in the darkness. She felt an electrical jolt and realized that he was looking at her. They locked eyes for a moment, and she felt something pass between them. He gave her a quick lopsided smile. She smiled back. He went back to scanning the audience. His body remained perfectly still.

'And on that note, I'd like to introduce my good friend Detective Archie Sheridan,' the mayor announced. Archie looked up, mildly startled, recovered and walked to the podium. He took his hands out of his pockets and rested them lightly on the surface of the podium. He adjusted a microphone. He ran his hand through his hair.

'Can I answer any questions?' he asked.

Kristy Mathers had been missing for almost twenty-one hours. Archie had spent the day interviewing the people who had seen her last at Jefferson, her friends, her teachers, her parents. He'd walked the route she would have taken home. He'd met with the crime-scene team that had searched the area the night before and found nothing. He'd approved flyers to distribute at the schools and in the neighbourhoods around the schools. He'd met with the chief of police and the mayor. He'd conferred with highway patrols in Washington and Idaho and California, conducted a conference call with both the American and Canadian border patrols, consulted with the private security firm brought in to secure the city's high schools, and he'd personally gone through the four-hundred-plus tips that had already been called in to the hotline. And there was still a lot more he could be doing that would be more productive than appearing at a press conference. But he was determined to make the best of it.

He had led hundreds of press conferences in his tenure as lead detective on the Beauty Killer Task Force, but this was the first since Gretchen. He surveyed the anxious faces in the audience. Many had changed in two years, but there were familiar ones, too. He searched the crowd for the person who would ask him the question he wanted, the one he needed for the soundbite on the evening news. Their hands strained to be highest, their faces pinched with determination. He willed his stomach to unclench and called on a young Asian woman who sat in the front row with a notebook poised.

'Detective, do you think you're mentally and physically fit to run the After School Strangler Task Force?' she asked.

'The After School Strangler?'

'That's what the *Herald* is calling the killer on their website.'

Archie winced. 'Right.' That didn't take long. 'I've never felt better,' he lied.

'Do you have any lasting physical effects from your captivity?'

'Some stomach problems. Probably on par with the mayor's ulcer.' There were some appreciative smiles in the audience.

He chose another hand. 'Do you think that the DA should have sought the death penalty for Gretchen Lowell?'

Archie sighed and went on autopilot. 'The plea bargain stipulated that she take responsibility for all the people she killed, not just the eleven we had enough evidence to take her to court on. Her victims' families deserve some closure.' He tried to look relaxed. In control. 'How about we talk about the current case? One serial killer at a time, ladies and gentlemen.'

He called on Quentin Parker. 'Do you think that Kristy Mathers is still alive?'

'We remain hopeful that she is, yes.'

Another hand. 'How many detectives will you have on the task force?'

'Full-time? Nine investigators, plus support staff. Seven of them worked on the Beauty Killer Task Force. In addition, we will work closely with other agencies, and pull in other personnel as needed.'

The mayor took an almost imperceptible step towards the podium. Archie tensed. He still hadn't got the question he wanted. He scanned the audience. *Come on. One of you ask it. It's obvious. It's the one you're all thinking. I need one of you to ask it.* His eyes came to rest on Susan Ward. She had wasted no time getting started on the story. Ambition – that was a good sign.

Archie had picked her out of the crowd right away. There was something in the way she was watching him. And the pink hair. Henry had mentioned something about that, but Archie had thought he was kidding. Susan was glancing around at the other reporters, too. She looked at him. He raised an eyebrow. She hesitated, then raised her hand. He called on her.

'How will you go about catching the killer?' she asked.

He cleared his throat and looked right into the television cameras. 'We will canvass every neighbourhood. We will interview every witness. We will explore every possible connection these girls might have had. We will use every scientific method available to us to uncover clues to the killer's identity.' He leaned forward, exuding, he hoped, confidence and authority. 'We will catch you.' He stepped back from the podium and waited a beat. 'Thank you.'

Ian led Susan into the task force offices. The press in attendance had rushed off to write their stories and edit their videos. Susan saw immediately why they had chosen to have the press conference outside. The office was in chaos. Half-unpacked boxes were everywhere. The bank transaction counter had been removed and what was left was a large open space with a few offices in the back and what Susan presumed was the old vault. The furniture was bank furniture – dingy mauve couches with oak armrests, cherry-laminate desks with shiny brass hardware, plastic floor mats and cloth task chairs. Fluorescent lights buzzed overhead. The industrial carpet was grey, with a worn footpath to and along the now-missing counter. The walls were painted a funereal pale rose. Detectives and support staff were unpacking boxes, nailing large dry-erase boards to the walls, plugging in computers and transforming the space into a police station. Susan wondered how much time they were losing setting up shop that might be used to find Kristy Mathers before she was murdered. Their faces were pinched; there was no small talk.

The mayor finished the soliloquy he was performing for a group of aides, and Ian stepped in to introduce Susan.

'Mayor, this is Susan Ward, the writer who will be doing the piece on the task force,' Ian said. Susan noticed that he used the word 'writer' and not 'reporter'.

The mayor's eyes widened at Susan's appearance, but he smiled and shook her hand firmly, placing his other hand on her upper arm. He was tall, with painstakingly sculpted, prematurely silver hair, and the kind of hands that are always warm. His fingernails were buffed to a bright sheen and he wore a grey suit that was just as luminous. Susan thought he looked like Robert Young in *Father Knows Best*, a TV show she loathed only because her own life had always seemed so tawdry in comparison. She made a mental bet with herself that he would be a senator within five years – assuming he was rich enough.

'It's a pleasure,' he said, his eyes positively brimming with paternal amiability. 'I've heard great things about you. I'm looking forward to reading the series.'

Susan felt a strange self-consciousness wash over her. She didn't like it. 'Thank you, sir,' she said.

'I want to introduce you to Archie Sheridan,' the mayor said. 'You know, I served on the Beauty Killer Task Force with him. Years ago. Before I was even chief. I was actually the first detective to lead the task force. Archie didn't have the seniority then. It was his first case. I was something of a hotshot in the department, so they put me in charge. I lasted three years. Hell of a thing. No one I'd rather work with than Archie Sheridan. There is no one out there I'd trust more with my daughter's life.' He waited a moment, and when Susan didn't open her notebook, he added, 'You can write that down.'

'You don't have a daughter,' Susan said.

The mayor cleared his throat. 'Figure of speech. Have you had a chance to look around?' He led her further into the bowels of the bank, his hand settled firmly just above the small of her back. 'As you can see, we're still setting up office equipment. When we're done, we'll have a working squad: interrogation room, conference room, state-of-the-art computer system, et cetera.' They reached an office with a large glass panel that overlooked the main room. The white Venetian blinds were closed. 'This is the old bank manager's office,' the mayor explained. 'But it appears our current bank manager isn't here.' He turned to a small dark-haired woman walking past with a badge clipped to the waist of her jeans. She was eating half a burrito wrapped in a paper towel and her lips were stained with hot sauce. 'Detective Masland? Where's Sheridan?'

She was caught mid-bite, and they had to wait while she finished chewing and swallowed. 'The school. Just left. He went over there to conduct some interviews and get the checkpoint set up. I'm heading over there now.'

A trace of agitation crossed the mayor's face. 'I'm sorry,' he said to Susan. 'I told him I wanted him to meet you.'

'I realize that he's busy,' Susan said. 'But eventually, I will have to meet him. I can't profile him without talking to him.'

'Come by tomorrow morning at nine a.m. I'll make sure he's here.'

I bet you will, thought Susan.

Ian and Susan drove back to the paper in silence. When they pulled into the parking garage, Ian swallowed hard. 'Can I come over tonight?'

Susan pulled at a wisp of pale pink hair. 'Where's Sharon?' she asked.

He looked at his hands, still gripping the steering wheel. 'Up in Seattle.'

Susan hesitated. 'Make it late,' she said. She felt a twinge of guilt, bit her lip and opened the car door. 'You'll find stomaching the whole adultery thing easier if we don't spend too much time together.'

9

There was another reason that Susan wanted Ian to come over late. As soon as she and Ian got to the fifth floor, she excused herself to go to the bathroom, doubled back downstairs, got in her car and drove across the river to Jefferson High School. There was no way she was going to let a night pass without getting to meet Archie Sheridan.

Portland was divided into quadrants: North-west, South-east, South-west and North-east. Which quadrant you were from said a lot about who you were. If you were from South-west, you lived in the hills and had money. If you were from South-east, you were liberal and probably a vegetarian. If you were from North-west, you were young and spent a lot on clothes. If you were from North-east, you had some money and a dog and drove a Subaru wagon. Then there was Portland's so-called fifth quadrant: North Portland. North Portland was carved out between North-east and the Willamette River. Only 2 per cent of Oregon's population was black. But you wouldn't know it walking down the street in North Portland.

Jefferson High was in this fifth quadrant, or, as it had been recently rechristened, 'NoPo'. The area was still recovering from heavy gang activity in the nineties. Teenagers were still occasionally shot dead on the street, but the empty lots thatched with dead grass that punctuated many blocks were getting fenced in and being transformed into multi-use development projects. Blame the gentrification on all the hipster white kids buying up or renting houses because they were cheap and close to downtown. The houses were usually bent with dry rot, but you didn't have to worry about neighbours calling the cops if your band played too loudly in the basement. The benefits of this renaissance – a bevy of trendy restaurants, boutiques and renovated old Portland four-squares – had not had much impact on the local school system, which boasted some of the lowest test scores in the state. Most of the kids who went to Jefferson were poor and most were black, and many were no strangers to violence.

Susan noticed the police cruisers parked out in front of the large institutional-looking brick school. She easily found a spot to park her car on a side street and walked the block back towards the campus, notebook in hand. There was some local news activity. Charlene Wood of Channel 8 was standing on the corner, interviewing a huddle of teenage girls in tight jeans and puffy coats. About half a block behind her, a man in a bright orange windbreaker was yammering into another microphone. Several teenagers, presumably fresh from extracurricular activities, loitered on the steps of the school, a nervous energy permeating their practised insouciance. A uniformed police officer and two crossing guards waited with them for parents or friends or buses or some other vessel of safety. On the other side of the river, the sky over the West Hills was ablaze with deep pinks and oranges, but on the east side it just looked grey.

Susan traced a line of vehicles up ahead to a police checkpoint, which was set up at the first intersection past the school. She could see a uniformed officer talking to the driver of the car at the front of the line. Then the officer waved the car through and the next car rolled forward. A large placard was set on a metal easel near the checkpoint. On it, Susan could just make out a photograph of Kristy Mathers and the words HAVE YOU SEEN THIS GIRL?

'Thanks for the question.'

Susan spun around. Archie Sheridan was standing a few steps behind her. He had his badge clipped to the breast pocket of his corduroy blazer and was carrying a red spiral-bound notebook and a paper cup of coffee. He was walking towards the checkpoint.

'I thought you were very convincing,' she said. 'With the speech. You're very intimidating.'

Archie stopped and took a sip of the coffee. 'A little posturing can't hurt.'

'Do you think he'll see it?'

He shrugged a little. 'Probably. It's a funny tic about

serial killers. They generally enjoy the attention of your profession.' A trio of tall teenage boys walked by, and Archie and Susan stepped aside to let them pass. The boys reeked of marijuana.

Susan watched Archie for a reaction. Nothing. 'I don't remember the pot I had in high school being that good,' she said.

'It probably wasn't.'

'You going to arrest them?'

'For smelling like a class-C controlled substance? No.'

Susan surveyed him playfully. 'What's your favourite movie?'

He didn't have to think about it. '*Band of Outsiders.* Godard.'

'Shut up! It's French. Your favourite movie is French?'

'Is that too haughty?'

'A little, yeah,' Susan said.

'I'll come up with something better for tomorrow.'

'She's dead, isn't she?'

If it was supposed to trick him into reacting, Susan had to admit it didn't work. But there was a chink. Archie glanced at his shoes so quickly that she would have missed it if she hadn't been looking so hard at his eyes. He recovered and gave her a wan smile. 'We have every hope that she is still alive,' he said without much conviction.

Susan tilted her head towards the commotion at the intersection. 'What's with the roadblock?'

'It's six-fifteen p.m. Kristy's friends say she left rehearsal at this time yesterday. We're stopping everyone who drives this route today between five and seven. If they're driving past here today at this time, chances are they may have been driving past here at this time yesterday. And they may have seen something. By the way, I got a call from Buddy. Sorry I missed our formal introduction.'

'Buddy? Are you and the mayor, uh, buddies?'

'We worked together,' he said. 'But you know that.'

'Is that why you agreed to the series? I mean, I know why Buddy the mayor agreed. He wants to be vice-president one day. But you must have had every writer in the country calling you wanting to write your story. "Hero Cop Saved from the Jaws of Death".'

Archie took another sip of coffee. 'You working on the headline already? I like it.'

'Why agree to a profile now, detective?'

'You're going to help me do my job.'

'You think so?'

'Yeah. But we can talk about that at that nine o'clock meeting I have been instructed not to miss.' He held up his red notebook. 'I've got to get back to work,' he said. He took a few steps. 'Susan, right?'

She nodded.

'You can call me Archie except when it seems like

"detective" might be more appropriate. Are you a morning person?'

'No.'

'Good.' He turned and walked off towards the checkpoint, tossing the empty coffee cup in a bin. 'See you tomorrow,' he called over his shoulder.

10

It was almost seven p.m. and it was dark and Archie's ribs hurt. It was all the standing around. Or the humidity. Or maybe just the mind-numbing boredom. Kristy Mathers had been gone for more than twenty-four hours. And after a day of interviews, searches and dead-ends, it had come to this: their best avenue of investigation was to stand there waiting for something to happen. The overwhelming sense of impotence was hard to stomach.

Archie used his thumb and forefinger to open the pillbox, still in his pocket, and slip out a Vicodin. He knew them from the other pills by touch: the size, the shape, the cut mark. He slipped it in his mouth. If anyone saw, it would look like a mint. Or an aspirin. He didn't really care. The bitter taste of stale coffee hugged the back of his tongue. He was wishing he had another cup when Chuck Whatley, a rookie patrol cop with a freckled face and a shock of unnaturally orange hair, waved Archie over with his flashlight. Dusk had settled, and there was a chill in the air despite the cloud cover. Archie walked quickly from where he was standing at the edge of the hubbub. He felt damp, even though it had only misted. That was how it was in the north-west: it rained just enough to get you wet, and yet somehow never enough that you could be bothered to don something waterproof or carry an umbrella. Officer Whatley was standing next to a maroon Honda. It had rust around the tyre wells and looked mottled where the wax finish had worn off. He stood like all patrol cops stand, with one thumb hooked on his belt, bent over talking to the passenger, periodically looking up excitedly as Archie approached.

Under the streetlight, the maroon Honda looked sequinned with rain. Officer Whatley's eyes were bright. 'She thinks she saw something, sir,' he said.

Archie kept his voice level. 'Ask her to pull over so these people can get by,' he told the officer. Whatley nodded and leaned towards the passenger, and the Honda pulled out of the line and next to a police cruiser. The driver's door opened and a young African-American woman tentatively stepped out. A pair of hospital scrubs hung loosely over her skinny frame and her neat cornrows were held back in a low ponytail.

'What's this all about?' she asked Archie slowly.

'A girl disappeared last night,' he said. 'You didn't hear about it?'

The skin of the woman's face seemed pulled too taut, the lines of her skull too evident beneath her flesh. She pulled at her fingers until they popped. 'I'm a nurses' assistant at Emanuel. I work nights, sleep days. I don't keep up on the news. Is it connected to those other girls?'

Officer Whatley broke in, no longer able to contain himself. 'She saw Kristy Mathers last night.'

'Thank you, officer,' Archie said with a stern glance. 'You on your way to work now?' he asked the woman, opening his notebook.

'Yeah,' she said, still eyeing them uneasily.

'And you worked the same shift yesterday?'

She shifted her feet. Her scuffed white clogs snapped against the wet pavement. 'Yeah.'

A few other uniformed officers had gathered around, curious and keyed up at the possibility of a witness. They stood on the balls of their feet, leaning in towards one another, waiting. Archie could feel the woman physically shrink at all the attention. He placed a hand lightly on her shoulderblade and guided her a few steps away from the small huddle. He tilted his head next to hers, his voice gentle. 'And you would have been by here about this same time? You weren't running late or early?'

'No. I never run late or early. I'm punctual.'

'We won't keep you long,' Archie reassured her. 'And you think you saw Kristy Mathers?'

'The girl in the photo? Yeah. I saw her. Up at Killingsworth and Albina. I waited for her to cross. She was walking her bike.'

Archie did not allow himself to react. He didn't want to startle the woman. To pressure her. He had talked to hundreds of witnesses, and he knew that if someone felt pressured, they would try too hard, and their imagination would fill what their memory couldn't recover. His hand remained lightly on her back. He was steady, unflappable – the good cop. 'She was walking it? Not riding it?'

'No. That's why I noticed her. My mother used to make me and my sisters do that – walk our bike across busy streets. It's safer. Especially in this neighbourhood. People drive like fools.'

'So the bike wasn't damaged. It didn't have a flat tyre or anything?'

She pulled at her fingers again. 'I don't know. Not that I noticed. Someone took her? Someone took this girl?'

Archie evaded the question. 'Did you notice anything else? Anyone following her? Anyone suspicious on the street? Any vehicles?'

She shook her head sadly and let her hands drop to her sides. 'I was on my way to work.'

Archie took down her contact information and her licence number and let her go on her way.

A moment later, Detectives Henry Sobol and Claire Masland walked up behind him. Claire was carrying two coffees in white paper cups with black lids. Both Henry and Claire, Archie noticed, were wearing waterproof jackets.

'What was that?' Henry asked.

'Witness saw Kristy walking her bike about three

blocks from here at' – he checked his watch – 'about six-fifty-five p.m. Her friends say she left rehearsal at six-fifteen. Which raises the question, where was she for that forty minutes?'

'It doesn't take that long to walk a bike three blocks,' Henry observed. 'Even walking real slow.'

Claire handed Archie one of the cups of coffee. 'Back to the friends,' she said.

Archie glanced down at the cup in his hand. 'What's that?' he asked.

'The coffee you asked me to get you.'

Archie looked non-committally at the cup. He didn't want coffee any more. He was actually feeling pretty good.

'No,' Claire said. 'I had to go eleven blocks for that coffee. And you're drinking it.'

'I'm pretty sure I asked for a non-fat latte,' said Archie.

'Fuck you,' said Claire.

11

The friends were Maria Viello and Jennifer Washington. Maria, Jen and Kristy had been inseparable since middle school, and high school had not yet soured their friendship. Maria's house was just a few blocks from Jefferson, so the detectives went there first. She lived in a rented 1920s wooden bungalow surrounded by a chain-link fence. The house needed painting, but the yard was neatly kept and the sidewalk out front was clean of the usual debris of litter that clotted much of the neighbourhood. Her father, Armando Viello, answered the door. He was shorter than Archie, with a square torso and hands rough from manual labour. His face was deeply ravaged by acne scars. He spoke English fluently, though with a heavy accent. His wife, to Archie's knowledge, did not speak English at all. They were probably illegals, a fact that escaped none of the cops who had called on the house in the last twenty-four hours, but did not make it into any of their reports.

Armando Viello stared gravely at Archie and the others through the battered aluminium screen door. The porch light flickered and then went out.

'You were here this morning,' Viello said.

'We have some new questions,' Archie explained.

Armando opened the door and the detectives walked in. It was a brave thing, Archie thought, to know you could be deported, but let cop after cop inside your house anyway, on the off-chance it might help find someone else's missing kid.

'Maria is in her bedroom,' Armando said, heading down a short hallway in his stocking feet. Dinner was cooking in the kitchen, something spicy. 'You want to talk to Jennifer too?'

'Jennifer's here?' Claire asked.

'They're studying. They did not go to school today.' Armando rapped on Maria's bedroom door and said something in Spanish. In a minute the door opened. Her elbow-length straight black hair was pulled into a ponytail and she was wearing the same purple velour sweatpants and yellow T-shirt that she had had on when Archie had interviewed her that morning after his less than inspirational staff meeting.

'Have you found her?' she asked immediately.

'Not yet,' Archie said kindly. Kids were often overlooked in police investigations. The thinking was that they made bad witnesses, but Archie had found that they noticed things that adults didn't. As long as they were interviewed appropriately, assured that they didn't have to know the answers, so they wouldn't make up what they thought the interviewer wanted to hear, kids as young as six could offer valuable observations. But Maria was fifteen. Teenage girls were unpredictable. Archie had never communicated well with them. He had spent most of his teen years attempting to start conversations with girls and flubbing miserably. He hadn't really got much better. 'Can we talk to you some more?' he asked Maria.

She looked at him and her eyes filled with tears. *Well, you've still got the magic touch*, thought Archie.

Then Maria sniffled and nodded. Archie looked at Claire and Henry and then the three followed Maria into her bedroom.

It was a square yellow room with a single-paned window that looked out into the window of the bungalow next door. A paisley twin-sized sheet was tacked up in place of a curtain.

Jen Washington sat on the bed, under the window, holding an old and well-loved stuffed alligator on her lap, a relic of childhood. Her hair was styled in a short Afro and she wore an Indian-style shirt and jeans with beaded fringed cuffs. She was a beautiful girl, but the lack of any spark dampened her prettiness.

They had all been in the high-school auditorium together. Jen was painting scenery for the play. Maria was in charge of props. They had all auditioned. Kristy was the only one who had been cast. So she was the one who had left early. The one who was, by now, most probably dead. But Archie didn't want to think about that. Didn't want them to see it on his face.

Maria walked over to the bed and flung herself

down on the Mexican blanket beside Jen, who laid a skinny arm protectively across Maria's calf. Archie walked over to the wooden desk next to the bed, flipped the desk chair around and sat in it. Henry leaned back against the door, arms folded over his chest. Claire perched on the Mexican blanket on the corner of the bed.

Archie opened his red notebook. 'Did Kristy have a boyfriend?' he asked softly.

'You already asked us that,' Jen said, twisting the alligator. She glared at Archie with contempt. Archie didn't blame her. Fifteen was too young to find out how fucked-up the world was.

'Tell me again.'

Jen glowered. The alligator looked bored. Maria adjusted herself into a cross-legged position, pulling her long ponytail over her shoulder and absent-mindedly wrapping it around her fingers. 'No,' she said finally. 'There was no one.' Unlike her father, she had no trace of a Mexican accent.

Claire smiled conspiratorially at the girls. 'No one? Not even someone maybe that her parents might disapprove of? Someone secret.'

Jen rolled her eyes. 'No one means no one.'

'And you're sure that Kristy left rehearsal at six-fifteen?' Archie asked.

Maria stopped fidgeting with her hair and looked at Archie, certainty flashing in her dark eyes. 'Yeah,' she said. 'Why?'

'Someone saw Kristy a few blocks away almost forty minutes later,' Archie explained. 'Any idea what she might have been doing?'

Jen lifted her arm from Maria's calf, sat up and shook her head. 'That doesn't make sense.'

'But you didn't see her ride off, right?' asked Claire. 'You just saw her leave the auditorium.'

'Right,' Maria said. 'They finished blocking all her scenes. Ms Sanders let her go.'

'And no one left with her?' Archie asked.

Maria shook her head. 'Like we said. All the actors got to go once their scenes were blocked. Kristy went first. Most of us had to stay until seven-thirty. But you talked to all of them, right?'

'No one saw her,' Archie said.

'So what was she doing all that time?' asked Jen, staring hard at the yellow wall. 'It doesn't make sense.'

'Does she smoke?' asked Claire.

'No,' Maria said. 'She hates it.'

Jen examined the plastic eyes of the stuffed alligator, scratching at an invisible imperfection on the hard black plastic of its pupil. 'Maybe she had trouble with her bike.' She shrugged, not looking up.

Archie leaned forward. 'Why do you say that, Jen?'

Jen smoothed the matted green fur of the alligator. 'She'd been having trouble with the chain coming off. It was a shitty bike. She had to drag it home a couple of times.' A single tear rolled down her brown cheek.

She wiped it away with her sleeve and shook her head. 'I don't know. That's probably a stupid answer.'

Archie reached out and gently put his hand on Jen's. She looked up. And he saw, in her hard eyes, a fissure and, behind it, a tiny bit of hope. 'I think it's a really smart guess,' he said. He squeezed her hand. 'Thank you.'

'So her bike is broken,' Claire said when they were back in the car. It was dark and the windows were silvered with rain. 'She tries to fix it for a while, then gives up and decides to walk it home. Our guy stops, offers her a ride, or to help fix the bike, and he grabs her.'

'But that's a crime of opportunity,' Henry said from the driver's seat of the unmarked Crown Vic. Henry hated Crown Vics, and yet somehow he always ended up with one. 'She fits his profile. You think he just drives around looking for high-school girls who look right enough to snatch? That he just got lucky?'

'He broke the bike,' Archie said quietly from the back seat. He pulled the pillbox out of his pocket and absent-mindedly rotated it between his thumb and fore-finger.

'He broke the bike,' Henry agreed emphatically, nodding. 'Which means he had her picked out. Knew she had the bike. Knew which bike was hers. Maybe even knew it was crappy. That she'd drag the thing home like usual. He's watching them.'

'Still leaves us with some missing time,' Claire said. 'Next kid left rehearsal at six-thirty. Didn't see her. The bike rack is right by the door.'

Archie's head throbbed. 'We'll do the roadblock again tomorrow. Maybe someone else saw her.' He extracted three pills from the pillbox and put them in his mouth one by one.

'You OK, boss?' Henry asked, glancing back at Archie in the rear-view mirror.

'Zantac,' Archie lied. 'For my stomach.' He leaned his head back on the seat and closed his eyes. If the killer had stalked Kristy, then he'd probably start looking for another girl soon. 'You sure the other high schools are secure?' Archie asked, eyes still closed.

'Fort Knox,' Claire confirmed.

'Set up surveillance at all four tomorrow,' Archie told them. 'Run the plates of every car that goes by Jefferson between five and seven.' He opened his eyes, rubbed his face with an open hand and leaned forward between the two front seats. 'I want to go through the autopsy reports again. And let's go door to door again tonight. Maybe someone's remembered something.'

Henry glanced over at him. 'We should all get some sleep. We've got people working tonight. Smart people. Awake people. I'll have them call if anything turns up.'

Archie was too tired to argue. He could do the

work back at the apartment. 'I'll go home,' he said. 'If you take me by the office so I can pick up the reports.'

'She's still out there, right?' Claire said. 'It's not all for nothing? There's a chance. Right?'

There was a long silence and then Henry said, 'Right.'

The phone was ringing when Archie got in. He had an armload of police reports and citizen tips he planned to read that night and he stacked them perilously on the hallway table, picked up the cordless, and set his keys on the table next to the charger.

'Hello?'

'It's me.'

'Hey, Debbie,' Archie said to his ex-wife, grateful for the momentary distraction. He walked through the kitchen, got a beer out of the fridge and opened it.

'How was your first day?'

'Futile,' Archie said. He unclipped his gun from his belt and set it on the coffee table and sat down on the couch in front of it.

'I saw you on TV. You were very intimidating.'

'I wore that tie you bought me.'

'I noticed that.' She paused. 'Are you coming to Ben's thing on Sunday?'

He swallowed hard. 'You know I can't.'

He could hear the sigh in her voice. 'Because you'll be with her.'

They had been through this before. There wasn't anything left to say. He let the phone slide down his face, his neck, until the base of the receiver rested against his breastbone. He pressed it hard against the bone until it hurt. He could still hear her, muffled and distant, like someone talking underwater.

'You know how sick that is, right?'

The vibration of her voice deep inside his chest made him feel better, like there was something alive in there.

'What do you two talk about?'

She had asked before. He had never told her, would never tell her. He lifted the phone back to his ear. He could hear her breathing. She said, 'I just don't know how you're going to get better until you cleanse her from your life.'

I'm not going to get better, he thought. 'I can't just yet.'

'I love you, Archie. Ben loves you. Sara loves you.'

He tried to say something. *I know.* But he wanted to say something more, and he couldn't, so he didn't say anything at all.

'Are you going to come out and see us?'

'As soon as I can.' They both knew what he meant. He felt the splinters of another headache starting. 'There's this reporter, though,' he continued. 'Susan Ward. She's doing a series about me for the *Herald*. She'll probably call you.'

'What should I tell her?'

'Tell her you won't talk to her. And then, later, when she tries again, tell her anything she wants to know.'

'You want me to tell her the truth?'

He ran his fingers over the nubby fabric of his cheerless couch and imagined Debbie sitting on their couch, in their house, in his old life. 'Yeah.'

'You want that published in the *Herald*?'

'Yeah.'

'What are you up to, Archie?'

He took a swig of his beer. 'Closure,' he said with a hollow laugh.

12

Gretchen doesn't let him sleep that first night, so he is already losing track of time. She injects him with some sort of amphetamine and then leaves for hours. Archie's heart races and he can do nothing but stare at the white ceiling and feel the pulse throb in his neck and his hands shake. The blood has dried on his chest and now itches. He is in excruciating pain every time he inhales, but it's the itching that is making him crazy. He tries for a while to keep track of time by counting, but his mind drifts and he loses the thread of numbers. Judging by the stink of the corpse on the floor beside him, he has been here for at least twenty-four hours. But more than that, he can't say. So Archie stares. And blinks. And breathes. And waits.

He does not hear her come in, but suddenly Gretchen is there, smiling beside him. She caresses his hair, which is wet with sweat. 'It's time for your medicine, darling,' she purrs. With a swift motion, she tears the tape off his mouth.

She is gentle as she pushes the funnel into his throat, but it still makes him gag. He fights it, jerking his head from side to side, trying to lift himself on his elbows, but she knots her fist in his hair and holds his head firmly in place. 'Now, now,' she scolds.

She has a handful of pills and she drops them down his throat one by one. He gags and tries to spit them out, but she extracts the funnel, presses his jaw shut and rubs his throat with her hand, forcing him to swallow them like a dog.

'What are they?' he croaks.

'You don't get to talk yet,' she says. She smooths another piece of tape over his mouth. He is almost thankful. What is there to say?

'What do you want to do today?' she asks.

Archie stares at the ceiling, his eyes burning for sleep.

'Look at me,' she says between clenched teeth.

He does.

'What do you want to do today?'

He raises his eyebrows in an expression of ambivalence.

'More of the nails?'

He can't stop himself from flinching.

Gretchen beams. He can tell his pain pleases her. 'They're looking for you,' she says in a sing-song voice. 'But they're not going to find you.'

Wherever they are, she is reading the paper, watching the news, he thinks.

She puts her face next to his, so he can see her smooth ivory skin, her huge pupils. 'I want you to think about what we're going to send them,' she says matter-of-factly. She runs her fingertips lightly along the skin of his arm, his wrist. 'Hand, foot, that sort of thing. Something nice to let them know we're thinking of them. I'm going to let you pick it out.'

Archie closes his eyes. He is not here. This is not happening. He tries frantically to conjure Debbie's face on the black canvas of his eyelids. He can see her as she was that last morning. He has already mentally catalogued every item of clothing she was wearing. The thick-cabled green-wool sweater. The grey skirt. The long coat that made her look like a Russian soldier. He conjures every freckle on her face. Her tiny diamond earrings. The mole on her neck, just above her breastbone.

'Look at me,' Gretchen orders.

He squeezes his eyes shut tighter. Her wedding band. Round knees. The freckles on her pale thigh.

'Look at me,' she says again, her voice airless.

Fuck you, he thinks.

She stabs him just under his left ribcage. He howls against the duct tape and wrenches in pain and his eyes fly open instinctively.

She holds his head firmly by a fistful of hair and bends over him so that her breasts are inches above his chest and she twists the scalpel further into his flesh. He gets a flash of her smell – lilacs, sweet sweat, talcum powder: it is a relief from the putrid stench of the corpse.

'I don't like to be ignored,' she says in a voice just above a whisper. 'Understand?'

He nods, straining against her hand.

'Good.' She pulls the scalpel out and drops it on the instrument tray.

13

Susan pulled into one of the freshly designated visitor parking spots at the task force offices. She was a half-hour early. Susan was never early. She didn't even like people who were early. But she had woken up at sunrise with that burning hum in her stomach she got when she was about to write a really good story. Ian had already left by then. If he'd woken her up to say goodbye, she didn't remember it.

A fog had settled on the city overnight, and the air was heavy and wet. The chilly humidity soaked into everything, so that even the inside of Susan's car felt like it might mildew as she sat there.

To pass the time now, she opened her phone, punched in a number and left a message on the voice-mail she knew by heart. 'Hi, Ethan. It's Susan Ward. From the alley.' From the alley? Christ. 'I mean the *Herald*. I was wondering if you'd had a chance to talk to Molly about me. I really think her story deserves to be heard. Anyway, give me a call. OK?' Ian had said not to pursue the story. That it was a time waster. But she had some time to kill, so why not do some background? Background wasn't really pursuit. Really.

She waited in the car for a few more minutes, smoking a cigarette and watching people go in and out of the building. Susan was usually a social smoker. She smoked when she was out. When she drank. And sometimes when she was nervous. She hated being nervous. She flung the cigarette out of the car window and watched the tiny explosion of sparks as it hit the pavement. Then she checked her appearance in the rear-view mirror. She was dressed entirely in black, with her pink hair pulled back into a low ponytail. *Jesus*, she thought. *I look like a punk-rock ninja.* There was nothing to be done. She bit on the bullet and went inside.

They had worked all night on transforming the bank into a working squad room. The boxes that yesterday had sat half unpacked were now flattened and stacked by the door, waiting to be hauled away. The desks sat in pairs, facing each other, each equipped with a computer and black flat-screen monitor. No wonder the public education budget was short. Enlarged school photographs of each of the girls, as well as dozens of snapshots, were pinned to a wall-sized bulletin board. Several city maps hung beside them, peppered with colourful pushpins. A copier was noisily spitting out paper. Coffee cups and water bottles sat on desks. Susan could smell coffee brewing. She counted seven detectives, all on the phone. A female uniformed officer sitting at a long desk immediately inside the door looked up at Susan.

'I'm here to see Archie Sheridan,' Susan said. 'Susan Ward. I have an appointment.' She pulled her press pass out of her purse and let it dangle from its lanyard a few inches above the desk.

The officer glanced at the press pass, picked up her phone, dialled an extension and announced Susan's arrival. 'You can go back,' she said, already returning to her computer monitor.

Susan made her way through the bank to Archie's office. This time, the white Venetian blinds were open and she could see him sitting at his desk, reading some papers. The door was ajar and she knocked lightly on it, feeling a slight flutter of nerves in her stomach.

'Good morning,' he said, standing up.

She went in and took the hand he offered. 'Good morning. Sorry I'm early.'

His eyebrows quirked up. 'Are you?'

'About thirty minutes.'

He shrugged slightly and just stood there. Susan counted four empty coffee cups on his desk.

Oh God. He was waiting for her to sit down first. Right. She scrambled into one of the burgundy vinyl armchairs that faced his desk.

He sat down. The office was small, just big enough for a large cherry-veneer desk with a built-in bookcase behind it and two armchairs in front of it. A small window overlooked the street, where cars sped by at a regular clip. He was wearing the same corduroy jacket from the day before, but today his button-down shirt was blue. She felt like she should be asking for a loan. 'So how do we do this?'

Archie placed his hands in front of him on the desk, palms down. 'You tell me.' His expression was friendly, welcoming.

'Well,' Susan said slowly, 'I'll need access. To you.'

He nodded. 'As long it doesn't get in the way of me doing my job, sure.'

'You don't have a problem with that? Me following you around while you're trying to work?'

'No.'

'And I'll want to talk to people around you.' She examined his face. It remained relaxed, unconcerned. 'Your ex-wife, for instance.'

He didn't flinch. 'Fine. I don't know if she'll talk to you, but you're welcome to ask her.'

'And Gretchen Lowell.'

His face constricted just a little. 'Gretchen doesn't talk to reporters.'

'I can be very persuasive.'

He traced an imaginary circle on the desk with his palm. 'She's in the state pen. Maximum security. She can only see her lawyers, cops and family. And she doesn't have any family. And you're not a cop.'

'We could exchange letters. Like in the olden days.'

He leaned back slowly in his chair and appraised her. 'No.'

'No?' Susan said.

'You can shadow me. You can talk to Debbie and the people I work with. I will talk to you about the so-called After School Strangler case. I will talk to you about the Beauty Killer case. You can interview my doctor if you want to. But not Gretchen Lowell. She's still the subject of a police investigation and asking her questions would be a distraction. It's a deal breaker.'

'Excuse me, detective. But what makes you think that, if I did write her, you'd even find out about it?'

He smiled patiently. 'Trust me, I'd find out.'

She stared at him. It was not the fact that he didn't want her talking to Gretchen Lowell that bothered her. He had been through some sort of hell. Of course he didn't want his tormentor interviewed for some stupid newspaper story. What bothered Susan was a growing certainty that this profile was a bad idea for Archie Sheridan. That he had things to hide, and that she was going to find them out. He should not have agreed to any of this. And if she realized that, then she was pretty sure that smart Archie Sheridan did, too. So why was he letting her do it?

'Any other deal breakers?' she asked.

'One.'

Here we go. 'Shoot.'

'Sundays off.'

'Is that when you have your kids?'

Archie glanced over her shoulder, out the window. 'No.'

'Church?'

Nothing.

'Golf?' Susan guessed. 'Taxidermy club?'

'One day of privacy,' he said firmly, focusing back on her, his hands now gripped in his lap. 'You get the other six.'

She nodded a couple of times. She could write this series, and she could write it well. Who was she kidding? She could write it brilliantly. The story was hers. The reasons why could work themselves out later. 'OK,' she agreed. 'Where do we start?'

'The beginning,' he said. 'Cleveland High School. Lee Robinson.' He picked up the phone on his desk and dialled an extension. 'You ready?' he said into the phone. He hung up and looked at Susan.

'Detective Sobol will be joining us.'

Susan tried to mask her dismay. She had hoped to have Archie Sheridan to herself, all the better to pick his mind. 'He was your partner, right? On the first Beauty Killer murder?'

Before Archie could answer, Henry appeared at the door to Archie's office, stretching his ill-fitting leather coat over his broad shoulders. He thrust a big hand at Susan. 'Henry Sobol,' he said. Just a big teddy bear.

She shook it, trying to match his grip. 'Susan Ward. *Oregon Herald.* I'm doing a story on—'

'You're early,' said Henry.

14

Fred Doud smoked a bowl on the beach. He was hunkered next to a large bark-stripped log that had washed ashore the winter before. Not that his discretion mattered: he hadn't seen anyone along the mile stretch of beach he'd just walked. He usually came out in the afternoon, but he had a court date later that day. He took one more extended drag off the small glass pipe and then put it back into the leather satchel. He tied the satchel shut, his long, bony fingers fumbling a little in the cold, and hung it back around his neck. He surveyed the skin of his arms, his thighs, belly, knees. It was bright pink, but he didn't feel cold any more. He liked winters on the beach. There were plenty of people the rest of the year, but during the winter he was often the only one. He lived with some college buddies a few miles away on the island, so it was an easy drive. Per beach rules, he wore a robe from the parking area down the path carved through the blackberry bushes. Then, once he was on the beach, he let the robe drop off his bony shoulders and stepped away from it, *au naturel*. He never felt freer.

The truth was that he usually turned back at that tree, but sometimes, every once in a while, he decided to go further, to the point where the beach went around a bend and he could see the lighthouse up ahead. Today, when he stood up, revelling in his stoned, naked body, Fred knew that it was one of those days.

He usually walked on the inner beach, where the sand was finer and more pleasant on bare feet, but when he went on the longer route he often walked closer to the water on the clay beds, where he had once found an arrowhead and hoped to again. Visibility wasn't bad. The fog had been dense when he started out, but all that was left now was a thick ridge of white that hovered over the river. The cold clay was slippery and the beach was rank, as it sometimes was. Dead fish washed up occasionally and rotted. Seaweed clumped and baked, infested with bugs. Birds eviscerated crabs and then left the carcasses to decompose.

Fred was walking along the clay, face pursed in absolute concentration, reddened eyes scanning the ground, studiously ignoring the mounting stench, when he found Kristy Mathers. He saw the bottom of her foot first, half submerged in the clay, and followed the foot to her leg and torso. He would have believed it sooner if he hadn't fantasized so many times about coming across a dead body on that beach. It just always seemed to him a probable event, somehow. Now, looking at the pale, almost unrecognizable figure at his feet, a horrible new feeling washed over him: sobriety. Fred Doud had never felt so naked.

Heart pounding, and suddenly thoroughly chilled, he turned and looked down the beach, where he had come from and then up towards the lighthouse. The isolation he had just minutes before been enjoying now filled him with terror. He had to get help. He had to get back to his truck. He started running.

15

Henry, Archie and Susan drove to Cleveland High in an unmarked police car, Henry behind the wheel, Archie in the passenger seat and Susan furiously scribbling notes in the back. They parked on the street in front of the three-storey tan-brick school and got out of the car. Henry waved at a couple of cops who sat in a patrol car directly in front of the school. One of them waved back.

The day had changed. The clammy morning fog had given way to a clear blue sky and tiny blazing sun. The temperature was in the mid-fifties. In this bright mid-morning light, Cleveland High looked grand and picture-perfect. Whereas Jefferson looked institutional, Cleveland had a sort of architectural elegance, replete with pillars, arched front doors and a sliver of front lawn. But it still made Susan think of prison.

'We're going this way.'

Susan glanced up. Archie and Henry were several steps down the sidewalk, and Archie was looking over his shoulder at her. She was still standing facing the school, lost in her own memories.

'Sorry,' she said. 'I went here.'

Archie raised his eyebrows. 'You went to Cleveland?'

'Ten years ago. Yeah.' She caught up with them. 'I'm still recovering.'

'Not a prom queen?' asked Henry.

'Hardly,' said Susan. She had been a troubled teenager, hysterical 15 per cent of the time. She didn't know how parents did it. 'Do you have kids?' she asked Henry.

'One,' Henry said. 'He grew up with his mom. In Alaska.'

'Is that where you're from?'

'Nah,' he said. 'I just ended up there.'

Archie grinned. 'It was the seventies. Back when he had a truck camper. And hair.'

Susan laughed and scribbled a sentence in her notebook. Henry's jolly face grew serious. 'No,' he said, looking between Susan and Archie. 'My life is off the record. Period.'

Susan closed the notebook.

'Henry doesn't want to be interviewed,' Archie said.

'I get that,' Susan said.

They continued walking, turning the corner along the side of the school. Susan could see in the large windows, replaced with new glass since she had been a student, where kids sat staring, in various states of repose, at the front of the room. God, she had loathed high school. 'Lee Robinson hated it here, didn't she?'

'Why do you say that?' asked Archie, peering up at the school.

'I saw her school picture. I remember what it was like being that girl.'

'That's the door,' said Henry, pointing towards the metal fire doors on the side of the building. 'Band rehearsal was on the first floor. She came out through there.'

Archie stood with his hands on his hips, looking at the door. Susan could make out a gun in a leather holster on one hip. He gazed up at the school and spun slowly around on his heels, absorbing every detail. Then he nodded. 'OK.'

Henry led them down the sidewalk. 'She walked this way.' Susan followed Archie, who was following Henry. They walked in silence. Susan stepped around a puddle that glittered in the light. It had been weeks since the sun had been out. Under the usual cloud cover, the world looked tamped down, flatteringly lit. Without it, every colour sparkled. The conifers were a darker, richer green, the bright leaf buds on the plum trees were verdant, promising spring and roses and riverfront festivals. Even the grey sidewalk, buckling in places from the gnarled roots of trees planted a hundred years ago, looked somehow more vivid.

Susan stepped around another puddle and squinted up at the sky. Sun in March in Portland, Oregon, was almost unheard of. It was supposed to be gloomy and overcast. It was supposed to rain.

When they came to a spot halfway down the fifth block, Henry stopped.

'This is it,' he said. 'This is where the dogs lost the scent.'

'So she got into a car?' asked Susan.

'Probably,' said Henry. 'Or on a bicycle. Or a motorcycle. Or she flagged down a bus. Or the rain washed her scent away. Or maybe the dogs just weren't tracking well that day.'

Again, Archie spun slowly around. After a few minutes, he turned to Henry. 'What do you think?'

'I think he was on foot.' Henry pointed to a thick laurel hedge that framed the yard of a house just behind the point where the dogs had lost Lee Robinson's scent. 'I think he was waiting for her behind there.'

'It would be risky,' Archie said doubtfully. He walked over to behind the hedge. 'This about how thick the foliage was?'

'It's evergreen.'

Archie considered this. 'So he waited for her behind the hedge,' he said, tracing his hand along the thick leaves of the bushes. 'Appeared. Then what? Talked her into a nearby vehicle?'

'A guy pops out from behind a bush and she gets into his car? Not when I was a teenager,' Susan said.

'No,' Henry said. 'He doesn't pop out.'

Archie nodded, thinking. 'He sees her. He comes out on the other side of the hedge. Over here.' He walked along the hedge to the far side, almost around the corner. 'Then he makes like he was just turning the corner,' he says, re-enacting it. 'Happens upon her.'

'He knows her,' said Henry.

'He knows her,' agreed Archie. They were quiet for a moment. 'Or – ' Archie shrugged – 'maybe he popped out and held a knife to her throat and forced her into the back of a van.'

'Or maybe that,' said Henry.

'You look for fibres on the leaves?'

'Four days of rain too late.'

Archie spun around to Susan. 'Did you walk home from school?'

'Just the first two years. Until I got a car.'

'Yeah,' Archie mused, his eyes on the hedge. 'That's when you walk, isn't it? The first two years.' He cocked his head. 'Did you like Cleveland?'

'I already told you, I hated Cleveland,' Susan said.

'No. You said you hated high school. Would you have hated high school anywhere, or was there something about Cleveland?'

Susan groaned. 'I don't know. There were some things I liked. I was in Drama Club. And, if you must know, I was on the Knowledge Bowl team. But only my freshman year. Before I ungeeked.'

'The drama teacher's been there awhile,' said Henry. 'Reston.'

'Yeah,' Susan said. 'I had him.'

'You ever go by?' asked Henry. 'Say hello?'

'Drop in on my old high-school teachers?' asked

Susan incredulously. 'I have a life, thanks.' Then a terrible thought struck her. 'He's not a suspect, is he?'

Henry shook his head. 'Not unless he got nine teenagers to lie for him. He was rehearsing a school play each of the evenings a girl was taken. So you don't have to take your apple back. How about the physics teacher, Dan McCallum? You have him?'

Susan opened her mouth to answer but was interrupted by Archie's cell phone ringing. He pulled it out of his jacket pocket, snapped it open, turned and walked a few steps away. 'Yeah?' he said. He listened for a minute. Henry and Susan watched him with rapt attention. Susan felt some almost imperceptible shift. She wasn't sure if it was in Archie's body language or a charge in the air, or maybe just a projection of her own mind, but she knew for certain that something had changed. Archie nodded several times. 'OK. We're on our way.' He snapped the phone shut, dropped it carefully back into his pocket, and slowly rotated back towards them.

'They find her?' asked Henry, his face impassive.

Archie nodded.

'Where?' asked Henry.

'Sauvie Island.'

Henry rolled his eyes towards Susan. 'You want to drop her off back at the bank?'

Susan stared at Archie, willing him to let her come along. *She can come. She can come. She can come.* She longed for his lips to form the words. Her first crime scene. A first-person account. It would make a great lead for the first story. What was it like to look at a murder victim? The stench of a corpse. The legion of investigators examining the scene. Yellow crime tape. She smiled, feeling that familiar hum in her belly again. Then caught herself and quickly forced the pleasure out of her face. But Archie had already seen it.

She looked at him, her eyes pleading, but his face showed nothing.

He started walking towards the car. Fuck. She'd blown it. Her first fucking day with him and he already thought she was some sort of bloodthirsty asshole.

'She can come,' he said, still walking. He turned and glanced purposefully back at Susan. 'But don't expect her to look like her photo.'

16

'You know, there are actually tons of dead bodies on Sauvie Island,' Susan said from the back seat. 'A lot of the gay guys who used to go to the nude beach died of AIDS and had their ashes scattered there. The upper beach? Above the tideline? All bone chips and charcoal.' She scrunched up her face in disgust. 'Sunbathers oil up and lie down and end up with tiny fragments of dead guy in their crevices.' She waited. 'I did a story about it. Maybe you read it?'

No one answered. Henry, she realized, had tuned her out about ten miles ago. Archie was on the phone.

She crossed her arms and tried not to yammer. It was the curse of the feature writer. Useless facts. And she had done plenty of stories about Sauvie Island: organic farmers, the cornfield maze, the nude beach, cycling clubs, eagles' nests, U-pick berry fields. *Herald* readers loved all that crap. Consequently, Susan knew more about the island than most of the people living on it. It was twenty-four thousand acres. A so-called agricultural oasis flanked by the Columbia and the polluted Multnomah Channel, and about a twenty-minute drive from downtown Portland. To preserve the island's natural wilderness, the state had set aside twelve thousand acres as the Sauvie Island Wildlife Area. It was there, far from the farmhouses that made the island seem like a slice of Iowa, that the dead girl had been found. Susan had never liked the place. There were too many open spaces.

The road turned to gravel. 'Yes,' Archie said into his phone. 'When? . . . Where? . . . Yes.' It didn't make for sensational note-taking. 'No . . . We don't know yet . . . I'll find out.' It was excruciatingly slow going on the gravel, and the steady spray of grit on the car was punctuated only by the occasional small rock that bounced off the windshield. Archie was still on the phone. 'Are you there now? . . . About five minutes.' Every time he hung the thing up, it rang. Susan let her gaze fall on the roadside, a thick wall of blackberry bushes backed by river oaks. It blinked by like a zoetrope. Finally, Susan could see a cluster of police cruisers, an old pick-up and an ambulance already parked along the side of the road up ahead. A Sheriff's Department vehicle was blocking the road, and a young state cop was stopping traffic. Susan craned her head to see more, her notebook open on her lap. Henry pulled to a stop and flashed a badge at the cop, who nodded and waved them through.

Henry pulled the car in next to a police cruiser and with one fluid motion he and Archie were out of the vehicle, leaving Susan to scurry after them, wishing that she had worn more practical footwear. She reached into her purse and dug out some lipstick. Nothing dramatic. Just a little natural colour. She put some on as she walked and immediately felt like a jerk for it. Beyond the police cruiser, a bearded young man in a terry-cloth robe stood with a patrol cop. He was barefoot. Susan smiled. He flashed her a peace sign.

The path to the beach had been trampled over time through a natural parting in the brambles and it cut diagonally through the tall dead grass down to the sand below. The sand was loose, and Archie had to secure his footing with each step. *All bone chips and charcoal.* Ahead lay the Columbia, still and brown, and, on the other side, Washington State. He could see a group of state patrol cops standing about a quarter-mile down the beach on the clay flats.

Claire Masland was waiting for them on the beach. She was wearing jeans and a solid red T-shirt, and had taken off her waterproof North Face jacket and tied it around her waist. Archie had never asked her, but he imagined that she hiked and camped. Maybe even skied. Hell, she probably snowshoed. Her badge was clipped to her waistband. Sweat stains had formed at her armpits. She matched their stride as they continued towards the body.

'A nudist found her at about ten,' she said. 'He had

to get back to his vehicle and then home to phone us, so we didn't get the call until ten-twenty-eight.'

'She look like the others?'

'Identical.'

Archie's mind was racing. It didn't make sense. The acceleration was too rapid. He liked to hold on to them. Why didn't he want to keep this one longer? Did he think he *needed* to dump her? 'He's scared,' Archie concluded. 'We've scared him.'

'So he watches the evening news,' Henry said.

They'd spooked him. They'd spooked him into dumping the body. So now what? He would take another one. He'd have to take another one. Acid rose in Archie's throat. He reached into his pocket, fished out an antacid tablet and chewed it fretfully. They'd rushed him. And now he'd have to kill another girl.

'Who's here?' Archie asked.

'Greg. Josh. Martin. Anne's running about ten minutes behind you.'

'Good,' Archie said. 'I want to talk to her.'

He stopped short and the group stopped with him. They were about fifteen yards from the crime scene. He listened.

'What is it?' asked Claire.

'News helicopters,' said Archie, looking up, face pained, as two helicopters cleared the treeline. 'Better get a tent up.' Claire nodded and hurried back towards the road. Archie turned to Susan. She was writing in her notebook, flipping pages frequently as she filled them with large cursive observations. Archie could sense her excitement and he remembered the feeling when he and Henry had responded to that first Beauty Killer case. It wasn't like that any more.

'Susan,' he said. She was working furiously to finish a thought in her notebook and made a motion with her finger that she would be with him in a second.

'Look at me,' Archie said. She looked up, her green eyes large. He felt, suddenly, very protective of this strange pink-haired girl who pretended to be so much tougher than he thought she was, and, at the same time, felt ridiculous for the presumption. He held her eye contact for a moment, until she focused on him. 'Whatever you think's going to be up there,' he said, gesturing to where Kristy Mathers lay naked in the mud, 'it's going to be worse.'

Susan nodded. 'I know.'

'Have you ever been around a corpse?' Archie asked.

She nodded some more. 'My dad. He died when I was a kid. Of cancer.'

'It's going to be different from that,' Archie said gently.

'I can handle it.' She lifted her head and sniffed the air. 'Do you smell that?' she asked. 'Clorox?'

Archie and Henry exchanged a look. Then Henry pulled two pairs of latex gloves out of the pocket of his coat and handed a pair to Archie. Archie looked out once more at the calm river glinting in the late-morning sun, took a deep breath through his mouth, and exhaled.

'Don't breathe through your nose,' he said to Susan. 'And don't get in my way.'

Squatting there beside Kristy's body, Archie felt absolutely lucid. His head cleared. His gut relaxed. His concentration focused. He realized that he'd actually gone a few minutes without thinking about Gretchen Lowell. He had missed this.

She had been strangled and then soaked in bleach, like the others. She lay five feet from the water's edge, on her back, head to the side, one plump arm tucked behind her torso, skin and hair coated with sand, as if she had been rolled a few feet. The other arm was delicately bent at the elbow, her curled hand resting just below her chin, chewed nails still flecked with glittery polish. That arm made her look almost human. Archie continued, taking in every detail, working his way from her head to her toes. One leg was slightly bent, the other straight, tangled in river weed. He noted the blood at her nose and mouth, the grotesquely swollen tongue, and the same horizontal mark low on the neck, indicating the use of a ligature they thought was a belt. The underside of her neck and shoulder showed the purplish stain of livor mortis, where her blood had settled after she died. A greenish-red coloration had started to bloom around her abdomen; her mouth, nose, vagina and ears were black. The bleach had slowed down the decomposition by killing some of the bacteria that caused distension and rupture of the soft tissues, so he could still see something of Kristy in the corpse. Something recognizable in the cheek and profile. But the bleach had not deterred the bugs. Tiny insects batted at her mouth and eyes and swarmed over her genitals. Crabs scrambled through her hair. Dark jelly was all that remained of one eye socket, the skin on her forehead and cheek torn from where a bird had stood, hooking its claws in the meat for leverage. Archie looked up to see a gull standing watchfully a few feet beyond the body. It met Archie's stare and took a few impatient steps before flapping back to a safer position.

Henry cleared his throat. 'He dumped her on the beach,' he theorized, 'not in the water.'

Archie nodded.

'How do you know?' Susan asked.

Archie looked up at Susan. Her face was pale, all lipstick and freckles, but she was holding together better than he had that first time. 'She'd still be out there,' he said.

'Corpses sink,' Henry explained. 'They pop up three days to a week later because of gases released in the body. It's only been two days since she disappeared.'

Archie looked up and down the beach. The helicopters circled overhead. He thought he caught the flash reflection of a telephoto lens. 'He must have dumped her out here last night, while it was still raining. Early enough that the rain and tide would wash away any trace evidence he'd left on the hike.'

'He wanted us to find her,' Henry said.

'Why is she like that?' Susan asked, her voice quavering for the first time.

Archie looked down at the body, the brown hair now a shade of pale orange, the skin burned. All identical to the crime photographs of Lee Robinson and Dana Stamp. 'He bleaches them,' he said quietly. 'He kills them, he sexually assaults them, and he soaks them in a tub of bleach until he decides to dump them.' He could taste it in his mouth, the eye-watering burn of the bleach blended with the putrefaction of flesh and muscle.

He saw Susan waver, just a small adjustment in her stance, a catch. 'You haven't released that.'

Archie gave her a tired smile. 'I just did.'

'So he kills them right away,' Susan said almost to herself. 'Once anyone knows they're missing, they're already dead.'

'Yep.'

Her eyes narrowed. 'You let everyone keep on hoping. Even though you knew she was dead.' Then she bit her lip and wrote something in the notebook. 'What a sick fuck,' she said under her breath.

Archie wasn't sure if she was referring to the killer, or to him. It didn't really matter. 'I think that's a fair assessment,' he said.

'If he did dump her here,' Henry said to Archie, 'he must have parked where we did. Used the same path. He couldn't have carried her from any other point. Unless he waded in from a boat.'

'Go door to door. See if anyone drove by, noticed a vehicle. Including a boat. Also have the Hardy Boys canvass the area for condoms. He may not have been able to resist.'

'You want them to search a nude beach for condoms?' asked Henry dubiously. 'And maybe while they're at it they could search a few college dorms for bongs.'

Archie smiled. 'Send anything you find to the lab. Then run the DNA through COIDUS. Maybe we'll get lucky.' Archie tucked another Vicodin in his mouth.

'Another Zantac?' Henry asked.

Archie looked away. 'Aspirin.'

17

On what Archie thinks is the third day, when Gretchen slams the funnel down his throat and drops the pills in, he swallows them without fighting it. She puts the funnel aside and quickly tapes his mouth shut again with a pre-cut piece of duct tape she has ready. She has said nothing today. She uses a white hand towel to wipe off the saliva that has run down his face, and then she leaves. He waits for the pills to kick in, every cell alert to change. It is another way to measure time. He doesn't know what the pills are, but suspects speed, a painkiller, some sort of hallucinogen. The tingling starts at his nose and creeps its way up to the top of his head. He forces himself to give in to it.

His mind is starting to go. He thinks he sees a dark-haired man in the basement with them. He is just a shadow. He flits behind Gretchen and then is gone. Archie wonders if the corpse has come to life, a walking man of rotting, bloated flesh and bone. But he tells himself that it is just a hallucination. Nothing is real.

He imagines the crime scene. Henry and Claire.

They would have traced him to the big yellow house that Gretchen had leased on Vista. Crime tape. Media. Forensics. Evidence markers. He moves through the scene, directing the task force as if he were just another Beauty Killer victim. 'It's been too long already,' he tells Claire. 'I'm dead.' They are all so grim and desperate-looking. 'Lighten up! It's all good! At least we know who the fuck the killer is! Right? Right?' They stare at him blankly. Claire cries. 'You have to see this is connected to the case,' Archie tells them, his voice reedy with anxiety. 'It's not a coincidence.'

They comb the entire property for clues. 'Piece it together,' Archie pleads. They would have Gretchen's name, her ID-badge photograph. He replays his visit, mining his memory for any surface he had touched, fibres he had left, some trace that he had been there. The coffee. He had spilled it on the rug. Archie points to the darkened stain. 'See it?' he cries to Henry. Henry stops, squats, waves a technician over. The lab would find traces of whatever she'd slipped him. It would confirm their suspicions. Had anyone seen him going in? What had happened to his car? Archie squats next to Henry. 'When the results come back, you have to do everything you can to connect her to the other murders. Release her photograph everywhere. When I'm dead, she'll leave the house. And when she leaves the house, you can catch her.'

'You're hallucinating,' Gretchen says.

He is wrenched from his dream back to the basement. She is there again, pressing a cool cloth against his forehead. He doesn't feel hot, but he realizes that he's sweating.

'You're mumbling,' Gretchen says.

Archie is grateful for the duct tape. Grateful that she can't hear his half-cracked ramblings.

'I don't know how you stand the stench down here,' Gretchen says, sliding her eyes to where the corpse still lies on the floor.

She starts to say something else, but he is tired of her, so he turns back into his mind.

And he goes to see Debbie.

She is sitting on the couch wrapped in a fleece blanket, eyes red from crying. 'Have you found him?' she asks quickly when Archie walks in.

'No,' he says. Archie gets a beer from the fridge and sits down beside her. Debbie's face is smooth and empty and her hands shake where she holds the blanket under her chin.

'He's still alive,' Debbie says adamantly. The steely optimism in her voice breaks his heart. 'I know it.'

Archie considers this. He wants to be kind to her. But he can't lie. 'Actually, chances are I'm dead,' he tells her. 'You have to prepare yourself.'

Debbie looks at him in horror, her posture hardening.

Flummoxed, he tries again to comfort her. 'It's for the best,' he says. 'The sooner she kills me the better. Believe me.'

Debbie's eyes fill with tears and her mouth gets small. 'I think you'd better go now,' she says.

'Look at me.' Gretchen. He is back in the basement again. Reality folds and skitters on the periphery of his vision. He doesn't want to give in to her, but he has learned his lesson, so he turns his head and gives her his attention.

There is nothing in her face. No anger. No pleasure. No pity. Nothing. 'Are you scared?' Gretchen asks. She dabs his forehead with the cloth, his cheek, the back of his neck, his collarbone. He thinks he sees a flash of emotion in her eyes. Sympathy?

Then it's gone. 'Whatever you think this is going to be like,' she whispers, 'it's going to be worse.'

18

The first thing Susan did when she arrived home from Sauvie Island was to unzip her tall black leather boots, kick them off and fling them on top of a pile of other shoes that had been abandoned at the door. Stained and reeking of bleach, the boots were ruined.

Susan lived in what she liked to call a loft but was actually a large studio apartment in the Pearl District, just north of downtown on Portland's west side. The building, once a turn-of-the-century brewery, had been redeveloped several years before. The facade still stood, hulking and brick, along with the old smokestack, but the rest of the structure had been replaced to provide residents with the most modern amenities. Susan's loft was on the third floor. Technically, it belonged to an ex-professor of hers who was on a year-long sabbatical in Europe with his wife, writing another book. He lived in Eugene, where he was the lauded head of the MFA writing programme at U of O, but he kept the place in Portland ostensibly as a writing getaway, though it was rarely used for literary pursuits. Susan had wanted it to be hers from that first weekend she'd spent there. The open kitchen had the latest appliances, a stainless-steel fridge and an impressive, gleaming range. It was everything the house she had grown up in wasn't. Sure, the countertops were Corian, not granite, and the range was a Frigidaire knock-off of a Viking, but from a distance the place still looked chic and urban. She loved the Great Writer's blue desk. She loved the built-in bookcase that took up an entire wall and was stacked with the Great Writer's books, two layers deep. She loved the framed photographs of the Great Writer with other great writers. The bed was walled off with a Japanese screen, leaving the rest of the space a living area, which consisted of a blue velvet sofa, a red leather club chair, a coffee table and a small TV set. Everything that was actually hers in that apartment could fit in two suitcases.

She tugged her shirt over her head, pulled off her black pants, her socks, her underpants, her bra. She could still smell it, the bleach. It was on everything, soaked into everything. God, she had loved those boots. She stood for a moment naked, shivering, her clothes a pile at her feet, and then she wrapped herself in the kimono that hung on a brass hook on the bathroom door, gathered up her clothes, the expensive beautiful boots, walked barefoot out into the hallway, down to the small rectangular door marked GARBAGE by the elevator, opened it, and threw the whole bundle down the chute. She didn't wait like she usually did to listen to the bundle fall; she went straight back to her apartment, into the bathroom, turned on the tub, let the kimono fall in the corner next to the door. Only an inch of steaming water had accumulated, but Susan climbed into the tub anyway, squatting in the hot water and watching her feet redden. She sat down slowly, wincing a little as she did, and then inched backward, stretching her skinny legs out in front of her. Her naked body only made her think of them. *Did he bleach them in a tub like this?* The waterline was just at her hips now and she leaned back against the cold porcelain, forcing herself to press against it until it warmed to her body temperature. Her arms were covered with goose bumps, and no matter what she did she couldn't seem to stop the damn shivering. She turned the faucet off with her toes, closed her eyes and tried not to think about the pale, bruised thing that had once been Kristy Mathers.

Archie sat at his new desk, listening to his taped interview with Fred Doud. Kristy Mathers was dead. And now the clock restarted. The killer would take another girl. It was just a matter of time. It was always a matter of time.

Archie had turned off the fluorescent overheads in his office and now sat in near-darkness, the only light streaming in from his open door. He had finally sent Henry to drive Susan Ward back to her car, and he and Claire Masland had followed the medical examiner's vehicle to the morgue, where they met Kristy's father and he identified her body. Archie had become an expert at shattering families. Sometimes he didn't have to say a word. They just looked at him and knew. Other times, he had to say it over and over again, and still they blinked at him, dumbfounded, heads shaking in disbelief, eyes stubbornly bright with denial. And then, like a wave, it would crash and the truth would flood in. It took a lot of effort to remind himself that he was not the cause of their anguish.

But Archie did not mind being around grief. Even the most blatant assholes seemed to function in a state of grace when confronted with the brutal loss of a loved one. They moved through the world differently from other people. When they looked at you, you had the feeling that they were really seeing you. Their entire universe was just this one thing, this one event, this one loss. They seemed, for a few weeks, to have things in perspective. Then the inconsequential shit of their lives would start to seep back in.

He looked up. Anne Boyd was leaning in his doorway, watching him in that way she had, like a parent waiting for a confession.

He rubbed his eyes, smiled wearily, and waved her in. Anne was a smart woman. He wondered if her psychological training allowed her to see through his pretence of sanity. 'Sorry. Daydreaming.' He punched the tape recorder off. 'You can get the light,' he added.

She did, and the room was flooded with jumpy

white light, causing the vice of pain that gripped Archie's head to crank a turn tighter. He stiffened, and stretched his neck until he heard a satisfying pop.

Anne flung herself down in one of the chairs facing him, crossed her legs and flopped a fifty-page document on his desk. She was one of the few female profilers at the FBI, and the only black woman. Archie had known her for six years, since the bureau had sent her out to profile the Beauty Killer. They had spent hundreds of hours in the rain going over crime sites together, staring at photographs of wound patterns at four o'clock in the morning, trying to get into the mind of Gretchen Lowell. Archie knew that Anne had kids. He had heard her talk to them on the phone. But they had never once, he realized, in all the time they had worked together, talked about their respective children. Their professional lives were too ugly. Talking about children seemed crude.

'That it?' he asked, nodding at the document.

'The fruit of my labours,' Anne said.

Archie's ribs hurt from sitting so long and acid burned in his stomach. Sometimes, he would wake up in the middle of the night and find himself in the right position, and realize that he wasn't in pain. He'd try to remain still, to stretch out the blissful interlude, but eventually he'd have to turn over or bend a knee or stretch an arm out, and then there'd be that familiar twinge or burn or ache. The pills helped, and sometimes he told himself that he was almost getting used to it. But his body still proved a distraction. If he was going to concentrate on Anne's profile, he needed some air. 'Let's take a walk. You can give me the topic sentences.'

'Sure,' she agreed.

They walked through the empty squad room, where a custodian was uncoiling a vacuum-cleaner cord, and Archie held the big glass bank door open for Anne and then followed her out on to the sidewalk. They started walking north. It was cold and Archie tucked his bare hands in the pockets of his jacket, and there were the pills. He was, as usual, underprepared for the weather. The streetlamps looked blurry in the dark, and the city looked dirty in the flat yellow light that they threw on the pavement. A car went by going ten miles over the speed limit.

'I think we're dealing with a budding psychopath,' Anne said. She was wearing a long chocolate-coloured leather trench coat and leopard-print boots. Anne always could put together an outfit.

'You like them?' Anne asked, noticing him looking at her feet. She stopped and lifted her long knit skirt a few inches to show off the boots. 'I got them in the "large and in charge" department. They're extra wide. For my enormous calves.'

Archie cleared his throat. 'You said he was a budding psychopath?'

'You don't want to talk about my calves?' Anne asked.

Archie smiled. 'I'm just trying to avoid a sexual-harassment lawsuit.'

Anne let the skirt drop and grinned at Archie. 'I do believe that's the first time I've seen you smile in two days.'

They started walking again and Anne continued her profile: 'He raped and murdered these girls but he feels remorse,' she said, her demeanour serious again. 'He cleans them up. Returns them.'

'But he kills again.'

'The need overpowers him. But it's about the rape. Not the murder. He's a rapist who kills, not a murderer who rapes. Even though he kills them first, it's not necrophilia. He kills them to spare them from experiencing the rape.'

'What a guy,' said Archie.

They walked past a darkened paint store, past a shuttered espresso drive-thru booth, past a hipster dive bar. The window of the bar was filled with neon beer signs: PBR, RAINIER, SIERRA NEVADA. A half-assed marquee advertised a band called Missing Persons Report. Nice. Archie glanced inside as they went past and caught a flash of people, mouths open wide, laughing, the sound of drunken levity.

Anne continued. 'I don't think the murder gives him pleasure *per se*. He doesn't linger with it. He doesn't use his hands. I think we need to look at where he came from. I think he's raped before. And if he has, it will be within the victim profile.'

Archie shook his head. 'We've pulled every unsolved rape over the last twenty years. No good fits.'

They came to an intersection. If Archie had been alone, he would have walked against the light, but because Anne was there he pushed the pedestrian button and waited.

'Look out of state. If you can't find anything, it means that the rapes weren't reported, which is useful in itself.'

Archie considered this. 'He has power over women.'

'Or used to,' Anne commented.

'He loses his power; he compensates with violence.'

Anne nodded several times, her jaw working. 'I'm thinking a steady evolution of sexual assaults, followed by some sort of stressor at work or home. He's probably had violent sexual fantasies since he was a child, but he was able to quell them with porn and the early rapes. Then he decides to take it further. Plans it. Carries it off. And he gets away with it.'

'So he does it again.' Archie sighed. The light changed, finally, and they walked across to the other side of the street and started heading back south. It wasn't much of a walk. But it felt good to move.

'Yes. And gets away with it again. So now the societal boundaries that he's always been uncomfortable with are seriously eroding. I think that part of him, that first time, fully expected to get caught. Maybe he even wanted to get caught, to be punished for his deviant fantasies. But he wasn't. So now he's thinking that the law doesn't apply to him. He's feeling special.'

'And the bleach? Is it a purification ritual or is he studiously destroying forensic evidence?'

He could see Anne bite her lip. 'I don't know. It doesn't fit. If he cares about them enough to kill them, why is he bathing them in corrosive chemicals? But it's overkill as a cleansing agent. And I think our guy is meticulous enough to avoid overkill. He would know exactly how much, and not use any more.'

'He dumped a body the day before Valentine's Day,' Archie said.

'It's not a coincidence.'

'The murders are intimate for him,' Archie said softly. 'He's choosing them.'

'This guy's smart,' Anne said. 'He's educated. He's got a job. He's transporting the bodies, so he has access to a vehicle. And probably to a boat. Based on his victim window, I'd say he works banker's hours. White, male. He would look unremarkable. Functional. Presentable. If it is an evolution, he's well into his thirties, possibly forties. He's detail-orientated and manipulative. He's taking an enormous risk snatching these girls off public streets. He's confident, arrogant even. And he's got a ruse. He's got a ruse to get these girls to go with him.'

'Like Bundy's cast?'

'Or Bianchi playing cop, or car trouble, or he says

he's a modelling scout, or says that the parents have been in an accident and offers to take the girl to the hospital.' She shook her head dismissively. 'But it's better that that. It's brilliant. Because whatever he's using, he got Kristy to go with him, after two girls had already been murdered.'

Archie thought of plump, brown-haired Kristy Mathers dragging her broken bike across the street, just blocks from home. *Where was the bike?* If he'd grabbed her, why take the bike? And if he did take the bike, then his car had to be big enough to get it in quickly. 'If she went with him voluntarily, she had to know him.'

'If we accept that premise, yes, she had to know him.' They were standing in the bank parking lot. 'This is me,' Anne said, putting her hand on the roof of a rented burgundy Mustang.

'I'm going to interview the teachers and staff again tomorrow,' Archie said. 'Just the men who fit the profile.' His headache was getting bad. It was like having a permanent hangover.

'You going home tonight, or are you going to sleep in your chair?'

Archie glanced at his watch and was startled to see that it was eleven p.m. 'I just need another couple of hours to finish up,' he said.

She clicked the car door unlocked and threw her purse in on the passenger seat, then turned back to

Archie. 'If you ever want to talk,' she said with a helpless shrug, 'I am a psychiatrist.'

'Who specializes in the criminally insane.' He smiled wanly. 'I'm going to try not to read into that.'

He noticed then, under the harsh security lights of the parking lot, how much she had aged over the last few years. There were lines around her eyes, and a few fine strings of grey in her hair. She still looked better than he did.

'Did she fit it at all?' she said.

Archie knew whom she meant. 'She manipulated the profile, Anne. You know that.'

Anne smiled darkly. 'I was convinced the killer was a man. That he was working alone. I didn't even consider the possibility of a female. Yet you suspected her. Despite the bad profile. The way she infiltrated her way into the investigation, it's textbook psychopathic behaviour. I can't believe I didn't see it.'

'She fed me exactly enough that I would need to go to her, and not enough that I would be careful. It was a trap. I went there because she played me. Not because of my investigative prowess.'

'She knew you wanted to solve that case more than anything. Psychopaths are excellent at reading people.'

You have no idea, thought Archie.

'In any case,' Anne said, sighing. 'I'm at the Heathman. If you change your mind. About talking.'

'Anne?'

She spun back. 'Yes?'

'Thanks for the offer.'

She stood there for another moment in her leopard-print boots, as if she wanted to say something more. Something like 'Sorry your life went to shit,' or 'I know what you're thinking about doing,' or 'Let me know if you want a referral to a nice quiet institution.' Or maybe she was just thinking about getting back to the hotel so she could call her children. It didn't really matter. Archie waited for her to drive off and then he went back into his office, snapped the tape recorder back on, closed his eyes and listened to Fred Doud talking about Kristy Mathers's terrible corpse.

19

Archie woke from a groggy, unsatisfying sleep to find Henry standing over him. The office light was on and Archie was still sitting in his desk chair.

'You spent the night,' Henry said.

Archie blinked, disorientated. 'What time is it?'

'Six.' Henry set a paper cup of coffee from the break room on Archie's desk.

Archie's ribs were sore; his head throbbed; even his teeth hurt. He rolled his neck to one side until he heard it pop. Henry was dressed in black pants and a crisp black T-shirt. He smelled like aftershave. Archie picked up the coffee and took a sip. It was strong, and he winced reflexively as it went down. 'You're here early,' Archie said.

'I got a call from Martin,' Henry said, sitting in the chair across from Archie's desk. 'He's been vetting the custodians. They work for a company called Amcorp that contracts with the district. The school board laid off all their janitors last year during the budget crisis. Then brought in Amcorp because it was cheaper. They're supposed to have criminal-background checks on file.'

'But . . . ?'

'They've got them for some, motor-vehicle checks for some,' Henry said. 'They're all over the place. Shoddy. Martin's been running names. One came back bad. Public exposure.'

'What school does he work at?' Archie asked.

Henry raised an eyebrow. 'Jefferson in the mornings, Cleveland in the afternoons. He's also worked at Lincoln.'

It was a lot of access. But there were a lot of people with a lot of access. 'Anyone talk to him yet?' Archie asked.

'Claire. After the first girl turned up dead. He said he was working. A few of the kids reported seeing him around after school. The contractor said he was clean.'

Archie had read the reports. The team had interviewed 973 people since the first girl had disappeared. Claire had interviewed 314 of them herself. Maybe she had cleared the custodian too quickly. 'But he was at Cleveland when Lee disappeared?'

'Right,' Henry said.

Archie placed his hands on his desk and stood. 'What are we still doing here?'

'Car's out front.' Henry looked down at Archie's wrinkled shirt. 'You need to go home and change?'

Archie shook his head. 'No time.' He grabbed his coffee and his jacket and let Henry walk out of his office first, so he could slip three pills in his mouth. He didn't like to take the Vicodin on an empty stomach, but he didn't see any breakfast in his immediate future.

Martin, Josh and Claire were already at their desks in the squad room. There were tips to track down, patrols to co-ordinate, alibis to check and double-check. School would be starting in a few hours, and their killer was still out there. A clock hung on the wall. A slogan printed on its face read TIME TO BANK WITH FRIENDS. Next to it someone had posted a sign scrawled on a piece of copy paper. REMEMBER: TIME IS OUR ENEMY.

'How did you know I'd be here?' Archie asked Henry as they exited the bank and walked into the parking lot. Dawn was just breaking and the air was cold and grey.

'Went by your place,' Henry said. 'Where else would you be?' He got in to drive and Archie walked around and got in the passenger side. Henry hadn't started the car yet. He was just sitting there.

'How many are you taking?' Henry asked. His hands were on the steering wheel and his eyes were on the windshield.

'Not as many as I'd like.'

'I thought you were going to cut back,' Henry said softly.

Archie laughed, remembering his worst days, a haze of codeine so thick he'd thought he might drown in it. 'I have.'

Henry tightened his fists on the wheel until they

went white. Archie could see the scarlet rising on his neck. Henry worked his jaw for a moment, his blue eyes hard. 'Don't assume that our friendship will prevent me from getting you back on medical leave if I start to think that you're too high to work.' He turned and looked, for the first time, at Archie. 'I've already done way more than I'm comfortable with for you.'

Archie nodded at his friend. 'I know,' he said.

Henry raised his eyebrows.

'I know,' Archie said again.

'This thing with Gretchen,' Henry said between gritted teeth. 'These weekly meetings. It's fucked up, my friend. I don't give a shit how many corpses she unearths for us. At some point' – he looked Archie right in the eye – 'you have got to let it go.'

Archie froze, afraid to show any reaction; afraid that Henry might see how much he cared. Henry was worried enough about him. Archie couldn't let Henry see how important those weekly meetings had become. Archie needed Gretchen. At least until he figured out what she wanted from him. 'I need more time,' he said carefully. 'I've got it under control.'

Henry pulled his sunglasses out of the pocket of his leather jacket, snapped them on and started the car. He sighed and shook his head. 'You better fucking well have.'

*

The custodian was named Evan Kent. Archie and Henry found him painting over graffiti on the north wall of the main building at Jefferson. The paint was a bad match and the fire-engine-red rectangle stood out on the faded bricks. The wall had been painted over many times through the years and was covered with dozens of uneven blocks of varying shades that formed a sort of *ad hoc* abstract painting. Kent looked to be in his mid-thirties, and he was fit, with dark hair and an attentively trimmed goatee. His blue coveralls were spotless.

It was still an hour before classes started, and the campus was quiet. An impromptu memorial had formed at the chain-link fence at the front of the school. Bouquets were twisted into the fence, ribbons hung limp, stuffed animals sat abandoned. Photographs of Kristy were glued on to cardboard signs and decorated with glittery stickers and puffy paint. WE LOVE YOU. U R ALWAYS R ANGEL. GOD BLESS. The eastern skyline was bubblegum pink and the first birds of spring sat dark and plump on the telephone lines, their chattering a distant music. A patrol car was parked on each side of the school, and private security guards stood at each entrance. The lights of the patrol cars were on to increase their presence, making the school look even more like a crime scene. Just another day of public education.

'I was taking a piss,' Kent said as Archie and Henry approached.

'Excuse me?' Henry said.

Kent continued to paint. The paint-heavy brush made a slapping sound against the bricks. Archie noticed a tattoo of the Virgin Mary on Kent's forearm. It was new, the colour brilliant. 'The indecent-exposure rap? I was taking a piss after a show got out downtown,' Kent explained. 'Maybe not my brightest moment. But I had to pee. I paid the fine.'

'You left it off the job application,' Archie said.

'I needed the job,' Kent said. He stepped back and examined the work he'd done. There was no trace of what had been written, only the smell of fresh paint and a new, glistening, blood-red rectangle. 'I've got a philosophy degree, so employment opportunities are not exactly plentiful. And I'm diabetic. Without insurance, I'm spending eighty bucks a week on insulin and needles.'

'Boo hoo,' said Henry.

Kent's posture stiffened defensively and he looked at Henry. 'Hey, man, health insurance is a real problem in this country.'

Archie stepped slightly forward. 'Where were you between five and seven on February second and March seventh?' he asked Kent.

Kent turned to Archie, his shoulders dropping. 'Working. I do afternoons at Cleveland. I'm generally on until six.'

'Then what?' Archie asked.

Kent shrugged. 'I go home. Or to band practice. Or to a bar.'

'You drink?' Henry said. 'I thought you said you were a diabetic.'

'I am. And I do,' Kent said. 'That's why I need the insulin. Look, the day the kid from Jefferson disappeared, my Dart broke down. I had to call my room-mate, and he came and gave me a jump. Ask him.' He gave Archie his room-mate's name and cell-phone number and Archie wrote the information down in his notebook. 'And why don't you do something about all the fucking media trespassing on school grounds? They're wigging out the kids. And they don't get their facts straight.'

Archie and Henry exchanged glances. How did Kent know which facts were straight?

Kent's face reddened and he jammed a toe into the grass. Then he asked, 'You going to tell Amcorp about my record?'

'That would be the cop-like thing to do,' Henry said.

Kent smirked. 'Where were the cops when those girls were taken off the street by some psycho?'

Henry turned to Archie and said loudly enough for Kent to hear, 'You like him for it?'

Archie made a show of examining Kent while the custodian stood shifting uncomfortably under the weight of his stare. 'He's handsome,' Archie conceded. 'I could see girls going with him. His age is in the profile range.'

Kent's cheeks coloured.

Henry widened his eyes incredulously. 'You think he's handsome?'

'Not as handsome as you,' Archie reassured him.

'I have work to do,' Kent said, picking up his bucket of paint and his brush.

'One thing,' Archie said to him.

'Yeah?' Kent said.

'The graffiti. What did it say?'

Kent looked at each of them a minute. '"We're all going to die,"' he said finally. He stared at the ground and shook his head. Then laughed and looked back up, his dark eyes flashing. 'With a goddamn smiley face.'

20

Susan sat at the Great Writer's blue desk near the window, watching the pedestrian lunchtime traffic go in and out of the Whole Foods that was catty-corner to her building. The first story was written and sent. She hated this part. She hated waiting for the affirmation from Ian, but she craved it. She hit REFRESH on her e-mail display. Nothing. She was filled with a sudden overwhelming certainty that he hated it. He abhorred her pathetic attempt at literary journalism. She had blown her one shot to write something big. They would probably fire her. She couldn't even bring herself to re-read it, sure that she would see every typo, every passive voice, every lame excuse for a sentence. She hit REFRESH again. Nothing. Catching the time on the monitor, she scrambled to the Great Writer's velvet sofa, curled up and turned on the midday news. Archie Sheridan's face filled the screen and a crawl announced that this was a special report. He looked tired. Or was the word *weary*? But he had shaved and brushed his dark hair and his lined, hang-dog face held a certain authority. She longed to feel that in control.

She watched Archie grimly confirm the death of Kristy Mathers, and then the screen switched back to a pair of daytime local news anchors who bantered in trepidation about the human monster at large and then segued right into a special report on the sudden dearth of rain in the Willamette Valley. The press conference had been at ten o'clock, which meant that it had been over for almost two hours. She wondered what Archie Sheridan was doing now.

The phone rang and Susan nearly tripped trying to get to it before the third ring, when the voicemail would pick up. She saw the caller ID and knew immediately who it was.

'I love it,' Ian said without introduction.

Susan felt the morning's tension bleed from her shoulders in an instant. 'Really?'

'It's great. That juxtaposition of walking in the dead girl's steps at Cleveland and then finding Kristy Mathers's body – it's exactly what we wanted, babe. There's not much about Sheridan in here. You've hooked us. Now I want Sheridan dismembered, so we can see his beating heart.'

'That's for next week,' Susan said happily, pouring herself a cup of cold coffee and putting it in the microwave. 'Leave the assholes wanting more, right?'

'The assholes?'

Susan laughed. 'The readers.'

'Oh,' said Ian. 'Right.'

Susan dressed for the day in cowboy boots, jeans, a Pixies T-shirt and a red velvet blazer. She put a reporter's notebook in the front right pocket of the blazer and two blue Bic ballpoints in the left. She even blow-dried her pink hair and put on make-up.

When she was ready to go, she opened her notebook to a poorly scrawled list of names and telephone numbers that Archie Sheridan had given her. She paused, wondering for a moment what he would think of that first story when it ran, then quashed her anxiety. He was a subject. She was a writer. One story down. Three to go. She dialled the phone.

'Hi,' Susan said brightly. 'Is this Debbie Sheridan?'

There was a slight hesitation. 'Yes?'

'I'm Susan Ward. With the *Herald*? Did your husband tell you I might be calling?'

'He mentioned something.'

She didn't correct the husband thing, thought Susan. She didn't say, *You mean my ex-husband. We're divorced. I'd have the marriage annulled if I could, the son of a bitch.* Susan wrote the word *husband* in her notebook, followed by a question mark.

She forced a big smile, hoping that Debbie could hear it in her voice. It was an old phone-interview trick that Parker had taught her. 'Well, I'm writing a profile about him, and I was hoping to ask you a few questions. Just to flesh him out a bit. Give the piece some personality.'

'Can you . . . can you call me back later?' Debbie asked.

'Sorry. You're at work, aren't you? Is there a better time I can call you back?'

There was a pause. 'No. I just need to think about it.'

'You mean talk to Archie? Because I asked him, and he said he didn't mind if I spoke to you.'

'No. No. I just don't like going over all those memories. Let me give it some thought.' Debbie's voice warmed. 'Call me later, OK?'

'OK,' Susan agreed ruefully.

She hung up, and immediately dialled the next number on the list before she lost her nerve. Archie's doctor was unavailable, so Susan left her name and cell-phone number with his receptionist.

She heaved a deep sigh, sank back down at the Great Writer's desk and Googled Gretchen Lowell. Over eighty thousand links came up. She spent a half-hour skimming through the interesting ones. It was astonishing how many websites were dedicated to the exploits of serial killers.

Susan was staring at an online case study recounting the Beauty Killer investigation when something caught her eye. 'Gretchen Lowell called 911 to turn herself in and call for an ambulance.'

Susan picked up the phone and dialled Ian on his cell.

'I'm in a news meeting,' he answered.

'How do I get a nine-one-one tape?' Susan asked.

'Which one?'

'Gretchen Lowell,' Susan said. 'Have you heard it?'

'They didn't release it. We ran a transcript.'

'I want the actual call. Can I get it?'

Ian made a clucking sound. 'Let me try.'

Susan hung up and Googled Oregon State Penitentiary. She copied the address of the prison on a piece of paper beside her computer and then opened a Word document. 'Dear Ms Lowell,' she wrote. 'I am writing a profile about Detective Archie Sheridan, and I am hoping to ask you a couple of questions.' She worked on the letter for almost twenty minutes. When she was done, she placed it in an envelope, stamped it and wrote out the address.

She paid a few bills and then drove to the post office and mailed them, along with the letter to the Beauty Killer. Then she drove to Cleveland High School. She wanted to open the next story with some personal anecdote, a memory of her own days at Cleveland. She thought going there might bring back some details she could incorporate. But the truth was that she had been avoiding it.

The final bell had just rung and the wide main hallway was thronged with students, cramming items from their lockers into their backpacks, standing in tight groups, making out against the wall, slugging back soft drinks, talking loudly and hurtling their way out of the building into the light. They moved with the loose-limbed ease of teenagers in their natural setting, something that Susan did not recall ever actually experiencing. The difference between the freshmen and seniors was staggering. The freshmen seemed so young. Which was funny to Susan, because at fourteen she had considered herself very much an adult.

A few of the kids sent sideways glances Susan's way as she passed. But most didn't even blink. In their world, pink hair was pretty ordinary. Susan took a few notes for her story, recording details and impressions of the school. Atmosphere.

When she reached the dark brown double doors that led into the theatre, she paused for a moment, hand on the door, overcome by a flood of teenage memories. She had left high school behind so long ago; it was amazing to her what mixed emotions the place now conjured. She ran a hand through her hair, put on her best grown-up face, and walked through the doors.

It smelled the same. Like paint and sawdust and orange-scented carpet cleaner.

The theatre sat 250 in red vinyl seats that terraced up from a small black stage. The stage lights were on, and a partially built set constructed out of plywood and canvas gave the vague impression of a turn-of-the-century parlour. She recognized the same old Queen Anne sofa that they had used in *Arsenic and Old Lace* and *Cheaper by the Dozen*. The sconces from *Murder at the Vicarage*. And the same staircase. Always the same staircase. It just switched sides.

She had hated high school, but she had loved this place. It floored her now to think of all the time she'd spent there, hours after school in rehearsal for play after play. It had been her whole world, especially after her father had died.

There wasn't anyone in the auditorium today. The emptiness of the place made her feel a splinter of sadness. She walked to the last row of chairs and knelt down to examine the underside of the second chair in from the aisle. There, scratched in the metal, were her initials: S.W. After all these years, her name was still carved into this place. She felt a sudden wash of self-consciousness and stood up. She didn't want someone walking in, finding her there. She didn't want any reunions. It was a mistake to have even come to Cleveland. The story was about Archie, not her. She took one last look around, and then turned and fled back into the hallway.

A voice called, 'Ms Ward.' She recognized it immediately. It was the voice that had launched a thousand detentions.

'Mr McCallum,' she said.

He looked the same. He was a short barrel of a man, with an enormous moustache and a ring of keys that pulled down one side of his pants, requiring constant adjustment. 'Walk with us,' he said. 'I'm just escorting Mr Schmidt to detention.' Susan then noticed the teenage boy walking behind McCallum. He smiled at her shyly, a painful trail of acne making its way up his neck.

Susan hurried along behind. The jostling kids in the hall parted for McCallum, who didn't break stride.

'I see your byline,' he said to Susan.

Susan cringed. 'Oh?' she said.

'Are you here about Lee Robinson?'

Susan brightened and opened her notebook. 'Did you know her?'

'Never laid eyes on her,' McCallum said.

Susan turned hopefully to the kid. 'You?'

The kid shrugged. 'Not really. I mean, I knew who she was.'

McCallum whipped around. 'What did I tell you, Mr Schmidt?'

The kid reddened. 'Not a word?'

'I don't want to see your mouth open or hear words come out of your face until sixth period tomorrow,' McCallum said. He turned to Susan. 'Mr Schmidt has a talking problem.'

Susan was about to fall prey to her own talking problem when she was distracted by a glass display case in the hallway. 'Look,' Susan said, pressing a finger against the glass. 'All the Knowledge Bowl trophies.'

McCallum nodded proudly, his chin and neck converging into one. 'We won state last year. So they were forced to move a few football trophies to make room in the display case.'

The case was full of trophies, the largest a wide silver bowl with the name of the school and the year engraved in fancy calligraphy. 'I really loved Knowledge Bowl,' she said quietly.

'You quit the team,' McCallum pointed out.

Susan swallowed a ball of sorrow in her throat. 'I had a lot going on.'

'It's difficult to lose a parent so young.'

She laid her hand flat on the glass. The trophies were polished to a shine and her distorted reflection stared back at her a dozen times. When she lifted her hand, a faint greasy palmprint marked where it had been. 'Yeah.'

'That's harsh,' the kid said.

McCallum looked at the kid, who shrank back.

The physics teacher spun back to Susan and jabbed a thumb at a brown door across the hall. 'This is us,' he said. He held out a thick, hairy hand. Susan took it. 'Ms Ward,' he said, 'I wish you the best in your future endeavours.'

'Thanks, Mr McCallum,' Susan said.

McCallum walked the kid over to the door and opened it for him. The kid waved limply at Susan as he was led inside.

'Sorry about bailing on Knowledge Bowl,' she called after them, but the door had already shut.

'You've got to be kidding me.' Susan stood with her hands on her hips, examining her old Saab. It had been booted. The metal device was firmly affixed to her left front wheel. She squeezed her eyes shut and emitted a low growl. She had parked in a reserved teacher spot, sure. But it was after school. And she'd been inside only fifteen minutes. She shuffled around for a few minutes, collecting herself.

'Booted, huh?'

Startled, Susan looked up to see a kid leaning against the hood of a boxy orange BMW parked a few spaces behind her. The kid was nice-looking: a mop of longish hair, clear skin, tall. But the car was beautiful, one of those old 2002 models from the 1970s. It was shiny tangerine, unmarred; the chrome details twinkled elegantly. The vanity plate read JAY 2.

'It's nice, isn't it?' he said. 'From my dad. To make up for leaving my mom for the real-estate lady.'

'Did it help?'

'It helped him.' He nodded at her car. 'You have to go inside to the admin office. Pay a fine. Then they'll call one of the custodians to unboot your car for you. You better hurry. There's a basketball game, so the office is closing early.' He pushed away from the car and took a few steps towards her. Looked at the ground. Then up at her again. Squinted. 'Listen. You wanna buy some weed?'

Susan took a small step back and glanced around to see if anyone was within earshot. There were cops everywhere. Two patrol cars were parked on either side of the school. Plus, Susan had noticed a man sitting in a sedan in front of the school, not thirty feet from where she now stood. Was he a cop? A dad waiting to pick up a kid? This was exactly how innocent reporters got themselves arrested. 'I'm a grown-up,' she whispered loudly.

His eyes travelled up to her pink hair, then down at her Pixies T-shirt, the cowboy boots, the beat-up car behind her. 'You sure? It's from BC.'

'Yeah,' Susan said. Then, more definitely: 'Yes.' She looked back at the clamp on her car. Why did these things always have to happen to her? 'The admin office?' she said.

The kid nodded.

'Thanks.' She turned and marched towards the building, passing the man in the sedan, who had produced a *Herald* and was suddenly studying it. Definitely a cop, Susan decided. She climbed the wide front stairs, pushed open one of the front doors, turned down the hall and found the admin office. But the door was locked. 'Seriously?' she demanded aloud. 'Seriously?' She slammed the door with the flat of her hand. The impact made a dull, loud thwap. Susan cried out and pulled her stinging hand to her chest.

'Can I help you?'

She spun around to face a custodian who was wheeling an enormous green plastic garbage bin through the hall.

'You can take the fucking boot off my car,' she said. The custodian had slick dark hair, a goatee and what they used to call a 'matinée idol' profile. The Cleveland custodians hadn't looked like that when Susan had gone there. In fact, he was almost handsome enough to distract Susan from her frustration. Almost.

His dark eyes widened. 'That's your Saab in the teachers' parking lot?'

'Yeah,' Susan said.

'Sorry,' he said with an apologetic shrug. 'I assumed that it belonged to a student.'

'Because it's crappy.'

He grinned. 'That, and the Blink One-Eighty-Two bumper sticker.'

Susan looked at the floor. 'That was on there when I bought it.'

'Anyway, we have a zero-tolerance policy on the teachers' spaces. Otherwise the students would all park there.' He was still grinning at her. 'But I guess I can cut you loose.' He pulled out the biggest ring of keys that Susan had ever seen. 'Come on,' he said, and started down the hall towards the front door of the building, leaving the garbage bin pushed against the wall. He stopped in front of the Knowledge Bowl trophy case, pulled a white rag out of his pocket and rubbed it on the glass. She caught a glimpse of a colourful tattoo on his arm: the Virgin Mary. He smiled at her and shook his head. 'Handprint. It's like cleaning up after apes sometimes.'

Susan busied her hand in her hair, on the off-chance that he might be able to match her palm to the greasy print, and then hurried to catch up with him. 'So, do you like being a custodian?' she asked, wincing even as the question left her mouth.

'I love it,' he deadpanned. 'Though it's just something to do while I work my way through my doctorate in French literature.'

'Really?' Susan said brightly.

He opened the front door and let her pass through. 'No.'

A cold wind was picking up, and Susan struggled to jam her hands into the tiny pockets of her velvet blazer. 'Did you know Lee Robinson?'

He seemed to bristle. 'Is that why you're here?'

'I'm doing a story for the *Herald*. Did you know her?'

'I cleaned her vomit up once in the nurse's office.'

'Seriously?' Susan asked.

'Yeah,' he said. 'And once she brought me a Hallmark card on National Janitor Appreciation Day.'

'Really?'

They'd reached the parking lot. The kid and the orange Beemer were gone. The guy in the sedan was gone too.

The hot janitor knelt down next to her car. 'No.'

'You're funny.'

'Thanks.' He bent over the boot, unlocked it and, in a swift, almost violent motion, pulled it off the front wheel. Then he stood, holding the heavy boot under one arm, and waited.

Susan fidgeted self-consciously with her purse. 'How much do I owe you?' she asked.

'I'll tell you what,' he said, his eyes turning cold. 'I'll let you off free and clear if you agree not to exploit a dead kid for a newspaper story.'

Susan felt like she'd been slapped in the face. She was speechless. He just stood there looking handsome in his coveralls. 'It's not really exploitation,' she stammered. She wanted to defend herself. To explain the importance of what she was doing. The public right to know. The beauty of shared humanity. The role of the witness. But suddenly she had to admit that it all seemed pretty lame.

He pulled a ticket out of one of his many pockets and held it out to her. She took it and flipped it over in her hand. Fifty dollars! And it would probably go to the fucking football team or something.

She wanted to say something clever. Something that would make her feel less like a bottom-feeder. But before she could, she heard the distant music of Kiss. She stopped and listened. It was the song 'Calling Dr Love'. She saw a flash of embarrassment cross the janitor's face as he fumbled in his pants pocket. It was his cell-phone ringtone.

And he thought *she* was a teenager.

He pulled the phone out of his pocket and looked at the caller ID. 'Better take this,' he said to Susan. 'It's my boss, calling to fire me.'

Then he lifted the phone to his ear and walked away.

Susan watched him go, puzzled, and then got into her car. The Kiss song rattled in her head. Something about being full of sin.

As she pulled her car out of the parking lot, she had an idle thought: janitors probably had a lot of access to bleach.

'What do they have in common?' Archie asked Henry.

They were walking along the Sauvie Island beach where Kristy Mathers had been found. It was Archie's default. No clues? No clear avenues of exploration? Return to the scene of the crime. He had probably spent whole years of his life walking in Gretchen Lowell's steps. It got him in the right headspace, and there was always a chance they'd find a clue. He needed a clue.

The river lapped at the beach, where a squiggle of foam and muck marked the tideline. A freighter with Asian characters on the side slid by in the distance. Above the Asian characters was the translation: *Sunshine*

Success. No one was on the beach. It was dusk and the light was low, though the winter sky in the north-west had a way of holding light so that no matter what time of night it was it always looked like the sun had just set. Still, it would soon be too dark to be out there. Archie held a flashlight so they could find their way back to the car.

'They look alike,' said Henry.

'Is it that simple? He stalks the schools? Picks girls out that fit a type?' After Archie and Henry had left Jefferson, they had spent the morning interviewing teachers and staff members at Cleveland who fitted the profile. There were ten in all. It had yielded nothing. Claire had tracked down Evan Kent's room-mate, who had confirmed his story about the jump-started Dart. But he put it earlier, more like 5.30. Which left enough time to get north to Jefferson.

'They're all sophomores.'

'So what do sophomores have in common?' Archie asked. Seven of the Cleveland staffers had alibis. Three didn't. He had gone over the alibis again and they had held up. That left three suspects in play at Cleveland: a school bus driver, a physics teacher, a maths teacher/volleyball coach, and Kent. Plus about ten thousand other perverts loose in the city. They would watch Kent, and check out the other three. The ten thousand perverts were on their own.

'They were all freshmen last year?' Henry guessed.

Archie stopped walking. Could it be that simple? He snapped his fingers. 'You're right,' he said.

Henry scratched his bald head. This time of day, it started to get a little grey stubble. 'I was kidding.'

'Tell me we checked to see if they all transferred from the same freshman class.'

'All three went to their respective schools the year before,' Henry said.

'Is there a test they all take freshman year?' Archie asked.

'You want me to see if some deranged proctor is killing them?'

Archie fished an antacid out of his pocket and put it in his mouth. It tasted like citrus-flavoured chalk. 'I don't know,' he said. He forced himself to chew the tablet and swallow it. He turned on the flashlight, holding it at an oblique angle against the sand. Several tiny crabs scrambled from the light. 'I just want to catch the motherfucker.' Archie liked to use a flashlight to go over a crime scene, even in broad daylight. It shrank his focus, made him look at things one square inch at a time. 'Throw more surveillance at the schools. I don't care if we have to drive every kid home.'

Henry hooked his thumbs behind his turquoise belt buckle, leaned back and looked up at the dark sky. 'Should we head back?' he asked hopefully.

'You have someone waiting for you at home?' Archie asked.

'Hey,' Henry said. 'My depressing apartment is nicer than yours.'

'*Touché*,' Archie said. 'Remind me how many times you've been married?'

Henry grinned. 'Three. Four if you count the one that was annulled, and five if you count the one that was just legal on the reservation.'

'Yeah, I think it's better to keep you busy,' Archie said. He swung the flashlight beam around, watching the crabs scatter. 'Besides, we haven't searched the crime scene yet.'

'The crime-scene investigators have already done that,' Henry said.

'So we'll see if they've missed anything.'

'It's dark.'

Archie shone the beam under his chin. He looked like a horror-show ghoul. 'That's why we have a flashlight.'

21

Susan woke up, shrugged on her old kimono, took the elevator downstairs and systematically dug through the pile of *Herald*s on the granite floor of the lobby until she found the one with her name on it. She waited until she was back upstairs in her apartment before she pulled the newspaper out of its plastic bag. She always felt butterflies when she looked for a story she had written. It was a mix of anticipation and fear, pride and embarrassment. Most of the time, she didn't even like to read her work once it appeared in print. But the hot janitor's smack-down had fanned the flame of her familiar self-doubt. The truth was, sometimes she did feel like a fraud. And sometimes she did feel like she exploited her subjects. She had pissed the hell out of a city councilman she had profiled and described as 'balding and gnome-like'. (He was.) But this was different.

The task force story was the first byline she had ever had on the front page. She sat down on her bed, and with a heavy, nervous breath unfolded the *Herald*, half expecting the story to have been killed, but there it was, below the fold, with a jump to the Metro section. The front page. A-1. An aerial photograph of the crime scene on Sauvie Island accompanied the story. With a startled laugh, she recognized herself, a small figure in the photo, and next to her, among the other detectives, Archie Sheridan. Screw the janitor. She was delighted.

She found herself wishing she had someone with whom she could share her little journalistic triumph. Bliss had cancelled her subscription to the *Herald* years ago, after the paper's owners had controversially clear-cut some old-growth forest. She would have bought a copy of the paper, if she'd known, but Susan hadn't told her about the series. And wouldn't. Susan traced the newspaper image of Archie Sheridan with her fingers and found herself wondering if he had seen it yet. The thought made her feel self-conscious and she shook it loose.

She got up and brewed herself a pot of coffee and then sat back down and flipped through the paper to find the Metro section, where the story jumped, and an envelope fell on the rug. At first, she thought it was a pack of coupons or some other silly promotion the paper had agreed to in exchange for advertising dollars. Then she saw that her name was on it. Typed. Not typed on a label. Typed on the envelope itself. 'Susan Ward'. Who typed an envelope? She picked it up.

It was a regular white business-size envelope. She turned it over a few times in her hands and then opened it. A piece of white copy paper was folded neatly inside. There was one line typed in the centre of the page. 'Justin Johnson: 031038299.'

Who the fuck was Justin Johnson?

Seriously. Who was he? And why, if she didn't know that, would someone slip her a secret note with his name and a bunch of numbers?

Susan was aware of her heart suddenly racing. She wrote the digits down on the edge of the newspaper in the hope that the act of writing them down would help her make sense of them. There were nine of them. It wasn't a phone number. Could a Social Security number start with a zero? She looked at it for a while longer and then she picked up the phone and called Quentin Parker's direct line at the *Herald*.

'Parker,' he barked.

'It's Susan. I'm going to read you some numbers and I want you to tell me what you think they are.' She read the numbers.

'Court-case file number,' Parker said immediately. 'The first two numbers are the year – 2003.'

Susan told Parker the story of the mysterious envelope.

'Looks like someone's got herself an anonymous source,' Parker teased. 'Let me call my guy at the courthouse and see what I can find out about your file.'

Her laptop was sitting on the coffee table. She opened it up and Googled the name Justin Johnson. Over 150,000 links came up. She Googled Justin

Johnson, Portland. This time, only eleven hundred. She started scrolling through them.

The phone rang. Susan picked it up.

'It's a juvie record,' Parker said. 'Sealed. Sorry.'

'A juvie record,' Susan said. 'What kind of crime?'

'Sealed, as in "cannot be opened".'

'Right.' She hung up and looked at the name and numbers some more. Drank some coffee. Looked at the name. A juvie record. Why would someone want her to know about Justin Johnson's juvenile record? Could it have something to do with the After School Strangler? Should she call Archie? About what? Some weird envelope she'd found in her newspaper? It could be about anything. It could be a prank. She didn't even know any Justins. Then she remembered the student pot dealer in the Cleveland High parking lot. His vanity plate had read JAY 2. The letter J squared? It was worth checking out. She dialled the number for the Cleveland High administration office.

'Hi,' Susan said. 'This is Mrs Johnson. We've been having some truancy issues and I was wondering if you could tell me if my son Justin had made it in to school today?'

The student office volunteer told Susan to hang on a minute and then came back on the line. 'Mrs Johnson?' she said. 'Yeah. No worries. Justin's here today.'

Well, what do you know? Justin Johnson went to Cleveland High. And he had a criminal record.

She punched in Archie's cell-phone number. He

answered on the second ring. 'This is going to sound weird,' she said, and she relayed the story of the parking lot and the envelope.

'He's alibied,' Archie said.

'You know this off the top of your head?'

'We looked into him,' Archie said. 'He was in detention. All three days in question. He's accounted for.'

'Don't you want the case number?'

'I know about his record,' Archie said.

'You do?'

'Susan, I'm a cop.'

She couldn't resist. 'Did you see my story?'

'I liked it very much.'

Susan hung up and squirmed with pleasure. He had liked her story. She set the envelope on a stack of mail on the coffee table. It was just before ten a.m. Justin Johnson would be out of school in about five and a half more hours. And she would be waiting for him. In the meantime, she was much more interested in Archie Sheridan. She poured herself some more coffee and called Debbie back on her landline. It was Friday, but Archie had said that his ex-wife worked at home on Fridays. Sure enough, Debbie picked up.

'Hi,' Susan said. 'It's Susan Ward again. You said to call back?'

'Oh, hi,' Debbie said.

'Is this a better time? I'd still really love to get together to talk.'

There was a brief pause. Then Debbie sighed. 'Can you come now? The kids are at school.'

Susan beamed. 'That sounds great. Where do you live?'

She got directions, pulled on skinny jeans, a red-and-blue-striped T-shirt and red ankle boots, grabbed her black pea coat and took the elevator downstairs. It was a gorgeous elevator, all steel and glass. Susan watched as the numbers blinked from 6 down to the subterranean garage, and then at the last moment she had an idea and hit L. The doors slid open and she stepped out into the lobby and walked into the building's chic administrative and sales office. Good. Monica was working.

Susan put on her best sorority-girl face (it was pretty good, even with the pink hair) and approached the bamboo counter where Monica sat frowning over a fashion magazine.

'Hi,' Susan said, stretching the word out to four syllables.

Monica looked up. She was a committed platinum blond. No roots. Ever. With the kind of automatic smile that becomes meaningless by definition. Susan wasn't sure what exactly she did besides read magazines. She seemed to function as bait for the building's sales team, like pumping a cookie-baking smell into a model home. Susan guessed she was in her mid-twenties, but with the amount of make-up she wore, it was hard to tell. Susan knew that Monica didn't know quite how to process her. The pink hair obviously confused the hell out of her. It must have appeared to Monica that Susan had engaged in some sort of self-mutilation. But this seemed to make her all the more determined to be nice.

'Listen,' Susan said. 'I've got a secret admirer.'

Monica perked up. 'No way!'

'Totally. And he left me a love note in my newspaper this morning.'

'Oh my God!'

'I know! So I was wondering if you could run through this morning's security video of the lobby so I can see who he is.'

Monica clapped her hands excitedly and rolled her *faux*-zebra-skin task chair over to a gleaming white monitor. This was the kind of project that gave her job meaning. She picked up a matching remote, and the black-and-white image on the screen began to jump back in time. They watched for a few minutes as people walked backward into elevators, until the lobby was quiet, the newspapers in their little stack below the mailboxes. Then a man walked backward into the building and bent down over the newspapers.

'There,' said Susan.

They rewound the tape a bit more and watched as a woman carrying a travel mug walked out of the elevator, through the lobby and out of the front door. As she exited, a man in a dark suit walked into the building and over to the newspapers, rooted through them and clearly deposited something inside. He'd been waiting out front and caught the door as the woman had gone out.

'He's cute!' squealed Monica.

'How can you tell?' asked Susan, disappointed. 'You can't see his face.'

'He's got a nice suit on. I bet he's a lawyer. A rich one.'

'Can you print this image for me?'

'Totally,' Monica gushed. She hit a button, rolled over to the white printer and waited while the image spat out, then handed the print-out to Susan. Susan examined it. Totally unidentifiable. Still, she'd show it to Justin Johnson and see if it sparked a discussion. She folded it up and slipped it into her purse.

'Thanks,' Susan said, already half turned to go.

'You know,' Monica said, her face a picture of helpfulness, 'you should dye your hair blond. You would look so much prettier.'

Susan looked at Monica for a minute. Monica looked back obliviously. 'I was thinking about it,' Susan said, 'but then I heard that story on the news about platinum hair dye causing cancer in lab kittens.'

'Lab kittens?' Monica said, eyes wide.

Susan shrugged. 'Gotta run.'

22

Debbie Sheridan lived in a stucco ranch-style house in Hillsboro, a few minutes off the highway. Susan had lived in Portland most of her life, and she could count on both hands the number of times she had been to Hillsboro. It was a suburb she drove through on the way to the coast; she didn't think of it as a destination. Just being in the suburbs made Susan nervous.

The house was typical for its neighbourhood. The lawn was green and well groomed, with the sharp edges and dearth of weeds that screamed professional maintenance. There was a box hedge, a Japanese maple tree, some blue spruce and several beds of ornamental grasses. A two-car garage was attached to the house. It was the picture of domestic bliss, and a home in which Susan could not even conceive of ever living.

She locked her car, walked to the medieval-looking front door and rang the bell.

Debbie Sheridan opened the door and thrust out a hand in greeting. Susan took it. Debbie was not what Susan had imagined. In her late thirties, she had stylish very short dark hair and a trim, athletic body. She was wearing black leggings and a T-shirt and sneakers. She was attractive and chic and not at all suburban-looking. Susan followed her into the house. It was filled with art. Large abstract oil paintings on stretched canvas lined the white walls. The floors were layered with Oriental rugs. Books were stacked on every flat surface. It was all very cosmopolitan. Very world-traveller. And very much not what Susan had expected.

'I like your art,' Susan commented. She always felt a little uneasy around women who were more sophisticated than she was.

'Thanks,' said Debbie amiably. 'I'm a designer out at Nike. This is what I do when I want to feel like an artist again.'

It was only then that Susan noticed the *D. Sheridan* scrawled in the corner of the canvases. 'They're amazing.'

'They keep me busy. Sometimes I think my kids are more talented.'

Debbie led Susan down a hallway, past framed black-and-white photographs of two attractive dark-haired children. Some of the photographs featured just the children; some were of Archie and Debbie and the children. They all looked deliriously happy and delighted with one another.

They reached a bright modern kitchen with French doors that overlooked a back yard with a big English cottage garden. 'Do you want some coffee?' Debbie asked.

'Sure,' Susan said, accepting a cup Debbie poured

from a French press and then taking a seat on one of the tall chairs at the kitchen bar. She noticed a completed *New York Times* crossword sitting out on the counter.

Debbie continued to stand.

There was a family room on the other side of the bar. It also had French doors that opened out on to the garden. Judging by the drafting table and wall of tacked-up sketches, Debbie used the room as a home office. But the floor was strewn with toys. Debbie noticed Susan looking at the sketches and smiled sheepishly. 'I'm designing a yoga shoe,' she explained.

'Aren't you supposed to do yoga barefoot?'

Debbie grinned. 'Let's just say that it's an untapped market.'

'Is that what you design mostly? Shoes?'

'Not the structural stuff. I just take what the lab guys give me and try to make it look pretty. I read your story today. It was interesting. Well written.'

'Thanks,' Susan said, embarrassed. 'It was just laying the groundwork. I want to go a little deeper in the next few. Do you want to sit down?'

Debbie put a tentative hand on a chair but then hesitated and removed it. She looked in the family room. At the toys on the carpet. 'I should pick up after the kids,' she said. She walked behind Susan around the bar into the family room and bent over to pick up a stuffed gorilla. 'So what do you want to know?' she asked.

Susan produced a small digital recorder from her purse. 'Do you mind if I record this? It's easier than having to take notes.'

'Go ahead,' said Debbie. She continued with her task, plucking up a stuffed cat, a rabbit, a panda.

'So,' Susan said. Dive right in. Full speed ahead. 'It must have been hard.'

Debbie stood up, her arms teeming with plush animals, and sighed. 'When he was missing? Yes.' She walked over to a small red table with two child-sized red chairs and began placing the stuffed animals on top of it one by one. 'He called me, you know, right before he went in to see her. Then he didn't come home.' She paused and looked at the gorilla still in her arms. It was the size of a baby. She spoke carefully. 'I thought it was traffic at first. It's close to Nike out here, but the commute on Twenty-six can be murder. I called his cell phone about a hundred times, but he wasn't picking up.' She looked up at Susan and forced a smile. 'This was not entirely unusual. I thought they might have found another body. But then . . .' She paused and took a breath that caught for a moment in her throat. 'Finally, I called Henry. Henry went to her house. They found Archie's car out front, but the house was empty. That's when it all started to fall apart.' She looked at the gorilla for another moment and then slowly placed it on the table, positioning it snugly between the panda and the cat. 'They didn't know what had happened, of course. That it had anything to do with Gretchen Lowell. But they were able to piece it together.' Her voice grew tight. 'But they couldn't find him.'

'Ten days is a long time.'

Debbie sat down cross-legged on the carpet and pulled a large wooden puzzle towards her. 'They thought he was dead,' she said matter-of-factly.

'Did you?'

She took two evenly measured inhalations. Then twisted her face as she said, 'Yes.'

Susan surreptitiously slid the digital recorder an inch closer to Debbie. 'Where were you when you heard that he'd been found?'

Debbie started putting the puzzle together with pieces that lay scattered around her. 'I was here,' she said, looking around. 'Right here.' She laughed sadly. 'In the family room. There was a couch. Coffee. So many cops. Claire Masland.' She froze, a puzzle piece still in her hand. 'And flowers. People had started leaving flowers. They showed our house on the news. And people came from all over to lay these bouquets in our yard.' She looked up at Susan, her face helpless and distraught and bemused all at the same time. 'Stuffed animals. Ribbons. Sad notes.' She glanced down at the puzzle piece still in her hand: a police car. 'And flowers. The entire front of the house was just thick with wilting flowers.' Her hand tightened around the puzzle piece and her forehead tensed. 'All these fucking condolences scrawled on scrap paper and bereavement cards. "Sorry for your loss." "Our deepest sympathies." I remember looking out the front window into this field of funeral arrangements. I could smell them from inside, that stink of rotting foliage.' She laid the police car in the puzzle and lifted her hand away and looked at it. 'And I knew that he was dead.'

She glanced back up at Susan. 'They say you're supposed to feel it, you know? When someone you love that much dies? I felt it. His absence. I knew that it was over. I knew, in my body, that Archie was dead. Then Henry called. They had found him. And he was alive. Everyone cheered. Claire drove me to Emanuel. And I didn't leave the hospital for five days.'

'How was he?'

Debbie took a long breath and seemed to consider the question. 'When he woke up? It took us a long time to convince him that he was out of that basement.' She paused. 'Sometimes I wonder if we ever did.'

'Did he talk to you about it?' Susan asked.

'No,' Debbie said.

'But you must have an idea of what happened?'

Debbie's eyes turned dark and cold. 'She killed him. She murdered my husband. I believe that a person knows. I know what I felt.' She looked at Susan meaningfully. 'And I know what he returned as.'

Susan glanced down at the recorder. Was it recording? The tiny red light above the microphone gleamed reassuringly. 'Why did she do it, do you think?'

Debbie sat perfectly still for a moment. 'I don't

know. But I think that whatever she was trying to do, she succeeded at it. She wouldn't have ended it until she had. She's not that type of person.'

'How long after it all happened did you two separate?' Susan asked.

'She took him around Thanksgiving. We were separated by spring break.' She looked away from Susan, into the back yard, a tree, a swing set, a hedge. 'I know that sounds terrible. He was a mess. Couldn't sleep. Panic attacks. I'm sorry, do you want more coffee?'

'What?' Susan looked down at her untouched mug. 'No. I'm fine.'

'Are you sure? It's no trouble.'

'I'm good.'

Debbie nodded a few times to herself and then stood up and carried the puzzle over to a four-shelf bookcase next to the little table and chairs. The bookcase was full of children's books, board games and wooden puzzles, and she slid the vehicle puzzle in on top of some others. Then she turned to examine the room. Everything was in its place. She let her hands drop to her sides. 'He didn't like to leave the house. Wasn't comfortable around the kids. He was on all this medication. He would sit for hours not doing anything at all. I was worried that he might do something to hurt himself.'

She let this hang in the air for a minute and then her face started to crumple. She put a hand over her mouth and turned her head and wrapped the other arm around her stomach. Susan stood up, but Debbie shook her head. 'I'm fine,' she said. She took another minute and then wiped the tears from under her eyes with her thumb, smiled apologetically at Susan, and walked over to the kitchen. Picked up the French press, pulled the plunger out and poured the rest of the coffee in the sink. Turned on the faucet.

'Three months after Archie was rescued, Henry came to see us,' Debbie continued. 'He told Archie that Gretchen Lowell had agreed to give up ten more bodies, people who were still missing, as part of a plea deal. But she said she would only give the locations to Archie. That was her deal breaker. Archie or nobody.' She rinsed the carafe out and opened the dishwasher and laid it on the top shelf. Then she held the plunger under the cold stream of water, head tilted, watching as the water washed away the grounds. 'She's a control freak. I think she liked the idea of having that control over him even from prison. But he didn't have to do it. Henry said so. Everyone would have understood. But Archie was determined.'

The plunger was rinsed clean, but Debbie kept washing it, turning it under the water. 'He had worked so long on the case that he had to bring closure to the families. Gretchen knew that, I suppose. Knew that he would have to agree. But there was more to it than that. Henry drove him down to Salem to see her about a week later. She kept her promise. Told them exactly where to find this seventeen-year-old girl she'd killed up in Seattle. She said that she would give up more bodies if he came to see her every week, every Sunday. Henry brought him back to the house later that day. And he fell asleep and slept for almost ten hours. No nightmares.' The look she gave Susan was withering. 'Slept like a fucking baby. When he woke up, he was the calmest I had seen him since it all started. It was like seeing her had made him feel better. The more he saw her, the more he pulled away from us. I didn't want him to keep going down there. It was not healthy. So I made him choose. Me or her.' Her choked laugh was humourless. 'And he chose her.'

Susan couldn't really think of what to say. 'I'm sorry.'

The plunger lay in the sink. Debbie was looking out of the window, her eyes glossed with tears. 'She sent me flowers. From one of those Internet places. She must have ordered them before she was arrested. A dozen sunflowers.' Her mouth twisted. '"My condolences on this sad occasion. With warm regards, Gretchen Lowell." They came to the house when he was in the hospital. I never told him that. Sunflowers. My favourite flower. I used to be quite the gardener. Now I have it all done by a service. I don't like flowers any more.' She smiled stiffly to herself. 'I can't stand the smell.'

'Do you still talk to him?'

'Every day over the phone. Ask me how often we see each other.'

'How often?' Susan asked.

'Every couple of weeks. Never more than that. Sometimes, when he is with Ben and Sara and me, I think he wants to carve his eyes out.' She glanced at the stuffed animals, the sink, the counter. 'I'm not usually this neat,' she said.

Susan took a long breath. She had to ask. 'Why are you telling me all this, Debbie?'

Debbie frowned thoughtfully. 'Because Archie asked me to.'

When Susan got back in her car the first thing she did was rewind the mini-tape in her recorder a few seconds and then hit PLAY to make sure that the interview had recorded. Debbie's voice came on immediately. 'Sometimes, when he is with Ben and Sara and me, I think he wants to carve his eyes out.' *Thank God*, thought Susan. She sat for several minutes, feeling her heart pound in her chest. A father and his small daughter walked hand in hand down the sidewalk past her car. The little girl stopped and her father picked her up and carried her into the house next door to Debbie's. Susan opened her window and lit a cigarette.

This story was for the greater good, right?

'Right,' she answered aloud. The role of the witness, she reminded herself. Shared humanity. *Right*.

She used her cell phone to check her messages at work. There was one message from Ian relaying the positive buzz around the building about her task-force story, and reporting that he was working on getting the 911 audio and would know something next week. Susan stared at the small digital recorder in her hand. The second story was writing itself. But there was no message from Archie's doctor's office. He was probably busy saving lives or overbilling Medicaid or something. She opened her notebook and found the number again and dialled it. 'Yeah,' she said into the phone. 'I want to talk to Dr Fergus. This is Susan Ward. I'm calling about a patient of his, Archie Sheridan.' She was, after all, on a roll.

23

'See something?' Anne asked.

She watched as Claire Masland stood on the cement walkway of the Eastbank Esplanade overlooking the Willamette, where Dana Stamp had been found. Claire had a Greek fisherman's cap pulled low over her short hair and she was gazing across the river to the west side of the city, where Waterfront Park formed a band of green around the mélange of new and historic buildings that made up the downtown corridor.

'No,' Claire said. 'Just smelling the river. Sewage has a special aroma, doesn't it?'

Anne had asked Claire to take her to the sites where they had found the bodies. It was something that she had picked up from Archie when they worked the Beauty Killer case. Walk the scene of the crime. They had been to Ross Island and Sauvie Island and now it was late morning and Anne's boots were wet and her feet were cold and it looked like it might rain. She sighed and pulled her leather coat tighter around her torso. A jogger ran past, not giving the two women a second glance. Below them, two enormous dirty seagulls paddled in circles in the muddy brown water.

'What do these sites have in common?' Anne mused aloud.

Claire sighed. 'They're all on the Willamette, Anne. He's got a boat. We know that.'

'It's not convenient. Ross Island. The Esplanade. Sauvie Island. He's working his way north. But why? Killers dispose of bodies in places they feel safe. Ross Island and Sauvie Island may be off the beaten path at night, but this place isn't.' She squinted behind her at the freeway overpass that squeezed above the Esplanade and up at the old-fashioned streetlights that illuminated the Esplanade at night. The sound of the traffic was deafening.

'You can't see the riverbank from here,' Claire said. 'If he was on a small boat, he would have been obscured from anyone walking by. So no one on this side could see him dump the body. And he'd be too far away for anyone to make out what he was doing from the other side.'

'But why risk it?' Anne asked. 'If you've got a boat. Why not dump the body somewhere safe like the other two locations?'

Claire shrugged. 'He wanted her to be found sooner than Lee Robinson?'

'Maybe. It just doesn't make sense. This guy's an organized killer. Maybe the first site is random, but after that, there'd be some method to it. Disposing of a body out in the open like this? It's risky. You don't do it unless you're familiar enough with the area that you think you can get away with it. There's some kind of method to it.' One of the seagulls suddenly squawked and flew off towards the Steel Bridge. The other one stared up at Anne with its beady little eyes.

'How long do we have, do you think?' Claire asked.

'Before he takes another girl? A week. Two if we're lucky.' Anne buttoned her coat, feeling a sudden chill. 'Could be sooner.'

Archie had read Susan's piece the moment he got up. It wasn't a bad article. It evoked a certain outsider's perspective of the investigation. The photo was good. But despite what he had told her over the phone, it was not what he had needed. Justin Johnson? That was interesting. He'd been busted, as a thirteen-year-old, for selling pot to an undercover cop. A pound of pot. And had got off on probation, which was interesting in and of itself. So they had checked him out. But his alibi was rock-solid, so the note concerned Archie less than the person who had left it. Someone was trying to manipulate Susan's story or the investigation. Someone with access to the kid's juvie record. Archie made a call and asked a patrol to make a few extra passes by Susan's place for the next couple of nights. It was probably overreacting, but it made him feel better. Now he sat at his desk in the task force offices, surrounded by photographs of murdered girls, barely aware of the bustle around him. His team was exhausted and growing demoralized. There were no new leads. Kent had been fired for lying about his record on his application and, according to the cops tailing him, had spent the last twenty-four hours playing his guitar. The Jefferson checkpoint had turned up nothing else. They had been unable to find any out-of-state rapes that fitted their MO, and so far none of the Sauvie Island condoms had matched the DNA of anyone on COIDUS. The phone on his desk rang. He glanced at the caller ID and saw that it was Debbie.

'Hello,' he said.

'Your biographer just left. Thought you'd want to know.'

'Did you tell her how fucked up I am?'

'I did.'

'Good.'

'I'll talk to you tonight.'

'Yes.'

Archie hung up the phone. He had taken six Vicodin and he had an unsteady buoyant sensation in his arms and at the back of his head. It was the first wave of codeine that was the best. It made all of the hard edges soften. When he was a patrol cop, he'd dealt with a lot of junkies. They were always breaking into cars to steal coins or whatever crap had been left on the back seat – books, old clothes, bottles that could be turned in for a deposit refund. They'd break a window and risk arrest for thirty-five cents. One of the first things cops learned was that junkies had their own system of reason. They would risk enormous consequences for even a slim chance of a fix. This made them unpredictable. Archie had never understood the mindset. But he thought he was getting closer.

The Hardy Boys appeared at his office door, forcing Archie to clear his mind and put on his cop face. Both were all jittery excitement. Heil took a few tentative steps towards Archie. Archie had pegged him for the talker. He was right. 'We checked the list of school staffers you gave us yesterday and one sort of stood out,' Heil announced.

'Kent?' Archie asked automatically. There was something about the custodian that made him wary.

'McCallum, the physics teacher at Cleveland. Turns out his boat isn't where it's supposed to be.'

'Where is it?'

'It burned down yesterday in that marina fire near Sauvie Island.'

Archie raised his eyebrows.

'Yeah,' said Heil. 'We thought that might be a clue.'

Emanuel Hospital was one of two trauma centres for the region and it was where Archie Sheridan had been taken after they got him out of Gretchen Lowell's basement. It was the hospital favoured by the city's paramedics and it was rumoured that many wore T-shirts printed with the words Take Me To Emanuel, just in case they threw a blood clot. The main structure had been built in 1915, but several additions had left the original stone building almost entirely obscured by glass and steel. It was also the hospital where Susan's father had died of non-Hodgkin's lymphoma the week before she got her braces off. She parked in the visitors' garage and made her way to the office building where Archie's doctor had agreed to meet her. When she took the elevator up to the fourth floor, she was careful to press the button with her elbow rather than her finger. Sick-people germs. You couldn't be too careful.

Dr Fergus made her wait for thirty-five minutes. It wasn't a bad waiting room. There was a view of the West Hills, Mount Hood, the meandering Willamette. But it smelled like every waiting room Susan remembered from her father's appointments. Like carnations and iodine. It was the soap they used to cover up the smell of people dying.

A pile of *InStyle* magazines was fanned out seductively on an end table, but Susan resisted the impulse to waste time and instead spent twenty minutes writing and then rewriting an intro to the next story in her notebook. Then she checked her messages. None. She speed-dialled Ethan Poole. Voicemail.

'Ethan,' she said. 'It's *moi*. Just calling to see if you've had a chance to talk to Molly Palmer yet. I'm starting to take this personally.' She noticed that the receptionist was giving her a very dirty look and pointing to a sign that had a picture of a cell phone with a line through it. 'Call me,' she said. Then she hung up and dropped the phone in her purse.

A *Herald* was laid out on a coffee table over a pile of *U.S. News & World Report*s. Susan had just pulled the front section from underneath the Metro section and put it on top, so her story would be properly displayed for anyone interested, when Dr Fergus appeared with a shrug of apology and a moist handshake and ushered her back past the examining rooms to his office. He was in his mid-fifties and wore his greying hair in a bristle cut, like some sort of Texas high-school football coach, and he walked quickly, at an eighty-degree angle, stethoscope swinging, his shoulders slumped and his fists in his white coat pockets. Susan had to hurry to keep pace.

His office was carefully appointed in classy baby-boomer style and overlooked the downtown skyline on the west side and the battered industrial buildings of the east side, with the wide brown river curving in between. On a clear day, you could see three mountains from Portland: Mount Hood, Mount St Helens and Mount Adams. But when people talked about 'the mountain', they meant Hood, and it was Hood that was visible out of Fergus's window, a perk that was not to be underestimated. Still white with snow, it looked to Susan like a shark's tooth tearing into the blue sky. But then, she'd never been much of a skier.

An expensive hand-made Oriental rug lay over the industrial carpet; a wall of bookshelves housed medical texts, but also contemporary fiction and books about eastern religions; and a large black-and-white photograph of Fergus leaning against a Harley-Davidson hung on one wall, dwarfing the medical degrees that hung beside it. At least he had his priorities straight. Susan noticed an expensive radio on his bookshelf, and bet that it was tuned to classic rock.

'So, Archie Sheridan,' Dr Fergus said, opening a blue folder in front of him.

Susan smiled. 'I assume you've spoken to him?'

'Yes. He faxed over a HIPAA waiver.' Fergus touched a piece of paper on his desk. 'We can't be too careful with the privacy issues today. The insurance companies get to know everything about you. But a friend or family member? Not without the proper paperwork.'

Susan set her digital recorder on the desk, lifting her eyebrows questioningly to Fergus. He nodded. She hit RECORD. 'So can I ask you anything, then?' she asked.

'I am willing to talk to you briefly about the injuries Detective Sheridan sustained in the line of duty in November of 2004.'

'Go.' Susan flipped open her notebook and smiled encouragingly.

Fergus traced through the information in Sheridan's file. His tone was brusque and businesslike. 'He arrived at the ER via ambulance at nine forty-three p.m. on the thirtieth of November. He was in critical condition. Six fractured ribs, lacerations to the torso, a stab wound to the abdomen, his tox levels were dangerously high. We had to do emergency surgery to repair damage to the oesophagus and stomach wall. When we got in there, the oesophagus was so damaged, we ended up having to rebuild it with a section of bowel. And, of course, she had removed his spleen.'

Susan was scribbling along when he got to that last part. She stopped writing and looked up. 'His spleen?'

'Correct. They didn't release that at the time. She'd done a decent job dividing the blood supply and suturing him up, but there was some minor bleeding we had to go in and clean up.'

The tip of Susan's pen remained motionless, pressed against the paper of the notebook. 'Can you do that? Can you just take someone's spleen out?'

'If you've done it before,' Fergus said. 'It's a non-essential organ.'

'What did she – ' Susan tapped her pen nervously against the page – 'do with it?'

Fergus exhaled slowly. 'I believe that it was sent to the police. Along with his wallet.'

Susan widened her eyes in disbelief and scribbled a sentence in her notebook. 'That's the most fucked-up thing I've ever heard,' she said, shaking her head.

'Yes,' he said, sitting forward, his professional interest clearly piqued. 'It surprised us too. It is major surgery. He'd gone into septic shock and his organs were failing. If she hadn't treated him at the site, he would be dead.'

'I heard that she did CPR on him,' Susan said.

Fergus examined her for a second. 'That's what the paramedics said. She also used digitalis to stop his heart, and then resuscitated him with lidocaine.'

Susan simultaneously cringed and craned forward. 'Why?'

'I have no idea. It happened several days before we got to him. That's about when she dressed the wounds. He was well taken care of.' He paused, catching himself, and ran a hand past his forehead. 'You know, from that point on. Clean bandages. Every wound stitched. She'd had him on intravenous fluids, given him blood. But there was nothing she could do at that point about the infection. She didn't have the proper antibiotics, or the equipment to keep his organs functioning enough for them to work.'

'Where'd she get the blood?'

Fergus shrugged and shook his head. 'We have no idea. It was O-negative, a universal donor, and it was fresh, but it wasn't hers. And the man she killed in front of Sheridan was AB.'

Susan wrote the word 'blood' in her notebook, followed by a question mark. 'You said his tox levels were high. What was he on exactly?'

'Quite a little cocktail.' Fergus glanced down at a page in his file. 'Morphine, amphetamine, succinylcholine, bufotenin, benzylpiperazine. And that's just what was still in his system.'

Susan was trying to figure out how to spell succinylcholine phonetically. 'What would have been the result of all those drugs?'

'Without knowing the order in which they were given, I have no way of knowing. Varying degrees of insomnia, restlessness, paralysis, hallucinations, and probably quite a nice high.'

Susan tried to imagine what that would be like. Alone, in pain. So high that your mind isn't functioning. Completely dependent on the person who is killing you. She examined Fergus. He wasn't exactly chatty. But she liked him for being protective of Archie. Jesus, someone had to be. She tilted her head and flashed her most radiant tell-me-anything smile. 'You like him? Archie?'

Fergus pursed his lips. 'I'm not sure Archie has friends any more. But if he did, I think he'd count me among them.'

'What do you think of me doing this? Writing this story? Writing about what happened to him?'

Fergus leaned back in his chair and crossed his legs. The mountain sparkled in the sunlight behind him. After a while, you probably stopped noticing it. 'I tried to talk him out of it.'

'How'd he react?' she asked.

'I was unable to sway him,' Fergus said.

'But you're not being entirely open with me either?'

'He never said I had to tell you everything. He is

my patient. And I will choose his well-being over your newspaper story. Regardless of what he thinks he wants. We had a lot of press crawling all over this hospital in the weeks after Archie was found. My staff referred them all to the hospital PR department. Do you know why?'

Wait, Susan thought, *I know this one!* 'Because reporters are vultures who will print anything without a passing thought to its relevance, significance or veracity?'

'Yes.' Fergus glanced at his five-hundred-dollar watch. 'If you want to know more, you can ask your subject. I've got to go. I'm a doctor. I've got patients. I've got to see about treating them. The hospital gets testy if I don't at least make an effort.'

'Sure,' Susan said quickly. 'Just a few more questions. Is Detective Sheridan still on any medication?'

Fergus looked her in the eye. 'Nothing that would interfere with his ability to do his job.'

'Great. And just so I understand, you're saying that Gretchen Lowell tortured Sheridan, killed him, and then resuscitated him and took care of him for a few days before calling nine-one-one?'

'That's what I'm saying,' Fergus said.

'And Sheridan confirms this?' Susan asked.

Fergus leaned further back in his chair and interlaced his fingers over his chest. 'He doesn't really talk about what happened to him. He claims not to remember much.'

'You don't believe him?'

Fergus looked deliberately at her. 'It's bullshit. And I've told him that to his face.'

'What's your favourite movie?' Susan asked.

'Excuse me?'

Susan smiled pleasantly, like it wasn't a strange question. 'Your favourite movie.'

The poor doctor seemed a little bewildered. 'I don't really have time to see movies,' he said finally. 'I ski.'

24

It was 3.30 and Susan found herself once again at Cleveland High School. She hadn't attended school this regularly when she was enrolled. Her plan had been to ambush Justin at his car, but now that she stood in the parking lot, the orange Beemer was nowhere in sight. Great. She sure as hell couldn't pretend to be his mom in person. Plus, she didn't want to go inside. She didn't want to run into any more of her old teachers. And she certainly didn't want to get lectured by that janitor again.

So now what? She had a lot she wanted to ask JAY 2, like what exactly he'd done to get himself a record and why she should care and, most important, why someone else would think she should care and who that someone might be.

And now she couldn't find him.

The kids were all dressed like it was summer – T-shirts, shorts, mini-skirts, sandals. The sun was bright and even the biggest puddles had dried up, but it was only fifty degrees. Most of the trees were bare.

The kids streamed around Susan to their cars, clutching enormous book bags and backpacks.

Then she saw a kid who looked like Justin. Same surfer haircut, similar clothes, same age. He was walking towards a Ford Bronco, punching a text message into a phone. Remembering the tribe mentality of high school, she took a chance that kids who look alike are usually friends.

'Do you know where I can find Justin Johnson?' she asked, trying not to look weird or dangerous.

He frowned. 'J.J.'s gone,' he said.

'Gone?'

'They took him out of sixth period. His grandpa died or something. He was going right to the airport to fly down to Palm Springs.'

'When's he going to be back?' Susan asked.

The kid shrugged. 'I'm supposed to get his homework for a week. McCallum was pissed. Said he was faking. That his grandpa had already died freshman year. Threatened to put him back in detention.' He examined Susan and seemed to come to some affirming conclusion. 'You looking for product?'

'Yes,' Susan said. 'And I've lost J.J.'s number. Can you give it to me?'

Archie sat across the table from Dan McCallum. He had the arson squad's report in front of him. McCallum was a small man with a lot of thick brown hair and a walrus-like moustache that hadn't been fashionable since before he was born. His arms and legs seemed too short for his thick torso and his hands were small and square. He wore his button-down shirt tucked into his brown pants, which were held up with a wide leather belt. The belt buckle was a brass cougar head. They were sitting in the vault-cum-interview room at the bank task force offices. Claire Masland leaned against the two-foot-thick door, arms crossed. McCallum was grading papers. His fingers had writing calluses on them.

'Can I interrupt a minute?' Archie asked.

McCallum didn't look up. His eyebrows looked like second and third moustaches. 'I've got a hundred and three physics tests to have graded by tomorrow. I've been a teacher for fifteen years. I get paid forty-two thousand dollars a year, not including benefits. That's five less than I got paid last year. Want to know why?'

'Why, Dan?'

'Because the state cut the school budget by fifteen per cent and they couldn't find enough janitors and school nurses to fire.' McCallum laid his red pen carefully across his stack of tests and looked up at Archie. The eyebrows lifted. 'Do you have kids, detective?'

Archie flinched. 'Two.'

'Send them to private school.'

'What happened to your boat, Dan?'

McCallum picked up the pen again and wrote a

'B –' on one of the papers and circled it. 'A marina fire burned it down. But I assume you know that.'

'Actually, it seems that your boat burned down the marina.' This got McCallum's attention. 'Burn patterns indicate that your boat was the origin. And that the fire was started with an accelerant. Gasoline, specifically.'

'Someone burned my boat?'

'Someone burned your boat, Dan.'

One enormous eyebrow started to twitch. McCallum tightened his hairy hand around his red pen. 'Look,' he said, his voice rising an octave. 'I told the detectives where I was when those girls disappeared. I had nothing to do with it. I'll give you a DNA sample if you want. I don't teach biology because I don't like to dissect frogs. Whoever you're looking for, it's not me. I don't know why someone would burn my boat. But it has nothing to do with those girls.'

Archie stood and leaned over the table, resting on his fists, so that he towered over the teacher. 'The thing is,' Archie said, 'the fire started in the cabin, Dan. Which makes us think someone had a key. Because why break into a boat to start a fire? Why not just splash some gas on the deck and start the fire there?'

McCallum's face darkened a shade and he glanced from Archie to Claire in mounting desperation. 'I don't know. But if that fire started in the cabin, then someone broke into the boat. I don't know why. But they did.'

'When was the last time you were on the boat?' Archie asked.

'A week ago Monday. I took it out for the first time this season. Just down the Willamette a few miles.'

'Anything been disturbed?'

'No,' McCallum said. 'It was all the way I left it. As far as I could tell.'

'Who knows you have a boat?' Archie asked.

'Well, I've had the boat for nine years. Multiply that times a hundred students a year. That's nine hundred Cleveland grads alone. Look. I'm not the most popular teacher. I'm tough.' He held up a handful of student papers as if to prove the point. 'I didn't give out a single A in my advanced physics class last semester. Maybe one of the kids got his nose out of joint. Decided to punish me. I loved that boat. They all know that. If someone wanted to hurt me, they might go after it.'

Archie scrutinized McCallum, who seemed to be growing sweatier with each passing minute. Archie didn't like him. But he'd learned long ago that not liking someone didn't mean that the someone was lying. 'OK, Dan. You can leave. We'll take the DNA sample. Claire will tell you where to go.'

McCallum stood and gathered up all of his students' papers and stuffed them into a scratched soft-leather briefcase. Claire opened the door. 'Wait for me in the hall for a minute, will you, Dan?' she said. He nodded and shuffled out.

Claire turned to Archie. 'We don't have any DNA to compare his to,' she said.

'He doesn't know that,' said Archie. 'Take a swab and let's make sure we've got a car on him from the time he leaves school at the end of the day until he's home in bed.'

'It was a boat fire, Archie.'

'It's all we've got.'

Susan sat in her car in the parking lot and dialled Justin Johnson's cell-phone number.

'Yo,' he answered.

She launched right into her rehearsed explanation. 'Hi, J.J. My name's Susan Ward. We met in the Cleveland parking lot. My car was booted, remember?'

There was a long pause. 'I'm not supposed to talk to you,' he said. And he hung up.

Susan sat looking at the cell phone in her hand.

What the hell was going on?

25

Susan had changed her outfit three times before heading to Archie Sheridan's apartment. Now she stood face to face with him in his doorway, wishing she'd gone with another look entirely. But he'd seen her, and now it was too late to go back to the car. 'Hi,' she said. 'Thanks for letting me come over.' It was just after eight o'clock. Archie was still wearing what Susan presumed were his work clothes – sturdy brown leather shoes, dark green jumbo-cords and a pale blue button-down over a T-shirt, unbuttoned at the neck. Susan glanced down at her own ensemble of black jeans, an old Aerosmith T-shirt worn over a long-john shirt, and motorcycle boots, her pink hair pulled up in pigtails. The look had worked well when she had interviewed Metallica backstage at the Coliseum, but for this it was all wrong. She should have gone with something more intellectual. A sweater, maybe.

Archie opened the door wide and stepped aside so she could enter his apartment. It was true, what she had said to him on the phone: she needed the interview. Her story was due the next day and she had a lot of questions for him. But she also wanted to see where he lived. Who he was. She tried not to let her face fall when she saw the empty environment he lived in. No books. Nothing on the walls. No family photographs or knick-knacks picked up on vacation or CDs or old magazines waiting to be recycled. Judging from the sad-looking brown couch and corduroy recliner, it looked like the place had come furnished. No personality. At all. What kind of divorced father didn't display photographs of his children?

'How long have you lived here?' she asked hopefully.

'Almost two years,' he answered. 'Sorry. Not much material, I know.'

'Tell me you have a television.'

He laughed. 'It's in the bedroom.'

I bet you don't have cable, Susan thought. She made a show of glancing around the room. 'Where do you keep your stuff? You must have useless crap. Everyone has useless crap.'

'Most of my useless crap is at Debbie's.' He gestured gallantly to the couch. 'Have a seat. Are you allowed to drink during interviews?'

'Oh, I'm allowed to drink,' Susan assured him. The coffee table, she noticed, was covered with police files. All gathered up and stacked in two neat piles. She wondered if Archie was one of those people who was naturally neat, or whether he just overcompensated. She sat on the couch and reached into her purse and pulled out a dog-eared copy of *The Last Victim*. She set it next to the files on the coffee table.

'I only have beer,' Archie called from the kitchen.

She hadn't bought *The Last Victim* when it came out, but she'd leafed through it. The trashy true-crime account of Archie Sheridan's kidnapping had been on all the supermarket paperback racks back then. Gretchen Lowell was on the cover. If beauty sold books, then beautiful serial killers made best-seller lists.

He handed her a bottle of mid-range microbrew and sat in the recliner. She watched as his eyes flicked down to the book. And away. 'My God,' Susan teased. 'An aesthetic choice. Careful. You might accidentally give someone some insight into your personality.'

'Sorry. I also like wine. And liquor. I just happen to only have beer. And no, I don't have a favourite brand. I just get whatever's on sale that isn't swill.'

'You know, Portland has more microbreweries and brew pubs than any other city in the country.'

'I did not know that,' he said.

Susan put her hand over her mouth. 'Sorry,' she said. 'I'm a data sieve. Occupational hazard of being a features writer.' She tilted her bottle in a small toast. Archie, she noticed, wasn't drinking. 'Here's to Portland. Incorporated in 1851. Population, five hundred and forty-five thousand, one hundred and forty.' She winked. 'Two million if you count the greater Portland area.'

Archie smiled weakly. 'I'm impressed.'

Susan took her recorder out of her purse and set it next to the book on the coffee table between them. 'Do you mind if I record this?'

'State bird?'

'Blue heron.'

'Record away.'

She waited for him to say something about the book. He waited for her to ask him a question. The book sat on the coffee table. Gretchen Lowell gazed daringly from under its gold-embossed title. She pressed RECORD and opened her notebook. She had hoped that the book might knock Archie off his game; provoke something, anything. Time for Plan B. 'I talked to your wife today.'

'Ex-wife.'

Well, Susan thought, he didn't take that bait. She'd have to try something more direct. She looked up. 'She still loves you.'

Archie's expression did not shift. 'And I love her,' he said, not missing a beat.

'Hey, I have an idea,' Susan said brightly. 'Why don't you two get married?'

Archie sighed. 'Our relationship is complicated by the fact that I am emotionally retarded.'

'Did she tell you about our interview?'

'Yep.'

'What did she say?'

'She was worried that she had been too honest

about . . .' he searched for the right words, 'my relationship with Gretchen.'

'Relationship,' Susan repeated slowly. 'Funny word.'

He shook his head. 'Not really. Criminal:cop. Kidnapper:hostage. Killer:victim. They're all relationships.' He twisted his mouth wryly. 'I don't mean to imply that we're dating.'

Archie was sitting back in the chair. Legs uncrossed, knees fallen apart. Feet on the carpet. Elbow on each armrest. But while he might have been trying to be casual, Susan thought, he was certainly not relaxed. Susan tried to observe him without staring, noting the angle of his head, the fit of his shirt, the heaviness under his eyes. His thick brown hair was all clumps and curls.

The truth was that Archie Sheridan made her feel off-kilter. It was something that Susan wasn't used to. The power in interviews was usually hers, but more and more, when she spent time with Archie Sheridan, she found herself longing for a cigarette. Or something.

He was looking at her. That was the thing with interviews. Everyone was always waiting for someone to say something. It was like one long first date. *So, where are you from? What did you major in? Any Huntington's in the family?* Or, in this case, 'Why did Gretchen Lowell kidnap you, do you think?'

'She's a serial killer. She wanted to murder me.' Archie's voice was level. They could have been talking about the rain.

'But she didn't,' Susan pointed out.

He shrugged. 'She changed her mind.'

'Why?'

Archie smiled faintly. 'Female's prerogative?'

'I'm serious.'

His expression returned to neutral and he picked at something microscopic on his pants leg. 'I don't know the answer to that question.'

'You've never asked her?' Susan said incredulously. 'All those Sundays?'

'It's never come up.'

'What do you talk about?'

His eyes lifted to meet hers. 'Murder.'

'That's not very forthcoming.'

'You're not asking the right questions.'

Susan could hear a child running above the popcorn ceiling over their heads. Archie didn't seem to notice it. 'OK,' she said slowly. 'I guess I'm interested in what was different about you. I mean, the torture was different, right? She killed all the others after a few days, right? You, she kept alive. So you were different. From the beginning. To her.'

'I was the lead investigator on her case. The others were all random. As far as we know, except for the accomplices she killed, she didn't know any of her victims. She and I knew each other. We had a relationship.'

Susan underlined the word relationship in her notebook. 'But she infiltrated the case to get to you. I mean, that's why she came to Portland, knocked on the task force door? She was after you.'

Archie lifted his arms off the armrests and folded and unfolded his hands in his lap. He was looking at the copy of *The Last Victim*. At Gretchen Lowell. Eyes heavy, unblinking. Susan glanced from Archie to the book and back at Archie. It was like once he looked, he couldn't look away. 'It's not that unusual for psychopaths to get close to investigations,' he said, gaze still fixed on the thick paperback. 'They enjoy watching the drama unfold. It makes them feel superior.'

Susan bent forward, resting her forearms on her crossed legs, and scooted a little closer to Archie. She always seemed to make the first move on first dates. 'But she risked a lot,' she said softly. 'To get to you. And then she didn't kill you.' He was still looking at the book. Susan was filled with a sudden impulse to reach out and fling it off the table. Just to see what he'd do. 'I'm confused by that. It seems out of character.'

'Excuse me,' Archie said. He stood up quickly and went into the kitchen. Susan twisted awkwardly in her seat so that she could watch him. She couldn't get a read on his face. He stood with his back to her, hands on his hips, facing a sad bank of white Formica cabinetry. And then he sighed and said, 'Will you do me a favour and put the book away?'

The book. Was it the photograph of Gretchen Lowell looking like a Breck Girl on the cover that bothered him, or was it what was inside? 'Sorry,' Susan called, pushing the paperback into her purse. She hunched her shoulders a little, feeling like a jerk. 'It was just a prop. For the interview.'

He didn't say anything. A hand went from his hip to the back of his neck. She wished he'd turn around so that she could see his face, see what he was thinking. She wanted to do something other than stare forlornly at the back of his curly head, so she started writing in her notebook. *What isn't he telling me about GL?* She circled the question several times, until the pen made an indentation in the paper. The question sat on the page, surrounded by blank paper.

He said something. She looked up, mortified. He was standing at the fridge now, looking at her, a beer in his hand. He had definitely said something.

'Excuse me?' she said, flipping over the page she had been writing on, so quickly it tore a little at the spiral.

'I said, you think she showed me mercy.'

Susan twisted around to face him again, lifting her legs under her on the couch, her motorcycle boots pressing a dent into the foam cushion. 'At the end,' Susan said, 'she killed everyone else she took. She killed you. But she brought you back.'

Archie stood alone in the kitchen and took a sip of the beer. She wasn't sure he'd even heard her. Then he walked back into the living room and sat down, placing the beer carefully on the coffee table in front of him. He did everything carefully, like someone who expected to break the things he took care of. He looked at his hands, thick, laced with veins, still folded in his lap. And then back at Susan. 'If Gretchen had been feeling charitable she would have let me die,' he said matter-of-factly. 'I wanted to die. I was ready to die. If she had put a scalpel in my hand, I would have stabbed myself in the neck and happily bled to death right there in her basement. She didn't do me any favours by not killing me. Gretchen enjoys people's pain. And she just found a way to prolong my pain and her pleasure. Believe me, it was the cruellest thing she could have done to me. If she could have thought of something crueller, she would have done it. Gretchen doesn't show people mercy.'

The heat kicked in. There was a rumble and then the slow blow of hot air from a vent that Susan couldn't see. Her mouth felt dry. The kid upstairs was still running. If Susan had lived there, she'd have killed that kid by now. 'But she ended up in jail. That couldn't have been part of the plan.'

'Everyone needs a career-exit strategy.'

'But she could have gotten the death penalty,' Susan said.

'She had too many bargaining chips.'

'You mean bodies?' Susan asked.

He took another sip of beer. 'Yes.'

'Why do you think she agreed to talk only to you?'

'Because she knew I'd go along with it,' Archie said simply.

'And why did you agree? When your wife made you choose? Why choose Gretchen?'

'She's my *ex*-wife. And I did it for the families. Because they deserve some closure. And it's my job.'

'And?' Susan asked.

Archie held the cold bottle next to his face and squeezed his eyes shut. 'It's complicated.'

Susan glanced at her purse. The spine of the paperback was still visible where she had tucked it in the main compartment, along with some loose tampons, her Paul Frank wallet, a plastic case of birth-control pills and about thirty pens. 'So, have you read *The Last Victim*?'

'God, no,' Archie said, groaning.

Susan blushed. 'It's not bad. You know, for a true-crime thriller. Not much in the way of actual journalism. I called the writer. She said that you refused to talk to her. Your ex-wife refused to talk to her. Your doctor refused to talk to her. The department refused to talk to her. She based the thing mostly on news accounts, public records and her own torrid imagination. There's this scene at the end where you talk Gretchen Lowell into turning herself in. You convince her that she can be a better person, and she is overcome by your grace and goodness.'

Archie laughed out loud.

'Didn't happen like that?'

'No.'

'What do you remember?' Susan asked.

Archie flinched.

'You OK?'

'Headache,' he explained. He reached into his pocket and produced a brass pillbox, withdrew three white oval pills and swallowed them with a pull of beer.

'What are those?' Susan asked.

'Headache pills.'

Susan threw him a dubious look. 'Do you really not remember those ten days?'

Archie blinked slowly and let his eyes settle on Susan. He looked at her for a million years. Then his eyes slid slowly to a digital clock that sat on a bookcase. The time was wrong, but Archie didn't appear to care. 'I remember those ten days better than I do the days my children were born.'

The heat turned off and the room fell quiet. 'Tell me what you remember,' Susan said. Her voice cracked like a teenage boy's. She could feel Archie appraising her. And she put on her best smile, the one she had learned to use so long ago, the one that made all the men understand that, no matter what their troubles, she could make them feel better. Archie wasn't buying.

'Not yet,' Archie said finally. 'You have three more stories, right? You don't want to spoil the suspense.'

Susan wasn't ready to let it go. 'What about the

“second man” theory? Some of the reports said that you said there was a man there. Someone who was never caught. Do you remember that?’

Archie closed his eyes. ‘Gretchen has always denied it. I never saw him. It was more of an impression that I had. But I was also not in the most stable mental condition.’ He reached up and rubbed the back of his neck and looked at Susan. ‘I’m tired. Let’s continue this some other time.’

Susan dropped her head in her hands in frustration.

‘We’ll get to it,’ Archie said. ‘I promise.’

She snapped off the recorder. ‘Can I use your bathroom?’

‘It’s off the hall.’

She stood up and walked down the hall to the bathroom. It was as unremarkable as the rest of the apartment. A fibreglass tub and shower combo with a sliding frosted-glass door. A cheap sink with plastic faucet knobs set in a pressboard cabinet. Two grey towels of an unimpressive thread count hanging limply on oak towel racks. Two more sat freshly laundered and folded on the back of the toilet. The bathroom was clean, but not too clean, not fastidious. She stood at the sink, staring at her reflection. Fuck. Fuck. Fuck. She was close to the biggest story of her career. So why did she feel so crappy? And what was she thinking with the pigtails? She pulled them out, combed her hair with her fingers, and tied her hair back at her neck. The light in the bathroom made her flesh look like raw chicken. She wondered how Archie Sheridan faced himself in that mirror each morning, sallow, every wrinkle shadowed. No wonder he was a headcase. She dug into her pocket, retrieved some lip gloss and slathered it on liberally. Did he want to be forced back on medical leave? Was that what this was all about?

She flushed the toilet and used the cover of the noise to open the door of the medicine cabinet. Shaving cream. Razors. Toothpaste and toothbrush. Deodorant. And two shelves of amber plastic pill bottles. She spun them around by their white lids to read the prescription information. Vicodin. Colace. Percocet. Zantac. Ambien. Xanax. Prozac. Large bottles. Small bottles. 'Nothing that would interfere with his ability to do his job,' Fergus had said. Right. There were enough pills in that cabinet to medicate an elephant. All made out to Archie Sheridan. Fuck. If he needed all this stuff to function, he was worse off than she thought. And a better actor.

She memorized the names, carefully turned the bottles back to their original orientation, closed the cabinet and walked back into the living room.

Archie didn't even look up at her. 'If I'd wanted you to not see the pills, I would have hidden them.'

Susan searched for what to say. *What pills?* But for some reason she didn't feel like lying. 'You're on a lot of medication.'

His eyes followed her into the room, but he remained still as a corpse. 'I'm unwell.'

Susan had the sudden unnerving sensation that everything she'd found out so far about Archie Sheridan was exactly what he wanted her to know. Every interview. Every lead. To what end? Maybe he was just tired of lying. Maybe he just wanted everyone to know all his secrets, so he didn't have to work so hard at keeping them hidden. Subterfuge could be exhausting.

She stowed her digital recorder and notebook in her purse and dug out a pack of cigarettes. 'I'm fucking my married boss,' she said to Archie.

Archie paused, mouth slightly agape. 'I'm not sure I needed to know that.'

Susan lit her cigarette and took a drag. 'Yeah, but as long as we're sharing.'

'OK.'

26

Anne Boyd ate all of the chocolate in the hotel minibar. She started with the plain M&Ms, then ate the Toblerone, then the peanut M&Ms. When she was done, she flattened the wrappers and placed them next to the photographs of the dead girls that lay on her hotel-room bed. Candy helped her think. There would be time to diet when people stopped killing one another.

She had memorized the girls' faces, pre- and postmortem, but there was something useful in seeing them all side by side. The school photographs. The crime-scene photographs. Family snapshots. She had outlined a victim profile in her report to Archie. The killer had a type: dark-haired white girls on the rocky side of puberty. Each from a different high school. *What is your fantasy?* she wondered. He killed this girl again and again. Then he raped her in the most controlling way possible. So who was it he was killing? A teenage girlfriend? His mother? A girl who broke his heart without even knowing? Whoever it was, it was someone he had not been able to control. Anne was growing more and more certain that this fact was key to identifying the person they were hunting.

She rolled off the bed, opened the minibar and found a Diet Coke. It was the last one. Her kids were already asking when she was going to come home. What they really wanted was the loot she'd promised she'd bring back from the Nike outlet store. She didn't know when she'd have time to get there.

The truth was that she didn't travel much for work any more. But she had asked to be assigned to this one. She'd considered quitting after the Beauty Killer case. Her profile had been wrong and it had nearly cost Archie Sheridan his life. She had been absolutely confident that the killer was a male and that he was working alone. The signs had been textbook. Because Gretchen Lowell had read the textbooks. Anne had been famously fooled, and she blamed only herself for it. She was a good profiler, one of the best with the FBI, which had the best profilers in the world. But her confidence had been shaken badly by Gretchen Lowell. Confidence was essential to profiling. You had to believe in your skill in order to make mental leaps.

So she had to find the leap. He was acting out a specific fantasy, one that had started many years before. So what had triggered the action? There were all sorts of triggers: financial, relationship or parental issues, trouble at work, a death, a birth, a perceived snub. He initiated contact with the victims. He chose them. The crimes were highly organized. He took pains to destroy evidence, but he still returned the bodies. Why did he return them? This time, she wasn't going to fuck it up. She couldn't undo what had happened to Archie Sheridan. But she could help him this time. And he needed help. Of that, she was quite certain.

She'd been on the job long enough to know that the only way you survived was if you could turn off the violence. But you had to have something to distract you, some other passion. If you didn't, if you were alone, it was harder to flip the switch. She recognized that Archie was cutting himself off from the people who could help him; she just didn't know what she could do about it.

She got up off the bed, walked to the window, pulled back the curtain and looked out over Broadway. The Friday-night traffic was heavy and streams of pedestrians in fancy clothes were making their way down from an event at the nearby concert hall. If there were any black folks among them, Anne didn't see them.

She let the curtain fall back into place and sat back down on the bed, where she took one last long look at the photographs of the dead girls and then turned them over one by one. Lee Robinson's week-old corpse, a yellow and blackened heap in the mud; Dana Stamp face-down in a bank of weeds; Kristy Mathers coated in wet sand, her body improbably twisted. The school photographs and birthday-party snapshots. When every image was turned, she got out her wallet and pulled out another photograph. This one was of a very handsome black man with his arm around two very handsome black teenage boys. She smiled at their grinning faces. Then she picked up her cell phone and called home.

'Mama,' her eldest son Anthony answered. 'You don't have to call every day.'

'Yeah, baby,' Anne said. The job was always hardest at night. When she was alone. 'I do.'

'You get us our Nikes?'

Anne laughed. 'It's on my to-do list.'

'What number is it?' her son asked.

Anne glanced back down at the photographs on her bed and then up across the room at the window that overlooked the bustle of downtown. The killer was out there. 'Two.'

After Susan left, Archie finished his beer and got back to work. First, he spread out the contents of the files on the coffee table. He had hurriedly shuffled them into two neat towers before her arrival. He wasn't cleaning up; he just didn't think she needed to see the autopsy photographs of three dead teenagers. He took three more Vicodin and sat down next to the coffee table on the beige carpet. It was staring at photographs like these that had helped him spot Gretchen Lowell's signature. He wasn't sure what he was looking for this time, but if it was there, he wasn't seeing it. The kid upstairs was singing. Archie couldn't make out the words, but he thought he recognized the tune from when his own children were toddlers.

He looked at the digital clock, did the maths. It was just after nine p.m. Gretchen would be in her cell for the night. Lights-out wasn't until ten p.m. This was the hour when Gretchen read. He knew that she borrowed books from the prison library, because her check-out history was forwarded to him every month. She read psychoanalytic tomes, from Freud to textbooks to pop-psych paperbacks. She read smart contemporary fiction, the kind of books that won awards and most people read only so that they could say so at dinner parties. She read true crime. Why not? Archie thought. It was her profession's trade publication. And last month she had checked out *The Last Victim.* He hadn't told Henry about that. The fact that Gretchen was reading the sordid true-crime account of Archie's captivity, with its cheap prose and gruesome photographs of the bodies, of Archie, of all of them, would have been more than Henry could handle. He would have had the book taken away, pulled from the library. He might even have gone through with his threat to stop Archie from seeing her. It wouldn't take much, a heart-to-heart with Buddy. Archie was barely convincing them all that he was functional. It was his insistence, combined with their guilt about what he'd been through, that kept him in a position to bargain. But he knew his footing was tenuous.

He looked at the girls' pallid bodies, gaping open on the morgue table, the ligature marks a slash of purple across their necks. That was one upside, Archie decided: he killed them right away. And there were worse ways to die than strangulation.

The kid upstairs jumped up and down and an adult walked over and picked her up. Archie could hear her shrieking and giggling.

27

Today, when Gretchen comes with the pills, Archie manages to get a sentence out when she removes the tape. 'I'll swallow them,' he tells her.

She sets the funnel on the tray and Archie opens his mouth and extends his tongue, like a good patient. She places a pill on his tongue and holds a small glass of water against his parched lips so he can drink. It is the first water he has had since his arrival and it feels good in his mouth and in his throat. She checks around his tongue to ensure that he has swallowed the medicine. They repeat the exercise four times.

When they are done, Archie asks, 'How long have I been here?'

'It doesn't matter,' she says.

He hears a buzzing. At first, he thinks it's in his head, but then he recognizes the sound: flies. The decomposing corpse on the floor. It reminds him of the other man, and for a moment he is a cop again. 'The second man who lifted me into the van,' he says. 'Where is he? Have you killed him too?'

Gretchen raises a bewildered eyebrow. 'Darling, you sound like a raving lunatic.'

'He was here,' Archie says, his mind foggy. 'Before.'

'It's just us,' she says impatiently.

But he wants to keep her talking, to get as much information as he can. He glances around at the windowless room. The subway tiles. The medical equipment. 'Where are we?'

She is done with his questions. 'Have you thought about what I asked you?' she says.

Archie has no idea what she's talking about. 'What?'

'What you want to send them.' This is delivered with thinly disguised irritation. 'They're worried about you, darling.' She runs her hand lightly along his arm to where his wrist is bound with a padded leather strap to the gurney. 'You're right-handed, yes?'

Archie has to think quickly, while he is still lucid, before the pills kick in. 'Why, Gretchen? You never sent anything from the other bodies.' Then it strikes him. Her victims. They were always killed within three days of their abductions. 'It's been four days,' he says. 'They're starting to think I'm dead. You want them to know I'm still alive.'

'I'll let you choose. But we need to do it now.'

The terror is building in his body, but he knows he can't agree to her terms. As soon as he does, he becomes a partner to it. 'No.'

'I've removed dozens of spleens,' she mutters. 'But only post-mortem. Do you think you can remain still?'

He starts to fold in on himself. 'Gretchen, don't do this.'

'It's moot, of course.' She picks up a syringe from the tray. 'This is succinylcholine. It's a paralysing agent, used for surgery. You won't be able to move at all. But you'll remain conscious. You'll feel everything.' She glances at him meaningfully. 'I think that's essential, don't you? If you're going to lose a part of your body, you should experience it happening. If you wake up and it's gone, how do you know if you feel any different?'

He can't stop it. He knows there is no reasoning with her. He can only protect the people he's left behind. 'Who are you going to send it to?' he asks her.

'I was thinking Debbie.'

Archie's mind lurches, imagining Debbie's face. 'Send it to Henry,' he asks. 'Please, Gretchen. Send it to Henry Sobol.'

Gretchen pauses with her preparations and smiles at him. 'If I do, you'll have to be good.'

'I'll do what you want,' Archie says. 'I'll be good.'

'The problem with succinylcholine is that it will paralyse your diaphragm.' She holds up a plastic tube that leads to a machine behind her. 'So first I'm going to have to intubate you.'

Before Archie can react, she inserts a curved steel blade into his mouth, depresses his tongue, and pushes the tube in behind it. The tube is large, filling his throat, and he gags violently and fights it. 'Swallow,' she says as she presses her hand against his forehead, pinning his head hard against the gurney.

He can feel his fingers splay, every muscle tensed as he fights the tube. She leans in close, tenderly, her hand still on his forehead. 'Swallow it,' she says again. 'Fighting it will only make it worse.'

He closes his eyes and forces himself to overcome the gag reflex and swallow the tube as she slides it further down his throat, deep into his body.

Then it is done. The air fills his lungs. It is calming, actually. It forces his breaths to equalize, his heart rate to slow. He opens his eyes and watches as she slides the hypo into his IV and adjusts the drip into his arm.

He feels suddenly, disturbingly calm. It is the resignation he has seen on the faces of death-row inmates. He has no control, so there is no point in fighting any of it. The sensation bleeds out of his body until it is just dead weight. He tries to move his fingers, his head, his shoulders, but nothing responds. It's a relief, really. He has fought so hard in his tiny career to order chaos, discourage violence, prevent crime. Now he can just let it happen.

She smiles at him, and he knows with that smile that he has been played. He has asked for and received a favour from his murderer. And more than that, he notes with dry detachment, he is grateful.

He can only stare at the familiar fluorescent lights and pipes on the white ceiling, vaguely aware of her movements as she washes her hands, prepares an instrument tray, shaves the hair off his abdomen. He feels the cold iodine on his skin and then she presses the scalpel into his flesh. It opens easily under the sharp blade in her hands, a slice and then a pop as it pulls through the muscle. He tries to distance himself from it; to talk himself out of the pain. For a moment, he thinks he's going to be all right. That he can stand this, that it's no worse than the nails. And then she inserts the clamp and prises open the hole she has made in him. It is a wrenching, ripping, nausea-inducing pain that makes Archie scream, only he cannot speak, cannot move his mouth, cannot lift his head. He still manages to cry out in his mind, a strangled howl that he carries with him into unconsciousness.

She lets him sleep. It feels like days, because when he wakes up his mind has constructed a tunnel of clarity. He turns his head and she is right beside him, face propped up on two stacked fists set on his bed. They are inches apart, nose to nose. The tube is gone from his throat, but his throat aches from it. She has not slept. He can tell. He can see the fine veins underneath the pale skin of her forehead. He knows her expressions. He is starting to know her face as well as Debbie's.

'What were you dreaming about?' she asks him.

Colour images flash through his mind. 'I was in a car in a city, looking for my house,' he says. His voice is hoarse, a cracked whisper. 'I couldn't find it. I'd forgotten the address. So I just kept circling.' He smirks mirthlessly, feeling his chapped lips crack. A hard nut of pain sits in his chest. 'I wonder what it means.'

Gretchen doesn't move. 'You'll never see them again, you know.'

'I know.' He glances down at the bandage on his abdomen. The pain pales compared to the ache of his ribs. His entire torso is bruised, the skin the colour of rotten fruit. His body feels like wet sand. He hardly notices the smell of decomposing flesh any more. It is a strange thing to be alive. He is getting less and less attached to the idea. 'They get it?'

'I sent it to Henry,' she says. 'They haven't released it to the media.'

'No, they wouldn't.'

'Why?'

'They'll want to confirm it's mine,' he explains.

She's perplexed. 'I sent your wallet with it.'

'They'll match the DNA,' he reassures her. 'It will take a few days.'

She lowers her perfect face next to his again. 'They'll know I took it out of you while you were alive. And they'll find traces of the drugs I've given you.'

'It's important to you, isn't it?' he asks. 'That they know what you're doing to me?'

'Yes.'

'Why?'

'I want them to know that I'm hurting you. I want

them to know that and not be able to find you. And then I want to kill you.' She places a hand on his forehead and holds it there, like a mother checking a child for fever. 'But I don't think I'll give you back, darling. I think I'll let them wonder. I like to let them wonder sometimes. Life shouldn't always be so cut and dried.'

He had squatted in the rain next to so many corpses, seen so much death. He had always wondered how many more she killed. Serial killers often killed for years before the police caught on to a pattern. He wanted to know. He had spent ten years living for the answer to two questions: who was the Beauty Killer? And how many had been murdered? He knows the answer to the first question. Now some part of him feels that if he knows the second, some door on the person he has been might close. It is as if the more she confides in him, the more he belongs to her.

Gretchen grows impatient. 'Just ask me how many people I've killed. I want to tell you.'

He sighs. The effort hurts his ribs and he winces. She is still waiting, her anticipation palpable. She is like an insistent child who must be indulged. It is the only way to make her go away. 'How many people have you killed, Gretchen?'

'You will be number two hundred.'

He swallows hard. *Jesus Christ*, he thinks. *Jesus fucking Christ.* 'That's a lot of people,' he says.

'I had my lovers kill for me sometimes. But I always

chose who it would be. It was always at my bidding. So I think I should get to count it, don't you?'

'I think you can count it.'

'Are you in pain?' Her face is shining.

He nods.

'Tell me,' she says.

He does. He tells her because he knows it will satisfy her, and if she is satisfied, she might give him some peace. She might let him rest. And when she lets him rest, he gets the pills. 'I can't breathe. I can't take a full breath without a searing pain in my ribs.'

'What's it like?' Her eyes gleam.

He searches for the right words. 'It's like razor wire. Like someone wrapped razor wire around my lungs, and when I breathe, it cuts deep into the tissue.'

'What about the incision?'

'It's starting to throb. It's a different kind of pain. More of a burning. It's OK if I don't move. My head hurts. Especially behind the eyes. The wound, where you stabbed me, it feels like it's getting infected. And my skin itches. All over. I think my hands are asleep. I can't feel them.'

'Do you want your medicine?'

He smiles, imagining the tingling wave of fog that follows the pills. His mouth waters for it. 'Yes.'

'All of it?'

'No,' he tells her. 'I don't want the hallucinations. I just see my life. I see them looking for me. I see Debbie.'

'Just the amphetamine and the codeine?'

'Yes.'

'Extra codeine?'

'Yes,' he says, choking.

'Ask me for it.'

'Can I have some extra codeine?'

She smiles. 'Yes.'

She empties the pills from bottles on a counter against the wall and returns with the water. She feeds them to him and lets him drink. She doesn't check to see if he's swallowed them because she doesn't need to.

It will be fifteen minutes before he feels the medicine, so he tries to divorce himself from the slow death of his body. She sits in a chair beside his bed, hands neatly on her lap, staring.

'Why did you decide to become a psychiatrist?' he asks her after a long silence.

'I'm not,' she says. 'I just read some books.'

'But you've got medical training.'

'I worked as an ER nurse. I went to medical school, but I dropped out.' She smiles. 'I would have been a great doctor, though, don't you think?'

'I'm maybe the wrong person to ask.'

They sit quietly again, but she is fidgety.

'Do you want to know all about my shitty childhood?' she asks. 'The incest? The beatings?'

He shakes his head. 'No,' he says thickly. 'Maybe later.'

He feels the first tingle bloom in the centre of his

face and begin its tidal surge across his body. *Just stay here in the room*, he tells himself. Don't think about Debbie. Don't think about the kids. Don't think. Just be in the room.

Gretchen is looking at him appreciatively. She reaches out and touches his face. It's a gesture he has learned often indicates that she is about to do something terrible.

'I want to kill you, Archie,' she says, her voice soft and sweet and untroubled. 'I've thought about it. I've fantasized about it for years.'

She runs her fingertips over the edge of his earlobe. It feels good. His breathing eases as the codeine softens the pain of his broken bones, his split flesh. 'So do it.'

'I want to use drain cleaner,' she tells him, as if discussing a wine they might serve at a dinner party. 'I've always done it quickly. Made them drink a lot of it at the end. Death comes very suddenly.' Her face is animated. 'But with you, I want to do it slowly. I want to watch you experience death. I want you to drink the drain cleaner slowly. A tablespoon a day. I want to see how long it takes. What it does to you. I want to take my time.'

He meets her stare. Amazing, he thinks, what psychopathic horror lives in that pretty, demure body.

'Are you waiting for my blessing?' he asks.

'You said you'd be good. I sent the package to Henry. Like you asked.'

'So that's part of the fantasy? I have to take the poison willingly?'

She nods, biting her lip. 'I'm going to kill you, Archie,' she says with absolute assurance. 'I can carve you up and send you piece by piece to your children. Or we can do it my way.'

He considers his options. He knows that she presents him with impossible choices, fully realizing that he can choose only one outcome. She wants total power over him. His only weapon is to retain some illusion of power himself. 'OK,' he agrees quietly. 'On one condition.'

'What?'

'Four more days. That's all I can do. If I'm not dead from it in four days, you find some other way to kill me.'

'Four days,' she concurs, her blue eyes bright with pleasure. 'Can we start now?'

He watches her body language change; her excitement palpable. He nods his surrender and she immediately jumps up and goes to the counter against the wall. She pours a glass of water, retrieves a beaker of clear golden fluid and returns to him. 'It will burn,' she instructs him. 'You'll have to resist a gag reflex. I'll plug your nose for you and follow the drain cleaner with water to wash it down.' She pours a tablespoon of fluid from the beaker and holds it at his chin. The familiar smell sickens him. 'Are you ready?' she asks.

He has no sense of consequence. It is not him who is there in the basement with Gretchen Lowell. It is someone else. He opens his mouth and she plugs his nose and thrusts the spoon far back into his throat and empties the poison. He swallows. She holds the glass of water to his lips and he gulps as much of it as he can. The burning is overwhelming. He feels it scald his throat and then flame into his gullet, and for a second he is back in his physical self, his nervous system in full panic. He screws up every muscle in his face and bites down on his tongue to keep from vomiting. Then, after a while, it passes and he lies panting on the bed, Gretchen holding his head in her hands.

'Ssh,' she says, soothing him. 'You did well.' She smooths his hair and kisses his forehead several times. Then she reaches into her pocket and pulls out six large white oval pills. 'More codeine,' she explains. 'You can have as much as you want from now on.'

28

Susan had spent Saturday writing and now the second story was in and she was taking a celebratory bubble bath. The Great Writer had a radio in his bathroom, but she didn't like to listen to it when she was in the tub. This was thinking time. Music was too easy a distraction. She had been in the tub for almost a half-hour and the water had cooled. Now she turned on the hot-water knob with her toes and let it run until the bath was as hot as she could stand it. Her skin pinkened under the water and she felt her face burn. That was how she liked it, heat the only sensation.

She jumped when the phone rang. She never took baths without her cell phone and her landline within arm's reach, but she was relaxed enough that it still surprised her. Now, in an effort to get to the ringing cordless that perched on the edge of the sink, she knocked over her half-full glass of Pinot Noir. It exploded on the tile floor, sending red wine splattering everywhere.

'Fuck,' she said aloud as she picked up the phone. She had broken five of the Great Writer's set of eight wineglasses. This was the sixth. Something about the way she moved through the world did not lend itself to the care of fragile objects. She fumbled with the receiver, nearly dropping it in the soapy water as she sank back into the tub.

'Ian?'

'No, honey, it's me.'

'Oh.' She tried not to sound disappointed. 'Hi, Bliss.'

'I saw your story.'

Susan sat up in the tub, bringing her knees to her chest. 'You did?'

'Leaf at the co-op gave me a copy.'

Susan's body hummed with pleasure. She didn't like to draw her mother's attention to her work. She didn't like to admit that it mattered.

'Listen, sweetie,' Bliss said. 'I know you know how to do your job.' She paused. 'But don't you think you might be exploiting these girls?'

The humming stopped. Susan could feel her teeth clench, the molars grinding into one another, another layer of enamel gone. It was remarkable how her mother always knew exactly the wrong thing to say. 'I've got to go, Bliss. I'm in the bathtub.'

'Right now?'

'Yep.' She splashed some water. 'See?'

'OK. We'll talk later.'

'Sure.' She hung up the phone and leaned back in the tub, letting the hot water fill her ears as she waited for her heartbeat to slow. She and Bliss had been close until the year Susan's father died, when Bliss had become impossible. Or maybe Susan had become impossible. It was hard to know. They had fought most over the bathtub. Back then, Susan liked to take two or three baths a day. It was the only place she didn't feel cold.

Susan smiled to herself. Archie Sheridan. She had to admit that she'd secretly hoped it would be him on the phone. He was right up her alley, after all. Not married, sure. But totally unavailable. Crap. She was a lost cause. But at least she knew she was a romantic train wreck. She had been since she was fourteen years old. Self-knowledge counted for something, right? When she climbed out of the tub ten minutes later and gathered up the small pieces of glass that lay scattered on the floor, she was so lost in thought that she stabbed her finger on one of the little shards. She grabbed one of the Great Writer's white washcloths and secured it around the wound. While she waited for the blood to stop, she called Archie and checked in on the case. He did not ask her out. By the time she was off the phone, the white washcloth was stained red, another thing she had ruined.

The plum trees in front of Gretchen's old house had bloomed. That was how it happened. One day the plum trees looked dead, skeletal, like something put out in the yard after a fire; the next they were heavy with pale pink blossoms, smug with their own prettiness.

'You just want to sit here?' the cab driver asked.

Archie dropped his cell phone in his pocket and glanced up at the driver. 'Just for a while.' The sun shining through the car window was warm, and Archie leaned his temple against the glass, enjoying the heat of it against his skin. The house was vaguely Georgian, a pale yellow plantation at two-thirds scale. The windows were flanked by tall white shutters. A brick path led from the sidewalk to a brick staircase and up a sloping hillside to the house. It was a nice house. Archie had always thought so.

Of course, it had never been Gretchen's. She'd been telling the truth when she told Archie that she'd leased it for the fall from a family who were spending the season in Italy. She had rented it online under a false name, just as she had rented the house in Gresham.

'You a stalker?' the cabbie asked, eyeing Archie in the rear-view mirror.

'A cop.'

The cab driver snorted, as if the two were indistinguishable.

Archie had spent the morning with Henry, reviewing a mountain of paper comprised of citizen tips. There were thousands: letters, transcripts from the tip hotline, even postcards. It was tedious work and Archie could have delegated it. But it gave him something to do. And there was a chance, a slim chance, that somewhere in all of that paper was the information that they needed.

After six hours they had gone through almost two thousand tips. And were no closer to finding the After School Strangler.

'It's Saturday,' Henry had said. 'Go home for a few hours.' And Archie had agreed. He didn't tell Henry that, as Sunday fast approached, he was having a hard time concentrating on anything but Gretchen.

And when the cab driver asked him his address he found himself giving this one instead.

So Archie gazed at the house, as if something about it could help him make sense of everything that had happened since that last time he'd walked through its front door.

A shiny black Audi wagon pulled into the driveway and parked in front of the garage, and a dark-haired woman got out with two dark-haired boys. She walked around the back of the car, opened the hatchback and handed the older boy a paper bag of groceries, and he went inside with the younger boy trailing after him. Then she got another bag of groceries from the back of the wagon, turned and walked towards the cab.

'She the one you're stalking?' the cabbie asked.

'I'm not stalking anyone,' Archie said. The woman with the groceries was clearly headed directly for them, intent on a conversation. Something like 'Why the hell are you idling in front my house?' maybe. He thought about telling the cabbie to drive away, but the woman was descending on them and he didn't want to rattle her further by roaring away in a cloud of exhaust. So he was sitting in a cab in front of her house. It was a residential street. There were a multitude of explanations. He would just have to pick one. Doing his best to look respectable, he rolled down the window just as she took her last few steps to the taxi. It was all moot.

'You're Archie Sheridan,' she said.

She had recognized him. That left little room to manoeuvre.

The woman gave him a concerned smile. She was wearing black leggings and a large black sweatshirt with the sleeves pushed up to the elbows. The sweatshirt had a Sanskrit symbol on it. Yoga clothes. Her curly black hair was swept up in a ponytail. She was in her forties, and wore it well; the fine lines around her mouth and eyes probably noticeable only in natural light.

He nodded. Archie Sheridan. Hopeless. Untethered. At your service.

She thrust a hand in his direction. Her forearms were lean and strong. 'I'm Sarah Rosenberg. Mind giving me a hand with the groceries?'

*

He followed her into the kitchen, his arms full of groceries from Whole Foods. He didn't remember the last time he'd done that; it reminded him of his family, of the pleasures of normality. But then there was the house. It looked exactly the same. The entryway, the hall, the kitchen. Archie felt as if he'd walked into a dream. The older boy, a young teenager, had already started unpacking the bags, and the contents were strewn over a large kitchen island: fresh tulips, leeks, apples, expensive cheese.

'This is Detective Sheridan,' Sarah said.

The boy took the groceries from Archie's hands.

'My son, Noah,' Sarah said.

The boy nodded at Archie. 'Some of my brother's friends won't come over here any more,' he said. 'They're afraid of her or something. Like she's still here. Like she's going to get them.'

'I'm sorry,' Archie said.

He felt Gretchen everywhere around him, as if she were there next to him, her breath on his neck. The room she had used as an office was through the kitchen, on the other side of the entryway. Archie realized that he was squeezing the pillbox in his pocket, and he forced himself to release the tension in his hand.

'It looks pretty much the same,' Sarah was saying as she loaded food into a large steel fridge. 'The police said that it happened in my office, right? She had moved a few things around, but it's mostly how it was the last time you were here.' She looked at Archie meaningfully. 'Feel free, if you want to take a look.'

'Yeah,' Archie said before he even realized it. 'I'd like that.'

She motioned with her head that he could go alone. Archie was grateful for that. He left Sarah and Noah in the kitchen and walked to the room where Gretchen Lowell had drugged him.

The heavy green velvet curtains were closed, but the sun streamed like a knife through a gap where they didn't quite meet. Archie turned on the chandelier, put two pills in his mouth and swallowed them.

The carpet was different. They had changed the carpet. Maybe the crime lab had cut the coffee stain out; maybe too many cops had tracked in too much mud; maybe they had just redecorated. The big wooden desk was on the other side of the room, against the wall, rather than in front of the windows where Gretchen had placed it. Other than that, it was the same: library bookshelves stacked two deep with books, the grandfather clock with its motionless hands still pointing to half-past three, the striped overstuffed chairs. He sank into the chair he had sat in that day with Gretchen. He could remember everything now. The black long-sleeved dress she had been wearing, the cashmere cardigan the colour of butter. He had admired her legs when she had sat down. A harmless observation and an obvious one. He was male, after all, and she was beautiful; he could be forgiven for noticing that.

'I've seen you out there a few times.' It was Sarah, standing in the doorway.

'I'm sorry,' Archie said. 'It's just that this place, your house, it's the last place I remember feeling all right.'

'You've been through a terrible ordeal,' Sarah said. 'Are you seeing anyone?'

Archie closed his eyes and leaned his head on the back of the chair. 'Oh God,' he said, smiling. 'You're a psychiatrist.'

'A psychologist, actually,' she said with a shrug. 'I also teach up at Lewis & Clark. That's how Gretchen Lowell found us. We'd posted the house through a faculty board. But I still have a practice.' She paused. 'If you're interested, I would love to have you as a patient.'

So that was why she had invited him in. A patient who'd been through what he had would prove endlessly interesting to a shrink. 'I'm seeing someone,' Archie said. He gazed at the spot on the carpet where he'd fallen, unable to move, everything suddenly, horribly clear. 'Every Sunday.'

'Is it helping?'

He considered this. 'Her methodology is a little unorthodox,' he said slowly. 'But I think that she'd tell you it's working.'

'I'm glad,' Sarah said.

Archie glanced around the room one last time and

then looked at his watch. 'I should be going. Thanks for inviting me inside. It was very kind of you.'

'I've always loved this room,' Sarah said, looking at the big window. 'When the curtains are open, you can see the plum trees.'

'Yeah,' Archie said, and as if they shared an old mutual friend he added, 'Gretchen liked that, too.'

29

Archie knew that Debbie would call him when she'd seen Susan's second story. It didn't matter that it was before seven on Sunday morning. She knew that he'd be up. There was a killer loose and the clock was ticking, and even though there was little he could actually do but wait for something to happen, sleep seemed an admission of defeat. As it was, he was sitting on his couch reading print-outs of Lee Robinson's mash-note e-mails. Nothing like going through the private thoughts of a dead teenager to make you feel like a voyeuristic asshole. He had been up long enough to have already had coffee and two runny eggs, but only to have food in his stomach so he could take some Vicodin. He always allowed himself extra Vicodin on Sundays.

'Have you seen it?' Debbie asked.

Archie leaned back and closed his eyes. 'No. Tell me about it.'

'She talks about Gretchen. What she did to you.'

They don't know half of what she did to me, thought Archie. 'Good. Are there pictures?'

'One of you and one of Gretchen.'

He opened his eyes. There were Vicodin on the table. He lined them up in a little row, like teeth. 'Which one of Gretchen?'

'The mug shot.'

Archie knew the one. It was the first time Gretchen had been in the system. She had been picked up for writing a bad cheque in Salt Lake City in 1992. She was nineteen and her hair was shoulder-length and teased, her expression startled, her face gaunt. Archie allowed himself a smirk. 'Good. She hates that picture. She'll be pissed. Anything else?' He picked up a pill and rolled it between his fingers.

'Susan Ward hints at sordid details to come of your much-speculated-upon captivity.'

'Good.' He put the Vicodin in his mouth, letting the bitter chalky taste sit on his tongue for a moment before washing it down with a sip of tepid black coffee.

'You're using her.' Debbie's voice was low and Archie could almost feel the heat of it against his neck. 'It's not fair of you.'

'I'm using me. She's just a vehicle.'

'What about the kids?'

The effects of the opiates made his skull feel soft, like a baby's. He reached up and touched the back of his head, feeling his hair beneath his fingers. Ben had fallen from the changing table when he was ten months old and cracked his skull. They had spent the whole night in the emergency room. No, Archie remembered, correcting himself, Debbie had spent the whole night. He had left the hospital early in the morning. There had been a call. They had found another Beauty Killer body. Just one of dozens of times he'd left Debbie for Gretchen. He could remember every one of the crime scenes. Every detail. But he couldn't remember how long Ben had been in the hospital. Or where exactly the fracture was.

'Are you there?' he heard Debbie's disembodied voice ask from the receiver. 'Say something, Archie.'

'Read it to them. It will help them understand.'

'It will scare the crap out of them.' She paused. 'You sound really high.'

His head felt like warm water and cotton and blood. 'I'm fine.' He picked up another Vicodin, rubbed it between his fingers.

'It's Sunday. You don't want to be high when you see her.'

He smiled at the pill. 'She likes it when I'm high.'

The truth. He regretted it as soon as the words were out of his mouth.

The line was heavy with silence, and Archie could feel Debbie let him go just a little more. 'I'm going to hang up now,' she said.

'I'm sorry,' he said. But she was already gone.

*

When the phone rang a few minutes later, Archie thought it was Debbie calling back, and he picked the phone up on the first ring. But it wasn't Debbie.

'This is Ken, down in Salem. I've got a message for you. From Gretchen Lowell.'

Bombs away, thought Archie.

30

It was almost nine a.m. by the time Susan awoke with a splitting headache and a stomach-turning wave of nausea. She had finished that entire bottle of Pinot on an empty stomach. Why did she do this to herself? She sat up gingerly, and then staggered into the bathroom, where she poured herself a big glass of water, took three ibuprofen and brushed her teeth. The Band-Aid on her finger had fallen off during the night and she examined the small wound, which had scabbed over into an ugly red crescent. She sucked on it for a minute, the blood coppery in her mouth, until the cut was almost undetectable.

Then she wandered naked into the kitchen, where she put on a pot of coffee and sat down on the Great Writer's blue sofa. It was too early for the light to make it in through her north-facing window, but she could see the blue sky beyond the building across the street. Long shadows loomed dark on the street and sidewalk below. Sunshine, to Susan, had always seemed ominous. She was halfway through her second cup of coffee when the doorbell rang.

Susan wrapped herself in her kimono and answered the door to find Detective Henry Sobol. His bald head, freshly shaved, gleamed.

'Ms Ward,' he said. 'Do you have a few hours?'

'For what?'

'Archie will explain. He's downstairs in the car. I couldn't find a fucking place to park. Your neighbourhood is awash with ambling yuppies.'

'Yes, they're ferocious. Can you give me a few minutes to change?'

He bowed nobly. 'I'll wait here.'

Susan closed the door and went back into her bedroom to dress. She realized that she was grinning. This was good. This meant a break in the case. This meant more material. She pulled on a pair of tight, distressed jeans and a long-sleeved black-and-white-striped shirt that she thought looked French and ran a hairbrush through her pink hair.

She grabbed a pair of cowboy boots from her closet, snapped up her digital recorder and notebook, stowed the entire bottle of ibuprofen in her purse and headed for the door.

Henry's unmarked Crown Victoria was idling in front of Susan's building, with Archie sitting in the passenger seat, gazing down at some files in his lap. The winter sun looked almost white in the pale, clear sky and the car shone and sparkled in its light. Susan glanced up in dismay as she climbed into the back seat. Another fucking beautiful day.

'Good morning,' she said, slipping on some oversized dark sunglasses. 'What's going on?'

'You wrote to Gretchen Lowell,' Archie said matter-of-factly.

'Yep.'

'I asked you not to.'

'I'm a reporter,' Susan reminded him. 'I was attempting to gather facts.'

'Well, your letter and your stories have intrigued her and she would like to meet you.'

Susan's headache vanished. 'Honestly?'

'Are you up for it?'

She leaned forward between the two front seats. 'Are you kidding? When? Now?'

'That's where we're headed.'

'Well, let's go,' she said. Maybe she would get a book out of this after all.

Archie turned around to face Susan, his face so serious and haggard that it successfully wrung the life out of her momentarily high spirits. 'Gretchen is mental. She's curious about you, but only in so far as how she can manipulate you. If you come, you're going to have to follow my lead and restrain yourself.'

Susan forced her face into a professional earnestness. 'I am known for my restraint.'

'I'm going to regret this,' Archie said to Henry.

Henry grinned, flipped down a pair of mirrored

aviator sunglasses from the peak of his forehead to the bridge of his nose, and pulled away from the kerb.

'How did you know where I live, anyway?' Susan asked as they pulled on to the freeway headed south.

'I detected it,' Archie said.

Susan was just glad that Ian hadn't been there. It's not like her apartment had all that many places to hide, and if Henry had seen him, he'd certainly have told Archie. Just because Archie knew she was screwing Ian didn't mean she wanted him to be reminded of it. In fact, she was hoping he'd forget she'd ever said anything. 'Well, it's a good thing I was alone,' she said. 'So I could drop everything at a moment's notice.'

Out of the corner of her eye, she thought she saw Henry smile. Archie's gaze didn't waver from the file he was reading. Susan's face grew hot.

It was an hour's drive to the prison. She crossed her arms, leaned back and forced her attention out of the window. It didn't last. 'Hey,' she said. 'Did you guys know that Portland was almost named Boston? Two founders flipped a coin for it. One of them was from Portland, Maine. The other guy was from Boston. Guess who won?' No one answered. Susan fiddled with the white string fringe around one of the holes in her jeans. 'It's ironic,' she said. 'Because Portland is often referred to as the "Boston of the West Coast".' Archie was still reading. *Why couldn't she stop talking?* She made a promise to herself that she wasn't going to say another word unless one of them talked to her first.

It was a quiet trip.

The Oregon State Penitentiary was a campus of gristle-coloured buildings located just off the freeway behind a wall topped with razor wire. It housed both maximum- and minimum-security inmates, male and female, and had the state's only death row. Susan had driven by it dozens of times on trips home from college, but she had never had occasion to visit, not that she would have jumped at the chance. Henry parked the car in a space reserved for police vehicles near the entrance of the prison. A middle-aged man in pressed khakis and a golf shirt stood on the steps of one of the main buildings, leaning against the railing, arms folded. He had soft features and a receding hairline and a belly that pressed insistently against his shirt. A cell phone in a jaunty leather case was clipped to the belt of his pants. A lawyer, thought Susan grimly. He stepped forward as Archie, Henry and Susan climbed out of the car.

'How is she today?' Archie asked him.

'Pissy,' the lawyer said. His nose was running and he dabbed at it with a white cloth hankie. 'Same as every Sunday. That the reporter?'

'Yep.'

He thrust a germy hand out to Susan, who shook it

despite that. He had a firm, precise handshake, like someone who intended to make good use out of it. 'Darrow Miller. Assistant DA.'

'Darrow?' she repeated, amused.

'Yeah,' he said without affect. 'My brother's name is Scopes. And that's the last crack we'll be making.'

Susan struggled to keep up as the group moved at a quick pace through the main building, taking corners and climbing stairs with the ease of people who had travelled the wide hallways so often that they had become a body memory. The group encountered two security checkpoints. At the first, a guard checked their identification, logged their names and stamped their hands. Henry and Archie surrendered their side-arms and moved past the guards without a break in their conversation. A male guard stopped Susan, who was still a few steps behind. The guard was small and wiry, and he stood with his fists on his hips, like an action figure.

'Did you not read your pamphlet?' he asked her with the slow enunciation of someone talking to a child. He was shorter than Susan was, so he had to look up.

Susan bristled.

'It's OK, Ron,' Archie interjected, turning back. 'She's with me.'

The little guard chewed his cheek for a moment,

slid a look at Archie and then nodded and stepped back against the wall. 'Nobody reads their pamphlet,' he mumbled.

'What did I do?' Susan asked when they were moving again.

'They don't like visitors to wear denim,' Archie explained. 'The prisoners wear prison blues, and it might lead to confusion.'

'But sure their denim is not as chicly torn as mine?'

'You'd be surprised,' he said, smiling. 'The trannies are very creative.'

They came to a metal detector. Again the men moved through without incident. Susan, however, was motioned to wait by a rotund female guard. 'You wearing a bra?' the guard asked.

Susan blushed. 'Excuse me?'

The guard stared at Susan, bored. 'No underwire bras – they set off the metal detector.'

Was it Susan's imagination, or was everyone suddenly staring at her chest? 'Oh. No. I am lacy camisole girl. I have a really hard time finding bras that fit right. Small cup size, broad shoulders. You know.' Susan smiled amiably. The guard's breasts were enormous. Like melons. She probably had all sorts of problems finding bras, too.

The guard stared at Susan another moment and then widened her eyes and sighed. 'Are you wearing an underwire bra?' she asked again.

'Oh. No.'

'Then go through the damn metal detector already.'

'Here we are,' Archie said. He opened an unmarked grey metal door and Susan walked in, followed by Henry and the lawyer. It was a cement-walled observation room, with an impressive plate of one-way glass that looked into another room. It was just like on TV. The room was small, with a low ceiling and a long metal folding table jammed next to the window, leaving a space a little wider than an aeroplane aisle in which to manoeuvre. A young Hispanic man sat on a stool at the table facing a computer monitor and a TV with a closed-circuit feed from a camera mounted on the ceiling of the room. He had a meal from Taco Bell spread out carefully in front of him. Bleached napkins stacked. Hot-sauce packets lined up. One taco half eaten, another in queue. The food filled the compact room with the smell of refried beans and cheap hot sauce.

'That's Rico,' Archie said, thrusting his chin towards the man.

Rico grinned at Susan. 'I'm the sidekick,' he said.

'I thought Henry was the sidekick,' Susan said.

'No, man,' Rico said. 'He's the partner. I'm the sidekick.'

Archie's smile was weak. 'Wait here,' he told Susan. 'I'll be back for you in a minute.' He turned around and walked out of the door.

'Meet the Queen of Evil,' Rico said to Susan, lifting his chin towards the room on the other side of the glass.

Susan approached the glass and got her first good look at Gretchen Lowell. There she sat. The picture of poise, incongruous in denim pants and a denim shirt with the word INMATE printed on the back. Susan had seen her picture, of course. The media had loved running photographs of Gretchen Lowell because she was beautiful. And a serial killer. A perfect combination. And aren't all stunning women capable of murder? the pictures seemed to ask. But Susan could see now that she was even more gorgeous in person. Her eyes were large and pale blue and her features were perfectly symmetrical, wide cheekbones, a long, sculpted nose, a heart-shaped face that ended in a dainty chin. Her flesh was bloodless. Her hair, which had been very blond at the time of her arrest, was now a darker shade of blond, and was combed back into a high ponytail, showing off her long, aristocratic neck. She was not pretty. That was not the word for it. 'Pretty' implied something girlish. Gretchen Lowell was beautiful in a very grown-up way, in a sophisticated, confident way. It was more than beauty; it was the power of beauty. She radiated it. Susan was spellbound.

Susan watched through the glass, riveted, as Archie entered the room, head down, file under his arm. He turned to close the steel door behind him and stood for a moment facing the closed door, as if gathering himself. Then he took a breath, straightened, and turned towards the woman at the table. His face was engaging and pleasant, a man meeting an old friend for some coffee. 'Hello, Gretchen,' he said.

'Good morning, darling.' She tilted her head and smiled. The sudden animation made her features sparkle even more. It was not a fake beauty-queen smile. It was a genuine expression of warmth and pleasure. Or, Susan reconsidered, she was really, really good at the fake beauty-queen smile. Gretchen lifted her hands from her lap to the surface of the table and Susan could see that they were manacled. Susan craned her head and noticed that Gretchen's feet were shackled too. Gretchen's large blue eyes widened playfully. 'Did you bring me anything?' she asked Archie.

'I'll bring her in here in a minute,' Archie said, and Susan realized with a shudder that they were talking about her.

Archie walked towards the table and very carefully opened the folder he carried and fanned out five eight-by-ten photographs in front of Gretchen.

'Which one is she?' he asked.

Gretchen held his gaze, her face still a careful facade of congeniality. Then, with barely a downward flicker of her eyes, she reached out and placed her hand flat on one of the photographs.

'There,' she said. Her smile widened. 'Can we play now?'

'I'll be right back,' Archie said.

He walked into the observation room and held up the photograph that Gretchen had picked. The image was of a Latina girl, maybe twenty, with short black hair and a silly grin. She had her arm around someone who had been cut out of the photograph, and she was flashing a peace sign. 'It's her,' he said simply.

'Who?' asked Susan.

Rico spun around on his stool. 'Gloria Juarez. Nineteen. College kid. She disappeared in Utah in 1995. Gretchen gave us her name this morning. She said she'd tell us where to find her body if we brought you down to meet her.'

Susan was startled. 'Why me?'

'Because of me,' Archie said. He blinked slowly and ran a hand through his dark hair and stared at the ceiling for a moment before continuing. 'She hasn't given up a body in almost six months. I thought a profile in the *Herald* would shake her up a bit. She gets jealous easily. I thought that if she knew I was getting close to a reporter, close enough to talk about things, she would react by giving me – ' he paused, as if considering his words carefully – 'a token of her affection.'

Susan looked around the little room. They all were

staring at her. Waiting to see what she would do. 'A body?'

'Yeah. She hasn't talked to anyone but me in the last year.' He shrugged helplessly. 'It didn't even occur to me that she'd actually ask to see you.'

She had been manipulated. Susan felt a prickly self-consciousness wash over her. Archie had used her. She took a step back, away from him. She had trusted him, and he had taken advantage of her. It was a weirdly familiar sensation. No one said anything. She reached up and pulled at her hair, knotting it around a finger until it burned. Darrow, the lawyer, rubbed the back of his ruddy neck and sneezed. Rico looked at his lunch. Henry leaned against the wall, arms crossed, waiting for some sort of cue from Archie. They all knew. That just made it worse.

Susan looked through the glass at Gretchen. Gretchen was looking at the table. A picture of comportment. Genetically superior. Why did she have to be so perfect-looking? 'That's why you agreed to the profile?' Susan asked Archie, keeping her voice level as best she could. 'You thought it would make her tell you where more bodies were?'

Archie took a step forward towards Susan. 'The more she thinks I'm sharing with you, the more she'll want to reinforce her control, and the more bodies she'll give me.' His gaze flickered through the glass at Gretchen and held. Then back at Susan. 'She's mentioned your stories. She reads your work. That's why I chose you.' Underneath heavy lids, his eyes were full of apology and determination, and something else. It was something in his expression, something a half a second off. That's when it hit Susan. *Jesus Christ*, she thought. *He's high.*

'Help me,' he said.

He was high on pills. She could see him see her register it. They were prescription pills. He was in pain. But he didn't offer any explanations. He laughed. 'Fuck,' he said, rubbing his eyes with one hand. He leaned his forehead against the glass and he looked at Gretchen Lowell. No one said a word. Susan thought she could hear someone's watch ticking. The lawyer blew his nose. Finally, Archie turned his head back towards Susan. 'I should never have brought you here. I'm sorry.'

Susan lifted her chin towards the window. 'What does she want with me?' she asked.

Archie looked at Susan. He ran a hand over his mouth, through his hair. 'She wants to size you up. See what you know.'

'About you.'

He nodded a few times. 'Yup.'

'What do you want me to tell her?'

He looked her in the eye. 'The truth. She has a marvellous bullshit detector. But if you go in there, she will fuck with you. She's not a nice person. And she will not like you.'

Susan tried to smile. 'I'm charming.'

Archie's craggy face was dead serious. 'She will feel threatened by you and she will be mean to you. You need to understand that.'

Susan put her palm on the glass, so that Gretchen Lowell's head rested in the crux between her thumb and forefinger. 'Can I write about it?'

'I can't stop you.'

'True.'

'But no pens,' Archie said definitively.

'Why?'

He looked in through the glass at Gretchen. Susan could see his eyes travel over her, her neck, her arms, her hands. It reminded her of the way someone might linger over a lover. 'Because I don't want her using it to stab you in the throat,' he said.

31

'Gretchen,' Archie said. 'This is Susan Ward. Susan, Gretchen Lowell.'

It suddenly seemed, to Susan, that there wasn't enough oxygen in the room. She stood stupidly for a moment, wondering if she was supposed to offer to shake Gretchen's hand, then remembered the manacles and thought better of it. *Just be calm*, Susan told herself for the tenth time in thirty seconds. She pulled a chair out so she could sit down across from Gretchen. The chair scraped against the floor, making Susan feel clumsy and awkward. Her heart was racing. She avoided eye contact with Gretchen as she sat down, conscious of her silly thrashed jeans, wishing that she had asked for a minute back in the hall to brush her hair. Archie sat down next to Susan. Susan forced herself to look across the table. Gretchen smiled at her. She was even more lovely up close.

'Well, aren't you cute,' Gretchen said sweetly. 'Like a little cartoon character.' Susan had never been more conscious of her stupid pink hair. Of her childish clothes. Of her flat chest. 'I've enjoyed your stories,'

Gretchen continued, with just enough lilt in her voice that Susan couldn't tell for sure if she was being genuine or sarcastic.

Susan plunked her recorder on the table and willed her heart to slow. 'Do you mind if I record this?' she asked, trying to seem professional. The room smelled antiseptic, like industrial-power cleanser. Toxic.

Gretchen tilted her head towards the window, where Susan knew the others were watching. 'It's all being recorded,' she said.

Susan met Gretchen's stare. 'Humour me.'

Gretchen raised her eyebrows gamely.

Susan pressed RECORD. She could sense Gretchen absorbing her. She felt like a mistress suddenly confronted with her lover's glamorous wife. It was a role to which Susan was well suited, an irony that did not escape her. She glanced at Archie for some indication of what to do next, how to behave. He sat leaning back in his chair, hands threaded on his lap, not taking his eyes off Gretchen. There was a level of comfort between them. As if they had known each other their whole lives. Debbie was right: it was creepy.

'She likes you,' Gretchen said teasingly to Archie.

Archie pulled a brass pillbox out of his pocket and set it on the table in front of him. 'She's a reporter,' he said, rotating the small box in a clockwise motion on the tabletop. 'She's friendly with her subjects so they tell her things. It's her job.'

'Do you tell her things?'

'Yes,' he said, looking at the box.

'But not everything.'

He glanced up at Gretchen meaningfully. 'Of course not.'

Gretchen seemed satisfied by this, and she settled her attention on Susan. 'What are your questions?'

Susan was startled. 'My questions?'

Gretchen gestured to the recorder. She wore the manacles like they were bracelets, lovely, expensive baubles to be admired and envied. 'That's why you've come here, right? With your little gadget and furrowed brow? To interview me? You can't write a story about Archie Sheridan without talking to me. I made him who he is today. Without me, he wouldn't have had a career.'

'I like to think I would have found some other megalomaniacal homicidal psychopath,' Archie said with a sigh.

Gretchen ignored him. 'Go ahead,' she said to Susan. 'Ask me anything.'

Susan's mind went blank. She had gone over this in her head dozens of times, what she would ask Gretchen Lowell if she had a chance. But she had never believed that she would have the opportunity. *Get a grip*, she chided herself. Come up with a question. Anything. Ask the first thing that comes into your head. 'Why did you kidnap Archie Sheridan?' she said.

Gretchen's skin glowed. Susan wondered if they allowed exfoliants in prisons. Maybe she was hoarding strawberries from the cafeteria and making her own masks. Gretchen leaned forward over the small table. 'I wanted to kill him,' she said with glee. 'I wanted to torture him in the most interesting, painful manner imaginable until he begged me to slit his throat.'

Susan had to swallow before she could speak. 'Did he?'

Gretchen looked adoringly at Archie. 'Do you want to take that one, darling?'

'I did,' Archie said without missing a beat. He placed the pillbox in his open palm on the table and looked at it.

'But you didn't kill him,' Susan said to Gretchen.

Gretchen shrugged and widened her eyes. 'Change of plan.'

'Why him?'

'I was bored. And he seemed to take such a genuine interest in my work. I thought it would be nice for him to get to see it up close. Now can I ask you a question?'

Susan shifted in her seat, struggling for an adequate response. Gretchen didn't wait for one. The question was directed at Susan, but Gretchen's attention was fixed on Archie. Archie was looking at the pillbox.

'You've met Debbie? How is she?' Her voice was tender, as if she were asking after an old friend.

Oh, Debbie! She's great! Just moved to Des Moines. Married, couple of kids. Sends her love.

Susan glanced over at Archie. He wasn't looking at the box any more; he was looking at Gretchen. But other than his eyes, he hadn't moved a muscle. The brass pillbox glistened in his palm. The sudden tension between them made Susan's stomach feel rigid.

'I don't think I should answer that,' she said. Her voice came out smaller than she had intended. She felt like a teenager. Like she was fourteen again. The feeling made her uncomfortably warm.

'There's a cemetery,' Gretchen announced. 'Off a state highway in Nebraska. We buried Gloria on top of one of the graves. Want to know where it is?'

No one moved for a minute. And then Archie finally looked at Susan. His eyes were glassy. *Now I see why you're high*, thought Susan.

'It's fine,' Archie said. 'Really. She likes to revel in what a thorough mess she's made of my life. We talk about it all the time. You'd think she'd get tired of it after a while.' He set the box back down on the table. He did it gently, like it was bruised. 'But it never ceases to entertain her.'

Susan wasn't sure what fucked-up game the two of them were playing, but she was hoping that Archie had it more under control than it seemed. She shrugged her assent. It was his call. She would play along. 'Debbie hates you,' she told Gretchen. 'She hates you for murdering the man she knew as her husband.' She glanced at Archie. No reaction. 'She thinks he's dead. And that Archie is someone else now.'

Gretchen looked pleased, her eyes bright, her cheekbones pronounced. 'But she still loves him?'

Susan bit her lip. 'Yes.'

'And he still loves her. But he can't be with her. And he can't be with his two adorable children. Know why?'

'Because of you?' Susan guessed.

'Because of me. And that's why you'll never be with him, either, pigeon. Because I've ruined him for other women.'

'You've ruined me for other human beings, Gretchen,' Archie said wearily. He slid the box off the table and put it back in his pocket, then scooted his chair back from the table and stood.

'Where are you going?' Gretchen asked, her voice betraying a sudden anxiety. Susan watched as her entire posture changed. Her face hardened. Were those crow's feet? Gretchen leaned forward towards Archie, as if attempting to close the space between them.

'I'm taking a break,' Archie answered, his fingertips still on the table. 'I'm not sure that we're being very productive today.' He looked down at Susan. 'Come on,' he said. He took a step back and Gretchen reached up, hands still shackled, and seized his hand.

'The name on the grave is Emma Watson,' she said quickly. 'The cemetery is on SR One Hundred, in a little town called Hamilton, eighteen miles west of Lincoln.'

Archie didn't move. He just stood, staring at his hand in hers. Not pulling away. Like someone gripping a live electric wire. Susan had no idea what to do. She looked around frantically at the observation window and, as if on cue, Henry Sobol burst into the room. He was at the table in three steps, and he reached a large hand around Gretchen Lowell's wrist and squeezed it until she winced in pain and let Archie's hand fall free.

'That's against the rules,' Henry said between clenched teeth. His face was red and his pulse surged under the thick skin of his neck. 'You touch him again and I swear to fuck that I'll end this bullshit, bodies or not. Got it?' Gretchen didn't recoil, didn't say a word, just looked at him, lips wet with saliva, nostrils flaring, eyes daring him to take a swing at her. Suddenly, she didn't look beautiful at all.

'It's fine,' Archie said. His voice was even, perfectly modulated, but Susan noticed that his hands were trembling. 'I'm fine.'

Henry looked at Archie, holding his gaze for a moment, and then turned his shaved head back towards Gretchen. He still had his meaty fist around her slender wrist, and for a moment Susan thought he might just snap it in two. Without letting his grip waver an iota, he turned to Archie. 'We've got the Nebraska state police on their way to that cemetery. We should know something in the next hour.' Then he opened his hand, dropped Gretchen's wrist and, without giving her a second glance, turned and walked out of the door.

Gretchen smoothed her blond hair with her manacled hands. 'I don't think your friends like me,' she said to Archie.

Archie sank back into his chair. 'You did send him my spleen.'

'And he won't let me forget it.' She turned back to Susan, all poise and tranquillity, as if the entire encounter had not happened. 'You were saying?'

Susan was still reeling. Would it be a show of weakness to vomit? 'What?'

'You were asking me questions, pigeon. For your story.'

And that's when Susan knew what to ask. 'What's your favourite movie?' Try to find a twisted answer to that. Susan settled back smugly.

Gretchen's answer was instantaneous. '*Band of Outsiders.* Godard.'

Well. That was unexpected. Susan looked at Archie searchingly, not even trying to mask the confusion that was surely screwed up on her face. 'That's Detective Sheridan's favourite movie,' she said.

'You can call him Archie,' Gretchen said lightly. 'I've seen him naked.'

'Have you two talked about Godard?' Susan asked Archie.

'No,' he said. And there was the pillbox again.

Gretchen smiled, all innocence. 'Isn't that a funny coincidence? Do you have any other questions?'

Susan examined Gretchen. She had heard stories that Gretchen had killed something like two hundred people. She had never believed it. Until now. '"The After School Strangler". Any ideas of what kind of person we're looking for?'

Gretchen laughed. It was a throaty laugh, like Bette Davis, full of sex and lung cancer. 'Want me to get inside his head for you? Sorry, Clarice. Can't help you.'

'You're both murderers,' Susan offered sweetly.

Gretchen shook her head. 'We're different.'

'You are?'

'Tell her, Archie.'

Archie's voice sounded unnaturally slow. 'He doesn't like the killing part. Gretchen does.'

Cold smile. 'See? Apples and oranges.'

'You didn't kill Detective Sheridan,' Susan pointed out.

'Yes I did.' Gretchen's smile widened around her perfect teeth. It was the most chilling smile Susan had ever seen. She suddenly felt an infinite tenderness for Archie, and even as she did she regretted it, because she knew that Gretchen could see it in her eyes.

'Has he rejected you yet, pigeon?' Gretchen asked, bemusedly. 'It will be hard for you. You don't get rejected often, do you? You're not used to that. You think sex is your power. But it isn't.'

'Gretchen . . .' Archie cautioned.

'Do you know what's more intimate than sex?' Gretchen asked. She shot a wicked smile at Archie. 'Violence.'

Susan felt all of the saliva in her throat evaporate. 'You don't know anything about me.'

'You're attracted to older men. Authority figures. Men with more power than you have. Married. Why is that, pigeon, hmm?' Gretchen tilted her head, and Susan could see a thought skate across her eyes and then settle. Gretchen smiled. 'How old were you when your father died?'

Susan felt like the wind had been knocked out of her. Had she flinched? She squeezed her thumbs as hard as she could under the table until the pain dried up the tears she feared would well at any moment. When the moment passed, she stood up and leaned over the table, her knuckles pressed against its cold aluminium surface. 'Fuck you,' she said to Gretchen. 'Fuck you, you fucking psycho killer.'

But Gretchen merely smiled. 'All that bubbling post-pubescent rage. Who did you end up fucking? Your English teacher?' She arched an eyebrow. 'Drama teacher?'

Susan couldn't breathe. She felt a tear slide down one cheek and she was furious at herself for it. 'How—' she began. She put a hand over her mouth to try to stop herself from speaking, but it was too late.

Archie turned slowly and looked up at Susan, his

eyes wide, forehead lined. 'The drama teacher at Cleveland? Reston?'

'No,' Susan stammered.

Gretchen shook her head at Archie. 'Textbook denial.'

'Susan,' Archie said, his voice stern, authoritative. 'If you had a sexual relationship with Paul Reston when you were a teenager, you need to tell me right now.'

Gretchen's blue eyes narrowed victoriously. Game. Set. Match.

Susan laughed, a horrible distraught half-chuckle, and then the floodgates opened. Hot tears on her cheeks, humiliated, she backed away, hunched, gulping for air. She fumbled for the buzzer, and when the door jerked open, fled into the corridor.

32

Susan stumbled a few steps down the hall, hugging her arms, before her bones seemed to give out and she fell against the wall. Archie was behind her in a moment, his hand on her shoulder. It was a comforting touch, nothing sexual about it. Susan wasn't used to that. She turned away, pressing her forehead against the cinder-block wall so that he couldn't see her blotchy face, the tears, her smeared lipstick. Archie moved around in front of her, never taking his hand off her shoulder, and then leaned back against the wall, put his hands in his pockets and waited. The sound of a door, then footsteps, and Henry was in the hallway too, a guard, the lawyer. God, they had all seen everything. Susan wanted to die.

'Why don't you give us a minute?' Archie said to them, and they all slid back behind the observation-room door, except for the guard, who glanced around awkwardly and then slipped into the interview room, where Gretchen Lowell still sat. When they were alone in the hall, Archie asked, 'When did it start?'

The cinder-block wall was painted with glossy grey

paint. It reminded Susan of an overcast winter sky, when the clouds appear solid, a canopy of ash. 'When I was a sophomore. I ended it when I went to college.' She mustered her dignity, drawing herself to her full height, lifting her chin. 'I was precocious. It was consensual.'

'Technically, no, it wasn't,' he said. She could see the colour in his face change as he tried to suppress his frustration, his fists tightening in his pants pockets. 'You should have said something. Did it occur to you that the victims were all fifteen-year-old girls? All raped?'

Susan shrank into herself. 'He didn't rape me,' she said. She felt defensive, ridiculous. 'And I was going to tell you. But it didn't seem relevant. You would have harassed him. He would have lost his job. Besides, you said he had an alibi.'

'Statutory rape is a crime. If the statute of limitations weren't up, I'd go and arrest him right now. Did anyone know? Your parents?'

Susan laughed sadly. 'Bliss? She didn't know anything.' She twisted her mouth up. 'She probably would have been supportive. She always hated setting boundaries.'

Archie gave Susan a dubious look.

And suddenly, with a little shock, Susan knew that she was wrong. 'No,' Susan admitted. 'She would have hated it. She would have made sure he went to jail.' She turned away. 'But she didn't know. I didn't tell her.' She pressed her knuckles against the cinder-block until she felt the rough cement break the skin. 'I think I was mad at her for not figuring it out.'

'Were there any other girls?'

Susan couldn't even look at him. 'Not that I know of.'

'I can't just forget we had this conversation, Susan. I have to report it. I will do everything I can to get him fired.'

'It was ten years ago,' Susan pleaded. 'I seduced him. My father had just died and I needed comfort. Paul was my favourite teacher. It wasn't his fault.' She looked away. 'I was hardly a virgin.'

'He was an adult,' Archie said. 'He should have known better.'

Susan began the work of cleaning herself up, wiping the tears off her face, tucking her tangle of pink hair behind her ears. 'If you report it, I'll deny it. And so will Paul.' She bit her lip so hard it felt like it might split. 'I just wanted to explain.'

'Explain what?'

Susan looked away, fingers splayed as she tried to find the right words. Her knuckles were pink from where she had dug them into the wall. 'Why I am the way I am. All those things Gretchen Lowell said in there. They're true.'

Archie looked her in the eye under his heavy brows. 'Gretchen says a lot of things in the hope that one or two of them will stick and make you suffer. Believe me, I know this. Don't give her that power. And don't give Reston that power, either. He's a creep. Adult men should not sleep with teenagers. Period. The ones who do have some serious issues.' He leaned close to her, so close that for a moment she had an impulse to press her forehead into his neck. 'And those issues belong to them, not you.'

'It's ancient history,' Susan said.

Archie gently took each of her wrists and lifted her hands away to reveal her tear-stained face. 'I have to go back in there now, and it's going to be a little while. Why don't you wait out here?'

Susan's face fell. 'Can't I wait in the observation room?'

Archie lifted his hand and wiped a tear that still hung on her cheek. 'When I go back in there, Gretchen is going to give me her confession,' he said. 'Every detail of how she tortured and killed Gloria Juarez.' His face darkened. 'You don't want to have to hear that if you don't have to.'

He gave Susan a last pat on the shoulder and started walking back towards the room where Gretchen sat waiting for him. Susan watched him as he walked, one arm extended, the fingertips of his hand dancing along the cinder-block wall.

She wondered if he was this high all the time, or just on Sundays. She decided this wasn't the time to ask.

*

The guard left as soon as Archie entered the room. Gretchen sat just as she had, in repose, her manacled hands folded on one knee, seemingly undisturbed and unimpressed by Susan's outburst. Susan's sleek silver digital recorder still sat in the centre of the table where she had left it, still recording. Archie pulled the metal chair out again, sat in it and faced Gretchen. Then, avoiding eye contact with her, he reached out, turned the recorder off and slipped it in the inside pocket of his jacket. He could still feel Susan's tears on his hand.

'You want to tell me how you knew about Reston?' he asked, looking up.

Gretchen's eyes widened innocently. 'Lucky guess?'

'You're intuitive,' Archie said, 'not psychic.'

Gretchen rolled her eyes and gave him a bored half-smile. 'She mentioned her dead daddy in a story in the *Herald* about a year ago. And just look at her. The pink hair. The clothes. She's completely arrested. It screams sexual abuse.' She leaned forward. 'The way she looks at you: that longing for a father figure to take her in his strong, protective arms. It was obvious. I just had to guess the right teacher.' She smiled, delighted with herself. 'And, darling, it's always the English or the drama teacher.'

Archie's head throbbed. He rubbed his eyes with his thumb and forefinger. 'It's a coincidence. That it might be related to a case I'm working on.'

'You're tired.'

That was a safe bet. 'You have no idea.'

'Maybe you should up your antidepressant dosage.'

'I'll defer to Fergus for my medical advice, thank you.'

She put her elbows on the table and rested her chin in her manacled hands. Then she glanced at the observation window before settling her attention back on Archie. 'I pulled her small intestine out. I cut an inch-wide hole in her abdominal wall with a scalpel and I pulled her small intestine out inch by inch with a crochet hook, slicing it from the mesentery an inch at a time. An H crochet hook. You want something big enough to be able to get a grip on the intestine because it's slippery and you don't want to perforate it.' She never looked away during the confessions. She maintained eye contact with Archie always. She never glanced to the side to recover some memory; never looked away in revulsion at what she had done; never allowed him a moment's respite. 'Seven metres. That's what they say the average length is. I've never been able to pull out more than three.' She smiled, licking her lips as if they were dry. 'It's beautiful, though. So pink and delicate. Like something waiting to be born. The metallic smell of blood: remember it, darling?' She sat forward, a blush of pleasure settling in her cheeks. 'When she begged me to stop, I started burning her.'

He tried to tune out for the confession. To shut off. Ignore the graphic images she tried to paint for him. He just watched her. She was very beautiful. And if he could manage to stop himself from hearing her, he could enjoy this part. He could enjoy the excuse to just sit and look at a beautiful woman. But he had to be careful when he did. That his eyes didn't slip from her face, didn't slide down her neck to her collarbone or breasts.

She knew, of course. She knew everything.

'Are you listening?' she asked, a smile flirting on her lips.

'Yeah,' he said. He pulled the pillbox out of his pocket and set it back on the table. 'I'm listening.'

33

Susan rolled off Ian and on to her back. She had called him as soon as she'd got home and he'd come over within the hour. She'd had him in her mouth before she even said hello. Susan found that sex was an excellent reliever of stress and if Gretchen Lowell had anything to say about that, she could go fuck herself.

Ian picked his glasses up off the bedside table and put them on. 'How'd it go?' he asked.

Susan did not consider for a moment telling Ian about Reston, or how Gretchen had emotionally filleted her without even looking like she was trying. 'It could have gone better,' she said. She rifled around on her bedside table until she found a half-smoked joint on a saucer on top of a paperback volume of William Stafford poetry. She lit it and inhaled. She liked smoking pot naked. It made her feel bohemian.

'Ever think you smoke too much dope?' Ian asked.

'We're in Oregon,' Susan said. 'It's our main agricultural export.' She smiled. 'I'm supporting local farmers.'

'You're not in college any more, Susan.'

'Exactly,' Susan said, annoyed. 'Everyone smokes pot in college. It's totally average. Smoking dope after college, now that takes a certain level of commitment. Besides, my mother still smokes pot.'

'You have a mother?'

Susan smiled to herself. 'I'd introduce you, but she distrusts men who don't have beards.'

Ian found his boxers on the floor beside the bed and pulled them on. He didn't seem that disappointed about not getting to meet Bliss. 'Did you learn anything from the serial-killer beauty queen?'

Susan felt a wave of nausea at the thought of her run-in with Gretchen and pushed it aside. 'It took you long enough to ask.'

'I was playing it cool,' Ian said. 'As if I might be more interested in your body than one of the biggest stories I've ever edited.'

Susan delighted in the double compliment, striking a cheesecake pose, arching her back and placing one hand on her nude hip. 'As if.'

'So what did you learn?'

Her stomach clenched again. She rolled on to her belly, stretched out diagonally across the bed and pulled a loose blanket over her naked body. 'That I'm a bad reporter. I totally let her get to me.'

'You've still got a story, though, right? Facing the cold stare of death and all that.'

She was up on her elbows, the joint held over the edge of the bed. A tiny chunk of ash drifted to the floor and landed on one of the Great Writer's Persian eBay carpets. Susan watched it fall without even the faintest thought of picking it up. 'Oh yeah. She gave up another body. Some college girl in Nebraska.' Susan remembered the smiling girl. The peace sign. The arm around her shoulder that belonged to some left-behind friend who had been cropped out of the photograph. She gave herself a mental shake and took another hit off the joint. 'They found her buried on top of an old grave in a cemetery off the highway.' The pot was smoothing all the hard edges, and she felt the stress of the day start to bleed from her body. With it went the need for her companion. 'Shouldn't you be getting home?' she asked, raising an eyebrow purposefully at Ian.

He had settled back on to the bed in his boxers, feet crossed at the ankles. 'Sharon's at the coast. I can't spend the night?'

'I've got to get up early tomorrow. Claire Masland is picking me up.'

'She's a dyke, you know.'

'Why? Because she has short hair?'

'I'm just saying.'

'Go home, Ian.'

Ian swung his feet on the floor and found the rest of his clothes. He pulled on one of his black socks. 'I thought I told you to leave the Molly Palmer thing alone,' he said, pulling on the other sock, not looking at her.

Susan was taken aback. Molly Palmer? 'OK,' she

said, raising her hands in mock defensiveness. 'You got me. I left a few messages for Ethan Poole.'

'I'm talking about Justin Johnson,' he said, an irritated edge to his voice.

It took a minute for Susan to process this. Justin Johnson? And then the confusion lifted and she thought, *Holy shit.* All this time, she'd thought that Justin had something to do with the After School Strangler case. She had connected him to the wrong story. Justin Johnson had nothing to do with Lee Robinson, nothing to do with Cleveland High – except when he sold grass in its parking lot. 'What does Justin have to do with Molly Palmer?' she asked.

Ian laughed. 'You don't know?'

She felt stupid, and stupid for feeling stupid. 'What's going on, Ian?'

He stood, and pulled on his black jeans. 'Ethan gave Molly your messages. She called the senator's lawyer. He called Howard Jenkins.' He zipped and buttoned the jeans, then bent and picked his black belt up off the floor and began to thread it through the belt loops. 'Jenkins called me. I told him that you weren't working the story any more. But apparently little Justin's mother hired a PI to watch him.' He finished buckling the belt and sat on the edge of the bed. 'She thinks he's dealing pot, see. And who shows up at school to talk to him but Susan Ward from the *Oregon Herald*. They recognized the pink hair.' He pulled on a black Converse, tied it. 'So now everyone thinks you're on the story. That it's all going to break wide open.' Pulled the other Converse on, tied it. 'So the lawyer gets the bright idea of slipping you a note with the kid's juvie-record file number on it. With the thought that if you know he has a record, you might not trust the little bastard's story.'

'Seriously?' Susan said, trying not to smile. 'That guy really was a lawyer?'

Ian stood up, half dressed, and faced her. 'You're going to get us both fired. You know that, right?'

Susan scrambled into a seated position, letting the blanket fall around her waist. 'What does Justin know about Molly Palmer?'

'He was the senator's son's best friend. When they were kids. Inseparable. Molly Palmer used to babysit them both. So I'm suspecting he saw or heard something he shouldn't. You might recognize Justin's mother's maiden name. Overlook?'

Susan's heart sank. 'As in the family who owns the *Herald*?'

'She's a cousin.'

'Senator Castle really did it, didn't he?'

'Oh, he did it. It's just not a story that will ever run in this town.' He reached into the pocket of his grey wool jacket, withdrew something and tossed it on the bed.

'What's that?' Susan asked.

'It's your nine-one-one tape. If I were you, I'd get back on the story we'll actually run, and dance with the fella who brung ya.'

Susan picked up the cassette and turned it over in her hands. 'Thanks.'

'Don't thank me. Thank Derek. He spent all day tracking it down for you.' Ian gave his Columbia Journalism School T-shirt a shake, the way he always did, to get out the wrinkles. 'I think he likes you.'

Susan took another drag off the joint. 'Well, if I ever want to fuck a frat boy ex-football star,' she said, holding the smoke in her lungs, 'I'll know who to call.'

'Whom,' said Ian.

After Ian was gone, Susan sat cross-legged in the middle of the bed. The worst of it was that the Molly Palmer story actually mattered. It wasn't exploitation. It wasn't advertising. It wasn't another disposable feature. It could make a difference. A teenager had been wronged, and the man responsible was going to enormous lengths to cover it up. A man with power. A man elected by a public who had a right to know that he was the kind of man who would take advantage of that power to screw a fourteen-year-old. So OK, yes, maybe she had something personal at stake. And now Susan had somehow both landed the Molly Palmer story and lost it at exactly the same time. Justin was in Palm Springs, or wherever. Molly wasn't talking.

Ethan wasn't even returning her calls. She wanted to nail Senator Castle. More than Ian even knew. She didn't care if it got her fired. She was going to get someone, somewhere, to go on the record. She looked down at the cassette tape in her hands. Gretchen's 911 tape. And that's when Susan Ward was filled with a sudden desire that was entirely foreign to her. She didn't care about prizes or prose or voice. She didn't care about a book deal. She didn't care about impressing Ian. She wanted, for the first time in her professional life, to be a good reporter.

She padded over to the living area and, sitting on her bare heels, popped the tape into the stereo. She had read the transcript of the call dozens of times. But it was still thrilling to finally get a glimpse into the real-time moment. She pressed PLAY.

'Nine-one-one. What is the nature of your emergency?'

'My name is Gretchen Lowell. I'm calling on behalf of Detective Archie Sheridan. Do you know who I am?'

'Uh, yeah.'

'Good. Your detective needs to get to a trauma centre. I'm at two-three-three-nine Magnolia Lane in Gresham. We're in the basement. There's a school two blocks away where you should be able to land a helicopter. If you get people here in the next fifteen minutes, he just might live.' She hung up.

Susan sank back into a seated position on the floor

and ran her hands over her forearms, which were scattered with tiny goose bumps. Gretchen had sounded so calm. When Susan had heard Gretchen's voice in her mind, it had been more panicked, frantic. She was, in effect, turning herself in to the police, giving up the ghost. She could have been killed. But she hadn't seemed concerned at all. Her voice did not bear a single tremor. She did not stammer or search for words. She was direct, articulate and professional. Her call almost sounded rehearsed.

Archie didn't ask Henry to go with him to interview Reston. It was Sunday afternoon and he felt bad enough about dragging Henry to the state pen every weekend, though he knew Henry would never let him go alone. He also wanted, if at all possible, to protect Susan's privacy. So he let Henry drop him off at his apartment.

He was numb and tired from the pills, so he made a pot of coffee. Then he checked his voicemail for messages. There were none, which meant that Debbie had never called back. Archie didn't blame her. It was a mistake to talk to her at all on Sundays. He had promised himself that he'd keep Debbie and Gretchen separate, compartmentalized; it was the only way this would work. But he was selfish. He needed Debbie, wanted to hear her voice, to be reminded of his old life. But the phone calls would have to stop eventually.

They both knew it. They just prolonged the pain of their emotional entanglement. He would stop the calls. He just couldn't bear to do it yet.

He called Claire and checked in. There were no leads. The tip line was quiet. Even prank callers took Sundays off. It had been four days since they had discovered Kristy Mathers's body. Which meant that the killer was probably already looking for another victim. Archie sat alone in his kitchen and drank half the pot of coffee, pausing only long enough to refill his cup. When he felt suitably revived, he took two more Vicodin and called a cab.

Reston lived in Brooklyn, a neighbourhood south of Cleveland High. It was a tangle of telephone wires and trees densely packed with little middle-class Victorians and eighties duplexes. A nice neighbourhood. Safe.

Archie told the cab to wait and then got out and began to climb the mossy cement steps that led up the little hill to Reston's one-storey house. It was late afternoon, and while the houses across the street still glowed in the sun, long shadows streaked Reston's terraced hillside. Reston was on the porch, painting a door that he had propped up on two sawhorses. He was wearing project clothes: paint-splattered work pants, an old grey sweatshirt, a Mariners baseball cap. His expression was relaxed, showing obvious pleasure in the task. He looked up when he saw Archie, and then he went back to painting. Of course he knew Archie was a cop. Archie looked like a cop. It didn't matter what he wore. (It wasn't always that way. The first few years, everyone had always been surprised when they found out what he did. He wasn't sure when the change had happened. He'd just noticed one day that he made people nervous.)

When Archie got to the top of the porch stairs, he sat down on the top step and leaned up against the square porch column, a few feet from where Reston stooped over the door. An old wisteria, still leafless, its branches as thick as human wrists, knotted up the post and along the railing.

'Ever read *Lolita*?' Archie asked.

Reston dipped the brush in some white paint and slid it along the door. The wall of paint fumes pushed away every other sensation. 'Who are you?' Reston asked.

Archie opened his badge and held it out. 'I'm Detective Sheridan. I have some questions for you about a former student of yours, Susan Ward.'

Reston glanced at the badge. No one ever bothered to look at it up close. 'She told you we had a relationship,' he said.

'Yep.'

Reston sighed and adjusted his stance so his eyes were level with the surface of the door. He applied more paint, a quick dab and drag along the wood. 'Is this on the record?'

'I'm a police detective,' Archie said. 'I don't do off the record.'

'She's confused.'

'Really.'

A rivulet of paint had collected and Reston smoothed the brush along the wood until the paint was perfectly dispersed. 'You know about her father? He died her freshman year. That was very hard on her. I tried to be kind. And I think she misunderstood my interest.' He frowned. 'Built it up in her mind.'

'You're saying that you never had a sexual relationship,' Archie said.

Reston exhaled. Looked off across the yard for a minute. And then carefully placed the brush on the paint can. The can was on top of a piece of the *Herald*, so that the wet end of the brush hung suspended above a corner of it, a thread of paint pooling on the newsprint. He turned to Archie. 'I kissed her, OK?' He shook his head sorrowfully. 'Once. It was bad judgement on my part. I never let it happen again. When I rejected her, she started a rumour that I'd had an affair with another student. It could have gotten me fired. But there was nothing to it. There was never a formal investigation, because everyone knew it was bogus. Susan was just – ' he searched the air with his hand for the right word – 'damaged. She was distraught by her father's death and lashed out. But I liked her. I always did. She was a charming, pissed-off, talented kid. I understood the pain she was in. And I did everything I could to help her.'

'How incomprehensibly generous of you,' Archie said.

'I'm a good teacher. For what it's worth.' He allowed himself a wry little grin. 'And it's not worth much these days.'

'You ever kiss Lee Robinson?' Archie asked.

Reston drew back, his mouth open. 'Jesus, no. I barely knew her. I was in tech rehearsal when she disappeared. It's all been verified.'

Archie nodded to himself. 'OK then.' He offered Reston a solicitous smile. 'Can I get a glass of water?' It was a lazy way to try to get inside, but if Reston said no, it would at least indicate that he had something to hide.

Reston stared at Archie for a moment. 'OK.' He stood up, brushed some muck off his paint-splattered pants, stamped a few times on the front mat and gestured for Archie to follow him. They walked into the house and Reston led Archie through a small cloakroom, then through the living room and dining room and into the kitchen. The thing that struck Archie was the level of organization. No clutter. Everything in its place. Surfaces clean of debris. No dishes in the sink.

'Ever been married?' Archie asked.

Reston pulled a glass down from a cabinet and filled it at the sink. Above the sink hung a framed print of a blond Varga pin-up girl. 'She left me. Took everything I had,' he said, handing Archie the glass of water.

Archie took a sip. 'Girlfriend?'

'Not currently. My last relationship ended suddenly.'

'Did you murder her?'

'Is that supposed to be funny?'

Archie took another sip. 'No.' He drained the last of the water and handed the glass to Reston, who immediately rinsed it and put it in the dishwasher. Archie noticed another blond Varga girl hanging on the other side of the kitchen. She was wearing tiny shorts and a tight blouse and stood in impossibly high heels, back arched, flirtatious smile on her red lips.

'You like blonds,' Archie observed.

'For Christ's sake,' Reston said, running an anxious hand through his hair. 'What do you want from me? I'm a teacher. I answered your questions. I've already been interviewed by two other cops. I let you in my house.' He looked at Archie plaintively. 'Are you going to arrest me?'

'No.'

Reston planted his hands on his hips. 'Then leave me the hell alone.'

'Fine,' Archie said, starting back towards the porch.

As he moved through the house, Reston a step behind him, Archie searched for any clue to the truth, any insight into the man. The house was a hundred years old, but decorated in a mid-century style. Original light fixtures had been replaced with chrome space-age fixtures that looked as retro as they did futuristic. The dining-room set looked like it was made out of thick plastic. On the table, a bouquet of daffodils sprang out of a round red vase. Archie couldn't tell if the furniture was expensive or if it had all come in a box from Ikea. But he knew enough to know that it was stylish. The living room was less photo-ready. The gold couch appeared to be a thrift-store find. Its gold-cord bottom fringe had detached in places and still hung un-mended. A rose-coloured corduroy chair and ottoman sat next to a space-age lamp. It was as if someone had offered to help Reston redecorate and then they'd had a falling out. It was still far nicer than Archie's squalid rental. The room still had the original built-ins. Archie scanned the shelves. Just a few books, perfectly straight and flush. But Archie knew that spine anywhere. It was *The Last Victim*. It didn't mean anything. A lot of people had that book.

'Look,' Reston was saying. 'Susan was very promiscuous in school. So she may have had a relationship with a teacher. It's very possible. I'm just saying that it wasn't me.'

'OK,' Archie said, distractedly. 'It wasn't you.'

'Where to?' the cabbie asked when Archie got back in the car.

'Wait here,' Archie said. The cab was non-smoking but reeked of old cigarettes and pine deodorizer. No one ever followed the rules. Archie pulled out his cell phone and called Claire. 'I want Reston's alibis double-checked. And I want surveillance on him,' he said. 'And when I say surveillance, I mean I want all entrances covered.' He squinted up at Reston's charming wisteria-covered house. 'I want to know if he even thinks about leaving that house.'

'I'll send Heil and Flannigan.'

'Good,' Archie said, settling back in the cab's sticky vinyl seat. 'I'll wait.'

It was dark by the time Archie made it home. Still no messages. He decided against more coffee and instead drank a beer. Was Susan lying? No. Could she have convinced herself that her story was true? Maybe.

Either way, Gretchen had seen it. He found a sort of solace in the fact that she could see through anybody. It wasn't that there was something intrinsically weak about him.

He stared at the merry face of Gloria Juarez. Another mystery solved; that was something at least. He touched her forehead and then stepped back from where he had tacked her photograph on his bedroom wall.

There were forty-two photographs on his bedroom wall, forty-two murder victims, forty-two families with answers. They stared at him from DMV photos and family snapshots and school pictures. It was a lurid, gruesome spectacle and Archie knew it. He didn't care. He needed to see them all, to give himself a reason why he went back to that prison week after week. It was that or admit to himself that Gretchen's draw was something else entirely. Something far more troubling.

Archie's head throbbed and his body felt heavy and

tired. But it was Sunday night and the week would start and girls would go to school, and that meant that their killer would be hunting.

He emptied the pillbox on his dresser and lined the pills up by type. Then he took off his shirt, undershirt, pants, until he was sitting on the edge of the bed naked. There was a big square mirror above the dresser and he could see his reflection from the mid-chest up. The scars that had so long been a brutal pale purple had lightened to a translucent white. He was almost starting to think of them as part of his body. He let his hand find the heart, the raised tissue sensitive beneath his fingertips, sending shivers down his thighs.

He settled back on the bed and let his memory of her smell wash over him. Lilacs. Her breath against his face. Her touch. His hand found its way lower. He had resisted this for a long time. Until he and Debbie had separated. And then he was alone. And he could think only of Gretchen. Every time he closed his eyes, there she would be, this ghostly presence, wanting him, so beautiful that it took his breath away. Until one day, finally, he gave in, and in his mind he pulled her to him, on to him. He knew it was wrong. That he was sick. That he needed help. But he was beyond help. So what did it matter? It wasn't real.

The pills grinned at him from the dresser. There weren't enough to kill him. But he had enough in the bathroom. He liked to think about that sometimes at night. It was cold comfort.

34

Susan had ground her teeth all night. She could tell the moment she woke up, because she could barely move her jaw, barely open her mouth, and her teeth felt like she'd spent the night chewing gravel. She held a heating pad against her face until she felt her sore muscles loosen and the pain in her face subside. But the heat left her face looking raw and sunburned.

It was only just getting light outside, and the forecast in the paper was a row of smiling yellow suns on squares of blue sky. Sure enough, a glance beyond the loft's wall of glass revealed fragments of clear blue behind the Pearl District's skyline of brick, glass, stone and steel. Susan was unimpressed. People didn't appreciate rain until it was gone.

She sat on her bed and watched the pedestrians struggle by with their paper coffee cups down below. She should have been working. The next story was due tomorrow. But the digital recorder that Archie had recovered for her still sat on her bedside table, and she had yet to listen to the recording of her encounter with

Gretchen Lowell. The thought of it made her a little sick to her stomach.

Claire rang the doorbell at exactly eight a.m. Next to her was Anne Boyd.

Despite the unseasonably warm forecast, Susan was wearing what she thought of as her TV-cop clothes: black pants, a crisp black button-down shirt, and an honest-to-God tan trench coat. She didn't care if it was going to be sixty-five degrees; she was wearing that coat. Claire was dressed, per usual, as if she had just come down off the mountain, and Anne was wearing a zebra-print blouse, black pants and leopard-print boots, and she had about a dozen gold bracelets squeezed on each wrist. 'I love your boots,' Susan said.

'I know,' Anne said. 'They're fabulous.'

'Yeah,' said Claire with a sigh. 'You two are going to get along fine.' She introduced Anne and Susan and the three women headed downstairs to where Claire's city-issued Chevy Caprice was parked.

The plan was to check on the security at the city's ten public high schools. Many parents were keeping their daughters at home; all kids were encouraged not to walk to or from school, or if they did, to have a buddy. The whole city was on edge. The anticipation was so palpable that it felt to Susan as if people were actually willing another girl to be taken so that they could watch it on the news. A good kidnapping and murder made for excellent televised entertainment as long as it didn't pre-empt anything more interesting.

They drove to Roosevelt High first. Claire had a paper cup of coffee from the place next door to Susan's building, and the nutty aroma filled the car, making Susan's mouth water. She got her notebook out and set it on her lap. She hated riding in the back. It reminded her of being a child. She unlocked her seat belt so she could lean forward between the seats, the better to ask questions.

'Uh-uh-uh,' Claire chided. 'Seat belt.'

Susan sat back with a heavy sigh and resnapped the belt in place. The front seats were light blue cloth, but the back seat was dark blue vinyl. Easier to clean up if someone you were transporting started vomiting. 'So this guy,' she said to Anne. 'You think he's a nut job, or what?'

'My professional opinion?' Anne said, looking out of the window. 'I think he may have an issue or two.'

'He's going to kill another girl?' Susan asked.

Anne leaned around to look at Susan, her expression sceptical. 'Why would he stop?'

Roosevelt was a large brick school with white pillars, a half-acre of green lawn and a steeple. It looked a bit like Monticello. Three patrol cars were out front.

'They should have called this one Jefferson,' Susan joked.

Claire rolled her eyes. 'I'm going to go check on things,' she announced. 'You guys want to wait here?'

Susan, seeing an opportunity for some one-on-one time with Anne, jumped at the opportunity. 'Sure,' she said. She unclasped her seat belt and leaned forward between the front seats so that she was inches away from Anne.

Claire got out of the car and walked over to one of the patrol cars.

'So you think he works at one of the schools?' Susan asked Anne.

Anne extracted a Diet Coke from her large purse and opened it. A tiny spray of sticky brown liquid shot out in a two-inch diameter. 'I don't know.' She gave Susan a look. 'And don't start with me about the Diet Coke. I know. I just have one a day. To kick-start my morning.'

'I think warm Diet Coke is delicious,' Susan lied. She pushed ahead. 'So do you like profiling?'

'Yeah.' Anne smiled and took a sip of the Coke. 'I'm good at it most of the time. And every workday is different.'

'How did you get into it?'

'I went to med school. I wanted to be a paediatrician. I thought they were so cool. They were always the nicest docs at the hospital. No ego. Weren't in it for the money.'

'So you wanted to be a paediatrician so you could hang out with other paediatricians?' Susan asked.

Anne laughed and her bracelets jingled. 'Basically.' She leaned her head back on the headrest and looked thoughtfully at Susan. 'The first day of my paediatrics rotation, I diagnosed a kid with lymphoma. Stage four. She was seven years old. Completely adorable. One of those kids with old souls, you know? I was devastated, and by devastated, I mean crying-in-the-bathroom devastated.' Anne was quiet for a minute, lost in thought. Susan could hear her soda fizzing. Then she shrugged. 'So I decided to go into psychiatry. My husband's people are in Virginia. He got a job there and I needed one and Quantico was looking to train some women in the dark arts. Turned out I wasn't bad at it.'

'Profiling seems like a weird field to end up in if you wanted to get away from death.'

'Not death,' she said. She licked her thumb and ran it over a tiny stain of soda spray on her black slacks. 'Pity.' She glanced up out the window. A kid flew by on a skateboard. She turned back to Susan. 'The victims we deal with are already dead. We do what we do to prevent other deaths. We catch killers. And I don't feel sorry for them.'

Susan thought of Gretchen Lowell. 'What makes a person do this sort of thing?'

'There was this study of prisoners serving time for breaking and entering. They asked them all the same question: "Would you rather run into a dog or a person with a gun?" You know what the majority of them said?' She spun the soda can slowly in her palm. 'The person with a gun. The dog won't hesitate. The dog will rip your throat out. Every time. Eight times out of ten, you can wrestle the gun right out of the person's hands or just walk away. Know why?'

'Because it's hard to shoot someone.'

Anne's black eyes were electric. 'Exactly. And that's broken in our guy. I don't think he works for the school district. I hope he does. Because if he does, we'll catch him. If he doesn't, I don't know.'

'But how does it get broken?'

She made a small toasting motion with the can. 'Nature, nurture, a combination. Take your pick.'

Susan hooked her clasped hands over her knee and leaned in even closer. 'But someone can break it for you, right? Like Gretchen Lowell did. How did she do that? How did she get people to kill for her?'

'She's a master manipulator. Psychopaths very often are. She chose particularly vulnerable men.'

'And she tortured them?'

'No,' Anne said. 'Much more foolproof. She used sex.'

Claire suddenly appeared at the car door. Her cheeks were scarlet. 'The fucker took another girl last night.'

35

Addy Jackson's family lived in a two-storey adobe house on a terraced hill on the corner of a busy street in south-east Portland. The house was painted pink and had a red-tiled roof and it looked as out of place surrounded by its Craftsman neighbours as it now did surrounded by police cars. Susan noticed a shiny black helicopter with the Channel 12 news logo on the side already circling overhead.

Claire took the cement steps that jack-knifed up the hillside to the house two at a time, followed by Anne and finally Susan. It was already getting too warm for the trench coat, but Susan kept it on so she could have her notebook at the ready in one of the deep pockets. She felt sick to her stomach at the notion of walking into a budding family tragedy and she didn't want to make herself feel worse by walking around clutching a reporter's notebook that screamed *Hello I'm with the media I'm here to exploit you.* I am a serious journalist, she told herself in an effort to mollify her growing unease. A. Serious. Journalist.

The house was full of cops. Susan saw Archie in

the living room on one knee in front of a stricken couple who sat holding hands on a small sofa. They looked at him as if he were the only person in the world, as if he could save them. Susan remembered seeing her mother look at Susan's father's oncologist with that very same expression. But the case was terminal then, too.

She looked away. The room was beautiful, full of mission-style furniture and stained glass and jewel-toned Deco velvet. Someone had meticulously stripped and refinished the wood moulding, which curved around built-in shelf nooks and over the arched doors. When she looked back at Archie, he said something to the parents, touching the mother lightly on the arm, and stood up and walked over to the entryway.

'She was gone this morning,' he said, his voice barely above a whisper. 'Last they saw her was last night around ten. The bedroom window's broken. Parents didn't hear anything. Their bedroom is upstairs. Nothing missing but the girl. The crime-scene investigators are in there now.'

He looked better than the day before, Susan noticed, more alert. That was a good sign. Then she remembered what Debbie had said about how he would sleep so well when he got home from seeing Gretchen.

'How'd he know which room was hers?' asked Claire.

A cop wearing a crime-scene-investigation jacket

walked by and Archie stepped out of the way to let him pass. 'Curtains were open. She was in there doing homework last night with the lights on. Maybe he was watching. Or maybe he knows her.'

'We sure it's our guy?' Anne asked, her face hard. 'This doesn't fit.'

Archie motioned for them to follow him into the dining room, where he removed a framed photograph from the wall and handed it to Anne. It was a photograph of a teenage girl with brown hair and wide-set eyes.

'Jesus,' Claire said under her breath.

'Why would he change his MO?' mused Anne.

'I was hoping you could tell me,' said Archie.

'Too much security at the schools,' Anne guessed. 'He's worried he won't be able to get to his victims. Maybe he followed her home. But this seems really risky. He's panicking. In the big picture, it's good news. It means he's getting less careful. We're closer.'

Susan leaned back on her heels and looked through the entryway into the living room, where the parents still sat, motionless on the sofa, another detective perched across from them on an ottoman, notebook in hand.

'What school did she go to?' Claire asked.

Archie jerked his head towards Susan. 'Her *alma mater*.'

'Cleveland?' Susan said, stomach dropping. She knew then, in a horrible rush of certainty, that Archie had confronted Paul. Of course he had. 'You don't think—'

'It wasn't Reston,' Archie told her. 'He was under surveillance from six on. Didn't leave the house.'

Susan's jaw ached again. Archie had put Paul under surveillance, made him a suspect, based on her dramatic performance at the prison. She mentally kicked herself for opening her big mouth. She shouldn't have let Gretchen get to her. She should never have even taken the story. Now there was no stopping what she had set in motion. 'You're watching Paul? Based on what I told you yesterday?'

'He fits the profile better than anyone right now. Except for his unerring ability to have an alibi at the time of the crimes.' Archie turned to Claire. 'Check in with our tail on Evan Kent. Then call Cleveland. Find out if anyone showed up today covered in blood and wearing a ski mask.' He smiled wanly. 'Or, you know, anything out of the ordinary.'

Claire nodded, pulled her cell phone off her belt, and walked outside to make the calls.

Susan stole another look at Archie. 'You went to see him,' she said.

Archie snapped his pen shut and dropped it in his coat pocket. 'Of course,' he said. 'What did you think I'd do?'

'What did he say?'

'He denied it.'

Susan felt her face flush. 'Good,' she said, her voice

faltering just a little. 'He's protecting himself. That's good.' And then: 'I told you he'd deny it.'

Claire reappeared. 'Kent's at home. But Dan McCallum didn't show today at Cleveland.'

Archie looked at his watch. 'How late is he?' he asked.

'Mr McCallum?' Susan said. 'There's no way.'

Claire ignored her. 'His first class started ten minutes ago. He didn't call in sick, just didn't show up. The school called his house and no one's answering.'

'I think that might be suspicious,' Archie said.

36

Archie knocked on the door of McCallum's 1950s bungalow so hard that he thought his knuckles might split. It was a diminutive one-storey tan-brick house set in the middle of an expansive and obsessively tended yard. A row of rosebushes, just returning after being cut back for winter, lined the paved walkway to the wide cement stoop at the front of the house. The door, in a lonely splash of personality, was painted a glossy red. A doorbell that looked like it had not been operational since shortly after the house was built was covered with a weathered piece of electrician's tape. Monday's *Oregon Herald*, untouched in its plastic sleeve, still lay in front of the door. 'Dan?' Archie called. He knocked again. The door had a large glass window, but it was curtained and Archie couldn't see more than a sliver of the interior of the house. He motioned with two fingers for the Hardy Boys to go around to the back door. Henry stood back on the steps. Claire stood beside Archie. Susan, attired in a yellow vest with the words RIDE ALONG emblazoned in black on the back, had wedged herself next to Claire.

Archie gestured for Susan to stand back, which she did. Then he drew his gun and knocked again. 'Dan, it's the police. Open up.' Nothing.

He tried the door. It was locked. A grey tabby appeared on the porch and snaked her way between Archie's legs. 'Hello, beautiful,' he said. Then he noticed the faint trail of pawprints she'd left behind. He knelt down and looked at the prints, pale red against the glossy mud-green paint of the stoop.

'It's blood,' he said to Claire. 'You want to get it?'

He stood up and stepped back as Claire shielded her face with her elbow and gave the door window a hard whack with the handle of her gun. The window splintered and broke into five pieces which slid from the framing and fell to the inside floor in an explosion of shattered glass. The moment the glass was broken, the stench of death hit them. They all recognized it. Archie reached inside and unlocked the door. He swung it open and raised his gun.

He carried a Smith & Wesson .38 Special. He preferred a revolver to an automatic. They were reliable and didn't require as much upkeep. Archie didn't like guns. He'd never had to fire his off the range. And he didn't want to spend half his waking hours at the kitchen table cleaning his service weapon. But a .38 wasn't as powerful as a 9mm, and Archie found his loyalty suddenly wavering.

'Dan,' he called out. 'This is the police. Are you in here? We're coming in.' Nothing.

The front door opened into a living room, which led into a kitchen. Archie could see pawprints straying diagonally across the linoleum. He turned to Susan. 'Stay here,' he said in his most commanding voice. Then he nodded to Claire and Henry. 'You ready?' They both nodded back.

He moved inside.

Archie loved this part. Even all his pills couldn't compete with a natural surge of adrenalin and endorphins. His body felt alive with energy. His heart rate and breathing increased; his muscles tightened. He was never more alert. He moved through the house, taking in every detail. Bookcases filled the far side of the living room. The shelves were stacked with books as well as other objects – old coffee cups and papers and what looked like mail that had been tucked into any available cranny. Four easy chairs of varying pedigrees and shades of green sat around a square coffee table, which was layered with newspapers. Framed line-drawings of tall ships hung on one wall, one on top of the next. Archie moved through the hallway, his back against the wall, with Claire following so close behind that he could hear her breathing. Henry followed behind Claire. Archie called out again, 'Dan? It's the police.' Nothing.

He turned the corner, gun raised, and immediately saw the source of the bloody pawprints.

Dan McCallum lay cheek-down on the oak kitchen table, his head resting in a pool of thick blood. One arm was stretched across the table; the other was folded at the elbow, the gun still in his hand. He was facing Archie, eyes open, but there was no question that he had been dead much of the night.

'Fuck,' Archie sighed. He reholstered his gun, threaded his fingers behind his neck, and walked in a small circle, willing himself to let go of his frustration. If McCallum was their killer, it was over. But where was the girl? He snapped back to the present. 'Call it in,' he said to Claire.

He could hear Claire on the radio behind him as he approached the body. Careful not to step in the blood that had pooled on the floor, he squatted beside the corpse. Archie recognized the gun in McCallum's hand right away. It was a .38. The heart can continue to pump for up to two minutes with a brain injury like that, which explained the extensive bleeding.

Archie had once found the body of a man who'd punched his fist through a plate-glass window after an argument with his wife. He'd severed the artery in his arm and bled to death because she had stormed out of the house and he was too proud to call an ambulance. The blood had sprayed in a wide arc across the kitchen when the artery was severed and then continued to throb out of his body despite the several dish-towels he'd tried to use as tourniquets. His wife had returned the next morning and called 911. When Archie got there, he found the man dead, slumped against a kitchen cabinet. Blood splattered the yellow kitchen curtains and the white walls and spread across the entire kitchen floor. Archie hadn't known that one body could produce that much blood.

Different kitchen. Archie leaned in close to examine the muzzle imprint of the contact wound near the mouth and the exit wound in the back of the head. A .38 will go right through the skull, whereas a .22 will bounce around for a while. McCallum's hazel eyes stared sightless, the pupils dilated, the lids pulling back in full rigor. His jaw, too, had tightened, giving his mouth a disapproving grimace. The skin of his face was bruised with livor mortis, like he'd laid his head down to rest after a bad fight. He was wearing red sweatpants and what appeared to be a Cleveland Warriors sweatshirt. His feet were clad only in white sweat socks, their toes wet with blood. There was no coffee cup on the table.

Archie's gaze returned to the body. Pawprints indicated where the cat had ambled across the table, leaving in her wake blood dusted with a fine grey cat hair. The brown hair above McCallum's left temple was flattened and wet where the cat appeared to have licked him. Poor thing. Archie tracked the pawprints from the table to a flap in the back door.

He stood up. It wasn't as easy as it used to be. Henry had opened the back door and the Hardy Boys stood waiting, along with Susan Ward. They were waiting for him to say something. 'Turn this place upside-down,' Archie said. 'Maybe we'll get lucky and she'll still be here.' But he didn't believe it. 'And call Animal Control,' he added. 'Someone's going to have to take care of that cat.'

37

It seemed to Susan that every cop in the city had descended on Dan McCallum's small house. Canary-yellow crime-scene tape zig-zagged around the yard to keep the growing throng of spectators at bay. In the distance, TV reporters positioned themselves in front of the action for their live-remote reports. Susan was sitting on a wrought-iron bench on McCallum's front stoop, smoking a cigarette She had her cell phone pressed against her ear, and was explaining the whole situation to Ian, when they found Kristy Mathers's bike.

A patrol cop searching the garage discovered it leaning up against the wall, hidden under a blue tarp. A yellow girl's bike, with a banana seat and a busted chain. The cops all gathered around it, scratching their heads and looking taciturn, while newspaper photographers snapped digital pictures and neighbours took snapshots with their camera phones.

Susan thought of Addy Jackson and where she was right then and felt sick. She was surely dead, half buried in some river muck somewhere. Charlene Wood from

Channel 8 stood in front of the house, her back to Susan, reporting live. Susan couldn't hear what she was saying but could imagine the cheesy dramatic graphics and local news hysteria. The state of humanity, it seemed to Susan recently, was looking pretty bleak.

After a while, Archie left the circle of cops and came over to where Susan sat.

'You not covering this?' he asked, sitting down next to her on the bench.

She shook her head. 'It's news. They want a reporter. They're sending Parker over.' She bent her knees, lifted them to her chest, wrapped her arms around her legs and took a drag off her cigarette. The RIDE ALONG vest sat in a heap beside her. 'So he killed himself?'

'Looks like it.'

'I didn't see a note.'

'Most suicides don't leave notes,' Archie said. 'You'd be surprised.'

'Really?'

Archie rubbed the back of his neck with one hand and looked out into the front yard. 'I think it's hard to know what to say.'

'I saw him the other day,' Susan said sadly. 'At Cleveland.'

Archie raised his eyebrows. 'Did he say anything?'

'Just small talk,' Susan said, ashing her cigarette off the side of the stoop.

'You're ashing on my crime scene,' Archie said.

'Oh shit,' Susan said. 'I'm sorry.' She ground her cigarette out on her notebook, folded a piece of the paper carefully around it, and deposited the package in her purse. She was aware of Archie watching her, but she couldn't bring herself to look at him. Instead, she looked at her hands. The skin around the small wound on her finger from the wineglass was red, like it was getting infected. 'Don't you want to ask me?'

'What?' he asked.

She lifted the finger to her mouth and sucked on it for a moment, a flash of salty skin and tinny dried blood. 'If it really happened.'

He shook his head, a tiny movement, barely noticeable. 'No.'

Naturally. He would be gallant about it. Susan wished she hadn't ground out the cigarette. She wanted something to do with her hands. She fidgeted with the sash of her trench coat. 'McCallum coached my Knowledge Bowl team. I quit the day before state. I was the only one who knew anything about geography.'

Archie hesitated. 'This thing with Reston. I'm going to report it to the school. He shouldn't be teaching, at the very least.'

Susan steeled herself. 'I lied. I made the whole thing up.'

Archie closed his eyes sadly. 'Susan, don't do this.'

'Please just leave it alone,' Susan begged him. 'I already feel like such a fool. I'm such a fucking moron when it comes to men.' She looked Archie in the eye.

'I had a crush on him. And I made the affair up. I wanted it to happen. But it didn't.' She held his gaze, her expression pleading. 'So leave it alone, OK? Seriously. I'm a fuck-up. You have no idea.'

He shook his head. 'Susan—'

'I made it up,' she said again.

Archie was motionless.

'Archie,' she said carefully. 'Please believe me. It was all a story. I'm a liar.' She stressed each word, each syllable, wanting him to understand. 'I've always been a liar.'

He nodded slowly. 'OK.'

She had fucked everything up. Royally. As usual. 'Don't feel bad. I'm a lost cause.' Susan tried to smile at Archie, but felt her eyes fill. She rolled them and laughed. 'My mother thinks that I just need to find a nice boy with a hybrid car.'

Archie seemed to consider this. 'Good gas mileage is an important attribute in a potential mate.' He smiled gingerly at Susan and then gazed back out into the yard, where Charlene Wood had just finished her live shot. 'I've got to get back to work, but I'll get someone to give you a ride home.'

'It's OK. I called Ian.'

Archie stood and then turned back towards Susan. 'You sure you're OK?'

She squinted up at the blue sky. 'Do you think this sunshine will ever break?'

'It'll rain,' Archie said. 'It always does.'

38

Archie was standing in the back yard with Henry and Anne when the mayor arrived with half a page of handwritten notes, ready for a press conference. Like the front yard, the back yard was mowed to within an inch of its life. It took a serious commitment to keep a lawn that manicured during the rainy season. A small ready-made aluminium shed sat in the back corner, its contents removed by police and stacked around its perimeter. A cedar fence with a lattice top ran along the property line. Archie saw the mayor spot him and head over. He was wearing a black suit and tie and his silver hair was plastered into place. Buddy had always been able to pull off the suit-and-tie thing. The first words out of the mayor's mouth when he reached Archie were 'This the guy?'

'Looks like it,' Archie said.

Buddy took a pair of black Ray-Ban sunglasses out of his interior coat pocket and put them on. 'Where's the girl?'

Archie glanced at Anne. 'In the river, probably.'

'Shit,' the mayor said under his breath. He took a

deep breath and nodded a few times, as if listening to a pep talk only he could hear. 'OK. So, let's focus on the fact he's off the streets.' He looked at Archie over his sunglasses. 'You look like shit, Archie. Why don't you throw some water on your face or something before we get started?'

Archie forced a smile. 'Sure.' He shot a wry look at Henry and Anne and walked back into the house.

Inside McCallum's kitchen, a voice said, 'You Sheridan?'

Archie had to stop and take a few slow breaths to acclimatize to the ripe odour. 'Yeah,' he said.

A young black man with shoulder-length dreads, wearing a white Tyvek suit over his street clothes, sat on the kitchen counter, swinging his legs and writing on a clipboard. 'I'm Lorenzo Robbins.'

'You're with the ME's office?'

'Yeah,' he said. 'Look, man, I just wanted to let you know that there are a few issues with your dead guy.'

'A few issues?' Archie asked.

Robbins shrugged and wrote something on the clipboard. 'A thirty-eight isn't a small gun,' he said.

'Right,' Archie said slowly.

'It's got a kick. With this sort of central-nervous-system injury, you expect to see one of two things. Either the gun's a few feet away or your guy suffers a cadaveric spasm, right, and his hand's frozen around the weapon.' He held a clenched latex-gloved hand out to demonstrate.

Archie turned and looked at where McCallum still lay face-down on the table. The gun was gone, already bagged. 'A death grip.'

Robbins let his hand drop. 'Yeah. If the body's fresh, you can tell. The hand's frozen. Body's not. But when I got here, he was in full rigor. Maybe a cadaveric spasm kept that gun in his hand. It's possible. Thing is, death grips are kinda rare. Something you see more in the movies.'

'So what does that mean?'

'Maybe nothing,' Robbins said. He started writing on the clipboard again. 'He's got a nice muzzle imprint, so the gun was definitely against his skin when it was fired.' He scribbled something else. 'Then again, there wasn't any blow-back on his hand. There was blow-back on the gun. But not on his hand.'

Archie reached out and plucked Robbins's pen out of his fist. 'Are you saying that this wasn't suicide? That someone shot him and put the gun in his hand?'

'No,' Robbins said. He looked at where Archie held his pen out, then at Archie. 'I'm saying that death grips are pretty rare and he didn't have blow-back on his hand. It was probably suicide. We'll cut him up and have a look-see. I'm just giving you a preview. Make it more exciting.'

'Shit,' Archie muttered, leaning his head back in frustration. The ceiling was white. A single globe light fixture hung over the middle of the room. The light was off. 'Did you turn off the light?' Archie asked.

Robbins looked up at the light fixture. 'Do I look like it's my first day? 'Cause it's not.'

Archie spun around and poked his head out of the back door. 'Anyone turn off the light in here?' he hollered. The cops in the back yard looked at one another. No one volunteered.

He shut the door and turned back to Robbins. 'So if we accept the premise that no one fucked up and hit the switch—'

Robbins took his pen from Archie's hand and casually slipped it behind his clipboard clamp. 'He probably didn't shoot himself in the dark. Sunset's around six, six-thirty. Sorta indicates that he did it before then.' He looked down at the corpse. 'But not by much.' He smiled. His brown skin made his teeth look especially white. 'Or maybe one of the dozen cops who've been through here turned off the light.'

Archie could taste the sour burn of stomach acid on his tongue. Addy Jackson had gone to bed at ten.

'You feel OK?' Robbins asked.

'I feel terrific,' Archie said. 'Never better.' He found an antacid loose in his pocket and put it in his mouth. Its sweet chalky taste was muted by the smell of rotting flesh.

39

'How does it feel?' Archie asks. The codeine had made things better. He is only barely present now. The wounds on his abdomen are red and hard with fluid. He can feel the burning pain of the infections, but he doesn't mind it. He doesn't even mind the heavy smell of decomposition that suffocates everything. Sweat clings to his clammy skin and his limbs lie lifeless, but to him, his body feels loose and warm, his blood gelatinous. There is Archie. And there is Gretchen. And there is the basement. It is like they are in a waiting room for death. So he makes conversation.

Gretchen sits in her chair next to his bed, her hand resting on his. 'Were you there when your children were born?'

'Yes.'

Her look grows distant as she tries to articulate her thoughts. 'I think it must be like that. Intense and beautiful and wretched.' She leans towards him until he can feel her breath against his cheek, and then brings her lips to his ear. 'You think they were random.

But they weren't. There was always a chemistry. I would feel it right away.' Her breath tickles his earlobe; her hand tightens around his. 'A physical connection. A death spark.' She turns and looks at their hands folded together, his wrist still bound by the leather strap. 'Like they wanted it. I would pluck them out of the universe. Hold their life in my hand. What astounds me is that people get up and go to work and come home and they don't ever kill anyone. I feel sorry for them because they aren't alive. They will never really know what it's like to be human.'

'Why did you use the men?'

She gazes at him flirtatiously. 'It was better when my lovers did it. I liked to watch them kill for me.'

'Because then you had power over two people.'

'Yes.'

Archie lets his eyes fall on the corpse on the floor. He can't see the head from his vantage point, only a hand, and he has watched the flesh darken and swell until it is unrecognizable, a dead bird at the end of a sleeve. 'Who's on the floor?' Archie asks.

She gives the corpse an uninterested glance. 'Daniel. I found him online.'

'Why did you kill him?'

'I didn't need him any more,' she says, running a delicate finger over the skin of Archie's forearm. 'I had you. You're special, darling. Don't you understand that?'

'Number two hundred. The bicentennial.'

'It's more than that.'

He is beginning to think he understands her. As if the further he gets from his life, the more she becomes clear to him. Had she been born? Or made? 'Who made you drink drain cleaner, Gretchen?'

She laughs, but the amusement is unconvincing. 'My father? Is that the answer?'

'Do I remind you of him?' Archie asks.

He thinks he sees her flinch. 'Yes.'

'End this,' he says fruitlessly. 'Get some help.'

Her hand flutters in the air for a moment. 'I'm not the way I am because of him. I'm not a violent person.'

'I know,' Archie says. 'You need help.'

She picks up the scalpel, still stained with his blood, from the tray and holds it against his chest. Then she begins to carve. He can barely feel it. The blade is sharp and she is not cutting deeply. He watches as his ugly bruised skin splits beneath the blade, the blood holding for a moment, oxygenating, before it flows bright red from the wound. That's the main sensation: the blood running down his sides, leaving trails of crimson that pool under his torso on the sweat-soaked white sheet. He watches her, her small brow furrowed with concentration, doodle on his flesh. 'There,' she says finally. 'It's a heart.'

'Who's it for?' he asks. 'I thought we were going to bury the body. Keep them guessing.'

'It's for you,' Gretchen says brightly. 'It's for

you, darling. It's my heart.' She glances sadly down at Archie's swollen abdomen. 'Of course it will get infected. It's Daniel. His corpse has desterilized everything. I don't have the proper antibiotics for a staph infection. The antibiotics I'm giving you will slow it down. But I don't have anything strong enough to kill it.'

Archie smiles. 'You worried about me?'

She nods. 'You have to fight it. You have to stay alive.'

'So you can kill me with drain cleaner?'

'Yes.'

'You're crazy.'

'I'm not crazy,' she insists, her voice a thin reed of desperation. 'I'm very sane. And if you die before I let you, I will kill your children, darling. Ben and Sara.' She holds the scalpel easily, as if it is an extension of her body, another finger. 'Ben is in kindergarten at Clark Elementary School. I will slice him up. You will do what I say. You will stay alive until I tell you. Understand?'

He nods.

'Say it.'

'Yes.'

'I'm not trying to be mean,' she says, her face softening. 'It's just that I'm worried.'

'OK,' he says.

'Ask me anything. I'll tell you anything you want to know about the murders.'

His throat and abdomen throb. Swallowing has become excruciating. 'I don't care any more, Gretchen.'

Her mouth falters. She almost looks a little hurt. 'You're the head of my task force. You don't want to take my confession?'

He stares past her, at the ceiling: the pipes, the ducts, the fluorescent light panels. 'I'm trying to fight my staph infection.'

'Do you want to watch the news? I could bring a TV down.'

'No.' The thought of seeing his widow on the television news fills him with dread.

'Come on. There's a vigil for you today. It will cheer you up.'

'No.' His mind searches for something to distract her with. 'Let me drink the drain cleaner.' He gives her a pleading look. It isn't faked. 'Come on.' He is so tired. 'I want to.'

'You want to?' She smiles with satisfaction.

'I want to drink the drain cleaner,' Archie says emphatically. 'Feed it to me.'

She rises and makes the preparations, humming softly under her breath. In the codeine haze, he is unattached to any of it. It is like watching it all happen in a rear-view mirror. When she returns, they repeat the exercise from the previous day. This time the pain is more intense, and Archie vomits on to the bed.

'It's blood,' Gretchen observes, pleased. 'The poison is eating through your oesophagus.'

Good, thinks Archie. *Good.*

He is dying. Gretchen has him on a morphine drip because he can't keep the pills down any more. He is coughing blood. He cannot remember the last time she left his side. She just sits there, holding a white washcloth to his face to catch the blood when he coughs, the drool of saliva he can't swallow. He can smell the corpse and he can hear her voice, but that is it. There is no other sensation. No pain. No taste. His vision has narrowed to a circle a few feet around his head. He is aware of her when she touches him, her blond hair, her hand, her bare forearm. There are no more lilacs.

Gretchen puts her face next to his and gently turns his head so that he can see her, her face shimmering and folding in the light. 'It's time again,' she says.

He blinks slowly. He is bathed in soft, thick, warm blackness. He doesn't even register what she has said until he feels the spoon in his mouth. This time, he cannot swallow the poison. She pours water down his throat after it, but he chokes and vomits all the fluid up. His entire body spasms, sending a black wall of pain from his groin to his shoulders. He fights for oxygen, and in his alarm his consciousness is forced back into his body and all of his senses come horribly alive. He screams.

Gretchen holds his head against the bed, her forehead pressed hard against his cheek. He lurches against her hand, screaming as loudly as he can, letting all the pain and fear drive out of his body through his lungs. The effort tears at his throat and the screams turn into choking and the choking to dry heaves. When his breathing returns to normal, Gretchen looks up, and slowly begins to wipe the sweat and blood and tears off his face.

'I'm sorry,' he gasps stupidly.

She sits, her attention fixed on him for a time, and then stands up and walks away. When she returns, she has a hypodermic. 'I think you're ready now,' she says. Gretchen holds the hypodermic up for him to see. 'It's digitalis. It will stop your heart. Then you'll die.' She touches his face tenderly with the back of her hand. 'Don't worry. I'll stay here with you until it's over.'

He is relieved. He watches as she injects the digitalis into his IV tube and then takes her seat at his deathbed, one hand resting lightly on his pale knuckles, the other on his forehead.

He does not think about Debbie or Ben or Sara or Detective Archie Sheridan or the Beauty Killer Task Force. He can't. He just concentrates on her. Gretchen is all there is. His only thread. If he can stay focused, he thinks, he will not be afraid. His heartbeat increases, coming faster and faster, until it loses all rhythm to him – so foreign and wrong that it doesn't even feel like his heart any more. It is just someone knocking, panicked, desperate, on a faraway door. Gretchen's face is the last thing he sees when the sudden pain seizes him by the chest and neck. The pressure grows. Then there is a blinding, excruciating, white burn, and finally peace.

40

Ian pulled into a parking spot in front of Susan's building. Susan picked a strand of ginger pet hair off her black pants, feeling it between her fingers for a moment before she let it float on to the floor mat below. Ian's Subaru smelled like Armor All and his wife's Welsh Corgi. Chic twentysomethings slumped in the afternoon sun outside the coffeehouse on the corner, smoking cigarettes and thumbing through alt weeklies. They worked as waiters or at galleries, or didn't have jobs, and always seemed to have a great deal of disposable time. Susan envied them. They were like some marvellous high-school clique that Susan's reputation kept her from joining. She looked up at the old brewery building with its large windows like yawning mouths. Its stone facade seemed embarrassed by all the glass and steel that surrounded it.

'Do you want to come up?' she asked Ian.

Ian made an apologetic face. 'I've got copy to look at.'

'Later?' Susan asked, carefully shaving the edge of neediness off her voice.

'Sharon's having people over for dinner,' Ian

explained. 'I've got to go right home after work. She's making some kind of meal that involves boiled chard. I said I'd stop and pick up cheese.'

'Boiled chard and cheese? It must be important.'

'Tomorrow?' Ian asked.

'Forget it.'

'No,' Ian said awkwardly. 'I mean you'll have the story for me tomorrow, right? The next instalment?'

Susan picked another dog hair off her pants and flicked it onto the floor mat. 'Oh, right. Sure.'

'By noon, OK? Seriously.'

'No problem,' Susan said. Then she got out of the car and walked inside.

Archie walked outside into the back yard. The mayor was nowhere to be seen, presumably off in a quiet corner preparing for the press conference. The Hardy Boys were standing with their hands on their hips in the door of the garage, and Anne was now standing with Claire near the shed. Archie saw Henry emerge from the garage with McCallum's grey cat in his arms, and he waved him over.

'They fingerprint the bike yet?' Archie asked.

The cat nuzzled its head under Henry's chin and purred. 'Yeah. It's clean.'

'Totally?' Archie asked.

'Yep,' Henry said. The cat gave Archie a suspicious, doubtful glance. 'Wiped down. Not a print on it.'

Archie chewed on his bottom lip and stood with his hands on his hips, facing the house. It didn't make sense. Why go to the trouble of wiping the bike down and then go ahead and keep it? If you were worried about evidence, why keep what amounted to a smoking gun? 'Why would he do that, do you think?' Archie mused aloud.

Henry shrugged. 'Neat freak?'

'They print the gun?'

'Not yet.' Henry gave the cat an absent-minded scratch on the head. 'They'll do that back at the lab, after they've picked the brain matter off.'

'Good idea,' Archie said.

The cat began the task of licking Henry's neck clean. 'You seen Animal Control?' he asked hopefully.

'Nope.'

Archie hopped off the stoop and walked over to where Anne and Claire stood near the shed in the corner of the back yard. A couple of toddlers, unimpressed by the police activity and the helicopters and the news vans, chased each other in circles beyond the fence. Their mother stood in the middle of her yard, hugging her arms and watching the show. Was he crazy to think that McCallum wasn't the guy? Anne and Claire were in the throes of conversation, but Archie didn't have time for niceties. He needed Anne's profiling skills. And he knew that she needed him to still need her.

'Does McCallum fit?' he asked.

Claire and Anne stopped talking, surprised at the interruption. Claire's eyes widened. Anne drew her jaw back slightly, then she tilted her head and said, 'Yes.' She stopped herself. The lines around her eyes deepened and she added, 'Except he's not *quite* right.'

'Not quite right?' Archie repeated.

She made a helpless gesture. 'If you were a fifteen-year-old girl and Dan McCallum offered to give you a ride, would you go with him? He looked like a toad. He wasn't well liked. And how did he know the girls at the other schools?'

Archie thought of the handsome custodian, Evan Kent.

'Jesus Christ,' Claire said. 'You think it isn't suicide.'

They all looked at one another, waiting.

Archie caught the grey cat streaking through the back yard in the periphery of his vision.

He raised his eyebrows apologetically. 'I don't know,' he said. 'I don't know.' He saw Mike Flannigan and called him over to join them. He'd pulled the Hardy Boys off Reston when they'd found McCallum's body. Now he was kicking himself for it. 'Anyone else not show up at Cleveland today?' he asked Flannigan.

Flannigan was chewing a fresh piece of gum that made him smell like he'd sucked down a tube of spearmint toothpaste. It was something they taught you at the academy: chewing gum to mask the odour of death. 'No,' Flannigan said. 'But that janitor you've got Josh tailing just hopped a train to Seattle with a backpack and a guitar case. And another thing's a little weird.' He jabbed his thumb at the house. 'We searched the house, and for an unpopular teacher, he sure dug his students.'

'What do you mean?' Archie asked.

Flannigan unwrapped another piece of gum and put it in his mouth. 'On the bookcases in the front room, he's got every yearbook for the past twenty years,' he said. He snorted and gave the gum a chew. 'That's quite a memory walk for a guy who supposedly hated his job.'

Archie raised a questioning eyebrow at Anne. She frowned a little and turned to Flannigan. 'Show me,' she said.

Archie ran his hand over his mouth. 'After that,' he said, 'I want you and Jeff back on Paul Reston.'

Flannigan's brows shot up. 'What about Kent?' he asked.

'It's not Kent,' Archie said.

'Why?' Flannigan asked.

'Because I say so.'

Flannigan worked the gum with his tongue. 'We were on him from six last night to nine-thirty this morning,' he insisted. 'I'm telling you, Reston didn't leave his house last night. He couldn't have taken the girl.'

Archie sighed. 'Humour me.'

'We always do,' Flannigan muttered as he and Anne walked away.

Archie walked over to where the mayor was in deep confab with an aide.

'I think you should cancel the press conference,' Archie said, breaking in.

The mayor visibly blanched. 'How about no?'

'This is going to sound crazy,' Archie said calmly. 'So I'm going to have to ask you to trust that I'm feeling exceedingly rational right now. But I'm having doubts as to whether McCallum's our guy.'

'Tell me you're kidding,' the mayor said, punctuating the statement by dramatically removing his sunglasses.

'I think there's a rather significant chance that it's a set-up.'

The mayoral aide was glancing around helplessly. His suit was cheap and looked shiny in the sun.

The mayor leaned towards Archie and spoke in an urgent whisper. 'I can't cancel the press conference. The story's out. A teacher's dead. A dead girl's bike is in his garage. They're live with it right now. It's on TV.' He gave 'TV' an agonized emphasis.

'Then hedge our bets,' Archie said.

The veins in the mayor's neck thickened and raised. '"Hedge our bets"?'

Archie reached out and patted the hood of the silver

Ford Escort that sat parked just in front of the garage. 'The car's not big enough,' he said to the mayor. 'How'd he get the bike and the girl in a compact, hmm?'

The mayor began to rub some imaginary object between his fingers. 'What am I supposed to say?'

'You're a politician, Buddy. Find a way to tell them that we don't know what the fuck is going on in a way that makes it look like we know what the fuck is going on.' Archie gave the mayor an I-know-you-can-do-this arm squeeze and backed away.

41

Susan sat on the couch with her laptop and a glass of red wine and started writing about Gretchen Lowell. As far as she was concerned, the After School Strangler story had ended with Dan McCallum's suicide. She was sure they'd find Addy Jackson's body somewhere. He'd killed her and dumped her like he had the others, and she was in the mud, waiting to be discovered by some unlucky jogger or Boy Scout troop. The image of Addy's half-buried corpse flashed in her mind, and she felt her eyes burn with tears. Crap. She was not going to let this get to her, not now. She wiped the image clean, but it was replaced by Kristy Mathers's damaged naked body twisted on the dark Sauvie Island sand. And then by Addy's parents, and how they had looked at Archie with such despair and expectation, wanting him to save their daughter, to save them. And then by her own father.

Her cell phone jumped and vibrated on the coffee table. The screen read UNKNOWN NUMBER. She picked it up and lifted it to her ear. 'Yeah?'

'My name's Molly Palmer.'

'Holy shit,' Susan said.

There was a pause. 'Look. I'm just calling to tell you that I don't want to talk to you. I have nothing to say.'

'It's not your fault,' Susan said quickly. 'He was an adult. There's no excuse.'

There was a bitter laugh. 'Yeah.' There was another pause. 'He taught me to play tennis. You can put that in the article you're writing. It's the only nice thing I have to say about him.'

Susan tried to control the desperation in her voice. Molly was the story. If she could get her to talk, the paper would have to run it; if not, she'd have nothing, and the senator would get off free and clear. 'Get it off your chest, Molly,' Susan pleaded. 'If you don't, it will just eat at you. It will just poison everything.' She twisted a piece of hair around a finger until it hurt. 'I know.'

'Listen,' Molly said, her voice catching. 'Do me a favour, OK? Don't call Ethan any more. This whole thing is starting to freak him out. I don't keep in touch with a lot of people from back then. And I don't want to lose him, too.'

'Please,' Susan said.

'It's ancient history,' Molly said. And she hung up.

Susan held the phone to her ear for a moment, listening to the dead line.

Ancient history. And without Molly, it would stay that way. Susan squeezed her eyes shut in frustration.

Ian could have got Molly to go on the record. Parker, too. Susan had had Molly in her hands, and she'd lost her. She put her phone down, took a deep breath, wiped her nose and eyes with the back of her hand, and poured some more wine into her glass. There was nothing more reassuring than a full glass of wine.

She considered calling Ethan again. He had clearly given Molly her messages. But then she thought of the pain in Molly's voice and how she just wanted to be left alone, to leave the past behind.

Was that so wrong?

Fuck it. She picked up the phone and punched in Ethan's number. Voicemail. Imagine that. 'Hi,' she said. 'It's me. Susan Ward. Again. Listen. I just got off the phone with Molly and I want you to tell her that I understand. I had an affair – ' she caught herself, 'or whatever – with my teacher when I was fifteen. And I've spent a lot of time justifying it. But you know what, Ethan? It's not justifiable. It's just not. So just tell Molly that. She'll understand. And I won't call you again.' Who was she kidding? 'At least not for a few days.'

She set the phone back down on the table and lifted her computer to her lap. She was on deadline and this story was about Gretchen Lowell. Gretchen, who was very much alive. Gretchen, who made Susan's teeth hurt. Susan was convinced that if she could get Gretchen down on paper, she could somehow understand Archie and McCallum and the rest of it. She could feel the story, shadowy and amorphous, in the room with her. It just needed to be gathered and shaped. She took a large sip of wine. It was from the Great Writer's collection, which she had found hidden in the back of his closet under a stack of remaindered hardbacks of his latest novel. Susan told herself he wouldn't mind. These were special circumstances. The wine was fragrant and leggy and she held it on her tongue, savouring its heat before she swallowed it.

When she heard the knock at the door, her first thought was that it might be Bliss. She had called her mother when she got home – Bliss, who was the only person in the world without a cell phone or voicemail. Susan had left a forlorn message on her mother's answering machine, which only occasionally recorded, and more often played back messages in a weird slow cadence that sent Bliss writhing in hysterics. So when Susan heard the knock, she had a brief fantasy that her mother had heard her message and had dropped everything to rush over to see if she was OK. Susan knew this was an absurd scenario. She had spent so much time when she was growing up taking care of Bliss; yet in her commitment to treating her daughter like an adult, Bliss had rarely taken care of Susan. Besides, Bliss refused to own a car and would have had to take two buses to get to the Pearl. No, Susan decided. It was Ian. She smiled at this idea, allowing herself a heartening smugness that he had, in the end, been unable to resist her feminine wiles.

They were powerful, her wiles. Yes. It was most definitely Ian.

He knocked again.

She got up and headed to the door in her socks, pausing to check her reflection in an old gilded mirror she passed on the way. The Great Writer had told her he'd bought it at a flea market in Paris, but she'd seen the same one at Pottery Barn. Gretchen Lowell was right: she was developing a furrow on her forehead. Susan didn't like the look of it one bit. Was it possible she had aged in the past week? She set her wineglass on the table in front of the mirror and held her thumb flat against the offending wrinkle until her forehead relaxed, and then she pulled at some wisps of pink hair and secured them behind her small ears. There. She put on her most dazzling smile and opened the door. But it wasn't Ian.

It was Paul Reston.

It had been ten years. He was now in his mid-forties. His light brown hair had thinned and inched back from the temples, and his belly had softened. He looked longer somehow, his back bonier, the folds in his face more pronounced. He had given up the rectangular glasses with the red plastic frames that Susan remembered and now wore wire rims with oval lenses. It surprised Susan to see that he was not the dashing young teacher she remembered. Had he ever been?

'Paul,' Susan said, taken aback. 'What are you doing here?'

'It's good to see you,' he said. 'You look great.' He smiled warmly and opened his arms for a hug, and she stepped forward and he wrapped his arms around her. He smelled like the Cleveland auditorium, like paint and sawdust and oranges. 'Paul,' she said into his maroon V-necked sweater. 'Seriously.'

He let go of Susan and looked at her, his brown eyes heavy with disappointment. 'A police detective came to see me.'

Susan flushed with shame. 'I'm so sorry about that,' she said. 'I took it back. I told him I made it up. It's all fine now.'

Paul sighed heavily and walked past her into the apartment, shaking his head. 'What were you thinking? Bringing that story up again. You know it could cause me all sorts of trouble at school.'

'It doesn't matter,' Susan said, trying to reassure him. 'There's nothing he can do if we both deny it.'

Frustration sparked in his eyes. 'There's nothing to deny. Nothing happened, Suzy.' He cupped her face in his hands and looked at her. 'It's the truth.'

Susan stepped back, so that his hands fell away. 'Yeah. Nothing happened.'

'You had a rough time as a kid. I get that. But you need to move past this.'

'I have,' Susan insisted. 'I will.'

He turned back towards her with an imploring look. 'So let me hear you say it.'

'Nothing happened,' Susan repeated in her strongest, most confident voice. 'I made it all up.'

Paul nodded a few times, relieved. 'You're a good writer. You have so much potential. You were always so creative.'

'I still am,' Susan said, a little annoyed. The door to the hall was still ajar. Susan didn't want to close it; the gesture seemed too much an invitation to stay.

'Come here,' he said, opening his arms. 'We're OK, right?' He smiled and his face softened and dimpled, and she saw her handsome favourite teacher as he had been, his hair to his shoulders, his velvet blazers and wisecracks and stupid poetry, and she almost went to him. Because some small part of her still loved him, still loved Paul Reston. But the best part of her knew that it was bullshit.

Her spine stiffened and she took a tiny step back as he came for her. 'I don't want to play this any more,' she said. Her voice suddenly sounded hollow and strange, not at all her own.

He stopped and let his arms drop to his sides. 'What's wrong?' he asked.

'This is weird, Paul.' She lifted a hand and flailed it around the loft. 'We're alone. We can talk about what happened. So why are we playing the whole "It never happened" thing?'

He cocked his head, an eyebrow raised. 'What do you mean, "playing"?'

Yeah. Now this was fucked up. 'Jesus, Paul,' Susan said.

He laughed, a quick, fierce bark, head back, face rosy. 'OK. I'm sorry. I was just having some fun. When did you get so serious?' He shot her a good-humoured look. 'You used to love role-playing.'

'Three girls are dead,' Susan said. 'Another is missing, probably dead.'

He walked to the door, closed it and leaned against it, his hands behind him, resting on the doorknob. His voice and demeanour were suddenly perfectly calm. 'I heard. Dan McCallum, huh? I never would have seen that coming.'

McCallum. She felt the hot sting of tears again. She still didn't understand how McCallum could have done it. He'd always seemed so demonstrably fair. A pain in the ass, sure, but always reasoned. You never knew what anyone was capable of.

And Paul. She had seduced her teacher, and then blabbed about it to a cop. After she had promised him again and again that she'd never say anything. He probably hated her now. 'At least it's over,' she said.

He brushed the back of his hand against her cheek, and she was grateful for his kindness. 'I figured that you might need some company. Let me make you dinner,' he said. He surveyed her kitchen sceptically. 'Do you keep food here?'

'Just cans of artichoke hearts and peanut butter,' she said.

'Well, I can whip something up.' He gave a fancy little bow. 'I can make a hell of an artichoke-heart-and-peanut-butter casserole.'

Susan glanced back at her laptop on the coffee table, longing suddenly for the comfort of her wine and her computer. 'I'm on deadline. I've really got to get some writing done tonight.' She caught a glimpse of her reflection in the Pottery Barn mirror. There was the furrow again. Her wineglass still sat where she'd left it on the curio table in front of the mirror.

'You have to eat.' He looked at her expectantly.

She turned to him. 'How did you know where I lived, anyway?'

'We've got access to Nexus at school. You can find anyone. Just by typing in their name.' Reston took a moment, as if considering his exact intent, wanting to get the words just so. 'It was hard for me after you graduated.' He glanced away. 'You didn't respond to my letters.'

'I was in college.'

He shrugged casually and shot her a handsome smile. 'I loved you.'

'That's because I was a teenager,' Susan said, trying to explain. 'I adored you. What's not to love about that?' She walked over to the mirror and picked her wineglass off the table and drained it. The photograph that Bliss had given her the week before was stuck in the corner of the mirror. Three-year-old Susan holding hands with her father. Safe. Happy.

Everything changes eventually.

'I've never stopped thinking about you,' Paul said.

Susan looked at her reflection. 'Come on, Paul,' she said to her own image. 'You don't even know me.'

He walked up behind her, his reflection serious and a little hurt. 'How can you say that?'

Susan picked her wooden hairbrush off the table and began to brush her pink hair. It didn't need it, but it gave her something to do. 'Because, when you knew me, I wasn't a fully formed person. I was a teenager.' She kept brushing, feeling the bristles drag along her skull, the blood rush to her scalp. Her bearded father stared at her from the photograph, his hand clenched protectively around the little girl's.

Paul touched the back of her head. 'You were never a teenager.'

She put the hairbrush down. She did it heavily, and the brush made a snapping sound against the wooden table, startling her. 'Look,' she said, glancing at her watch. 'You have to go. I'm on deadline.'

'Let me take you out to dinner.'

She turned away from the mirror, from the photograph, from her father, and looked at him. 'Paul.'

He gave her that handsome smile again. 'One hour. I'll regale you with stories of Dan McCallum. For your story. Then I'll drop you off and you can get your work done.'

Susan felt like she was fifteen again. Incapable of

disappointing him. Besides, she didn't have the energy to argue. 'One hour.'

'Cross my heart.'

The elevator took a thousand years to get down to the parking garage in the basement of Susan's building. Paul didn't speak, and for the first time in Susan's life she didn't try to fill the silence. Paul just stood there with a soft smile on his face, watching her as she fiddled with the sash of her trench coat and shifted her weight on her feet and studied the illuminated numbers above the elevator door. Susan could see both their reflections in the wall's steel sheeting, a distorted mesh of colours refracting off the metal.

The doors opened and Paul let her exit first.

'I'm this way,' he said, and he pointed off to a car on the far side of the garage, away from the elevator, far from the other parked cars. Well, Susan thought, at least there'd be time to suck down half a cigarette. She fumbled in her purse for one and lit it.

'So, did you know Lee Robinson?' Susan asked, taking a drag.

Paul drew his face back in disgust. 'You still smoke?'

'No,' Susan said, flustered. 'Just in social situations.'

He looked around the parking garage. 'Is this a social situation?'

Susan groaned. 'You're not my teacher any more, Paul. Don't lecture me.'

'Four hundred and forty thousand people die a year in the United States from smoking. That's fifty people an hour.'

Susan took another careful drag on the cigarette. 'How well did you know Lee Robinson?' she asked again.

He reached up and touched his head, like he had a sudden headache. 'Not well at all,' he said.

Susan pulled at her sash, untying it and retying it. 'But you were pretty tight with McCallum, right? I thought I remembered you telling a story about going fishing or something with him on his boat.'

'Suzy,' Paul said with an exasperated smile. 'That was twenty years ago.'

'So you used to hang out.'

'We went fishing together once twenty years ago.' He reached over and put his arm around her shoulder, and she took an extra step forward and shrugged it off.

Susan laughed nervously. 'Could you have parked any farther away?' she asked.

Paul shrugged and put his hands back in his pockets. 'It was crowded when I got here.'

'Well, if I collapse because of my poor lung capacity, just leave my body for the rats,' Susan joked.

'Smoking isn't funny. It's a very dangerous addiction. It will kill you.'

The car, finally. Susan had never been so happy to see a ten-year-old silver Passat wagon. She smiled at the two stickers affixed neatly side by side on the back bumper. One read SAVE OUR SCHOOLS. The other read IF YOU'RE NOT OUTRAGED YOU'RE NOT PAYING ATTENTION.

Paul got in on his side first, leaning over and unlocking Susan's door. She climbed in and pulled her seat belt into place and took a final drag on the cigarette. Then she looked for the ashtray to put it out in. It was the cleanest car she'd ever seen. The dash was so clean, it shone. There wasn't a Corgi hair or a pen or an old pack of ketchup to be found. She reached out and opened the ashtray in the centre console. The ashtray in her car was filled with old gum and ashes. Paul's ashtray was empty. You could eat out of it. Susan examined her cigarette; it seemed a shame to sully his sterile ashtray with it. Paul had turned his head and was leaning between the seats to root for something in the back. She didn't want to just drop the cigarette on the parking-garage floor – she was trying to be better about the whole littering thing. Maybe Paul had something in the glove compartment she could wrap the cigarette in and then she could put it in her purse. She opened the glove compartment. Inside was a flashlight and a single folded map. 'Jesus, Paul,' she said. 'Clean much?' The car even smelled disinfected, like a freshly scrubbed public bathroom.

'What did you do? Dip your car in bleach?' she asked. 'Because it smells like' – she pulled the map out and turned it over in her hands. It was a nautical map of the Willamette – 'Clorox.'

He grabbed her from behind just as she reached for the door handle. She clawed at the door, but he hit an all-lock button and the electronic locks bolted into place with a mechanical thud. She scrambled to get to the button on her door handle, but he had a forearm around her neck and something over her mouth and nose and she couldn't get free of him. She fought, all knees and elbows, but it wasn't enough. He had leverage on her. She thought of all sorts of things: how she wished she'd done that story on self-defence classes; how she should have worn her shit-kicker boots, the ones with the steel toes; how she should have kept her nails long, so she could rip his fucking eyes out; how, somehow, none of this surprised her at all. She managed to get the lit cigarette up, grinding it hard into his neck until he howled and wrenched her wrist so that she dropped it. She had wanted to kill him with it, but she would settle for it burning a hole through his spotless floor mat. That would be her legacy: a burn spot on an otherwise pristine surface. *Fucking perfect.* It was her last thought as the darkness engulfed her.

42

Anne sat on the carpet in Dan McCallum's dark little living room, surrounded by Cleveland High School yearbooks. She wasn't sure what she was looking for. But Archie suspected Reston and she was going to find him something to move on. The books had been arranged chronologically and Anne had started with the most recent volume, flipping through the pages, hoping for something to catch her eye. Page after page of goofy club photographs, sporting events, school plays, class photos, teachers, and plaintive senior messages, and then, halfway through the 1994 yearbook, she found exactly what she was looking for. She pulled the 1995 yearbook off the shelf and searched frantically through it until she found the next picture she needed to confirm what she was thinking. It did.

She scrambled up off the floor, holding both the books cradled to her chest, and fled through the house to find Archie.

He was in the kitchen, watching as they zipped McCallum's corpse into a black body bag and prepared to wheel him out of the house. Anne pulled him to the back stoop and thrust the first yearbook into his hands, open to the photograph of the Cleveland High School drama club. There at its centre was Susan Ward, and next to her Paul Reston. Susan, fourteen years old, before the pink hair. She had not yet come into the beauty that was waiting for her. She was still an awkward-looking, thin, brown-haired girl.

'Jesus Christ,' said Archie, his colour draining. 'She looks like all the others.'

'Why did you suspect Reston?' Anne asked.

She could see Archie hesitate for a moment. He touched the photograph of the young Susan, as if his fingertips could somehow protect her retroactively. 'Susan told me yesterday that she had a sexual relationship with him when he was her teacher. Today, she denied it.'

Anne harboured no doubt that Susan had slept with Reston when she was a teenager. 'It's him,' she said simply.

'He's got an alibi,' Archie said, leaning against the back of the house. 'We can't pick him up based on an old photograph and a crime with a long-passed statute of limitations.'

Anne laid the next yearbook over the one he held and opened it to Susan's sophomore-year photograph. She was a different kid from the one in the first picture. She wore a black T-shirt and black lipstick. Her eyes looked helpless and sad and hard all at the same time. And she had bleached her hair. But she hadn't used Clairol. She hadn't gone to a salon. She'd used what she could find under the sink. She'd used Clorox.

'It's all about her,' Anne said. She catalogued the morgue photos in her mind, the girls' marbled faces, their haemorrhaged corneas, the cruel yellow-orange of their once-brown hair. 'He bleaches them because it completes the transformation.'

Archie's eyes didn't lift from the page. She could see him processing all of it. 'You've got to be kidding me,' he said almost to himself. Then he looked up at Anne, his face flushed with urgency. 'Where are Claire and Henry?'

'I'm here,' Claire said, coming up the back steps, cell phone still in her hand. 'Jeff just called,' she said, face tense. 'Reston isn't at home. He left school at the usual time, but hasn't come home yet. They don't have any way to find him until he shows up. Should I have them wait?'

The back door burst open and Anne saw the back of a jacket that read MEDICAL TRANSPORTATION SERVICES, and then a college-age man backed out, pulling the metal gurney that carried McCallum's bagged body. Anne held the screen door open for him as he and another man moved the body out on to the stoop.

'Find him,' Archie said to Claire, handing the yearbooks back to Anne so that he could get to his cell phone. 'Arrest him. He's our guy. Get a warrant to search his house. And get some uniforms over to Susan Ward's apartment. Now.'

43

Susan awoke with a start to the smell of gasoline. The odour was so strong that it reached down through the ocean she was under, grabbed her by the hair and dragged her to the surface of her consciousness. She came to with a start, but it was so dark that it took her a few moments to realize that her eyes were open. Her hands and feet were bound. She sat up and hit her head on something hard just above her. The impact sent a shock wave of pain through her skull and she sank back down into a lying position.

'Paul?' she said. Her voice came out in a whimper.

The room lurched. Susan was caught off balance and rolled back against a wall. It wasn't so much the lurching room that tipped her off as the thud her body made against the fibreglass. A boat. She was on a boat.

It was then that she panicked.

She started to scream. She used her bound hands and feet to bang on the fibreglass. She found strength she didn't know she had. 'I'm down here,' she shrieked. 'Help me. Someone.'

'Susan.'

She froze and every hair on her body stood up. He was down there. With her. In the dark.

'Susan.' His disembodied voice was strained and brutal. 'You need to be quiet.'

'Let me go, Paul,' she pleaded into the darkness.

She felt him fumble for her and she forced herself not to cringe under his touch as his hand found her leg and moved up her thigh and stopped. He was right next to her. His breath was hot against her face.

'I thought we'd spend some time together,' he said, and his voice caught. 'Like you said, I barely know you.'

44

When Susan didn't pick up her landline or cell phone, Archie's thoughts grew dark. They were already in Henry's car, Archie in the passenger seat, Henry behind the wheel, on their way to the Pearl. Claire and Anne were following close behind. He left identical troubled messages on Susan's voicemails and then let the phone rest in his palm on his lap, willing it to ring. It was nearly half-past seven, so the sun had long ago slipped behind the West Hills, but the purple late-winter sky was still half lit with dusk. It was going to be a cold night.

'Could be anything,' Henry said, gripping the steering wheel. 'Could be she's in the shower. Anything.'

'Right,' said Archie.

'Maybe she's taking a nap,' Henry added.

'I get it,' said Archie. He noticed then that Henry's wrist was bleeding. 'What happened to you?'

Henry shrugged. 'Fucking cat scratched me.'

Archie's walkie-talkie buzzed and he answered it. The patrol cops were at Susan's apartment. She wasn't answering the door. 'Find out if her car's in the parking lot,' he told them. 'Knock on her neighbours' doors.

See if anyone saw her come home or go out. And check if there's a security camera in the parking garage or lobby.' Then he dialled Information and got Ian Harper's telephone number.

A child's voice picked up at the Harper residence. 'Is your dad at home?' Archie asked.

The boy went off to get his father and Archie could hear music and the sounds of adults eating and laughing. In a minute, Ian Harper picked up the phone.

His voice was annoyed. 'Yeah?'

Archie wasn't feeling very generous towards Ian right now and he was in a hurry, so he skipped the niceties. 'Ian. Archie Sheridan. Did you drop Susan at her apartment this afternoon?'

Ian hesitated. 'Yeah.'

'What time?' Archie asked.

'What's going on?'

Henry whipped around a slow pick-up truck on the Ross Island Bridge. He had the Crown Vic's lights on but not the siren. The downtown skyline was a postcard to the north. Archie pulled the pillbox from his pocket and rotated it between his fingers. 'What time did you drop her off?' he asked again.

'I don't know,' Ian said. His voice wavered. 'About five-thirty?'

'Was she planning on going out this evening?' asked Archie. 'Or having anyone over?'

'Not that she said.' Then Ian added, authoritatively, 'She's got a story due tomorrow.'

'You know anything about an anonymous source mentioning a Cleveland student to her?'

'Yeah,' Ian said instantly. 'It's another story. Nothing to do with the Strangler.'

'You sure?'

'Yes,' he said definitely.

None of this was making Archie feel any better. He started to open the pillbox, caught Henry's disapproving glance and shoved the box back in his pocket. 'And you saw her go inside the building?'

'Yeah.' Ian paused. Archie could hear his guests laughing again in the background. 'Has something happened to Susan?'

'I'm just trying to find her. If you hear from her, you tell her to call me, OK?'

Ian's voice lowered an octave. 'Should I come over?'

'No, Ian.' Archie sighed, thinking about Susan's confession. 'Stay with your family.'

When Henry pulled in behind a patrol car in front of the old brewery building, one of the patrol cops was waiting for them. 'Car's here,' he said. 'There's a security camera in the lobby. It feeds into a monitor in the concierge's office.'

'Concierge?' Archie asked.

The patrol cop rolled his eyes. 'I think she's the building spokesmodel.'

Archie, Henry and Anne followed the officer

through the building's black-and-white modernist lobby to a small room decorated entirely in shades of brown, where a young woman with a platinum ponytail stood behind a bamboo counter. She held an egg-shaped white remote in her hand and was reviewing grainy footage of the parking garage on a glossy white monitor. A stack of photocopies sat on the counter. Archie glanced at the top one. It had a picture of a cat and in big letters said STOP LAB KITTEN ABUSE.

'There,' she said. She leaned forward on her elbows and pressed a manicured forefinger on the screen on top of an image of Susan Ward and Paul Reston. 'That's Susan Ward.'

The five of them watched the jerky image as Susan and Reston made their way from the elevator, across the parking garage and out of range of the camera. The time code on the video read 6:12 p.m.

'Find them,' Anne said to Archie and Henry. 'He'll kill her if you don't.'

Archie stood in Susan's apartment. The spokesmodel had let them in. An expensive-looking gilded mirror hung just inside the front door. A wineglass sat empty on the table in front of it. Beside the glass was a wooden hairbrush, a single bright-pink hair tangled in its bristles. Archie examined the glass without touching it. The base was coated with gritty red-wine sediment; traces of lipstick were visible on the lip. They had just missed her. She'd drunk a glass of wine and she'd left with him and who the fuck knew where they were now? Archie had put a broadcast out for Reston. Highway Patrol in four states would be looking for his car. But a lot of people had looked for Archie once, too. He fingered the pillbox in his pocket. He was feeling that sort of uneven overcaffeinated vibration that meant it was time to take some Vicodin. Soon the headache, then the slow burn under the skin that would turn to cold sweats, the body aches.

He slid open the box and removed three of the large oval pills by touch and then slipped them into his mouth. He held them in his cheek as he walked into Susan's kitchen nook, where he filled his cupped hand with water from the faucet and washed the pills down.

He'd even grown to like the bitter taste. He'd run into addicts who shot saline when they couldn't get their intravenous drug of choice. The fact that someone would inject a needle into a vein for the hell of it had puzzled Archie then. Now he understood that the familiar pain acted as a sort of placebo.

'That a good idea?' Henry asked.

Archie looked up. Henry was standing on the other side of the kitchen bar, as inscrutable as ever. 'It's maintenance,' Archie said, turning away from Henry. 'They won't make me high.'

He could feel his body loosen up, already anticipating the codeine in his system. It was psychosomatic: the pills didn't work that fast. But he didn't care. He had to focus. To think. How had Reston managed to get to Addy? And why kill McCallum? It had to be connected to the boat. Reston and McCallum taught at the same school, knew each other, and McCallum had said that everyone knew he had a boat. Maybe Reston had been using the boat and set fire to it to destroy evidence or divert suspicion. If he knew that McCallum had been questioned, then a suicide could provide a final frame-up. It was sloppy. Desperate. And that worried Archie.

He turned and walked the ten steps that separated the kitchen area from the living-room area, where Anne stood looking out of the large window. He hoped that she was thinking about Reston and not considering a real-estate investment in the Pearl. He could feel Henry a step behind him, his constant shadow. Archie stood next to Anne and looked out of the window, too. Across the street sat another brand-new condo building, each loft a brightly lit doll's-house room in the darkness.

'How desperate is he?' he asked Anne.

She moved a stray braid out of her eyes. 'He's obsessed with a former student,' she said. 'An affair that ended ten years ago. I would say that he's very desperate. If you're asking me if there's a possibility he'll kill himself, I'd say there's a strong one.'

A woman in one of the lofts across the street turned on a TV. 'So you don't think he's killed her already?' Archie asked.

'No.' She paused. 'But I could be wrong.'

'So where would he take her?' asked Henry.

Anne considered this. 'He'll take her somewhere where he feels safe. Where did he take the others?' she asked rhetorically.

'The boat,' answered Archie.

'McCallum's boat,' Henry echoed. 'But it's gone.'

Archie considered this. Below them, on the street, someone in an SUV was attempting to parallel park. 'Unless he's got another boat.'

'No,' Claire said, joining them. 'We checked the State Marine Board for all faculty and staff at the schools who fitted the profile back in November. And again in February. And again in March. McCallum had only one boat registered. And he was the only one with a captain's licence.'

'He said he bought this boat a few years ago,' Archie said. 'Maybe he kept the old one but let the registration lapse.'

'Can you do that?' asked Claire.

'Call the people,' Archie told her.

Claire pulled her phone off the waist of her pants. 'Yep.' She stepped away to make the call.

'You OK?' Henry asked Archie.

Archie realized that he was standing with his hands on his hips staring at the wood floor. Susan Ward was being held by some crazy jackass who was going to kill her if he hadn't already, and Archie wasn't sure that he could save her. 'I just need a minute,' he said.

Archie stood in Susan Ward's bathroom. He could feel Henry's worry wrap around him like a shroud. Keep it together, Archie thought. Then he said it out loud: 'Keep it together.' He splashed some water over his face from the faucet and dried off with a hand towel that hung next to the sink.

He checked his watch. It was almost nine. *An hour of reading and then lights-out.* He stopped himself. Don't think about her. Not now. He had to focus on Susan. His nose itched. It was a nervous-system response to the Vicodin that his body had mostly quashed but which still occasionally surfaced. He gave it a vigorous rubbing. Great. Now, on top of everything, they were all going to think that he was a cokehead. And there was Gretchen again, clear as day in his mind, lying in repose on her prison cot, propped on one elbow, *The Last Victim* in her hands. His wedding photograph was in that book.

'Boss?' Henry knocked gently at the bathroom door.

Archie blinked a few times at his bleary reflection and opened the door. Henry and Claire stood outside the bathroom.

'What do we have?' Archie asked.

Claire checked her notebook. 'He registered the boat

that burned down five years ago. Before that, he had another boat registered, a 1950 Chris-Craft Catalina. That registration lapsed eight months after he registered the new boat. But if he'd sold it locally, it would have been registered by someone else. And it hasn't been.'

'So maybe he sold it to someone across the river,' Archie said.

'Maybe,' Claire agreed. 'But according to the nice lady at the OSMB, until they clarified the rules in 2002 you didn't have to keep current registration on a boat that wasn't "in the water", which is to say, if you had a boat moored at a marina but weren't actually taking it out, you could save having to pay the state fifteen bucks a year.'

Archie nodded. 'The cheap bastard kept the boat.'

Henry crossed and uncrossed his arms. 'That's the one Reston would have used, because it's the one that McCallum would have been less likely to notice was amiss.'

'"Amiss"?' Claire said.

'I can't use a fancy word?' Henry said.

Claire continued: 'If we're right, the boat would be at the same marina, right? I mean, most likely?'

'Let's go,' Archie said.

Anne had walked up beside Henry. 'Be careful. Because if you send in the cavalry and spook him, he's likely to hurt her.'

'If we're right and he's even there and she's even still alive,' Archie said.

Anne nodded a few times. Behind her, in the loft across the street, the woman shut off her television set. Nothing on. 'I need a Diet Coke,' Anne said.

Then there was a sound from behind them, a sort of gasp, and every cop in the room turned to look at the front door. A middle-aged woman stood there. She wore a ridiculous hand-made hat and a leopardskin coat and tall lace-up platform boots. Her hair was a tangle of long blond dreadlocks. Her dark red mouth was open in a sort of surprised grimace.

'Who are you people?' she asked. 'And where is my daughter?'

45

'You killed those girls,' Susan said into the darkness.

Reston's voice was strangled with sadness. 'I'm sorry.'

Susan's breath felt like the loudest thing in the world to her. Like tiny atom bombs. She willed herself to slow the intake of oxygen, to relax, to make him think that she was not afraid. She had to convince him that she was strong. That she could control the situation. 'You're sorry? Paul, you're sick. You need help. I can help you.'

'You shouldn't have left me,' he said, slipping something over her head, around her neck. She could feel the smooth leather strap of it against the skin below her hairline at the base of her scalp, and then in the front, above her clavicle, something cold and hard – a belt buckle. The purple ligature marks around Kristy Mathers's neck flashed in her mind and she frantically reached up to get her bound hands under the belt, but it snapped tight around her throat. She gasped and grappled with it, but Reston pushed her hands down and pulled the belt tighter. Her head throbbed and filled with fire. He pulled her down so hard that her kneecaps hitting the floor made a crack like an axe hitting wood. She was spinning untethered in space, and then all of sudden she was still. All of her senses slammed to life, and at that moment her eyes adjusted just a bit to the darkness. She could see him in front of her. Not a person, but a dark shape, the shadow of a person. She could feel his thumb on her mouth, tracing her lips. His thumb was ice. Her lips were shaking.

'You have a beautiful mouth,' he said.

Susan's mind was clarifying, ordering information. Kidnapped. Boat. Paul. Killer. And now: Addy. 'Paul,' Susan rasped. 'Where's Addy?'

She felt him hesitate for a moment, then he stepped back and the strap loosened. The lights came on. Susan recoiled and reflexively closed her eyes, overcome by the sudden brightness. When she forced them open again, a moment later, Reston was back in front of her and he held a gun pointed at her forehead. Susan steeled herself against a sudden wave of nausea, swallowing the sickly warm saliva that rose in her throat.

She had been right. They were on a boat. In some sort of sleeping quarters. The walls and low ceiling of the room were white. It was a cramped space, only five feet wide at most. Cubbies and drawers filled one wall. Built into the opposite wall was a sturdy wooden bunk bed. On the top bunk, above where Susan herself only moments ago had lain, was Addy Jackson.

She was semi-conscious and naked except for a pair

of pink underpants, and her forearms and ankles were bound with duct tape. Her eyes were slits, her mouth was wet with saliva, her hair matted with sweat. She stirred and scratched at her tear-stained cheek with her bound hands. And then Susan recognized herself in them. Lee. Dana. Kristy. Addy. The brown hair. The wide-spaced eyes. The small breasts. She knew then with devastating clarity that it was about her, that it had always been about her. And she knew that he would kill them. Both of them. There was no question now. She looked at Addy, who appeared unfocused and unaware of her surroundings, and she envied her.

'It's your fault,' Paul explained, running his hand along the back of Susan's neck. 'You shouldn't have been such a cunt to me.'

It was then that Susan made a silent pledge: she was not going to die. No way. Not at the hands of her fucking drama teacher.

46

The manager of the River Haven marina did not live on a boat; she lived in a manufactured home up the hill from the boats. The temperature had dropped ten degrees and night had officially fallen. Archie could taste the river, like tinfoil in his mouth, as he waited on the stoop of the flat tan house with the word OFFICE burned on to a piece of polished driftwood that had been nailed on to the siding. His nose itched. *Answer the fucking door*, he thought.

Henry and Claire stood beside him. Behind them were three unmarked police cars. He had ordered the patrol cars and SWAT vehicles to park up on the old highway, out of sight. He craned his head to look down at the marina, where several dozen boats bobbed in gloomy silence.

A dog barked and the door opened. An older woman emerged, and Archie caught a flash of bouncing fur before she managed to push the dog behind her and close the door. She now stood, on the stoop, between the closed interior door and an aluminium screen one that she kept protectively between herself and the detectives. Archie lifted his badge up and showed it to her.

'I know who you are,' she said, eyes level. 'I've seen you on TV.' She took off her glasses. Her hair was dyed chestnut and tied in a loose knot at the base of her neck and she was wearing a turtleneck tucked into blue jeans. She was holding a paperback thriller, the place where she'd been reading marked with one thumb. The glasses left a sore-looking red impression on the bridge of her nose. 'You're that cop who was kidnapped by Gretchen Lowell.'

Gretchen's name sent a stab of electrical current down Archie's arms. His fist tightened around the pillbox in his pocket. 'I need to know which boats Dan McCallum has moored here.'

She looked away and rattled the handle of the screen door a little. 'Dan's boat burned down.'

'Is there another one?'

She hesitated.

'It's important,' Archie said.

'I let him keep it here, even though it's not registered. He's a good tenant.'

'It's OK,' Archie assured her. 'You're not in trouble. Where is it?'

She studied Archie for a moment, and then she came out from behind the screen door and pointed down to the docks below. 'Slip twenty-eight. Down there. Second boat from the end, on the left.'

*

'You can do what you want to me,' Susan said. 'But you have to let Addy go.'

Reston's face was all shadow and light. The corners of his mouth twitched. 'I can't.'

It took everything Susan had to keep her face composed. 'You're going to kill her?'

'I have to.'

Susan felt the small room close in on her. Even if she were unbound, she wouldn't be able to get around him, get to the door, get out of the boat. And then what? Swim? The porthole above where Addy lay was the size of a dinner plate. There was no way out. 'And me?'

'Look at her.' Reston reached out tentatively and touched the girl's hip, letting his finger trace the deep curve down to her slender waist and over the bones of her ribs. Outside, water lapped at the hull. The boat rocked, uneven skittish bumps and rolls. 'Isn't she beautiful?' Reston asked.

Susan couldn't understand how he had done it. 'They said they were watching you. They said you didn't leave your house.'

'I didn't kidnap her, Suzy,' he said softly. 'She came to me.' He closed his eyes. 'I told her we could be together. I told her to break her bedroom window from the outside. I told her what bus to take to get out here. I told her to wait on the boat until I got done with school.' His eyes fluttered open and he gazed at Susan with a hatred she had never seen before. The boat rocked and the door to the room rattled in its hinges. 'She did exactly what I told her to do.'

'You're crazy,' Susan said.

He smiled to himself as he ogled the semi-conscious girl. 'Rohypnol. I got it on the Internet.'

Susan was disgusted that she'd ever let him touch her. She saw every encounter, every fumble; the images ticked through her brain, a sad slide show of her sad adolescence. She had wanted so badly to be in control. She had convinced everyone she was. The truth was so much more pathetic.

His breathing became more rapid and his face flushed with his arousal. He was touching Addy's breast now. He circled her small pink nipple with his thumb. She stirred. 'I only want them so badly because they remind me of you.'

Susan told herself to be strong, to get out of this. 'That's self-justifying bullshit. You've always had a hard-on for teenage girls.'

'No,' he said, his voice cracking. 'No. You made me into this. I never lusted after students. Not until you. You did this to me.' He slid his hand from Addy's breast back down over her ribs, her waist and her hip, and then down along the waistband of her underpants.

'Don't do that,' Susan said, turning her head, unable to look. 'Please.'

'Did I mean anything to you?'

Susan squeezed her eyes shut. 'Of course.'

'I think about that day after school all the time.

How you were standing, what you were wearing, what we said. You made me that tape, remember?' He touched her face, and she jerked away and felt the belt tighten, gagging her again, forcing her to remain still, afraid to move. *Don't cry*, she told herself. *Just don't fucking cry.*

'Your favourite songs,' he said, and she felt his lips brush against her cheek. It made her want to vomit. 'I still have it. There was a Violent Femmes song, "Add It Up", with the line "Why can't I get just one kiss?" You handed it to me and you said, "This is who I am." You gave yourself to me.' He kissed her again, dragging his bottom lip up the side of her face, leaving a path of wet saliva. 'You had handwritten all of the titles of the songs. They were so carefully lettered. It must have taken you hours.'

She squeezed her eyes tighter, until they felt like fists. 'It was for rehearsal, Paul. I volunteered to make a tape for rehearsal. For the warm-up.'

'It was that day in my classroom. After school. When we first kissed.'

She could smell his sweat, sweet and acrid in the small space. 'No.'

'I listened to the tape on my way home and I couldn't believe it – how much alike we were.' She felt his wet lips on her mouth and fought to turn her head but couldn't. The black canvas of her eyelids was filled with stars. 'I listened to the words of the songs, and I knew what you were trying to tell me,' he said, his lips dancing on hers. 'I knew that it was wrong for us to be together.'

He pulled away and she could feel the belt loosen, but she was still afraid to open her eyes, afraid of what she might see. 'I was married. I was your teacher. But you were so mature for your age, so wise beyond your years. I wrote you a letter. I should never have done it, should never have put my feelings into words. But I took a chance. I gave it to you in class the next day and told you to read it after school, and you did.' He made a halting sighing sound that turned into something like a sob.

'And you came to me after the cast party. And we made love.' He grabbed her head in his hands then and she felt his lips on her mouth, his tongue pushing against her sealed lips. The belt tightened. 'Open your mouth.'

Susan flung open her eyes and stared up at him, enraged. 'That's not how it happened, Paul,' she said. Finally saying it. Finally telling the truth. 'I got drunk,' she spat at him. 'I got drunk for the first time at the cast party after a stupid school play and you offered me a ride home and you fucked me in your car.' She leaned her head sadly against the bunk. 'I was a kid. My dad had just died. I let it go on. I didn't know any better. And you were my favourite teacher.'

47

The Kevlar vest forced Archie to breathe differently. The Velcro straps were snug and the weight of the thing constricted his chest, causing his ribs to throb and making every movement of his torso a mental victory. He tried to inhale air deeply, visualizing the oxygen moving through his windpipe and down into his lungs, feeding his heart. It gave him something to think about as he and Henry and Claire made their slow way along the cement drive that zigzagged down the hillside to the boats below. An old silver Passat was parked at the bottom of the hill. Reston's car. They walked at a casual pace, their vests under their civilian clothes, guns tucked away, but their bodies were tense, and anyone who happened to see them would be an idiot not to be alarmed. But there wasn't anyone. Just the boats.

They reached the dock. It stretched into the river in a T shape, with boats on either side. The security lights that lined the gangways provided a lazy white glow that bounced off the black water and made everything look especially sharp. It was the cooler air,

Archie supposed. It made everything look harder. He unsnapped the safety strap on his holster and let the smooth metal of the .38 press against the skin of his palm.

The numbers of the slips ran even on one side, odd on the other. Archie knew the boat wouldn't be there even before they got to number twenty-eight. He just wasn't that lucky.

'Fuck,' said Archie as they stood in front of the empty slip.

'What does that mean?' Claire asked.

'It means they've gone sailing,' said Archie.

'Boating,' Henry said. 'It's a powerboat. You say boating.'

'Fuck,' Archie said again.

Archie was standing on the deck of a twenty-eight-foot twin-screw hard-top cabin cruiser. He didn't like boats. But he knew what kind of boat this one was because one of the river-patrol deputies had told him. The county river-patrol unit wore green uniforms, painted their boats emerald and called themselves the Green Hornets. Their winter staff consisted of one lieutenant, one sergeant, eight deputies and a full-time mechanic. Within a half-hour of Archie's call, every one of them had reported for duty.

Within forty-five minutes, five Green Hornet boats were in the water, and two police helicopters and a

Coast Guard helicopter were in the air looking for the Chris-Craft. 'It's a boat,' one of the pilots had told Archie confidently. 'It's on a river. We'll find it.' And they did. An hour later, one of the pilots had radioed to say that he had spotted a Chris-Craft anchored just off the channel on the Columbia side of Sauvie Island.

Archie relayed the location to SWAT. Reston would have noticed the ten-thousand-megawatt police helicopter searchlight as it slid past. He'd either anchor up and try to flee, in which case the helicopter would track him, or he'd hunker down. It was a hostage situation, and Archie didn't want to take any chances. But it would take SWAT time to get there, and the Green Hornet cabin cruiser wasn't far, and, after all, didn't they need to confirm that it was the right Chris-Craft? Didn't want to send a SWAT team to burst into the wrong boat and ruin a family fishing holiday. So Archie instructed the three deputies on the Hornet boat with Henry, Claire, Anne and him to circle around the island and see if they could get close.

And there she was. The running lights were off, but her cabin lights were on. Rick, a deputy about Archie's age, with short-cropped hair and a salt-and-pepper beard, aimed a searchlight mounted on the deck of the cruiser at the Chris-Craft. The helicopter circled in the black sky above.

'That's your girl,' he hollered over the engine.

'I've got SWAT and a hostage negotiator on the way,' Archie hollered back.

'There's not a lot of time,' Anne cautioned Archie. Her braids were whipping in her face and she held them back with one leather-gloved hand. 'He's going to want to end this.'

'How close can you get to him?' Archie asked Rick.

'Close enough to board.'

'Do it.'

Henry, Claire and Archie had their guns drawn as the Hornets slowed the engine to a crawl and they made their way next to the Chris-Craft. Two of the men secured lines around the patrol cruiser's cleats and stood at the starboard side of the boat. When the cruiser got close, Rick shut off her engines and they drifted the last few feet. When they were close enough, the two other deputies grabbed her railing and secured their lines to her cleats.

The two boats bobbed and knocked together. No one spoke. It was cold on the water and Archie brought his cupped hands to his mouth, blew warm air on them and then flexed them a few times to keep the blood flowing. His cheeks burned from the wind that blew over the river. There was no movement on the Chris-Craft. Archie scanned the river. No other lights on the water.

'I'm going aboard,' he announced.

He handed his gun to Henry, butt first.

Henry wrapped his fist around the gun, but placed his other hand firmly over Archie's so the gun was locked between them. He leaned forward, his big face pinched. 'You going in there because you think it's the smart thing to do,' he whispered to Archie, 'or because you've been feeling sorry for yourself?'

Archie looked his friend in the eye. *You can't save me*, Archie thought. 'Don't come in unless you hear a shot. I'll try to signal you if I think SWAT needs to take him out.'

'Take a vest,' Henry said.

The vest. Archie had taken it off when they first got on the boat. It seemed counterintuitive to wear something heavy when you were supposed to be wearing something buoyant. He pulled his hand away, leaving his gun in Henry's fist. 'Hurts my ribs,' he said, and he turned and heaved himself over the railing of the cruiser and on to the old Chris-Craft before anyone could stop him. The rubber soles of his shoes stuck to the fibreglass deck of the boat and he managed to scurry, knees bent, hunched, a few yards to the door of the cabin.

'Reston!' he shouted. 'It's Detective Archie Sheridan. I'm going to open the hatch so we can talk, OK?' He didn't wait for an answer. What was he going to do if Reston said no? Just keep moving. Keep talking. Keep him off guard. Archie fumbled with the latch; it was unlocked. He swung the square wooden hatch open. A sign on the doorjamb warned: WATCH YOUR STEP.

Archie could make out part of the interior of the wooden cabin – a small corner galley and a dinette.

But no Reston. No Susan. No Addy Jackson. 'I'm unarmed. I'm going to come in so we can talk, OK?' He waited. Nothing. That was a bad sign. Maybe they were all already dead. He took a deep breath, bracing himself for any coming scenes of carnage. 'I'm coming in.'

He squeezed in through the hatch and lowered himself down the four steps that led straight into the main cabin.

He squinted in the light. It was what passed aboard a boat for a living room. A small floral sofa and a rattan chair with matching floral cushion sat in front of a round rattan coffee table that was painted white and topped with glass. The carpet was the colour of Astroturf. The ceilings were low and the space was cramped, but the walls appeared to be panelled with teak and the wood shone warmly in the yellow interior light. A large wood and brass barometer hung decoratively above the sofa. Just beyond the sitting area lay the small dinette and corner galley he had seen from above.

Reston stood next to the sofa, in front of an entryway that led deeper under the hull. He was wearing khakis and a T-shirt. His eyes were black holes. He had one arm firmly around Susan Ward's waist and he held a gun underneath her left jaw. A brown leather belt hung loosely around her neck. Archie had no doubt that it would match the ligature marks around the dead girls' necks. Susan's forearms and ankles were bound with duct tape. But she was alive. And awake. And, judging by her drained but withering expression, furious.

'Ahoy,' Archie said.

'Addy's in the back—' Susan managed to spit out before Reston snatched the end of the belt and wrenched it tight, choking her. He kept the gun flush against her head as she fell to her knees.

'Shhhh,' he said ferociously. 'Why did you have to do that? Why won't you be nice to me?'

Susan flailed at the belt with her bound hands but couldn't get her fingers behind it to loosen the noose. Her face was distorted, blotchy, her eyes frozen wide, mouth wider, sputtering. Archie had about two minutes.

It was all he could do to stop himself from rushing Reston. He had a gun to Susan's head. If Archie lunged at him, he might shoot her. Her weight was on the floor, so Reston probably wasn't going to break her neck. A successful strangulation was harder than it looked. It wasn't the lack of air alone that killed you; it was the compression of the vascular structures of the neck. If Archie did nothing, she was going to die. But that would take a few minutes. And a few minutes was a long time. That gave Archie a chance.

He turned away from Reston and Susan and walked the few feet to the corner galley. There was a small stove and a steel sink set in a green countertop. The cupboards were painted white. Archie opened a few of them until he found some glasses. He took one out and poured himself a glass of water. He couldn't hear Susan struggling any more. Had she lost consciousness? Had he blown this, too? And then, at once, there came an enormous choking gasp. Reston had let go of the belt. Susan was breathing. She coughed, hoarse and rasping. Archie closed his eyes, feeling his blood rush to his fingertips. It had worked.

'What are you doing?' Reston asked him.

Archie waited a few breaths before he answered. Let the bastard wonder. 'I have to take some pills,' he explained, his back still turned. 'I can take them without water, but they work faster if I wash them down with something.' He turned back to Reston and gave him a courteous smile. Then he sat on the tan upholstered bench at the green fold-down dinette table, careful not to slide his knees under the tabletop, so that he could move quickly if he had to. He set the glass of water on the table. Archie could see the lights of the Coast Guard boat through the tiny porthole over the dinette. Which meant that they could see him. Good.

'I'm going to reach into my pocket now and get the pills,' he said, and before Reston could respond, he reached slowly into his pocket and retrieved the brass pillbox. He opened it and counted out eight pills and lined them up one by one on the dark-green tabletop. Even in this situation, he felt a surge of endorphins just looking at them. 'I know it looks like a lot,' he said to Reston. He raised his eyebrows wryly. 'But I have a high tolerance.'

Reston had Susan by the waist again. She was still coughing as her airway tried to convince itself that it was clear. But she had managed to pull the belt off her neck and it now lay in a heap at her feet. Good girl, thought Archie.

'Susan,' he said pleasantly. 'You OK?'

She nodded, raising her head to look at him, eyes flashing with defiance again. Reston pulled her tighter towards him. Archie picked up a pill, put it on his tongue and washed it down with a drink of water from the glass. Then he set the glass back down on the table. 'You got Addy to come to you,' he said to Reston.

Reston nodded. 'She needed someone who made her feel special.'

'But you took the other girls,' Archie said. 'So how did you fake your alibis?'

'It was easy,' Reston said. 'I watch rehearsals from the light booth. The kids can't see inside. We'd do a run-through. I'd give notes. Then we'd do another run-through. They'd see me go into the booth before they started and out of the booth when they were done. I would leave a few minutes into the first act.' He smoothed Susan's tangle of hair like one would a doll's, and she recoiled at his touch. 'I could find them, talk to them and kill them, and be back by curtain. The girls would be dead under blankets in my car and I would be giving the actors notes I had made up. I didn't even need to see the run-through. They made the same fucking mistakes every time.' Reston looked down at Susan and then back up at Archie. 'I'm not going to let you take her out of here,' he said.

Archie glanced around the cabin. 'This is a nice boat.'

'It's Dan McCallum's.'

'Right,' Archie said. 'Dan McCallum. The suicidal serial killer.'

Reston gave Archie a fleeting smile. 'I just wanted to buy some time.'

Archie picked up another pill, tossed it in the air, caught it on his tongue and washed it down with more water. He set the glass back on the table.

'I could kill you if I wanted to,' Reston said, his voice hollow and tremulous. 'I could shoot you and her before they got inside.'

Archie ran a hand through his hair and tried to look bored. 'You're not scary, Paul.' Then he added, 'I've seen scary.'

Reston was unravelling before Archie's eyes, shifting his weight from foot to foot and squeezing his eyes shut in a hard blink, an involuntary tic. He grappled with Susan, continually adjusting his grip on her, fidgeting with the gun, moving it a fraction of an inch in Archie's direction, then back, not wanting to waver from Susan. Susan kept her eye on the gun. Her whole body was shaking, but she appeared to be keeping it together. The tears had stopped. Reston leaned his head close to hers and kissed her on the cheek. 'Don't be afraid,' he told her. 'It'll be quick.' She flinched, and Reston squeezed her tighter. Then Reston turned to Archie. The pits and neck of his shirt were stained with sweat. He stank of it. 'Do you recognize me?' he asked Archie. His expression was pleading, hungry.

No question. Reston was definitely losing it. 'From yesterday on the porch?' asked Archie. Reston's eyes narrowed. 'Think back.'

Reston looked so serious, so certain, that Archie actually found himself searching his memory for what he might be talking about. Had he arrested Reston before? No, he didn't have a record. A witness he'd interviewed? Lord knew, he interviewed thousands of witnesses in connection with the Beauty Killer case. He shook his head blankly, coming up with nothing.

Reston was growing increasingly unwound. 'I've killed four people,' he announced.

That meant that Addy was still alive.

Archie heard the engine of another boat approaching. The helicopter. Bright light glowed beyond the cabin's portholes.

He picked up another pill. Washed it down. Put the glass back on the table. His own twisted Japanese tea ceremony. 'Did you like it?' he asked.

Another involuntary blink. 'I had to do it. I didn't want to do it. I didn't have a choice.' Reston's jumpiness worried Archie. Reston wasn't nervous enough about what was going on outside. The other boat. The lights.

He wasn't worried about being arrested, and to Archie that meant one thing: he'd already decided to die.

And if SWAT rushed the boat, the first thing Reston would do would be to kill Susan Ward.

'But did you like it?' Archie asked again.

'The first one was hard. After that, it got easier.' He worked his mouth into a sick grin. 'I didn't like having to kill them. But I liked it afterwards.'

'How did you choose them?' Archie asked.

'They all auditioned for the district-wide musical last year.' Reston laughed at the ridiculousness of it. 'They're expensive, musicals. Because of budget cuts, none of us could afford to launch one on our own, so the high schools got together and co-sponsored one.'

There was the connection, thought Archie. Henry was right – they had all been freshmen last year. A district-wide musical? How could they have missed it?

'I was the director. I didn't cast any of them. They weren't good enough. But I remembered them. And they remembered me. They all wanted to be stars. I told them I wanted them each in my next play.'

'Young girls are easily manipulated,' Archie observed flatly.

Reston smirked. 'I'm a very popular teacher.'

Susan rolled her eyes. 'Please,' she said.

Archie took another pill.

'What are the pills for?' Reston asked.

A smile skated across Archie's lips. It just might work. He ran his finger around the lip of the glass, never taking his eyes off Reston. 'I have dark fantasies.' There was Gretchen again. Her hand against his cheek. The lilacs.

Then Archie had a thought. He could probably get Reston to shoot him. Provoke him a little more. Needle him until he became so enraged at Archie that he was willing to train the gun away from Susan long enough to take a shot. Archie bet he wasn't a good shot, probably never been to a range. But if Archie got close enough, Reston might be able to hit him in the head or neck. It was an easy way out. In the line of duty. Everyone would understand that. Henry would know. Debbie, too, probably. But everyone else would just chalk the tragedy up to his dark fate. *Poor Archie Sheridan. It's probably for the best. He was never quite the same after his ordeal.*

But then there was Susan. Reston would kill her. The second after he'd fired at Archie, he'd shoot her in the head, and he wouldn't miss. SWAT wouldn't be able to take him out in time, not where he was standing. They'd storm in after the first crack of gunfire, but Susan would be dead by then and Reston would maybe be able to get the gun in his mouth, fire it. Or they'd tackle him. Take the gun away. Arrest him. Archie and Susan would be dead and Reston would survive. That didn't seem fair.

Back to Plan A. The plan in which Reston got the bullet through the skull. *It was a better plan anyway*, thought Archie.

Time to alert the cavalry. Archie placed his elbow on the table and rested his chin in his right hand, the side that faced the porthole. He curled his pinkie and ring finger and extended his index and middle fingers straight, like the barrel of a shotgun, right to the temple. They would be watching him; he had been sitting there long enough, a goldfish in a bowl, a girl watching TV at night in an apartment. Henry would understand. The portholes were made out of some sort of thick double-paned acrylic. The best shot would be through the hatch, which Archie had left open. If the sharpshooters had even arrived. If anyone had seen his signal. If he could get Reston in the line of fire.

Reston took a tiny step forward, the gun still pressed against Susan's skull. 'Do the pills help?'

'No,' Archie said truthfully. 'But they make you feel less guilty.'

'Give me some,' Reston demanded.

Archie picked up a pill and looked at it. 'Do you have a prescription?'

'I'll kill her.'

'You're going to kill her anyway.'

'I'll kill you.'

Archie set the pill back on the table. 'Still not scary, Paul.'

Reston grabbed a handful of Susan's pink hair and rammed her head into the teak-panelled wall of the cabin.

'Fuck!' she yelled.

Archie stood.

Reston levelled the gun on him, still holding Susan by the hair. Her forehead was bleeding, but she was conscious, fighting. Reston was infuriated, his face beet red, eyes searing. His chest heaved and his features transformed into something misshapen, deformed with rage.

'OK,' Archie said. He picked up a pill and tossed it towards Reston. It landed on the green carpet, halfway between the two men. Reston scrambled forward, dragging Susan by the hair, gun still levelled at Archie. He got to where the pill lay and, unwilling to drop the gun or Susan, lowered his head, eyes still raised at Archie, and picked up the pill in his teeth. With a victorious grin at Archie, he swallowed it. Then, there was a crack of a sniper's rifle through the open hatch, and Reston's head jerked forward and he slammed into the carpet. Susan screamed and scooted backward, her mouth open.

The SWAT team rushed in, weapons drawn, their black gear making them look like creatures that had just risen out of the Willamette. Susan had her bound hands in front of her face and she was saying, 'Fuck. Fuck. Fuck.'

'Check through there,' Archie said, pointing down the hallway. But he didn't move. There were still three pills on the table. He brushed them into his hand and dropped them in his pocket.

48

Archie was high. He stood at the river's edge, hands in his pockets, a fine mist of rain settling on his shoulders. One of these days, he was going to get one of those waterproof jackets that everyone kept recommending. It was nearly two o'clock in the morning. But he wasn't tired. The right dose of Vicodin kept him in a state of perpetual in-between. Not tired, not awake. It wasn't such a bad state of mind once you got used to it.

Behind him, about fifty feet from the river's edge, was the downtown branch of the Green Hornet River Patrol office. Rectangular, with brown plastic siding, the building looked like something that had come in a box and been put together in an afternoon. Henry, Claire, Susan and the others were inside. They were talking to her first; then Archie would be up. He had sneaked out to get some air. The Chris-Craft had been towed to the dock, and Archie watched now as the crime-scene techs set up 1,800-watt lights that lit the exterior of the boat up like a movie set.

Addy Jackson was stable and on her way to Emanuel. The Rohypnol fog was already lifting, and she was conscious, though confused and unable to answer questions yet. Archie hoped that she would be blessed with the drug's more amnesiac properties.

The press had yet to arrive. They would have heard the police call by then, but Portland was still a small market, and the TV stations worked skeleton shifts at night. Archie imagined them pulling on their news slickers, racing to the scene, prepared to go live with the story for as long as they could wring the drama from it. It would start all over again.

Archie heard the man behind him before he saw him. A few footsteps, and then the silhouette of a fat man appeared in the dark. Archie didn't even need to turn his head. He recognized the faint smell of liquor and stale cigarettes.

'Quentin Parker,' Archie said.

'Heard you caught yourself another one.'

'You working this?'

'I've got a kid with me,' Parker said. 'Derek Rogers. Plus Ian Harper's on his way.'

'Ah.'

Parker snorted. 'You think he's a twit now. Wait until you meet him in person.'

The two stood side by side for a long moment, watching the Chris-Craft, the lights, the black river. Finally, Archie spoke. 'You never came to see me in the hospital. Everyone else was scrambling to sneak into my room, begging for interviews, sending flowers, impersonating doctors. Not you.'

The big man shrugged. 'Never got around to it.'

'It was appreciated,' Archie said.

Parker fumbled for a cigarette, lit it, and took a drag. It was tiny in his hand, the tip glowing orange in the darkness. 'You're going to be famous again.'

Archie looked up at the sky. The moon was a smear of light behind the cloud cover. 'I'm thinking of moving to Australia.'

'Watch yourself, Sheridan. Those stories Susan did have stirred things up. The whole "tragic hero" thing goes over well, but pretty soon they'll want more. The pills. Your weekly sit-downs with Gretchen Lowell. We'll eat you alive for that shit. The mayor, Henry – they can only do so much to protect you. If the fourth estate smells blood, there's gonna be a blood-bath.'

'Thanks for the advice.'

'Bad call, huh?' Parker said, bringing his fist to his mouth, the cigarette a tiny lantern.

'What?' Archie asked.

'Becoming a cop,' he said, looking at the cigarette in his hand. 'Should've been an academic.' He ashed the cigarette with a delicate flick of his big wrist. 'Taught school somewhere.'

'Too late now,' Archie said.

'Me, I wanted to be a car salesman.' He looked into the distance and smiled. 'Oldsmobiles.' He gave Archie a shrug and studied the cigarette. 'Got sidetracked as a copy boy. Tenth grade. Nineteen fifty-nine. Never went to college. They used to print the paper right there. In the basement. I used to love the smell of the ink.' He brought the cigarette to his mouth again, took a drag, exhaled it. 'These days? Paper won't hire someone for an unpaid internship unless they've got an Ivy League degree.'

'Times change.'

'How's our girl?'

Archie looked up at the office. 'Pissed.'

'She's a hell of a kid.'

'Can I have a piece of gum?' Susan asked. She was in a back room in the patrol office with Henry and Claire. There was a desk in the room, and a task chair. The walls were covered with nautical charts. The desk was stacked with black binders with the city seal on them, and white and pink pieces of paper that appeared to be various forms and reports: boxes checked, explanations filled in, stamped, certified, signed. It was a man's office. Colour photographs of him hung on the walls in cheap diploma frames. Fishing. Standing around with other men in green uniforms. Formal Sears portraits with the family. He had a moustache and an exuberant expression. In some of the more recent pictures, he had a beard. To the left of the desk was a four-shelf metal bookcase, stacked with books about marine law and Oregon history. On top of the bookcase was a jar of fat pink bubble gum.

'Sure.' Claire plucked a piece of gum from the jar and handed it to Susan.

Susan unwrapped it and put it in her mouth. Her hands were still sore from the tape, and her wrists were raw. The gum was sugary and hard. 'It's stale,' Susan declared sadly.

'Just a few more questions,' Claire said. 'Before your mother breaks down the door.'

'My mom's here?' Susan asked, surprised.

'Outside,' Henry said. 'They practically had to put her in a half-nelson to keep her out of here while we wrapped up.'

Bliss was there. Bliss had come and was waiting for her. It was something a mother would do. Susan imagined the cops having to deal with her. Bliss was probably bossing everyone around, threatening to go to the Citizen's Police Action Committee. Susan smiled happily.

'What?' said Claire.

'Nothing,' Susan said. 'Go ahead.' They had been going over the same questions for almost an hour. Susan felt that she had recounted, minute by minute, every interaction she'd had with Paul Reston since she was fourteen years old. She had told them how he had manipulated Addy. Now she didn't want to think about him any more. Her head throbbed. The paramedics had used butterfly bandages to tape the cut on her forehead shut, but she was going to have a hell of a black eye in the morning. She wanted a cigarette. And a bath. And she wanted her mother.

Claire was leaning against one wall, Henry against the other. 'You're sure he didn't mention any other girls, girls we might not know about?' Claire asked.

'I'm sure,' Susan said.

'And you didn't save any letters that he sent?'

There had been hundreds of them. She had tossed them in the bonfire on her dead father's birthday while she was still in college. 'I got rid of them all. Years ago.'

Claire gave Susan a careful appraisal. 'And you're OK? You don't need to go to the hospital?'

Susan touched her neck, where an ugly red mark had formed. It stung, but it would heal. 'I'll be fine.'

There was a knock at the door and Henry opened it and Archie Sheridan walked in.

'Maybe we can wrap this up in the morning?' he asked. 'Let Susan go home and get some sleep?'

'Sure,' Henry said. He glanced at his watch and turned to Claire. 'You still up for heading back to McCallum's?'

'For what?' Archie asked.

'He wants to see if he can find that goddamn cat,' Claire said. She made a face at Archie. 'He's such a softy.'

'What?' said Henry as he and Claire left the office. 'I like cats.'

Archie's hair and clothes glistened with condensation. He looked like something that had been left in the yard overnight and was now covered with dew.

Susan wanted to leap into his arms. 'You're all wet,' she observed.

'It's raining,' Archie said.

'Thank God,' Susan muttered. And then she started to cry. She felt Archie kneel down next to her and put his arm around her and pull her into his wet corduroy blazer. She let herself sob. Not because she wanted to, but because she couldn't stop it. Her whole body shook, gasping for air. She hid her face. Archie smelled like rain. His sweater scratched her cheek, but she didn't care. After a few minutes, she looked up and saw that Henry and Claire were gone.

'Feel better?' Archie asked softly.

Susan held her hands out in front of her and watched them quiver. 'No.'

'Afraid?' he asked.

Susan considered this. 'The expression "scared shitless" comes to mind.'

Archie looked her in the eyes. 'It'll pass,' he said.

She examined his face, his eyes full of kindness, his pupils tiny. That had been quite a performance on the boat. If it had been a performance. 'What are you afraid of, Archie?' she asked.

He slid her an amused, suspicious glance. 'Is this for your story?'

'Yes.' She looked at him for a minute and then laughed. 'But we can go off the record if you want.'

He was thoughtful and then his face grew dark and

he seemed to shake some prickly idea from his head. 'I think I'm done being a subject for a while,' he said.

She nodded, and in that moment she realized that Archie had never told her anything, never let her see anything, that he didn't want her to know. It didn't matter. He could have his secrets. She was done with hers. 'He said that I was his person,' she told him. 'He said that we all have people in the world we belong to. Connect with. And that I was his. He said that there was no denying it.'

Archie laid his hand on her arm. 'He was wrong.'

She rested her fist on Archie's chest. 'Well, anyway,' she said, 'this is going to sound dorky, but thanks for saving my life.'

'It doesn't sound dorky at all.'

She leaned forward and kissed him. It was a light kiss on the lips. He didn't move. He didn't reciprocate, but he didn't pull away either. When she opened her eyes, he smiled at her gently.

'You've got to get over that,' he said. 'The older-men-in-authority thing.'

She made a face. 'Right. I'll get right on that.'

Susan walked out into the foyer of the patrol office. She saw her mother before her mother saw her. Bliss's red lipstick was faded and she looked small in her big leopard-print coat. Quentin Parker, Derek the Square and Ian Harper were huddled a few yards away from her, and Bliss stood by herself against the wall. Ian saw Susan and smiled, but Susan barely gave him a glance as she went straight to her mother. Bliss looked up and burst into tears and wrapped her arms around Susan. She reeked of menthols and wet old fur and pressed against Susan like they might merge into one person. Susan was aware of her colleagues watching, but she was only slightly mortified.

'They told me about Reston,' Bliss said in a shaky whisper. 'I'm so sorry, baby. I'm so sorry.'

'It's OK,' Susan said. She peeled her mother off her and kissed her on the cheek. 'I think it's going to be OK now.'

She squinted past them through a bank of rain-splattered windows and for a second she thought it was daylight, until she realized that the lights were from the TV cameras. She was news and they all wanted a shot of her for the local morning shows. She was definitely going to have to do something different with her hair. Maybe dye it blue.

'Hey,' Susan said to her mother. 'Can I bum a cigarette?'

Bliss's brow furrowed. 'You'll get lung cancer,' she said.

Susan fixed her steely gaze on her mother. 'Give me a cigarette, Bliss.'

Bliss dug a pack of menthols out of her enormous

purse and held one out towards Susan. Then withdrew it when Susan reached for it. 'Call me Mom,' she said.

'Give me a cigarette . . .' Susan paused and scrunched her face up with effort. 'Mom.'

'Now try "Mother dearest".'

'Give me the fucking cigarette.'

They both laughed and Bliss handed Susan the cigarette and then pressed a plastic lighter into her hands.

Parker stepped forward. 'We need to talk,' he said to Susan. 'And only partially because I want to scoop the assholes waiting outside.'

'I'll give you the facts,' Susan said. 'But I'm filing a harrowing personal account in the morning.'

There was Ian. He was wearing a Yankees sweat-shirt and jeans, clearly pulled on after a middle-of-the-night phone call, and all she could think was: *You went to sleep when you knew I was missing? You asshole.*

But he looked at her like nothing had changed. Like she hadn't changed. Well, she hadn't changed. But she planned to. She put the cigarette in her mouth, lit it and handed the lighter back to her mother. She only vaguely noticed that her hand was still trembling.

She took a drag of the cigarette, putting a lot of elbow in it, like she had seen in old French movies, and she appraised him – arrogant, condescending, professorial. And she saw in Ian every boss, every teacher, she'd ever slept with. Yeah. It was probably time to consider therapy. She wondered idly if the paper's health-insurance policy covered it. This probably wasn't the time to ask. 'Once this whole thing is done,' she said to Ian, 'I want to work on the Molly Palmer story. Full-time.'

'It's career suicide,' Ian protested. Then, in a final attempt at dissuasion, he added, 'It's tabloid journalism.'

'Hey,' Bliss said. 'My daughter—'

'Mom,' Susan warned, and Bliss was silent. Susan was composed, indomitable. 'Molly was a teenager, Ian. I want to find out what happened. I want to get her side of the story.'

Ian sighed and rocked back on his heels. He opened his mouth as if to argue, then seemed to think better of it and threw his hands in the air. The smoke from Susan's cigarette was getting in his eyes. She didn't move it. 'You won't get her to talk,' he said. 'She hasn't talked to anyone. But if you want to try . . .' He let that trail off.

Bliss didn't drive, and Susan's car was back in the Pearl District. 'I don't suppose you have money for a cab?' Susan asked her mother.

Bliss frowned. 'I don't carry money,' she said.

'Your purse,' Parker said to Susan, extracting her small black bag from the pocket of his coat and handing it to her. 'They found it in Reston's car.'

'I'll drive you both home when you're ready.' It was

Derek the Square. He hadn't had time to blow-dry his hair, and it protruded straight out from his skull like grass.

'I'm going to need you to file the story, kid,' Parker said. 'Get it up online before we get scooped. You go home early, don't expect to see your byline.'

Derek shrugged, throwing a glance at Susan. 'There'll be other stories.'

'I need a new mentee,' Parker said to Ian. 'This one isn't working out.' But Susan could tell he didn't mean it.

'What do you drive?' Susan asked Derek. 'Let me guess. A Jetta? No. A Taurus?'

Derek dangled a ring of keys from his fingers. 'An old Mercedes,' he said. 'It runs on biodiesel.'

Susan tried to ignore the slow grin she could see spreading on Bliss's face.

'First I'll need to go to my apartment for my laptop,' Susan told Derek, as she took a drag off her cigarette. 'Then I want to go home. To Bliss's.' Derek's eyebrows shot up. 'My mom's house,' Susan explained quickly, digging through her purse for her cell phone. 'She lives in South-east.' She looked at her cell-phone screen. She had eighteen new messages. The phone vibrated in her hand and she jumped, startled. It was an incoming call.

'Bliss?' Derek said.

Bliss held out a hand. 'How do you do,' she said.

Susan was going to say something clever, but she got distracted by her voicemail. The first message was from Molly Palmer.

Anne shrugged on her long leather coat. She wasn't needed, but she always liked witnessing the wrap-up. It gave her a sense of closure. She dug for her car keys as she exited the patrol office. The damp north-west weather had officially returned. Anne didn't know how the natives stood it. It just made her feel like the entire world was rotting away around her.

'Good job today.' It was Archie, standing in the drizzle just outside the door.

Anne smiled. 'You want a lift?' she asked. 'I'm headed back to the Heathman. I can drop you.'

'No. I've got a cab coming.'

Anne looked inside, where Claire and Henry were conferring with the crime-scene techies. 'Someone here will drive you.'

Archie shrugged. 'I've got to make a stop.'

'At this time of night?' Anne asked. She had an idea where he was going. She had gone to see Gretchen Lowell herself, in those first few days when Archie lay in a medically induced coma. Anne's bad profile had stung, and she'd thought she might learn something from the Beauty Killer. But Gretchen had refused to talk. She'd sat mutely for an hour in her cell while Anne peppered her with questions. And then Anne had got up to leave, and Gretchen had finally spoken. One sentence: 'Is he still alive?'

'You heading back tomorrow, or are you going to stick around for all the congratulatory press conferences?' Archie asked.

Anne let him change the subject. 'I'm on the red-eye.' You couldn't force it, she knew, until he was ready for help. But it hurt her to see him suffer, and it hurt her more to not be able to do anything for him. 'So I'm around during the day,' she said. She was going to skip the press conferences. There were two pairs of size-fourteen sneakers at the Nike outlet with her sons' names on them. But she added, just in case, 'If you want to talk.'

Archie fingered something in his coat pocket and looked at his shoes. 'I need to talk to someone.'

'But not to me,' Anne guessed.

Archie glanced up and smiled at her. He looked exhausted to Anne, and she wondered if she looked similarly worn.

'Have a nice flight,' he said warmly. 'It was good to see you.'

Anne took a small step towards him. 'Anything that happened. While you were with Gretchen. Anything you felt or did. You can't judge it. It was an extreme situation. She constructed an extreme situation. To push you.'

He looked away, into the night. 'I gave up everything I loved in that basement.' Archie's voice was low, controlled. 'My children. My wife. My work. My life. I was going to die. In her arms. And I was all right with that. Because she would be there.' He looked right at Anne. 'Taking care of me.'

'She's a psychopath.'

A yellow cab pulled into the small parking lot behind the office. 'Yeah,' Archie said, taking a step towards it. 'But she's my psychopath.'

49

Archie wakes up completely disorientated. He is still in the basement. He is still in the bed. But everything is different. The bed has been moved against the wall. The stench of rotten meat is gone. He looks for the corpse. It has vanished; the cement floor is washed clean. His bandages are fresh. The sheets have been changed. He has been bathed. The room smells like ammonia. He searches the fractured images in his mind for some recent memory.

'You've been asleep for two days.' Gretchen appears from behind him. She is wearing a fresh change of clothes – black pants and a grey cashmere sweater – and her blond hair is clean and brushed smooth into a shiny ponytail.

Archie blinks at her, his head still muddy. 'I don't understand,' he manages to say, his voice weak.

'You died,' Gretchen explains. 'But I brought you back. Ten milligrams of lidocaine. I wasn't sure it would work.' She shoots him a twinkling grin. 'You must have a healthy heart.'

He lets this sink in. 'Why?'

'Because we're not done yet.'

'I'm done,' he says with as much authority as he can muster.

Gretchen gives him an admonishing look. 'You don't get to choose, though, do you? I get to make all the decisions. I get to be the one in charge. All you have to do is go along.' She leans in close, her face inches away from his, her warm hand on his cheek. 'It's the easiest thing in the world,' she says soothingly. 'You've worked so hard for so long. Always on call. All that responsibility. Everyone always looking to you for answers.' He can feel her breath against his mouth, tickling his lips. He doesn't look at her. It's too hard. He looks through her. 'They all think you're dead now, darling. It's been a long time. I don't keep anyone alive this long. Henry knows that. I would think you would be pleased. No one needs you any more.' She smiles and kisses him on the forehead. 'Enjoy it.'

He feels that kiss even as she peels back the bandage covering the surgical incision that stretches from his xiphoid process to his navel. Even as he catches a glimpse of the black sutures that hold his flesh together. She looks pleased. 'The swelling's gone down as well as the redness,' she comments.

He stares unblinking at the ceiling. There is no escaping. She could keep him alive down here for years. He is at her mercy.

But he has to know. 'What are you going to do with me?'

'Keep you.'

'For how long?' he asks.

Gretchen leans over him again, this time eye to eye, so he can't help but look at her, her blue eyes wide, one eyebrow slightly arched, skin glowing. She smiles and is radiant. 'Until you like it,' she says.

When he wakes up, she has the X-Acto knife out again and she is cutting into his chest. It hurts, but he doesn't care. It's a minor nuisance, a mosquito bite. But it reminds him that he is alive.

'Do you want me to stop?' she asks, not looking up.

'No,' he says. 'I'm hoping you'll nick an artery.' His voice is frail, his throat still aflame with pain.

She puts her palm on his cheek and leans in close to his ear, as if they are about to share a secret. 'What about your children? Don't you want to live for them?'

Ben and Sara's sweet faces flash before him and he wipes the image clean from his mind, until there is nothing. 'I don't have any children.' He turns his head towards the wall.

'How long has it been?' he asks her. His slide in and out of consciousness has allowed time to slip away altogether. How long have they been there? Weeks? Months now? He has no idea. He has been spitting up blood again. He knows that it worries her. Her exquisite face has become taut and she is always there, always at his side. It is the one thing he can count on. He wants to stop spitting up the blood, to please her, but he can't help himself.

She is seated beside him. She puts a piece of blond hair behind her ear and presses her fingers against his wrist to take his pulse. She's been doing this a lot, and he realizes that it is because he is dying. He knows that she will touch his wrist for fifteen seconds, and it is the only thing he looks forward to. There is something about her touch that consoles him absolutely. He savours those fifteen seconds, memorizing the feel of her skin against his so that he can imagine her fingers there when she lifts her hand.

'Untie me,' he says. He has to take several breaths to get enough oxygen to speak, and even then his voice is a faint rasp.

She doesn't even think about it. She reaches down and unfastens the leather bindings that trap one wrist, and then undoes the other. He's too weak to raise his arms even a few inches, but she lifts his hand to her mouth and kisses his palm. He feels the warm tears on her face before he sees them. She is crying. And it breaks his heart. The tears rise in his own eyes even as hers cool on his rough hand.

'It's all right,' he says, comforting her.

He smiles. Because he believes it. Everything is all right. He is right where he is supposed to be. She is so beautiful and he is so tired. And it is almost over.

50

Archie called the prison from the cab, so by the time he had paid his $138 fare and made his way through security, Gretchen had been roused and placed in the interview room to wait for him. She was sitting at the table when he came into the room, hair loose, no make-up, yet still somehow put together. Like an actress made up to look unkempt.

'It's four in the morning,' she said.

'I'm sorry,' he said, sitting across from her. 'Were you in the middle of something?'

She glanced warily over her shoulder at the panel of two-way glass. 'Is Henry here?'

'I'm alone. There's no one behind the glass. I told the guards to wait on the other side of the door. So it's just you and me. I took a cab.'

'From Portland?' Gretchen asked sceptically.

'I'm a hero cop,' Archie said wearily. 'I have an expense account.'

She gave him a slow, sleepy smile. 'You must have caught him.'

Archie could feel himself finally relaxing. It was

more of a surrender, really. He used up so much energy keeping up appearances, and with her it didn't matter. She knew exactly how damaged he was. So he could let his muscles loosen, his eyelids fall heavy, his voice thicken. He could scratch his face if it itched. He could say what came into his head without worrying if it shed too much light on what he was really thinking. 'A sharpshooter plugged him in the head about three hours ago. You would have enjoyed it.' He raised an eyebrow in reconsideration. 'Except that he died instantly.'

'Well, aren't you the serial-killer bloodhound? Did you come to brag?'

'I can't drop by and say hi without an ulterior motive?'

'It's not Sunday.' She cocked her head and examined him, and a tiny little line formed between her eyebrows. 'Are you OK?'

He laughed at the ridiculousness of the question. He was definitely not OK. He has an exhausting, stressful, rewarding day at work, and where does he go? The state pen. 'I just wanted to see you.' He rubbed his eyes with his hand. 'How fucked up is that?'

'Do you know the origin of the term "Stockholm Syndrome"?' Gretchen asked sweetly. She reached out her manacled hands and laid her palms flat on the tabletop so that the tips of her fingers were inches from where Archie's right hand lay on the table. 'In 1973, a petty criminal named Janne Olsson walked into the

Kreditbanken bank in Stockholm with a machine gun. He demanded three million crowns and that a friend of his be freed from prison. The police released the friend and sent him into the bank and he and Olsson held four bank employees hostage in a vault for six days. The police finally drilled a hole into the vault and pumped in gas, and Olsson and his friend surrendered.' She slid her hands across the table, closer to Archie. Her hands were smooth, the nails cut short. 'All the hostages were freed, unharmed. Their lives had been threatened, they had been forced to wear nooses around their necks, and yet to a person they defended Olsson. One of the women said that she had wanted to run off with him. Olsson served eight years in prison. You know where he is now?' Gently, slowly, she brushed Archie's thumb with her fingertips. 'He runs a grocery store in Bangkok.'

Archie looked down at where their hands touched, but he didn't move a muscle. 'They should consider stiffer sentencing in Sweden.'

'Stockholm is lovely. The Bergianska botanical garden has a greenhouse that has plants from every climate zone in the world. I'll take you there one day.'

'You're never getting out of prison.'

She raised her eyebrows non-committally and drew a tiny circle on the crook of his thumb with her finger.

'It's funny,' Archie said, watching her finger on his thumb. 'How Reston waited ten years to start killing. Anne says there must have been a trigger.'

'Oh?'

Archie looked up. 'How did you meet him?'

Gretchen smiled. 'Meet him?'

'Reston,' Archie said. He threaded his hand in hers. It was the first time he had ever made an effort to touch her, and he thought he saw a flicker of surprise in her eyes. 'He was one of your accomplices. Maybe one you were training,' he said, letting himself enjoy the heat of her hand in his. 'He was there that day. He was the second man who lifted me into the van. And then you went to prison. And he festered. And it set him off. How did you meet him?'

She looked at him, and in that moment Archie realized that Gretchen had never told him anything, never let him see anything that she didn't want him to know. She had always been in control. She had always been one move ahead.

'I picked him out, just as I did all the others,' she explained happily. 'His online profile was perfect. Long divorced.' She smiled. 'I like the divorced ones because they're lonely. He didn't have any hobbies, passions. High IQ. Middle-class.' She gave a dismissive little roll of her eyes. 'He tried to pass a Whitman poem off as one of his own. Classic narcissism.' She leaned forward. 'Narcissists are easy to manipulate because they're so predictable. He was depressed. Obsessed with fantasy.' A smile spread on her lips. 'And he liked blonds. We dated. I told him that I was married and that we had to keep our love a secret and I gave him what he wanted. Power. Submission. I let him think he was in control.' *Sound familiar*? thought Archie. 'Once I'd gotten him to tell me about his little teen lust, it wasn't hard to help him express his rage.'

Archie threaded his fingers even deeper between hers, so that their hands were tightly entwined. His mouth felt dry. He could barely look at her, but he didn't want to let go. It was all becoming horribly clear. 'You let me think I'd come up with bringing Susan in. But Reston had told you about her. You recognized her byline. You planted the idea. Stopped giving me bodies. Dropped her name. You set us all up.' Archie shook his head and chuckled. 'And then you sat back to watch.' It sounded absurd even as he was saying it, paranoid, the delusions of a drug addict. 'I just don't think I can prove it.'

She smiled at him indulgently. 'The important thing is that you've gone back to work,' she said. 'Gotten out of that apartment.'

Henry would believe him. He knew what Gretchen was capable of. But then what? Henry would make sure that Archie never saw Gretchen again.

'You should be grateful to Paul,' Gretchen continued wickedly. 'He donated two pints of blood to you.'

Archie turned his head, nauseous. The image of Reston on the boat's Astroturf-green carpet, head bloody meat, flashed in his head. 'Do you really like Godard?' Archie asked her.

'No,' she said. 'But I know that you do.'

He was starting to wonder if there was anything left that Gretchen Lowell didn't know about him.

'Now you answer a question for me,' she said. She placed a hand on top of the hand she was already holding, so that he was entirely in her grasp. 'Were you attracted to me, that day we first met? When I was the psychiatrist writing a book?'

'I was married.'

'So cagey. Be honest.'

He had already betrayed Debbie utterly. Why not this too? 'Yes.'

She pulled her hands from his and sat back. 'Let me see it.'

He knew what she meant, and hesitated only briefly before reaching up and slowly unbuttoning his shirt. Then, when it was open, he pulled the shirt apart so she could see his ravaged torso.

She leaned forward over the table, her knees on her chair, perched on her elbows on the table, so she could see. He didn't move, didn't flinch, as she reached forward and ran her fingertip over the heart she had carved on him. But he wondered if she could see the pulse in his neck quicken. He could smell her hair. Not like lilacs any more, some industrial prison shampoo, harsh and lemon. She moved her fingers to the vertical scar that divided his chest, and Archie felt the muscles in his stomach, and lower, tense.

'Is this from the oesophagus surgery?' she asked.

He nodded.

Then the fingers danced to the midline scar that divided his lower torso.

'This isn't my incision.'

He cleared his throat. 'They had to open me up again. There was a little bleeding.'

She nodded and moved her fingers over the smaller scars now, from the X-Acto knife she had used to doodle on him. Her fingers traced the half-moon scars along his scapula, then across his nipples, underneath to the hash-mark scars in the tender skin of his flank. It had been more than two years since he'd been touched. He was afraid to move. Afraid of what? That she'd stop? He closed his eyes. He would give himself this one brief moment of pleasure. What could it hurt? It felt good. And he hadn't felt good in longer than he could remember. Her fingers skated lower. Blood rushed to his groin. She was unfastening his belt now. *Fuck.* He opened his eyes and grabbed one of her hands by the wrist and held it there.

She looked up, eyes shining, cheeks pink. 'You don't have to pretend to be good with me, Archie.'

He held her hand there, centimetres from his hard-on.

'I can make you feel better,' she said. 'Just let my wrist go. No one has to know.'

But he held on to her. Every cell in his body begged him to let her touch him. But what was left of his mind knew that, if he did, it would be the last thing, that she would have some last part of him. It would be over. She would own him entirely. She was amazingly good. She could torture him without even touching him. He laughed at that, and pushed her hands away.

'What's funny?' she asked.

He shook his head. 'You've done one hell of a job fucking me up,' he said. He got the pillbox from his pants pocket, opened it and dumped a handful of pills into his hand. Then he popped them into his mouth one at a time and swallowed them.

'You're already high,' Gretchen noted.

'Careful,' Archie said. 'You sound like Debbie.'

'You have to watch the pills. The acetaminophen will kill you. Do your kidneys hurt yet?'

'Sometimes.'

'If you experience fever, jaundice or vomiting, you need to get to an emergency room before your liver gives out. Are you drinking?'

'I'm fine, sweetheart,' Archie said.

'There are easier ways to kill yourself. I'll do it for you.' She caught his eye. 'If you bring me a razor.'

'Yeah,' he said with a sigh. 'You'd kill me, and the first three guards who came in after me. Don't let my erection confuse you. I still know what you are.'

She reached out and touched his face. Her hand was warm and gentle, and he turned into it almost by instinct. 'Poor Archie,' she said. 'I'm just getting started with you.'

She really was beautiful, Archie thought through

his pill haze. There was something delicate about her. The luminous skin. The perfect features. Sometimes he could fool himself into thinking that she was almost human. He turned his cheek, and her hand fell away. 'How many men like Reston do you have out there?' he asked. 'How many time bombs?'

Gretchen leaned back in her chair and smiled. 'Including you?'

Archie felt the room slip around him and he reached out to steady himself on the table. 'You had it planned all along. To call nine-one-one. To save me. To turn yourself in.'

It was hot in the room. Archie felt the moist burn of sweat under his clothes. Gretchen looked cool and calm. Maybe it was just the pills. He cracked his neck and wiped the sweat off his upper lip. He could feel the heart scar throb under his shirt, his real heart beating underneath it. 'It was a good plan,' he managed. He planted his hands on the table and stood. 'Except that I'm not like Reston and the jackasses you got to murder for you. I know what you're capable of.' He looked around the room, the cinder-block tomb they met in every week. She had manipulated him again and again. They had manipulated each other. But he had one power. The card she thought he wouldn't play. 'You made one other miscalculation,' he said. 'You got yourself locked up.' He raised an eyebrow and lifted his hands off the table. 'And you can't fuck with me if I'm not here.'

Gretchen was unimpressed. 'You'll stay away a few weeks. But you'll need the bodies.' She tilted her head at him and smiled, radiant. 'You'll need me.'

Probably, Archie thought. 'Maybe,' he said.

She shook her head sympathetically. 'It's too late. You won't feel better.'

Archie laughed. 'I don't need to feel better,' he said. His tone turned cold. 'I just need you to feel worse.'

She leaned forward, her blond hair brushing her shoulders. 'You'll still dream about me. You won't be able to touch another woman without thinking of me.'

He put a hand back on the table and lifted the other to his throbbing temple. 'Please, Gretchen.'

She smiled wickedly. 'You'll think about me tonight, won't you?' she said. 'When you're all alone in the dark. Your cock in your hand.'

Archie hung his head for a moment. And then he laughed to himself, looked up, and walked around the table to her. She glanced up, surprised, as he stood over her and reached out and touched her hair, the blond slick beneath his fingers. She started to speak and he put a finger on her mouth and he said quietly, 'You don't get to talk yet.' And he cupped her face in his hands and leaned down and he kissed her. He moved one hand behind her neck in her hair as their tongues met, the heat of the kiss momentarily overwhelming him. In that kiss he could taste the bitter pills, the salt of his own sweat, and in her mouth a sweetness almost like lilacs. He had to force himself to disentangle his fingers from her hair, wrench himself away, his lips moving from her mouth, across her smooth cheek, finding her ear. 'I think about you every night,' he whispered.

Then he straightened up and said, 'Now it's over.'

He hit the buzzer by the door with the heel of his fist. The door opened and he walked through.

'Wait,' she said, her voice faltering.

His heart was pounding in his chest, the taste of the kiss still in his mouth. It took everything he had not to look back.

51

Archie was sitting at the coffee table, studying his cab receipts, wondering how he was going to explain them, when the doorbell rang. He hadn't slept. His blood felt thick and warm, his brain muddy. He looked, he thought, even worse than normal. He half expected to find a reporter at his door, a TV camera, microphones. But in his heart he knew that it would be Debbie. He hoped it would be her.

'You caught him,' she said when he opened the door. She was dressed for work: a grey skirt and a fitted black turtleneck under her long double-breasted coat. They were almost the same clothes she'd been wearing that last morning he'd seen her, two years ago, that day he'd gone to Gretchen's house alone.

'Come in,' he said.

She moved past him, pausing a few feet inside to look around the living room. She had only been at his apartment a few times. She tried to act as if his sad little residence didn't depress her, but he could see it in her eyes. She turned back to face him. 'The news said that there was a hostage situation. With that reporter. That you went in.'

Archie closed the door. 'It wasn't that dangerous. He would have killed her before he killed me.'

She stepped forward, cupping his face with her hands. 'Are you OK?'

He didn't know how to answer the question. So he avoided it. 'Do you want some coffee?'

She let her hands drop. 'Archie.'

'I'm sorry,' he said, rubbing his eyes. 'I haven't slept.'

She took off her coat and laid it on the back of the beige recliner. Then she walked to the sofa and sat down. 'Sit with me,' she said.

He sank down beside her and rested his head in his hands. He wanted to tell her, but he was afraid to say it out loud. 'I'm going to try to stop seeing her,' he said.

Debbie closed her eyes for a moment. When she opened them, they were shining with tears. 'Thank God,' she said. She kicked off her shoes and curled her legs up on the sofa.

Rain slapped against the living-room window. *So much for the forecast*, Archie thought. The pillbox was on the coffee table. It had been a gift from Debbie. The day they'd let him out of the hospital.

'I think you should come home,' Debbie said. 'Just for a few days,' she added quickly. 'You can sleep in the guest room. It would be good for the kids.' And then, looking around, she added, 'I don't like to think of you in this terrible apartment.'

Archie leaned forward, picked up the pillbox and placed it on his palm. It was a pretty little thing. The kid upstairs was awake. Archie could hear her scamper from her bedroom into the living room, squealing. Then a TV came on. The kid did a little jig above their heads as the bright, loud voices of cartoon characters filled the room.

Debbie sighed and the air seemed to catch in her throat. 'What is it about us that makes it so hard for you?'

Archie felt all the pain and guilt he kept so carefully tranquillized begin to burn in his stomach. How could he even begin to explain? 'It's complicated.'

She laid a hand on his, covering the pillbox. 'Come home.'

He let their faces into his mind then. Debbie, Ben, Sara. His beautiful family. What had he done? 'OK.'

Debbie's eyebrows shot up, disbelieving. 'Really?'

He nodded a few times, trying to convince himself that this was the right thing, that it wouldn't just make things worse for everyone. 'I need to sleep. Then go into work. I can get Henry to drive me out tonight. He'd love it. He thinks I'm going to kill myself.'

Debbie touched the back of his neck. 'Are you?'

Archie considered this. 'I don't think so.'

The kid began to dance again, stamping her feet,

jumping. The pounding of her feet echoed through Archie's apartment.

Debbie glanced up at the white popcorn ceiling. 'What's that sound?' she asked.

Archie was tired. His eyes burned and his head felt heavy. He leaned back on the sofa and closed his eyes. 'The kid upstairs,' he said.

He felt Debbie rest her head on his shoulder. 'It sounds like home.'

He smiled. 'I know.'

Yes. He could give up Gretchen. He could do that. He could move home and rebuild his family. Maybe keep the task force together, as a special-crimes unit. He could even cut back on the pills. He could try. One last go at salvation. Not for himself. Not for his family. But because if he could do it, he'd win. And Gretchen would lose.

The thought kept the smile on his face as he surrendered his sore, tired body to sleep. He felt his hand relax around the pillbox. The last thing he was aware of was Debbie lifting it out of his hand and putting it back on the table.